LEGACY OF THE FEATHERED SERPENT

Book Two of the Children of Fire Series

Alica McKenna-Johnson

Cover and formatting by Sweet 'N Spicy Designs
http://sweetnspicydesigns.com

Copyright © 2015 by Alica McKenna-Johnson
Publishing by AMJ Publishing 2015

This book is dedicated to my Grandmother who recently left us.
I love you oceans and oceans.

Many thanks to my loving family, my critique partners Kilian, Kim, and Mary, Jill who helped edit, and my friends. All of them listened to hours of my plotting, ranting, and whining about this book. I couldn't have done it without their support!

Theresa thank you for your encouragement and support in helping for stay focused on my dreams.

And special thanks to Gisselle who helped me with information about Argentina and Peru!

Chapter One

"In every conceivable manner, the family is link to our past,
bridge to our future."
Alex Haley

Llamas spit.

"Oh my god, this reeks!" my uncle Gavin said, gagging as he tried to wipe the llama spit off his face. His skin turned pink from the irritating green goo.

"Oh, gross." I tossed him a packet of wet wipes. "You were told not to scare them."

My empathy picked up the llama's happiness at his victory. The female llamas surrounded him, making odd cooing noises. Understanding what animals felt and thought didn't freak me out anymore, thank goodness. Animals have a very different view of humans than we think. It didn't surprise me to find out that when some cats when they slither around your feet while you're walking, *are* trying to kill you.

The mountains of Patagonia, Argentina loomed above us, beautiful and desolate. Craggy rocks, spindly shrubs, and grass less than an inch high covered the steep slopes. Far below, the brownish gray mountainside gave way to stripes of bright green, terraced crops.

"Is not spit," Sasha said, his Russian accent making him

sound harsh and arrogant. "Is digested food."

"Thanks for sharing," I said. Sasha looked less like a ballet dancer and more like a bear in his navy winter coat, heavy black boots, thick wool hat, and scarf.

"When is their father going to be home?" Sasha paced in front of me wrapping his arms around himself.

Since Sasha's Phoenix gift of dreaming brought us here, why was he complaining? I sighed and strengthened my empathic shields against Sasha's boredom, frustration, and worry. We had a common ancestor four thousand years ago, a Phoenix King, and now our 'gifts' brought us together.

I looked over at the mother and her two young children sitting in front of their mud brick hut. They glowed against the gray rocks with their smiling dark, ruddy faces and thick wool clothes woven by their mother from bright colors.

"The sun is getting lower, and it looks like the mom has started to prepare dinner, so I bet it won't be too much longer."

Wind coming off the top of the snowcapped mountains of the Andes whipped around us. I snuggled deeper into the itchy wool poncho.

"Papa, he's coming. Listen," said the youngest, a girl about four or five years old.

I followed the girl's happy gaze, but couldn't see anyone.

"What did she say?" Gavin asked. A red splotch marked his face, but at least the nasty green goop was gone. His Phoenix gift of regeneration would heal that mark in a few minutes.

"She says her father is coming. But I don't see anything."

I began to get a headache as I always do whenever I translate foreign languages into English. Thank goodness my gift only works with other descendants of magical beings. Otherwise I'd have a constant migraine as we traveled.

"Can be she heard something," Sasha said.

A gust of wind blew over us from the valley, carrying with it the soft bleating of sheep.

"I think I hear them," I said.

Ten minutes later, the echo of the sheep and the sharp yips

of dogs became clear. Five minutes after that, the first black-faced, woolly sheep appeared. *Sheep look so cute. And smell.* I didn't know sheep smelled. My nose wrinkled at the pungent, musky odor.

The son, who looked about five or six, ran over to the large paddock and opened the gate. The sheep trotted inside. A few tried going another way, but one of the sheep dogs herded them into the pen with little fuss.

Their father rode up over the hill, on a sturdy horse with a heavy coat. He watched over his flock, sitting tall in a colorful, heavy wool poncho, a leather cowboy hat, and holding a child in his arms.

"Is everything all right?" the mom asked reaching her arms up to take the child.

"He fell rescuing a pregnant ewe. I wrapped it but haven't had time to do anything else."

Their oldest son moaned as they shifted him.

"Hello, my name is Lichuen, what can I do for you?" the man called in Mapuche, an ancient language long forgotten by the Spanish-speaking people of Argentina. His wild protective energy skimmed my shield as if trying to figure me out.

"Good afternoon, Sir," I said, trusting my Phoenix gift for languages would work. "My family and I would like to speak with you, if we may."

His eyes widened, and I could feel his surprise bounce off my empathic shields. "Yes, of course. Let me clean up and make sure my son is all right first."

Sasha poked me. "We must help son. He won't trust us or give us jewelry from Akasha if we don't."

I groaned and rubbed my temples. We needed the jewelry Sasha dreamed about.

Gavin sighed. "Sasha, if you knew this, why you didn't you say so? None of us is a healer."

Sasha crossed his arms. "I tell you what I remember of my dreams."

"Do you happen to remember how we heal him?" I asked.

We were all learning how to manage our Phoenix gifts. I can't expect perfection, especially when I'm constantly messing up.

"Nyet."

"Sapphire, can you connect to Akasha?" Gavin asked. "Can we connect to Miu somehow?"

"Then what?"

Gavin shrugged. "We hope something good happens."

I closed my eyes. "Well, I guess it's a plan. A terrible plan, but we'll see what happens."

I turned towards the fire where they placed their son. "May we try to help your son?"

His turquoise eyes narrowed, his distrust pinged against my shield. "How?"

I pulled my fire pendant out, hoping he would recognize the symbol. He didn't. "We are Children of Fire, descendants of the Phoenix King. I'm hoping by connecting to him, we can heal your son."

His distrust didn't lessen. "I dreamed of this. You're here for my family's legacy, for the gifts given to my family before white man came, from the god Quetzalcoatl himself."

Not good, I hadn't meant to upset him. "Yes, I'm sorry but we are here for them. Sasha saw them in a dream given to him by Shamash."

"His leg is broken and bleeding badly," the mom said.

Lichuen looked at his wife in silent communication.

"What's happening?" Sasha wasn't as patient.

"I don't know yet."

"You will heal him," the father said, a commandment not a question.

"Of course." I turned to Gavin and Sasha. "We're being given a chance. Now what?"

"We'll sit next to him and do our best to connect to the energy of Akasha."

Sasha dug through his pockets pulling out three cases. "I did remember that we should take out our contacts. Seeing the fire in our eyes will help convince him."

I took a case and removed a glove, gasping as the bitter cold wind hit my skin.

"I'm not sure this is a good idea," Gavin said as I removed my contacts.

"We need the jewelry, right?"

Gavin frowned but went along with it.

I put the case in my pocket and looked up. Lichuen's eyes widened, then he nodded.

I sat next to the injured boy and almost threw up. The jagged edge of his bone tore through his lower leg. I looked up at the mountain peaks waiting for the wind to blow away the coppery smell of his blood.

Once my stomach calmed, I looked down at the boy. His ruddy face looked ashy, and his eyes were bright from pain. The jewelry didn't matter.

"We're going to help you." My necklace began to warm up as the connection to Akasha opened. The boy moaned. A wave of pain and fear cut into my shield. I cupped my hands and held them up, letting the energy from Akasha fill them.

Gavin and Sasha opened their connection and channeled more energy to me. My hands lit up with purple flames. I tipped my hands and let the flames fall like water onto the boy's wound.

He cried out as the bone snapped back into place. Lichuen moved closer and grasped his son's hand while his wife held onto their younger kids. The muscle and skin began to repair. Sweat beaded on my forehead. I looked away. *How could Miu handle stuff like this?*

The energy faded as the skin finished healing over, leaving nothing but a pink scar. I slumped, trying to catch my breath. My hands, red and blistered, ached. I watched as cool blue flames danced on the red skin healing the burns.

"Thank you," his mother said as she ran her hands over her son's leg.

"I can't fix the blood loss," I said.

The shepherd smiled, lines carving into his weathered face,

his eyes bright. "My wife knows herbs. He'll be fine. Please let us get him settled and join us for tea." He scooped their son up and took him into the small home. His wife followed them.

I turned to the others and let them know what happened.

Sasha pursed his thin lips, his thick blond eyebrows coming together as he frowned. "What do you think they will serve us?"

"We will be polite and grateful for whatever they give us," Gavin said. "They don't have a lot and what they share with us will mean less for them later."

Sasha's wind chapped cheeks turned even redder as he flushed with embarrassment. "Of course. I was curious only."

We moved to the logs which surrounded the fire. Gavin tucked his long legs close so his feet didn't land in the coals. Sasha, being five-six, had a little more room than Gavin At five foot two, I was a little taller than our hosts, and I settled on the worn log without a problem.

The mother passed out cups of maté and plates of homemade bread and cheese made from sheep's milk. I liked the salty white cheese and chewy bread. She served the tea in gourd cups with metal straws. The straws had flat bottoms with holes in it like a tea strainer so you didn't have to worry about drinking the tea leaves.

The little girl came over and stared into my eyes, her face so close to mine that our noses bumped.

"You have fire in your eyes."

"Let me see," said her brother.

"No." She grabbed my face, her little hand rough with callouses.

He pouted but went over to Gavin. He didn't dive in like his sister, but looked from a distance. Gavin leaned forward once I told him what they wanted. The boy gasped and moved in closer, looking into Gavin's pale green eyes.

"Children, please let our guests enjoy their tea in peace." Their father sat down and sipped his tea through the metal straw.

When finished, Lichuen picked up a small bundle wrapped

in leather.

"This has been passed down in my family since the beginning of time."

He unwrapped the bundle, his thick, work-worn hands showing the greatest reverence. His family scooted closer to see. Clean raw llama wool filled the bundle. The rancher brushed the wool aside to reveal his family's treasures.

"This is a feather from Quetzalcoatl." He held out a beautiful iridescent feather. The green in the middle faded to yellow at the edges. Lichuen laid the feather against his arm with the quill at his elbow and the tip falling over his fingers.

I could feel a magical connection to Akasha radiating from the feather.

"It's beautiful, and very powerful."

"What is it?" Sasha asked, his eyes glued to the magical feather.

Oops, I need to remember to translate. "Sorry, it's a feather from Quetzalcoatl.""These were given to my ancestor, by a man from another world who was born from people of fire."

Lichuen paused until I told the others.

"He passed these along to his son and his son to his son and now they are in my care."

He held out his weathered hands palms up. A silver arm band glinted in the pale light. Metal curved in delicate swirls with a liquid-looking red line flowing down the center of each swirl of silver. In the other hand was a thick wrist cuff of hammered gold with symbols carved into it.

The silver arm band hummed with an energy that told me that Shamash had given it as a gift. The other one felt different. It vibrated with the energy from Akasha, but something more— something wild and windy.

"May I see the writing on the gold cuff, please?" I asked.

Lichuen turned it, but did not hand it to me.

"The cuff says, 'To a most treasured son, love Quetzalcoatl,'" I said, first in Aztec then in English.

"I didn't know other beings brought things from Akasha to

Earth," Gavin said, his fingers twitching with the desire to touch the amazing piece.

"When I received these, my father told me we needed to hold onto them until the Ones of Fire came again. The cuff from Quetzalcoatl will help you get into a secret room where he slumbers." Lichuen paused and stared at me. *What? Why is he staring at me?* Sasha nudged me. *Oh, yes.* I translated. He started speaking again as soon as I nodded.

"Many, many years ago Quetzalcoatl walked among our people. He admired the beauty of the Aztec and Toltec women and blessed many of them with children. The people built Quetzalcoatl shrines, worshiped his children, and the priests created elaborate rituals and celebrations to honor him.

"One day his red brother, Camaxtil, came and took him away. Legend says they went to battle giants and other gods who would harm the Aztec and Toltec."

Lichuen's voice drew me in, and his gestures emphasized the importance of his words. I translated each time he paused, so the others could follow the story.

"During Quetzalcoatl's absence, drought ravaged the land and the crops did not grow. A priest had seen Quetzalcoatl cut once, and he did not bleed. The priests decided that the gods must need blood because they didn't have any of their own. When their normal sacrifices didn't bring rain, the priests decided to hold a huge sacrifice in honor of Quetzalcoatl, hoping it would make him happy and end their suffering.

"The priests sacrificed prisoners on the summer solstice, along with the devout who felt called to offer themselves to the gods, and a virgin from each household. Including the king's youngest daughter, Quetzalcoatl's great-granddaughter. Both Aztec and Toltec temples and pyramids ran red with blood that day. They drummed and sang to drown out the screams of terror as they took prisoners to the altar and cut their living hearts from their chests.

"During the ceremony, Quetzalcoatl did come. He flew over the people, a large magnificent feathered serpent, like a beacon of hope in the sky. Here is where the stories and the myths part ways. According to the priests, Quetzalcoatl, screamed out in joy and blessed earth with his tears. The rivers filled, the crops sprang to life, and the wells filled with sweet clean water once again. The people danced and cheered and the sacrifices continued," he said.

We leaned forward, engrossed in his tale. Even Gavin and Sasha, who had to wait for me to translate, hung on his every word.

"My ancestors knew something different. They knew Quetzalcoatl cried for his grandchild. Her lifeless turquoise eyes looked up, as if in her last moments of life she looked for Quetzalcoatl to return and save her. No one ever saw Quetzalcoatl again. People reported seeing him, and the priests still sacrificed people to honor him, but never again did he bless the people with children or wisdom."

I blinked to fight back the tears. My throat dry, and I cleared it several times in order to finish translating the story.

Lichuen leaned back and looked at the sun. He twisted his cup in his hands while his wife finished the tale.

"My family says that Kukulcan or Quetzalcoatl tried to find a doorway to Xilbalba, the spirit world. But something went wrong, and now Quetzalcoatl sleeps in a hidden city waiting to be sent home," she said.

"I am sad to give up my family's treasures, to not be able to pass them on to one of my own children, but this is what must happen. You need the cuff to free Quetzalcoatl." Lichuen stroked the silver arm band and beaten gold wrist cuff. His turquoise eyes were bright and watery.

Over the past few months, Uncle Gavin taught me about our family as he felt a strong connection to our family's history. I didn't feel that connection, but it would break my heart to have to give up the journal my mother left with me when I was five. I knew from one of her entries that my mother also felt connected to our magical past.

Family ancestry shapes who you are and who you'll become. It's more than genetics. It's quilt patterns, recipes, holiday decorations, and secrets. For some people their ancestry shows up in special gifts and abilities passed down over centuries. While I grow, learn, and try new things, the ties I feel to our ancestors ground me and help me feel connected even when I am alone.

"I'm sorry," I said. "I wish there was another way. Even if we didn't need it, there is an evil force, the Sons of Belial, who might find you and your family and try to take the jewelry."

Gavin tugged on my sleeve. "Tell him we would like to offer him a gift, for keeping these important pieces safe."

"My uncle would like to offer your family a reward for keeping the arm band and cuff safe." I twisted the hem of my poncho.

"It was an honor to have such magical items in my care," Lichuen said, his voice proud.

"We do not wish to offend you," I said. I'd managed to loosen a strand of yarn and kept wrapping and unwrapping it around my finger. "We would like to do something, a gift of friendship and family."

Husband and wife shared a look. She smiled, her teeth bright against her red-brown lips. "We could accept a gift from family, but you need to hurry. It's getting late."

Gavin practically vibrated next to me. "What did they say?"

"They said they can accept a gift from family, but to hurry."

"Tell them we'll be right back," Gavin said, jumping up with Sasha following.

Delighted squeals echoed over the mountain as the kids unpacked the baskets we brought. We gave them toys, fruit, spices, several pots, combs and brushes, beans, and grain.

"They are lovely gifts and very appreciated." She began to repack the spices. "But the sun is close to setting, and navigating the mountain is difficult in the dark."

"Yes, very difficult." Lichuen glanced at the sun sinking below the horizon and stood up. "How did you find us?"

"The family who rented us the horses drew a map to the base of your hill. They wouldn't come up, something about you both being curanderos or witches. And Sasha's dream told him where to go the rest of the way," I said.

"Ah yes, my wife is a seventh daughter, and a curandera or healer. I'm surprised you're here tonight. It is the full moon, and well known that I am a seventh son and a werewolf."

My whole body stiffened, and for a moment I couldn't breathe. *A werewolf—was he serious? Lichuen turns into a snarling vicious monster?* "What?"

"You did not know." He sighed and rubbed his rough hand over his face. "In about half an hour the moon will rise, and I will change into a werewolf. You need to be going."

"How do your family and your animals stay safe?"

And more importantly how would we stay safe?

"Sapphire, what's wrong?" Gavin asked.

"Give me a minute, he's explaining something to me," I answered, holding my hand up to keep him from talking.

"I do not become a mindless monster, wolves are not blood-thirsty animals. They do kill for food, but they also protect and nurture." Lichuen reached over and mussed his son's hair. "I could never hurt my family. However, strangers on my land might not be so lucky."

I looked up at the sky. A sunset of pinks and oranges lit up the wispy clouds.

"It will take us a while to get down the mountain in this dim light. We should go."

"I would invite you to stay for dinner, but I am concerned for your safety," Lichuen said.

His wife smiled and took her husband's hand in hers. "You must come back and tell us all about how you save Quetzalcoatl. Come back when there isn't a full moon, and we'll have a feast."

"Thank you, I look forward to when we can come back." I turned to Gavin, and switched languages. My head ached from switching between Mapuche and English.

"We need to leave."

"Why?" Gavin's green eyes became serious as he looked

between me and the family as if he could somehow determine what was going on.

I cleared my throat. Despite everything I'd seen already, I couldn't believe what I was about to say.

"He's a werewolf, and the moon rises in less than half an hour. We have to leave his territory by then."

"Sasha we need to go," Gavin said. "Sapphire, please thank them for us."

"Thank you for tea and for the gifts of your ancestors." The words rolled off my tongue. *Am I being taught proper manners in my dreams when I visit Akasha?*

"You are most welcome. Careful going down the mountain. The trail is narrow, and there isn't much light. You need to be quick," Lichuen said.

As we walked to the corral icy fear swirled through my body. I wasn't happy with riding the horses during the day, I didn't know how I would cope in the dark. It felt wrong to try and force an animal that big to do what I wanted. The woman who rented them to us assured me my horse would follow the one in front of it, all I had to do was stay on.

"Come on, Sapphire, it's time to go," Gavin said, standing next to my horse. For a moment I considered seeing my first werewolf instead of getting on the horse. Gavin made the decision for me when he picked me up. I managed to keep my hands on the reins instead of clinging to the horse's mane as we started down the mountain.

A sliver of moon peeked over the horizon, and I welcomed its light while worrying about what dangers it would bring. We were not far enough from Lichuen to be safe yet. I could still hear the laughter of his children and the bleating of sheep on the icy wind.

I couldn't see the ground clearly, and the wind tugged at my clothes. "Gavin, are you sure we should be moving this fast?"

"I have excellent night vision," Gavin bragged. "You don't need to worry. Anyway we're just going at a walk."

I didn't feel reassured. It's great that Gavin can see rocks and holes in the path, but what about me? I didn't feel like falling down the side of a cactus-filled mountain with a horse!

"Sapphire," Sasha said, "horses have excellent night vision."

I reached out a shaking hand and patted the horse's neck trying to let her know I trusted her with my safety. Maybe I should call her by name. What was it again?

"Do you remember my horse's name?" I asked.

Gavin laughed. Rude.

Sasha sighed, as if I offended him and turned in his saddle showing off his skill and comfort on the large black animal he rode. "Her name is Bonita."

"Cool, thanks." Sasha jerked his head, which normally would have made his shaggy hair flip about in a very dismissive way, but with a hat on, Sasha looked like he had some weird tic.

The dark night encouraged silence to avoid alerting anything hiding in the inky blackness where we were. The moon rose, glowing pale yellow in the sky. Unfortunately, it wasn't high enough yet to light the rocky trail we descended.

Rocks tumbled as something large came our way.

"Gavin! Sasha! Sapphire!" Taliesin called out.

Thank goodness, maybe Taliesin could talk to the werewolf and keep us safe.

"Taliesin, what are you doing here? Is everyone okay?" Gavin said. We had left Taliesin and the others back at the ranch where we were staying, since there weren't enough horses available for all of us. I had to go, Gavin insisted on going, and since Sasha was the one who knew where we were going he came along, which meant the rest had to stay behind.

Taliesin came close enough that I could see him, and even in the cold and riding a horse, he looked GQ perfect. He's so irritating.

"Everyone's fine."

"Then why you are here?" Sasha sneered as he straightened his posture.

"Something is wrong." Taliesin looked around. "I was reading in my room."

"Our room," Sasha muttered.

Taliesin rolled his eyes. "Anyway, I knew I needed to get to you. So what kind of trouble are you in now?"

He looked right at me. *Rude!*

Gavin rubbed a hand over his face. "The man we visited is a werewolf, and the full moon is rising."

A howl echoed over the mountain. We all froze, maybe if we didn't move he wouldn't sense us. The sound of rocks falling down the mountain followed the next howl. The horses whinnied and began to stamp their feet, ready to get away.

"He's coming," I whispered.

"I can't reach him," Taliesin said, after a moment. "The werewolf is focused on getting the intruders out of his territory and protecting his family. We need to leave."

"We are leaving. Have you told him that?" I said.

"Of course," Taliesin flipped his white braid over his shoulder. It caught the moonlight and glowed silver. "But he doesn't care. We have to hurry."

"Can you make the horses understand what we need to do?" Gavin asked. "We need them to take over and get us down the mountain safely."

"I'll try." Taliesin bowed his head. No one moved or made a sound while we waited. After the longest minute ever, Taliesin looked up. "They understand and will help us."

We murmured our thanks and settled back into our seats. The horses took off - right down the side of the mountain. This time human cries echoed through the air.

My eyes stung as cold wind whipped around my face. I clung as well as one can to a massive beast careening down a mountain. Rocks kicked up around us, hitting our legs and the horses. They didn't want to stay around the werewolf either.

"Sapphire!" Gavin screamed. I want to yell that I was okay, but I couldn't breathe, couldn't move. All I could do was cling to Bonita.

She swerved to the right. Sliding in the saddle, I dropped the reins. Desperate to stay on I grabbed her mane. I screamed when my dangling leg hit a cactus and the sharp spines pierced my skin through my jeans. My arms shook as I hauled myself back into the saddle. The stirrups flopped about, but I managed to shove my feet into them. I waited for my life to flash before my eyes.

"Please," I begged. "Please keep me safe."

Through the panic coming off Bonita I felt determination, strength, and a little bit of protectiveness.

Good enough for me. I put my trust in her and held on with the best of my ability. My stomach roiled as Bonita jumped. I screamed. My legs protested as I clenched them even tighter around her back. Bonita's powerful muscles bunched and stretched under me as she ran from the monster behind us. We had to be close to the edge of its territory, right?

A fierce howl echoed around me. Nope, we weren't far enough away yet.

Bonita jerked to the right.

"Sapphire," Gavin yelled. We ran along the edge of a deep ravine. I couldn't see the bottom, only blackness. Everyone else raced down the other side of the ravine. *No. Oh, god, no.* I couldn't do this alone. Frantic, I grabbed at the reins while I tried to remember how to get the horse to go where I need to.

"I'll get her, Gavin," Taliesin said. He turned his horse sharply around, then headed back up the mountain.

"We're going the wrong way," I said to the horse, the reins staying out of reach. "Please, we need to stop and go back."

Energy as soft as a moonbeam flowed over us. Bonita snorted and stopped, prancing in place, turning around. Taliesin came towards us, his forehead glowing blue-silver under his hat.

"Come on," he whispered to the horse. "Come on, girl, this way. We'll be safe, but we need to go."

Never have I felt so glad to see Taliesin. My eyes fill with tears. "Thank you."

"We're not safe yet." Taliesin turned looking up the mountain. "I don't see the werewolf, but we need to hurry."

"Thank you for coming back for me, and for sending the

others on," I said.

Taliesin shrugged. "Their horses are listening more to me than them right now." Taliesin turned the horse's head back up the mountain to the top of the ravine.

Bonita screamed and reared up on her hind legs. My fingers tangled in her mane, holding on. I smiled as she lowered her bulk back down to the trail. *I did it! I held on! Go me!* Something slammed into me, knocking me from the horse and into the rocky ground. My chest burned as my breath was forced out of me. A snarling, gray werewolf pinned me down.

Chapter Two

"Don't find fault, find a remedy."
~Henry Ford

Okay, what the hell should I do now? I couldn't breathe as the beast's weight held my chest down and rocks dug into my back. I tried my best to look non-threatening and gross tasting. Lichuen howled. I whimpered. He lowered his head, teeth bared.

A hat hit Lichuen on his snout. Taliesin's hat, but now with a huge hole through it. Glowing hooves stopped next to my head. Taliesin had turned into a unicorn! Snorting, he lowered his head and used his horn to force the werewolf to back up.

As soon as the huge paws moved, my chest expanded and I gulped in a painful breath. Coughing, I rolled to the side, trying to breathe through the burning pain. Taliesin's body glowed silver and majestic as he forced the werewolf away from me.

Lichuen howled one last time then ran up the mountain.

"Taliesin," I whimpered sitting up. Everything hurt. I needed my backpack, there had to be something in there to help get the piece of cactus off my leg. Looking around the moonlit desert I couldn't see it. Shaking, I found a stick and after several painful tries managed to pry the cactus pad off my leg. I pulled needles out of me as Taliesin walked over.

"Thank you. You saved my life. I didn't know what to do," I said. Taliesin reached down and rubbed his velvety nose against my damp cheek, his soft unicorn magic calming me down.

"What are we going to do? The horses are gone, and it looks like your clothes are all torn up."

Taliesin walked over and kicked the pile of shredded cloth. Snorting, he tossed his head and walked back to me.

I stood up and took stock of my injuries. Nothing felt broken, but I was definitely bruised and scratched. My leg stung from all the cactus needles. I'd need to take my jeans off to get them all, and that wasn't happening here.

"I guess we'll walk. I can't even hear the others anymore."

I took a very small and pathetic step, almost falling on the loose rocks under my feet.

"You should run and get the others."

Taliesin neighed and shook his head. Standing next to me, he slid his head under my arm. I leaned against him and we began to walk.

"Thanks, again."

I sighed and looked up at the moon. I wondered if I would ever look up at its beauty again without thinking of the snarling face of the werewolf.

"Do you think the others are safe?"

Taliesin nodded his head.

Told the horses to run until they reached their home, I heard Taliesin say in my head.

I stumbled and would have fallen had I not held on to the young unicorn.

"Oh wow, that is seriously weird. You can't read my thoughts can you?"

Taliesin shook his head, making his horn glitter in the moonlight. Six inches long, his horn looked like twisted crystal. Taliesin didn't look full grown. His shoulder would be above my head at his full size. While I would have loved to let Taliesin carry me down the mountain, he hadn't offered, and I didn't ask.

"Taliesin, can you find the others?"

He snorted, I guess my question offended him.

"Do you know how to turn back into a human?"

Taliesin didn't answer, but his worry squirmed around me making me feel sick and scared. My shield was gone. Apparently being hurt and almost killed by a werewolf destroys my empathic protection.

I leaned into Taliesin and rubbed my hand on his neck, hoping it would comfort him.

"Don't worry, we'll get it all figured out."

Taliesin stayed quiet.

Every step took all my concentration and energy. My muscles trembled as I clung even tighter to Taliesin. My shirt stuck to my back, where blood had dried, each movement pulled at the new scabs. My calf burned and itched from the cactus needles. I didn't know how long we walked. The moon rose higher, and the plants changed, the grass became greener and thicker. It had taken us more than three hours to ride from the ranch where we rented the horses to Lichuen's home. We rode at least an hour when we reached the tall grassland, so at least my pathetic stumbling steps were getting us somewhere.

"We're about half way there right?"

Taliesin nodded his head.

"Thank goodness." My shoulders relaxed a little and some of the fear left. "Do you think the others will come looking for us?"

Gavin won't leave us behind, Taliesin sent into my head. It echoed, making my brain twinge, and a shudder ran down my spine.

"The people at the ranch did seem scared of Lichuen and his family. Of course, now we know why."

Taliesin sent a *"ya think?"* feeling. He was without a doubt the snottiest unicorn ever.

My toe caught on a small rock, and my legs collapsed under me. I didn't even try and save myself from falling. I wrapped my hands around my head and fell, whimpering as my body hit the hard, unforgiving earth.

Taliesin whinnied and nudged me with his nose.

"I can't. I'm sorry. I can't go any further right now. I need to rest." I shifted my arm and curled into a ball to keep warm.

"You can reach the ranch faster on your own. I'll stay here, and you can run ahead. We must be well beyond Lichuen's territory now. I'll be safe."

Taliesin looked in the direction of the ranch. Good, he could bring back help. I closed my eyes and waited for the unicorn to make a decision. Taliesin took a few steps away from me. He was leaving me. I began to tremble, my heart pounding. He needed to go. It was for the best that he go and get help, but I didn't want to be all alone. I wanted to beg Taliesin to stay, but I kept silent.

Coyote yips and howls filled the air. Whimpering, I curled up tighter and clenched my teeth together so I wouldn't beg Taliesin to stay. My eyes filled with tears. I tried to force them back by closing my eyes tight. I needed that water.

Hush, Taliesin sent to me. *Hush. You're safe. I'm not going to leave you.*

"Thank you," I whispered, ignoring the pain in my head. "I need to rest for a little bit, and then we can start walking again."

Taliesin lay down and huffed his hot breath on my neck and scooted a bit closer. Surrounded by the soothing unicorn energy, I began to breathe. I counted to five as I inhaled, held my breath for five counts, slowly exhaled to five counts, and counted to five before inhaling again. After a few breaths I added in my Phoenix powers, pulling the fiery energy up my spine as I inhaled and down to the base of my spine as I exhaled.

I opened my eyes to the full moon hanging overhead. The painful tiredness faded. My scrapes and bruises felt a little less tender, until I moved and my shirt pulled at the scabs.

"Thank you, Taliesin. I think I can walk again. We can't be too far away." I stood.

Are you sure? Taliesin asked. The echo of his voice threatened to bring back the headache I'd just gotten rid of.

"Yes. We need to get back." I needed water, food, and a

bed. Taliesin moved to my side, allowing me to lean on him again.

They're coming. I have to go, I will meet you back at the ranch.

"Who?" I asked.

Taliesin ran, his body a silver blur through the grass heading for the trees in the distance.

"Sapphire!"

"Uncle Gavin, I'm over here," I yelled. Thank goodness, all of this was over.

The riders came into view. Never had hoof beats sounded so welcome. Gavin leaped off his horse.

"Sapphire, are you okay?"

"Yes, I'll be fine."

Gavin ran his hands over my head and arms as if looking for injuries. I flinched when he touched a sore spot.

"Are you sure?"

"Uncle Gavin, I'm sure. Do you have any water?"

"Yes, of course," Gavin said, going over to his horse and pulling a water bottle out of the saddle bag. "Is Taliesin all right?"

"I think so, he changed to protect me from the werewolf."

I drank as much water as I could.

"He said he'd meet us back at the ranch."

"Can you ride?" Gavin looked me over again, his worry started to feel suffocating.

"I can do whatever you need me to if it gets me the hell out of here." I walked over to the horses. One of the ranch hands hopped down off his horse and helped me up onto mine. "How did you know I would need a horse?"

"Your horses showed up, and I was able to get someone to help me come and find you. I wanted to come right away, but they were all afraid of the werewolf." Gavin's voice cracked. "I'm sorry we couldn't get here earlier."

"I understand, don't worry about it. Taliesin kept me safe," I said as we began to ride back to the ranch.

The two men spoke to each other in soft Spanish. If they

had a magical lineage I would know what they were saying, instead I was left to wonder what they thought happened to us.

It didn't take long before I saw the warm yellow lights of the ranch.

"They're back," Anali called out. My aunt stood on the porch. Her pink sari fluttered in the cool breeze. Miu, our healer, stood next to her. Her black hair pulled back into two high pigtails, and she wore one of her lacy, school-girl styled outfits.

Uncle Gavin dismounted with more grace than I had on my best day and helped me down.

"I'll take Miu to Taliesin, I saw him by those trees, and see if we can help him turn back," Gavin said. "You go and get something to eat, okay?"

How many times would I have to tell Gavin that I was all right?

"I'm sure Anali will take very good care of me." I squealed as someone grabbed me.

"Little sister, are you okay? I was so scared when the horse came back without you," Kayin said, his voice deep and rich. His ebony arms wrapped around me.

I hugged him back and relaxed. "Hey, big brother, I'm okay."

Kayin raised an eyebrow, his dark brown eyes showed disbelief.

"Let's get her cleaned up and give her something hot to eat," Anali said. "Kayin, bring Sapphire inside."

Miu walked over to us. "I'll come and see you as soon as I've helped Taliesin."

"I will ask Señora Villescas to heat something," Sasha said, his fire red streaked blond hair fluttering down into his eyes.

"Thank you. I really am okay, and I can walk," I said, as Kayin held me and walked towards the house.

Kayin huffed and carried me through the courtyard and into my room in the back corner.

Anali followed us into the room. "Thank you, Kayin, I'll

help Sapphire from here."

Um, hello, didn't I say I was fine? "I don't need any help. All I want is a shower and something to eat."

"Let me check to make sure your injuries aren't serious," Anali said, in her soothing 'mom' tone.

I wanted to be alone. I could take care of myself. Anali's light brown eyes were calm, yet firm. I wouldn't get out of this. I began to take off all my layers.

"Here's the first aid kit." Sasha brought in a large tackle box, which Gavin filled with everything we could possibly need. "Let me know if you need anything else."

Once the boys left and the door shut, I undid my jeans and peeled them off. My calf had dozens of small red dots on it, some with thin cactus needles sticking out of them.

"Oh, Sapphire," Anali said, her thick dark eyebrows wrinkling around her red bindi. "What happened?"

"Cactus."

Anali began to dig through the first aid kit, her shoulder-length brown hair falling around her face.

My beat up fingers dug into the blanket as Anali yanked the large needles from my skin, then went over the area with duct tape to pull at the smaller ones. Cacti are evil. I will never go near another one again, ever.

"I'm sorry," Anali said, rubbing a patch of needle-free skin.

I nodded. "It's okay."

"Do you want a break or should I keep going?"

Nasty needles still stuck out of my calf. I turned away, afraid I would get sick if I watched. "Please finish, I need it to be over with."

My eyes watered, which made the mess on Miu's bed look like a kaleidoscope. We'd gotten to the ranch yesterday afternoon. I had no idea how Miu managed to get all of her clothes, bath stuff, accessories, and stuffed animals scattered over her side of the room.

"I think that's the last one." Anali ran a brown hand over my calf checking for any missed needles. "Let me check your back."

"I'm sure it's fine." I tugged my tee shirt down. I trusted Anali, but still, my pink leopard print underwear wasn't something I wanted to share.

Anali raised an eyebrow and twirled her finger. I turned around. My shirt still stuck to my back.

"Sapphire, I think you're going to have to keep your shirt on in the shower and let the water soak it loose. I'll stay out here in case you need help getting it off."

She intended to wait no matter what I said, so I shut the door but didn't lock it and turned on the water.

It didn't take long for the water to warm up, and soon the pounding spray relaxed my stiff muscles. I hoped the water would loosen my tee shirt. I pulled the wet cloth up, tugging it loose in a few places where the cuts were deeper. "Anali, I took my shirt off," I said, dropping the dirty wet shirt on the floor. "You can go now."

Anali chuckled. "All right I'll go, but I'll check your back in the morning."

I rolled my eyes and braced myself as I soaped up, flinching as the bubbles stung all of my cuts and scrapes.

Putting on my flannel pajamas with the purple and green stripes and a black bathrobe, I tidied up. Kayin was in my room, I felt his worry seeping through the bathroom door. I tried to put a bubble around myself to block the intensity of his feeling, but exhaustion flooded my body and the aches and pains were too distracting. Oh well. I stepped out and saw Kayin sitting on my bed facing the front window.

"Hey, little sister, are you dressed?" Kayin asked.

I smiled at his back. His hair was the same black highlighted with fire red streaks like mine, but his small, tight curls looked studded with little rubies. On someone else it might have looked silly, but with his wide nose, high cheekbones, full lips, and ebony skin, Kayin looked like an African prince.

"You can turn around, big brother." I poked him in the shoulder with my one finger not covered with bruises and cuts.

Kayin turned and held out a tray. "I've brought you dinner."

I sat in the middle of the bed and took off the cover. My mouth began to water. Señora Villescas had made me two fried cheese empanadas and a thick soup of vegetables, beans and quinoa.

"Tell me what happened."

I shrugged taking a bite of the crispy gooey pastry. "Not much, separated from the others, saw the werewolf, and Taliesin saved me."

Round brown eyes narrowed in irritation. Apparently, my explanation didn't satisfy him. Eating the delicious soup, I tried to ignore Kayin. It wasn't that I didn't want him to know, but I didn't want to think about that huge, gray beast pinning me to the ground. The skin on my back tearing against the rocks. Sharp claws threatening to pierce my flesh. Snarling puffs of hot breath hitting my face.

"I hope you are dressed," Sasha called through the door, waiting a second before walking in. His arm was wrapped around Miu's waist as he helped her to her bed.

Her porcelain skin looked pale, and her peridot green eyes shone glossy with fatigue.

"What happened? What's wrong?" I asked.

"Anali said she needs rest." Sasha sat her on the messy bed.

Kayin grabbed an extra blanket and covered Miu. She gave him a tired smile and closed her eyes.

"What happened?" I asked again.

Sasha sat on one of the small wooden chairs, looking graceful and chic even, as he ran a tired hand through his messy hair. "Miu tried turning Taliesin back to human." Sasha reached up, fiddling with his fire pendant—the one the Children of Fire gave him two years ago when he turned fifteen.

"Her pendant glowed with energy from Akasha. Then she collapsed. She said she could not fix because he is not broken."

"He's in a natural state," Miu mumbled from her bed not bothering to open her eyes. "There's nothing to heal, nothing broken, or ill, or wrong with Taliesin."

"That makes sense. So what do we do now?" I asked, before

finishing the soup and scraping the spoon on the bowl—such a sad sound.

Sasha shrugged. "We wait until Taliesin can do it himself, or get help when he sleeps."

Three sharp knocks echoed through the door.

"Come in," I said, not willing to get up and answer the door.

Señora Villescas' son came into the room holding a covered tray. His brown eyes sparkled and his mouth curved in a sexy smile. "Hello," he purred. Xavier always flirted. He didn't seem to care if he flirted with a boy or a girl or how old or attractive they were. Any person will do.

Miu sat up and began straightening her ponytails. "Hi, Xavier."

He set down the tray on the table and looked at Miu with great appreciation for her delicate beauty. "Good evening, my dear. I've brought you a special treat." He rolled his Rs in a way that made my stomach flutter and Miu giggle and blush.

"What you bring?" Sasha asked, his Russian accent sharp in comparison with Xavier's soft vowels.

Xavier gave him a wink and took the wicker cover off the tray revealing four ice cream sundaes. "Mama asked me to bring you dessert."

Argentinian ice cream tastes divine. It's made with *dulce de leche*, a thick sweetened cream. It brings ice cream to a whole new level of amazing. Miu could have Xavier, I wanted the ice cream sundae.

"Thank you." I held out my hands.

Xavier smiled, his hips swaying as he walked, as if any moment he might begin to dance the tango. "It has calafate berry sauce on it. They say one taste of calafate guarantees you will come back to Patagonia to get more."

Kayin grunted and took the offered dessert.

Xavier smiled at Kayin. "If it works, you'll have to come back here and let me know."

Kayin's eyes widened, eyebrows shooting up towards his hair. He didn't know how to deal with the flirting.

"Ignore Xavier, he'd flirt with anyone. He doesn't mean it," I said.

Kayin calmed a bit, but still seemed upset. "Come on, we have ice cream, let it go." I moaned as the flavors exploded on my tongue. I would return to Patagonia for another taste of these berries.

More soft moans followed mine as the others tasted the dessert.

"My favorite sound," Xavier teased, as he left the room.

Sasha's gray eyes hardened as he glared at the door. "I do not like him."

"He's cute," Miu said twirling the end of a pony tail around her finger.

Kayin cleared his throat. "Forget about Xavier, what happens next?"

They all looked at me for an answer. My least favorite part of being the Jewel—people assumed I knew what I was doing. "Well, Sasha's dreams led us here and to the artifacts, so maybe he'll dream of where we should go next."

Miu went from bubbly and cute to ninja assassin as she turned to glare at Sasha. "Yes, and following his dream almost killed Sapphire."

"Is not my fault! I am not perfect."

"I've known that all along." Their eyes met and their anger rose.

"Stop," I said, in a firm 'mom' tone. "We are not going to argue about this. What we do isn't safe, we all know this, and we all do the best we can." My mom's advice always helped me solve a problem, but I never tried to use it with anyone else before.

You can spend hours, if not days, blaming other people for a problem. It's easy and requires no skill. It also does no good. Let go of the how/who/why a problem has come about and work on fixing the problem. Later you can figure out if things could have been done differently, but life happens, mistakes happen, and you need to deal with what 'is' and not what 'should be'. Take a deep breath and think of what the first step is—

do you need paper towels, to make a call, to hunt your pockets for change? Take the problem one step at a time without blaming anyone and you will be able to solve it.

"We can research Quetzalcoatl to see if we can find anything on where he sleeps," Kayin said.

I reached over and used the napkin to wipe away some of the red calafate berry sauce from his chin. "Before we do anything else we need to get Taliesin back to human, I don't think he'll fit into the RV right now."

"We research unicorns, too." Sasha said.

"Sounds like a plan to me," I said, thankful the conversation was over so I could focus on my dessert.

Chapter Three

"Time is neutral and does not change things. With courage and
initiative, leaders change things."
~Jesse Jackson

Miu interrupted the birds mid-chirp by talking in her sleep. I
enjoyed listening to her muttering in Japanese almost as much
as the chirping. Stretching, I moaned. The skin on my back was
healed but still tender. One of my favorite things about being
the Jewel is healing while I sleep.

Grabbing some sweats, I stumbled into the bathroom to get
ready for the day. Brushing out my hair, I braided my curls. I
knew we would work out this morning, and my waist-length
hair would get in the way. I avoided looking in the mirror, a
challenge as it covered half of the wall. I hated mirrors. They
always sent me into a spiral of questions, insecurity, and deep
pondering about who and what I am.

Before Gavin came along, I would stare in the mirror,
wondering which parent I looked like. I didn't grow up with
pictures of my parents, so I didn't know if my hair came from
my mom, or my dad's dad. Did an aunt or uncle also have big
almond shaped eyes? Did any of my grandparents have
dimples?

Now I knew that the shape of my mouth came from my
mom and my eyes from my dad. My coloring, though, came

from Shamash and Aya some four thousand years ago. My skin was a blend of Aya's rich middle-eastern copper and Shamash's milk white. His flame-red hair streaked the midnight black curls from Aya, and her peridot green eyes were flecked with metallic gold from his.

It disappointed me to find out that knowing where my features came from did nothing to help me figure out who I am.

A bang on the door made me jump. "Hurry up," Miu said, through a yawn. "Anali said we are going running in thirty minutes."

"All done." I opened the door and took a moment to make my bed and tuck my pajamas into my bag. Spending most of my childhood living in group homes had trained me to be very tidy, unlike Miu who blew the stereotype of the neat, proper Japanese girl into pieces.

In the courtyard, Anali stretched alongside Kayin and Sasha. A pitcher of orange juice and some glasses sat on a mosaic table.

"Good morning, little sister. How are you feeling?" Kayin rumbled. As he stretched, his forehead touched his shin while he placed his hands flat on the ground.

I smiled, pouring a glass of juice. Kayin and I both had a hard time accepting our fate as Children of Fire. We traveled around the world opening portals to Akasha to send the magical beings trapped on Earth back to their home. Granted, Kayin coped much better than I did, but still we had bonded initially over our confusion and fear.

Sasha and Miu knew they were Children of Fire from a young age and felt honored at having enough power to help send the magical creatures home. Most Children of Fire possessed very little of the Phoenix gifts and even fewer had any coloring marking them as Shamash and Aya's descendants.

"I'm good, all healed up." I chugged the juice and joined them in stretching. "So we're running today?"

Kayin chuckled. "Yes. And, yes, I know you hate running."

Scowling, I decided not to answer.

"Is important to keep in shape. We do not want injury," Sasha said.

I rolled my eyes. I knew that. We traveled with Cirque du Feu Magique, a small circus performing in parks, schools, town squares, and small theaters. I enjoyed being part of the circus. I wasn't very good yet, and I didn't perform with any of the big acts but I did enjoy the training and practice. Except running—I hated it. I don't know why, it just sucks. Thankfully, we only ran when there wasn't a good place to do yoga or strength conditioning.

Gavin stumbled out of his room in worn sweats, his hair a wild mess of red which fell past his shoulders. With his eyes barely open, he poured himself some juice and began to warm up.

Miu emerged from our room five minutes before we left. Her pink Hello Kitty jogging suit was too bright to look at directly.

"Good morning everyone. How's Taliesin this morning?" Miu asked.

Taliesin. I forgot about him. Guilt settled hard and cold in my belly. *Sure he's a snot, but he saved my life last night, so shouldn't I have thought about him? What kind of a person am I?*

"He's fine," Anali said. "He's still a unicorn, but he's good. We'll figure out how to help him today. Don't worry." Anali patted my arm. I didn't bother to say anything; she knew what I felt. Her empathy wasn't as strong as mine, but I couldn't hide my feelings from her.

"Come on, we can talk about it while we run," Gavin said, leading us out to the dirt road.

Taking a deep breath I forced myself to run, well closer to jog, but still horrible. "Last night we talked about researching unicorns to see if we could find a way to help him," I said.

"Good plan," Gavin said. "Sasha, did you dream anything?"

Miu snorted. "We trust his dreams after what happened last night?"

Sasha ignored her, which would make things worse in the

end. "No, I was too tired. Did anyone else have dream?"

Miu's pony tails shook as she said no. "I never remember my dreams clearly. That's your job."

Before Sasha answered I jumped in. "I don't remember anything. I know I spent time in Akasha because I woke healed. I'll go to bed early tonight and see if I can do better."

"Sorry," Kayin said. "I'm like Miu—I never remember my dreams."

"I think there is a ritual, or tea, or something we can do to increase our dreams." Gavin sped up a bit now that our muscles warmed up.

"My grandmother gave special tea to drink," Sasha began.

"Please, we don't want to use some old wives' tale that won't work, we need something proven to help aid dreaming," Miu snapped.

Sasha's shaggy hair whipped around his face as he glared at Miu, his gray eyes icy. "You do not know what you talk about." Anger thickened his accent.

Anali looked back at me. "Deal with this," she said, as she and Gavin began to run faster.

I glared at them. They were the adults—why did I have to fix this? But I knew the answer. Miu and Sasha saw me as the leader, and they wanted me to pick whose rituals we would now use. They had started arguing once we left the Guardians, a Native American group of Children of Fire who led the ritual we used to open the portals to Akasha throughout America. Together, we sent many amazing beings home to Akasha: small fairies, masked dancers, monstrous flying snakes, animals dressed as humans, and even a few Sasquatch.

Miu's high voice cut through my happy memories. I guess I should do something. She began cussing at Sasha, thankfully she swore in Japanese. He wouldn't like what Miu said about his mother and a monkey.

Both Sasha and Miu learned different meditations and rituals to help them. Sasha's grandmother taught him rituals flavored with their Russian Jewish ancestry. Miu's family is Japanese

Shinto, so all of her rituals entwine with those teachings. This had led to a lot of fighting over whose way was better.

Personally, I don't care. The point of these rituals is to connect everyone in the group and have them focusing on the same thing at the same time. Both Miu and Sasha wanted me to care, and wanted me to pick which ritual I liked best. They both sounded interesting, and I'm sure both rituals would work.

At one point I told them that and even went so far as to suggest we tradeoff who leads the ritual. No one received that well, so now I stayed out of it. But as soon as Sasha began to understand Miu was cussing at him, he made a foul comment about Miu's grandfather and a pig in Yiddish. I decided I needed to do something. I had no idea what, but I would do something.

Kayin sighed. "One of them will get hurt soon."

"What am I supposed to do?" I asked, watching as Sasha and Miu's body language became more aggressive.

Things do not get better with time, they get better with action. You must do something: write and burn an angry letter, forgive yourself and others, or set aside your ego and try to understand the other side of things. There are many actions you can take, but you will need to choose something. Sometimes a friend is trapped in anger, grief, fear, or sadness, and you might find yourself able to help by encouraging and supporting an action they can take. You don't have to do something huge and you don't have to fix everything at once. What one thing can you do today which will help make things better?

Okay, my mom's advice would work here, but what one thing could I do? Gag them both? Wipe their memories? Let them beat the crap out of each other and declare the winner right? Tempting, but I thought I'd have to do something else.

"Sasha, Miu, enough! The point of a ritual is to bind us together, and all of this arguing isn't helping." I glared, trying to make it look like I was angry and not that I stopped talking in order to catch my breath. I hate running.

"I have decided what we're going to do. Both of you are going to write down the ritual you have learned. I want to know the space you need, the time, and any materials." I let that sink in while I took a breath. "Then I will decide in which situations which ritual would work better."

"What?" Miu said turning to glare at me. She almost fell tripping over a rock in the road.

Sasha growled.

"We aren't able to open the portal and help magical creatures if we can't combine our energy. And we won't be able to connect if you two are so angry at each other," Kayin said, his breathing smooth and even.

"She is impossible ... " Sasha began.

"He's a jerk and ... " Miu snapped.

I stopped running, put my hands on my hips and panted for a moment. Kayin didn't say anything. Miu and Sasha stopped arguing, but they pierced my shields with sharp cold needles of anger.

"Stop it," I said before they said anything else. "Write your rituals out. Then I will decide where and when each ritual will work better." I gave my best 'unhappy mom' look. "This discussion is over, let's finish our run."

The silence that followed was refreshing.

* * *

My head ached from spending all day hunting books for answers. We found that a unicorn's parents would help them if they became stuck in a form, and that Taliesin at sixteen was too young to have changed forms. I snuggled into the bed and closed my eyes. Hopefully, someone would get an answer in their dream and we would help Taliesin tomorrow. I didn't know how long he could hide in the woods surrounding the ranch. Sighing, I felt myself slip into sleep and Akasha.

The Phoenix fire my Grandfather created died away leaving my body healed and refreshed. "Thank you, Adadda." He liked it when I called him Grandfather in Babylonian, the language of his children.

"You are most welcome," Shamash answered, his flame-red hair

fluttering around his face. "Come let's swing, and you can tell your Grandmother and me what happened yesterday. You fell asleep after I healed you last night."

"Good evening, Amagal," I said as Aya transformed from a purple, blue, and green phoenix into a beautiful Babylonian woman.

Her face lit up as she smiled at me. "Hello Sapphire, come sit, and tell us everything."

We sat on the moss-covered wood bench that the fairies made into a swing and I told them about Lichuen and his family and their children. Looking out over the meadow as we swung, I wondered if I would ever get used to the beauty of Akasha, with its turquoise sky, vibrant grass, delicate flowers, and magical creatures. A group of satyrs lounged in the meadow while a flock of nightingales flew overhead singing their magical song.

"Then Lichuen showed us a beautiful feather from Quetzalcoatl," I told them.

Shamash placed his milk-pale hand on top of mine. "Did he say anything else about him?"

"Yes, Lichuen gave us a bracelet from Quetzalcoatl, and said that we would need the bracelet to get into where he is sleeping."

"So they think he still lives?"

"Yes," I turned and looked into hopeful gold eyes. "Is he really your brother?"

"Yes. It's been more than two thousand years since I have spoken with him." Shamash sighed. "At first I thought my brother was angry because I kept telling him what to do. Once the doorways between Akasha and Earth closed, I tried to find him. I flew all over Akasha checking the oceans, mountains, deserts, every cave, jungle, forest, and the crystal labyrinth."

"We will help you in any way we can," Aya said.

"Well, Lichuen's wife told me Quetzalcoatl tried to find a doorway to Xilbalba, something went wrong, and now he's sleeping in a hidden city."

"If my brother tried to force one of the dying portals open it could have exploded and rendered him unconscious, but why didn't he wake up?"

I didn't know if my Adadda knew about his nieces and nephews, or the human sacrifices. I fiddled with my mother's ring.

"Sapphire, do you know something?" Aya asked, her voice soft and

soothing.

I kept my eyes down, unwilling to look at my many times great grandparents.

Thin fingers carded through my hair. "Sapphire, dear, it's okay, we won't become angry with you. None of this is your fault."

I didn't look up, as I began to talk. "Did you know Quetzalcoatl had children with some of the Aztec and Toltec women?"

Shamash sighed. "I suspected he did, but I never met any of them."

"Well once when Quetzalcoatl left there was a drought, and the people decided that their normal prayers weren't enough to get his attention. They made him into a god." I cleared my throat, wishing I didn't have to go on. "So they gathered and began to pray, celebrate, and sacrifice hundreds of people including a great granddaughter of Quetzalcoatl. Lichuen said the temple steps ran with blood."

"Poor Quetzalcoatl," Aya whispered.

Shamash's voice sounded rough. "I warned him, I knew if his actions hurt others, it would break his heart. I know he made mistakes, but it was him enjoying life and being playful. Quetzalcoatl didn't see how his actions would affect humans."

"Our Sapphire will find him," Aya said, patting my hand.

Shamash looked out over the meadow. "I have a few ideas of where he could have gone. I'll let Sasha know when I find something. He's getting much better remembering his dreams."

"Does Taliesin dream here?" I blurted out.

"No. We don't block him, but he has never come here in a dream. Why?" Shamash answered.

"He turned into a unicorn to protect me from a werewolf, and now he can't turn back."

"Is that where your injuries came from?" Aya asked.

I nodded and told them the rest of the story.

"I can give you enough energy to help Taliesin turn back. You will need to keep a connection open between us, and Taliesin will need to focus on what it feels like to be human," Shamash said.

"I think I can do that. Maybe."

"We can work on it together," Aya said. "And if it doesn't work the first time, we'll try again."

I nodded. "Okay, what do I need to do?"

"Stay open to me," Shamash said. "I want you to wake up keeping me firmly in your mind. Find a place where you can do what you need to do on Earth but you can still feel me."

Um, was that supposed to make sense? *"Okay."*

Shamash closed his eyes and dropped into meditation, I could see the power he pulled into himself; his skin glowed with it.

Aya began to run her fingers through my hair. "Imagine where you are sleeping and allow yourself to go back into your body."

I followed Aya's instructions and found myself waking, yet still feeling her fingers in my hair and the pleasant hum of magic. I opened my eyes into thin slits and closed them as I felt Akasha slipping away. After a few deep breaths, I tried again. I managed to keep my eyes open. Step by step, I walked out of the room towards Taliesin.

The tiles outside my door felt cold against my bare feet. I shivered. Closing my eyes I focused on Aya's fingers in my hair. Once I strengthened the connection, I began to walk. I shuffled half way into the court yard when my bare toe banged into a chair, and I lost Akasha. Grabbing my toe I cussed softly, not wanting to wake anyone up. I looked back to my room, I knew once I fell back to sleep I would go right back to Akasha and we'd start it again. But I hadn't even gotten half way to the trees. This might work better if I slept next to Taliesin.

I went into the bedroom and grabbed a pillow and blankets. I tried to not make a sound but doors creaked, pebbles crunched, and several twigs snapped under my feet. They sounded so loud in the night. I found Taliesin sleeping under a bush in a grove of trees. I spread one of the blankets next to him.

What are you doing? Taliesin asked telepathically.

"Shamash says he can help change you back, but I have to remain connected to Akasha and I can't walk from my room to you and stay connected to him without hurting myself. So I thought I would sleep here." I placed my pillow far enough down on the blanket so it wouldn't get in the grass and dirt, and laid down.

Oh. Well, thank you. Taliesin watched me for a moment. *I mean it. You can't enjoy sleeping out here. Thank you.*

"You did save my life, it's only right that I help you." I laid down, closed my eyes, and tried to ignore the rocks poking through the blanket.

"You're so smart," Shamash said, as I appeared back in Akasha.

I blushed and shrugged. "Can we try again? I don't know how long I'll be able to sleep."

"Of course dear, come here." Aya patted her lap.

I laid my head down sighing as my Amagal began to run her fingers through my hair. Shamash settled back into his meditation while Aya once again talked me through waking up without losing them.

I didn't bother to open my eyes this time as I heard Taliesin breathing. I reached him and placed my hands on his back. He snorted awake. "Think about how it feels to be human, imagine it in your mind," I said.

Moonlight cool energy flowed through me and into Taliesin. In the past, any energy spike felt fiery hot, but unicorn energy felt very different. Under my fingers Taliesin's muscles twitched, but nothing else happened. I waited as patiently as I could, allowing the energy to build and grow. I began to worry nothing would happen when his muscles began to slide and shift under my hands. It felt so gross. It took all my willpower to keep my hands on him. Stomach-churning pops and cracks echoed as his bones changed back into his human form. The soft hair disappeared and damp skin replaced it.

Aya's fingers left my hair, and she pressed a soft kiss to my forehead as the energy stopped. Opening my eyes, I smiled. Taliesin had shifted back and . . . "Oh my god, you're naked!" I put one hand over my eyes and reached out for my blanket with the other flinging it in his direction. "Please cover up!"

"You're so overreacting," Taliesin said. I heard the fabric rustle. "Okay, there, I'm covered up."

I turned and peeked through my fingers. "Thank goodness, can we go to bed now?"

Taliesin raised an eyebrow as he grinned at me.

"Eeewwww, that is so gross. I didn't mean together." I might not help him next time if he was going to be rude.

"I forget how young you are," he said, standing up and keeping careful hold of the blanket.

"Fifteen isn't that young. Not wanting to see you, or any other boy naked, doesn't mean I'm young, just wise." I gathered up my stuff and turned. The eastern sky turned pink as the sun began to rise.

"Good morning," Señora Villescas greeted us in English. Turning, her eyes widened, and she began to shout at us in Spanish—very fast, angry Spanish.

"What is she saying?" Taliesin asked, clutching the blanket around him.

"I have no idea, she's not magical." Señora Villescas stormed towards us, grabbed our upper arms and began dragging us back to the ranch. "What? Where are we going?"

"To your uncle," she said. She banged on the door, tapping her foot until it opened.

Gavin yawned as he opened the door. "Yes?"

"I found these two coming out of the woods looking like this." Señora Villescas pursed her lips and shoved me and Taliesin at Gavin. "You need to leave this morning. I won't have a werewolf staying here, even if the moon isn't full tonight."

"Yes, of course. You two get in here," Gavin said, and shut the door. "How did you turn back?"

"Sapphire helped," Taliesin said, with a shrug.

"Gavin, get Taliesin something to wear, then you can tell us what happened." Anali slipped on her saffron yellow robe and sat on the edge of the bed. She patted the bed next to her. Sighing, I sat down and began to explain what happened last night.

"What a great idea. I'm glad you figured out what to do," Gavin said. "I wasn't looking forward to sneaking a unicorn into Buenos Aires."

"Dear," said Anali, "none of those ideas would have worked."

Gavin placed a hand against his heart his pale green eyes wide in fake shock. "What? Some were pure genius."

"Anyway, can I please go to bed?" I stood up and moved towards the door.

"Yes, of course. I'm sure we can all use some more sleep. But we'll have to pack and leave after breakfast which is in two hours," Gavin said.

I nodded and shuffled to my room. Two hours was better than nothing.

Chapter Four

Cartazonon rubbed his temple as the buzzing echoed through his brain. It had begun to fade, but now vibrated through his head making his teeth ache. Pushing past the pain, Cartazonon followed the energy, the call to Akasha. He followed along to Buenos Aires before the bright, pure call became too painful.

Turning, he grabbed the garbage can, barely managing to not throw up on his Persian rug. What in the world had caused this?

"Are you all right, Khan?" Lee asked holding out a bottle of mineral water.

"Send people to Buenos Aires. Send some walk-ins, and General Saran—tell him he can take whatever he needs."

"Of course. May I tell him what is waiting for him there?" Lee asked.

Cartazonon groaned and slid long, bony fingers into his coarse black hair. His hands hid his narrow, pale face. When he looked up, his black eyes flashed with pain and anger. "I have no idea, something is sending out a call, an invitation to magical beings, and it's Akashic in origin."

"I'm sure General Saran will bring back something good to eat. A call this intense should attract some large, powerful magical creatures," Lee said, going to the cabinet and pulling out a bottle of Excedrin. "Here, take two of these."

Cartazonon smiled, showing square white teeth. "Thank you. Make sure he knows to bring me some *dulce de leche* ice cream back with whatever creatures he finds."

Lee chuckled, his thin brown eyes narrowing and pulling at the scar across his face. "Khan, everyone knows to bring you that ice cream."

Cartazonon shuffled paperwork to buy a small fishing village in Greece. "As they should, I have to get some benefits for all I do for you people."

Lee laughed, a ragged gasping laugh that always made Cartazonon smile. Two thousand years and he still hadn't grown tired of the old Mongolian warlord.

Chapter Five

"Our life is March weather, savage and serene in one hour."
~Ralph Waldo Emerson

Shante had poked me on Facebook ten times since I last logged in. I commented on each and every post, and all the pictures from her sixth birthday party. I copied the photo of Shante holding up the handmade cloth doll I bought her in Pennsylvania. Shante and I had lived in Hope House together, the nicest of the group homes I had lived in. I took care of Shante, helping her with chores, picking out clothes, reading stories to her, and holding her when she cried for her mother. Shante's mom, Sophia, had done the same for me when I entered the group home system at five.

It always felt disconcerting stepping back into the 'normal' world, even over the computer. A few minutes later, I posted a heavily edited update with some pictures for Shante to see the next time she went to Cordelia's house.

"Sapphire, are you on Facebook?" Taliesin asked.

"Yes, why?"

"My mom posted some fabric samples on her page and wants us to look over them for new costumes," he said, crossing the RV in three easy steps and sitting next to me at the small table. I stumbled when I tried to walk while the RV was moving, but Taliesin moved with the grace of a unicorn even in

43

his human form. The RV looked like a tiny apartment, two couches, a table with a bench and chairs, a kitchen, and a very tiny bathroom. In the back, four beds pulled down from the wall. If desperate we could sleep in the RV, but it wouldn't be comfortable.

"I don't need a new costume. Did you see the pictures from Shante's birthday party?" I said. Gavin arranged for Taliesin's mom Cordelia to become Shante's mentor when I left Hope House. When that happened, I knew that Gavin hadn't been looking for the Jewel of Akasha or even his sister's child, he searched for me, his beloved niece. Gavin had shown me in that one action that he listened to me, that he paid attention, and wanted me to be happy. I had trusted Gavin ever since and done my best to act like a good niece.

"*I wish you were here, Sapphire.*" Shante had written under a picture of herself blowing out her candles. My throat tightened and my vision swam with tears.

"She understands why you couldn't go to her party," Taliesin said.

I blinked back the tears and cleared my throat. "Does she? Because I promised her I would never willingly leave her."

"And you didn't."

"I made the phone call. I asked Five to let me go and live with Gavin and Anali."

Taliesin leaned in and whispered. "If I remember correctly you were having nightmares about the Sons of Belial at the time. I know you, Sapphire, you left Shante and Hope House to protect them. I'd bet you weren't ready to move in with your aunt and uncle. I'd bet you sacrificed yourself, in a small way, to protect the others in your group home from being hurt."

"The Sons of Belial killed my parents. I couldn't let them kill anyone else I loved. And moving in with my super nice and rich aunt and uncle wasn't much of a sacrifice." That and I still felt like I had betrayed Shante even if I had tried to protect her.

Taliesin shook his head. "Of course. Moving in with adults you barely know and leaving behind people you love isn't a sacrifice at all."

I shrugged and looked out the window.

"I'll leave you alone in a second. Do you know what's happening with Shante's case?" Taliesin asked. He stared at a picture of his mom holding Shante on her lap. "Last time I talked to my mom she said she wanted to adopt Shante."

I looked at the two of them together smiling, Shante's dark skin and black curls contrasted with Cordelia's pale skin and honey-blond hair. "I have no idea. Shante has been in the system over a year, and last I heard Sophia was still doing drugs, and no one knows who her dad is. So they might give her mom another six months to a year to get her stuff together."

Taliesin grunted and walked away.

I caught up with my other Facebook friends, including the three apprentices to the Guardians we traveled with over the summer. Storm and Elijah posted about everyday stuff, but Rebecca had started her own online store for her bead work.

"Those are lovely," Kayin said, looking over my shoulder. "Rebecca's?"

"Yes, I'm thinking of having her make a pair of beaded hair clips in every shade of pink possible for Shante."

"That would make a lovely gift." Kayin touched the pendent Rebecca made for him. Rebecca gave us each a necklace or hair clip beaded in the same pattern. Tiny seed beads expertly placed made beautiful rings representing Earth, Air, Water, Fire, Mother Earth, Father Sky, and in the center Spirit and the doorway to Akasha. "My little sisters would love something like that."

Kayin hadn't spoken about his family in a long time. "What if you sent them something?"

"I doubt my mom would let them have anything I'd sent. She thinks I'm a *muroyi*, possessed by an evil spirit." Kayin ran his hand over his hair. The morning he woke up with red curls scattered through his black curls was the last time he saw his family. "Did you know, I'd never lived anywhere but my ancestral land before? Once my mother chased me from our hut and out of the village, the Children of Fire protected me and took me off the nature preserve my village cares for."

"I'm so sorry," I lay my head on Kayin's shoulder. We stared out the window. The woods were filled with tall trees with spring green leaves and rough bark that looked like gray alligator skin, small bushes, ferns, and the occasional bright colored bird.

"Do you ever wish you were like them, growing up knowing about the Children of Fire?" Kayin asked, in a rough whisper nodding to Sasha and Miu. "What would it have been like to wake up on our fifteenth birthday and celebrate these changes instead of fear them?"

Cold jealousy settled in the pit of my stomach. Sasha grew up with faerie tales of magical beings and stories of the Phoenix King and Queen. While his changes surprised him, his family celebrated them. Miu's family knew their heritage since before the samurai ruled Japan. These changes blessed their lives. Kayin and I haven't decided about our lives yet.

Wallowing in self-pity and listing everything you don't have or how things could have been, is a sad way to spend your time. Life happens, and sometimes it's painful. But you have to deal with it. You still need to get up and live your life. Nothing lasts forever. Even the worst parts are only a moment of your life, and will pass. Hang in there and try your best to find things to feel grateful for. Focus on what you have, on the times of joy, on your blessings.

My mom's words echoed in my mind. "I have you," I said. "I have you, and I wouldn't want my old life if it meant giving you up."

"I am very glad to have you as my new family." Ebony arms wrapped me in a hug. "You have Gavin and Anali too."

"I guess. Life with them is so weird. I feel like I can't figure out how to act or who they want me to be. There are no rules or clear routines. Outside of travel times and show times everything else is kind of a free-for-all." I picked at the hem of my shirt. "They don't treat me any differently than you or Taliesin."

"I think Gavin doesn't know what to do," Kayin said. "He

does look at you differently. His eyes soften when he talks to you. And when a boy he doesn't know talks to you he glares and moves close to you."

"Seriously?" I couldn't remember any of those things ever happening.

"Yes, little sister, I'm serious. It will work out. The three of you will figure out how to live as a family."

"I guess so." Maybe if I had any idea of how a real family worked, I would have more luck figuring out how to act.

"How are you guys doing on your studies?" Anali asked, turning her chair around. I felt queasy looking at her with the front windshield behind her.

None of us bothered to answer, instead the others took their laptops out and started to work. Gavin and Anali signed us up for a 'virtual academy' where we did our schoolwork online and teachers graded us. I took more classes, and the expectations were higher than at my old school. I caught up on all of my classes except for history. I hate history classes which focus on dates and wars. Learning about how people lived, art they created, and even new discoveries I enjoy, but dates and wars are so boring!

I needed to complete three lessons in history and take a test before I could do anything else. Whatever, getting A's at the group home earned me more privileges and rewards. There are scholarships for kids in the system. So far, other than reminding us to do our work, Gavin and Anali hadn't said anything about grades. Maybe they didn't care?

I clicked on the first lesson. Skim the reading, try and remember the dates as best as I can, and take the test. Who cares what my grades were like? My future had been decided.

After a lunch of sandwiches and fruit, we took a break from studying. Kayin and Anali sewed juggling balls to sell while Taliesin and Sasha played *Go*. I didn't see Miu. Maybe I'd luck out and she was napping. As the only other girl in our group, Miu frequently sought me out to do girly stuff.

Miu plopped down and set a metallic pink box in front of

me. "Let's do our nails, even our toes. It's hot in Buenos Aires, and we'll wear sandals. We need to have cute toes."

"Sure, do you want me to do yours first?" *I can do nails. As long as you don't want to give me a makeover, I'm fine.*

Miu nodded, her high pony tail bouncing. "Yes please. Can you do flowers?"

"Sure."

Clapping, Miu opened the box and pulled out polish. "I'd like my nails frosty blue with sunrise lavender flowers."

Guh, even the names were cute and girly. I painted her fingernails while she told me the latest gossip about her friends back in Japan. I made the appropriate noises of interest and even asked a few questions. She didn't expect much as I focused on painting her nails.

"I miss my family. I've missed so many celebrations this year. I know that being a powerful Child of Fire is important. My family danced around me and then we went to the shrine to give our thanks to the ancestors when I woke up with peridot green eyes and my skin a paler shade." Her eyes fill with tears. "My little brother fell and scraped his knee that afternoon. I helped him clean it, as I always have, and it healed. My family was beside themselves with joy, and for three days family from all over Japan came to celebrate."

I set her foot down and picked up the other one. The blue had to dry before I put on the flowers. "It sounds great."

"It was. I spent the next eight months preparing to travel. Learning myths, rituals, the history of the Children of Fire, and everything else my grandparents and parents thought I might need." Miu took a lace hanky out of her pocket and wiped her eyes, careful not to ruin her make-up. "I was so excited that I never thought about how much I would miss home."

"I'm sure we'll go to Japan. I know your family protects Mt. Fuji and the surrounding forests and the magical creatures who live there." I began adding the pale lavender flower on her big toe.

"Do you think so? That would be so much fun! I can take

48

you all over Tokyo and you can meet my friends."

I smiled at Miu and held in a shudder of fear. Oh, God. I had seen pictures of her and her friends all dressed up in cosplay and Lolita at the park. Would she make me go, too?

"Okay pick your colors, and I'll do your nails," Miu said.

I hunted through the box, bottles clinking as I shifted them around. Through all of the bright and glittery bottles of colors that I would hate on me, I found one dark bottle. Holding it to the light I smiled. I had found a purple so dark it looked almost black. It sparkled—I could live with sparkle.

Miu clapped. "I knew you would like that color when I saw it in the store."

Now I felt like crap. "You bought this for me?"

"I thought it would look better with your clothes."

I looked down at my dark gray shirt and blue jeans. "Thank you."

"You're welcome. Now give me your hand."

By the time we arrived in Buenos Aires my nails looked great, and Miu's happiness hummed against my empathic bubble.

I sighed with relief when I saw the houses. The Cirque du Feu Magique performers divided themselves among three large row houses. We stayed in a smaller one next to them. The theater we performed in was a few blocks away, and the dance schools where different performers offered workshops were all within walking distance. These past three weeks offered a much needed break from the constant traveling. While I enjoyed traveling, it was nice to stay in one place for a while.

When Gavin first mentioned how we would travel with the Cirque du Feu Magique, I pictured Cirque du Soleil. We were a much smaller troupe. We kept the acts simple but well done, and everyone performed in at least two acts. Most of the crew could do three if needed. We hired local people to run the ticket booth and sell food and drinks.

Traveling with Cirque du Feu Magique allowed us to hide the paperwork trail and mask our Phoenix energy by surrounding ourselves with normal people. We also had Nyota, a wizard with electronics. I could feel the protection when we entered the range of the large damping field and my shoulders relaxed. Nyota made a small damper for the RV but the larger, more powerful one made me feel safer. I had no idea how she did it, something about vibrations and frequencies and some energy the Children of Fire give off. All I knew was science kept us well hidden.

"Welcome back," said Michael, our manager, ringmaster, and Nyota's father. He made sure everyone trained well and rested. He organized the acts and set up the shows. Michael, Gavin, and Philip, Michael's brother and owner of the San Francisco Center for Circus Arts, worked together to decide where we traveled next. The final decision was based on juggling the needs of the circus, information from the dreamers, and requests for help from Children of Fire who watched over magical creatures.

"We have a show in four hours. Will you guys feel up to performing, or do I need to do the modified schedule?" Michael asked. Michael looked a lot like his brother, Phillip, stocky, muscular, and golden skinned. He wore his brown hair cut short, and he made no effort to hide his receding hair line, where Philip wore his salt and pepper hair in a Mohawk.

"We can perform. I'm sorry about not making it back in time for the shows," Gavin said.

Michael held up hand. A thick scar bisected the palm. "Gavin, don't worry about it. We have a back-up plan for a reason."

"How did the rest of the troupe take it?" Anali asked.

Michael shrugged, his crooked nose wrinkling with his grin. "There was some grumbling, but the consensus is that because Gavin signs the paychecks and pays for everything, you guys can be eccentric. They are a bit confused as to why Taliesin, Miu, Kayin, and Sasha go with your family."

Gavin sighed. "Well, I guess that's not too bad. I don't want the others to think we're not committed to the troupe."

Michael ran a hand over his short brown hair. "Hey, you guys have a higher purpose. The others will be fine, let me worry about morale. We'll leave here at six-thirty. Make sure to eat and rest before we leave."

"We will," Anali said. "And I'll make sure everyone is on time."

Gavin looked away as if he wasn't the one who always ran late.

* * *

"Sasha, will you help me up?" I asked, holding out my hands.

Sasha grasped my hands and placed his feet in front of the stilts tied to my feet. It felt like butterflies fluttered inside me, as it always did until I found my balance. I took a deep breath and steadied myself, taking in the familiar scent of make-up, hair-spray, and popcorn in the air.

"Thank you," I said, tying the long skirt around my waist, covering the aluminum stilts.

"You are welcome." Sasha crossed his arms and looked out onto the stage. "I think I could do that."

I stepped over a cable and looked out. The audience watched in silence as Gavin held Anali's hands, lifted her over his head, then she moved into a handstand. "Why don't you? I'm sure Gavin and Anali would teach you."

Gavin lowered Anali until the back of her shoulders rested against his shoulders. They balanced perfectly and Gavin began to turn.

Sasha snorted. "I might injure myself. My parents want me to be in ballet like them. Their whole life, my whole life, is ballet. So instead I spin glowing balls in circles." He held up the poi, shaking the LED balls at the end of the chains, as if they were to blame that he couldn't do something more exciting.

Gavin and Anali finished their statue routine with Anali holding onto her feet and creating a circle with her body. Gavin held her above his head then tossed her up bringing his hands together so she could slide down him like a ring falling over a pole. He spread his feet, stopping her from hitting the ground. They bowed to loud applause, and the clowns went on stage to distract the audience while riggers set up the silk.

In vibrant costumes, wild hats, and make-up which highlighted their natural faces, the clowns pretended to re-do the statue act. They fumbled, fell, and faked the complex poses. What the audience didn't know is that the silly clowns were all talented enough to do any of the acts they wanted to. People underestimate you when you act silly.

"Are you guys ready? We're on after Taliesin," Ralph the stilt leader asked. As he strode over, his black and white striped pants skimmed the ground.

"Yes," I said.

"Good, I'm going to check on the others."

"I should walk on stilts." Sasha glared after Ralph. "It does not look hard. I am at top of class at the Vaganova Academy of Russian Ballet in St. Petersburg. I should be star, not. . ." Sasha began to speak in Russian. I tuned him out and focused on warming up and going through the routine in my head.

I shivered as if a slick oily film coated my stomach. This isn't my normal pre-show jitters. Did I eat something bad?

Playful piano music faded as the clowns scattered off the stage. The first note from the cello echoed through the hall and pale blue fabric fluttered down from the ceiling. The audience's eyes focused on the fabric and didn't see Taliesin walking onto the stage. When the silk touched the ground Taliesin began to climb up. Grasping both sections of the fabric in his hands, he pulled himself up hand over hand, his body and legs motionless.

The silver and ice-blue ribbons which made up his costume shimmered in the spotlight. Taliesin wound himself up in the fabric, then grasped the tail end and began to twist. Soon, he spun in mid-air. Curling into a ball, he spun faster and faster. Then he stretched out and slowed down. I held my breath knowing what came next. Taliesin flipped, loosened one of the loops, then let go completely. He rolled out of the loops of fabric to the floor, stopping inches above the hard wood. The audience gasped and clapped.

Sasha put his hand over mine, startling me. "Sapphire, you are going to hurt yourself."

I had scratched myself, leaving vivid red marks. *Oh crap this isn't good.*

"Can you go and get Gavin for me please?"

"Something bad is happening, yes? I can feel something is wrong." His gray eyes darted around.

"Yes. Please get Gavin."

Sasha frowned but did as I asked. Closing my eyes, I focused on the sick, evil feeling that came from the Sons of Belial. It felt much too weak, not the way I remembered how Cartazonon or his generals felt. *Maybe a walk-in, but how did they find us with Nyota's damping field?*

"Sapphire, what's wrong?" Gavin asked. Half of his face glowed in blues and purples, and his hair was gelled into a tight French braid.

"I think a walk-in is in the audience," I answered. "Can you feel it?"

"Walk-in? Evil spirit thing is here?" Sasha asked looking into the audience.

"A spirit being who inhabits the body of someone who owes the Sons of Belial a favor. Remember?"

Sasha nodded, "Da, is odd word."

"My stomach feels a little queasy," Gavin said peering over our shoulders.

"Do we need to leave?" Sasha asked, as he shifted back and forth. His nervousness tugged at my shield.

"It doesn't feel very strong." Gavin scanned the crowd as if he could find the walk-in. "Are you both wearing your contacts?"

Touching my eyelid I felt the contact. The Sons of Belial couldn't trace a Child of Fire unless they saw the flame in our eyes, a reflection of the Phoenix power within us. Using a special ritual, Children of Fire filled the contacts with power from Akasha so the Sons of Belial couldn't see the flames in our eyes. My parents might still be alive if these contacts had been around ten years ago.

"Yes."

"Da."

"I'll make sure the others have their contacts in, and I'll ask Nyota to make sure the damping field is working properly. As long as we don't do anything that shows we are Children of Fire, we should be fine." Gavin patted my arm and squeezed Sasha's shoulder. "It's about time for your act. Don't worry."

Sasha scowled, he didn't look convinced, and his nervousness increased. When we traveled with the Guardians, Elijah their dreamer always knew when the Sons of Belial came too close so we could avoid them. Neither Miu nor Sasha had felt them before.

"I do not like this."

"I know, but this is something small. It won't sense us as long as we don't use our powers," I said. Sasha arched an eyebrow at me. "You're a performer right? Can't you fake it and get through this?"

Sasha stood tall, his shoulders back. "Da, I can do that."

"Good, because it's time."

Taliesin bowed low. His cello music faded as our New Orleans jazz piece began to play. Spinning our poi, we stepped out onto the stage. The LED lights glowed, creating circles in the air.

Focusing on the routine, I forced myself not to react as I moved closer to the walk-in. It was definitely one of the people in the front rows of the audience.

In front of me, Sasha stopped for a moment. His nervousness changed to cold fear. I worried he would run, but he kept spinning his poi and stepped forward, continuing with the routine. Taking a breath, I kept my balance on the stilts and slid back into the performance.

I tried to figure out which person the Sons of Belial's walk-in possessed, but I couldn't see the audience in the dim light. Why were they here? Did it feel us? Would more come here? Was our cover with the circus blown? What would we do now?

My fire pendant began to warm. In my panic I must have reached out for Akasha. I pulled in my power, careful not to shut it down completely.

As the last trombone notes echoed through the theater and the lights came up, I saw a plump, middle-aged woman staring at a young woman in front of her. The young woman's hair sparkled with tiny braids decorated with beads and shells. The walk-in didn't blink. Her hands flexed into claw shapes. The walk-in didn't come here for us. She was hunting someone else.

Chapter Six

"I believe in you."
~Mom

My body shook as I walked off the stage. I needed to help the woman with the braids. If I didn't, the Sons of Belial would kill her by pulling all of the magic and life out of her body to feed their own rituals for protection and immortality.

"Sapphire, do you need some help?" Shin asked, his blue-streaked bangs were gelled back over his buzzed black hair so they wouldn't get in the way.

"Sasha?" I looked around. How long had I stood back stage? On stage Miu danced a traditional Japanese fan dance. The geisha make-up and pearl gray silk kimono embroidered with cherry blossoms made her look timeless. Each movement was slow and graceful—a complete change from the hyperactive girl I knew. I always thought Miu somehow channeled a great-great grandmother when she danced.

"He went to get Gavin." Shin held up his hands. "Let me help you down and we'll get the stilts off."

"Okay."

"Sapphire, what's wrong?" Shin's thin dark eyes held mine as he lowered me to the ground. We'd become friends over the past year. I met him when I went to winter camp at the San Francisco Center for the Circus Arts where he taught me beginning acrobatics. I didn't want to lie to Shin, but he wasn't a Child of Fire, so I didn't have much choice. One of the many drawbacks to being a magical being in a secret society.

"I need some water. After spending time in the mountains I think the heat got to me."

"Hold on I'll get you some." Shin grabbed a cold bottle of water from one of the coolers we stored backstage. "You should take better care of yourself."

"Thanks."

"Will you be able to do jump rope?"

"Sure. Miu's on right now, then your act, and then the clowns." Guilt gnawed at me for lying to Shin.

Shin began to stretch his arms in preparation for doing Chinese pole, the solid muscles in his arms stretched and flexed as he moved. "My mom sent me a box with several jars of kim-chi, do you want one?"

Um, hello, I'm not stupid. "Yes, of course I want one. Is she still bugging you about how you're wasting your life and should go to college?"

Shin laughed and stepped closer to me to let the clowns pass by. A normal girl would probably flush and stammer being so close to a handsome buff man, but at this point I had buff body immunity. With all of the hours I've spent around buff bodies and pressed against them during practice, I could now keep my cool and not stammer like an idiot. "Not in this letter. This time it was a reminder to stay away from women of loose morals because I need to marry a proper Korean woman once I come to my senses and return home to start my life."

"I'm sure the girls will be very upset to hear you're not available."

Shin shrugged as he warmed up his wrists. "I'm not interested. Anyway my older brother got accepted to law school and is dating a proper Korean girl. I think if I can wait until he gives my mom a grandchild before I go home, maybe she'll lay off me."

I raised an eyebrow. Was he joking? His mom mothered

everyone. Gavin got an earful of advice at the going-away party they held for Shin. Apparently he wears his hair too long, and he should get rid of his earrings.

Shin laughed. "Yes, I know, but I'm hoping a bunch of grandchildren will distract her and she won't yell so loud."

"Good luck. I'm glad I don't have to worry about stuff like that," I said, untying my stilts.

Shin's brow furrowed. "Stuff like what?"

"Like people caring about what I do with my life."

"Doesn't Gavin care?"

"I don't know. He's never said anything about it." Of course having a prophesied destiny did kind of override any other hopes and dreams.

"Hey, I'm being waved at. I'll see you later," Shin said, patting my shoulder

I watched Shin join the group for Chinese pole. Taliesin's mom had made them costumes of skin-tight fabric which looked like white overalls with bright splotches of paint. Shin put on a painter's hat to complete the look. I envied his normal life. At least I guessed it's a normal life with normal problems. Having grown up in group homes and foster care, I wasn't sure how normal families acted or what problems they dealt with. *I bet it's better than fighting evil spirits who possess people and hunt and kill magical creatures.*

I wrapped up my stilts and put them away then went back to watching the walk-in and the woman in braids. The walk-in still stared at Braids, who watched Miu and didn't seem to notice the evil lurking behind her, if her happy smile was anything to go by.

"Is everything all right?" Gavin asked, Nyota in tow.

"I found the walk-in," I said.

They leaned over my shoulder to look out into the crowd. "Where?"

I pointed to the third row on the right side. "Do you see the woman with all the small braids?"

"Yes."

"Two rows up and three seats to the left—the middle-aged woman staring at her like a hungry cannibal."

"Gross." Gavin wrinkled his purple painted nose. "I see her. Thank goodness she isn't after any of us."

"She doesn't even know you're here." Nyota said, tucking a dark brown dreadlock behind her ear. "I was wondering if you would feel the Sons of Belial or if the damping field would block them too. I've never had the chance to test it before now. Does the walk-in feel different from normal?"

I shrugged and turned to face Nyota. Her light, amber-brown eyes sparkled brighter than her multiple eyebrow piercings. "Well, the sick feeling seemed sudden, but it could have been masked by my normal pre-show jitters."

"Interesting." Nyota sucked on the barbell piercing in the middle of her bottom lip.

"How far does the damping field reach?" I asked.

Nyota shrugged. "It covers part of the parking lot. I wouldn't go past the tables where you guys sign stuff while the walk-in is here. Why?"

"We need to protect Braids."

Gavin stepped away from me. "I'm not sure there is anything we can do. None of us can risk exposure. She'll have to take care of herself."

I froze unable to catch my breath. Letting Braids die by having her power and life sucked out of her was not an option.

Gavin grabbed my shoulders and stared into my eyes for a moment before speaking. "I know you want to save her, but we can't get caught. Thousands of magical beings are counting on us to save them."

I let my cold glare speak for me.

"Let me know if you need anything else." Nyota stepped away her light brown skin blending into the shadows.

Gavin's fingers tightened around my shoulders. "Promise me you won't put yourself or anyone else in danger. Promise me, Sapphire, or I'll drag you out of here right now."

My eyes narrowed and Gavin's face blurred through my

eyelashes. "I promise."

"I know you're not happy, but sometimes we have to make choices based on what's for the greater good."

I didn't answer and turned to watch Braids. Gavin sighed and walked away. I would protect her. I would find a way to protect her without breaking my promise.

The crowd gasped, Braids leaned forward in her seat as the Chinese Pole act took the stage. I couldn't help but smile as delight bubbled from the crowd when the Chinese Pole troupe began to climb the six wooden poles. They seemed to skip up the twenty foot tall polls as they climbed up.

As soon as they were up, they used their arms to spin around the poles and slowly moved back down. Another group climbed the poles and at the top stretched out to the beat of the music. They held onto the poles with their hands and held their bodies perpendicular to the pole. My abs ached in sympathy.

Looking back to Braids I frowned. The walk-in didn't even look away from her prey as the performers leapt from one pole to another in perfect rhythm.

* * *

"Everyone has five minutes and then I want you out in the parking lot to sign posters and talk with the kids," Michael said, after the show. He patted his face with a rag trying to sop up sweat without smearing his make-up.

Everywhere we went Gavin arranged for children in group homes and orphanages to see our show for free. After the show we talked to the kids and signed their programs.

I slipped through the crowd linking my arm through Shin's once I found him. "Hey there."

"Hey Sapphire. What's up? Do you need some water?"

"Nope I'm good. I just felt like hanging out with you tonight."

"Sure." His voice said he didn't believe me. "Should we go sign programs?"

"Absolutely." I scanned the parking lot hoping to find Braids. *Damn it.* I couldn't see her anywhere.

Children swarmed around us, bouncing and waving their programs. Armed with Sharpies, each of us signed our names under our picture, smiling as we thanked the kids for coming to see us. Some of the performers even wrote nice sayings like, 'Reach for your dreams' or 'Do the impossible.'

I wrote, 'I believe in you.' It was one of the quotes in my mom's journal, one of the few directly from her. Some days it helped the most.

I believe in you, my darling. I believe you are strong, intelligent, and wise. I believe you'll learn and grow and you will always try your best. I believe you have love, compassion, and courage enough to face any challenge. Trust your instincts, listen to your wisdom, follow your heart, and remember I believe in you.

Fearing I lost Braids, as only a few people hung around, I scanned the parking lot one last time. I found her as she walked past an empanada vendor. The walk-in followed close behind. I grabbed Shin's arm. "I need your help. I have a bad feeling." *Really, a 'badfeeling' that's the best you can do?*

Shin's forehead wrinkled, and his black eyes were serious. "What do you need?"

I couldn't believe he accepted this so easily. "See that woman with her hair in braids and that woman following her? Something isn't right?" I was vague and sounded stupid. *You're on fire tonight.*

Shin looked at the two women for a moment. "Should we go over there? It's better to be safe than sorry, right?"

"Thanks," As we began to walk towards Braids, the walk-in reached out and grabbed her upper arm.

"Let go of me," Braids said, as the walk-in tried to drag her backwards.

"Hey!" Shin yelled. "What are you doing?"

People turned, some even began walking towards the two women.

"She's my daughter," the walk-in said, looking the part of the middle aged woman it possessed.

"I am not," Braids said, trying to pull away. "I don't know you. Let go of me."

Following behind Shin, I made sure the walk-in couldn't see me.

"Ma'am, please let go of her and we'll get this all sorted out," Shin said his voice calm yet firm.

"Yes, let go." Braids pushed at the walk-in's hand as she jerked her body backwards.

"You need to let go of her," a man said, placing his hand on top of the walk-in's arm.

Braids pulled free of her grip. I reached out to steady her. "Come with me," I said.

Braids nodded, and I guided her through the crowd gathering around the now hysterical walk-in.

"I have a bike over there," Braids said pointing to the far end of the parking lot.

"Can you run?"

"Away from her, yes, absolutely." Holding hands we ran through the parking lot, sliding between cars and around groups of friends talking.

"There—the silver moped."

I looked around, no one followed after us. She shoved her helmet on, the beads and shells in her braids clinking against the hard plastic.

"I don't see any one, hurry and go," I said.

"You should come with me. What if she tries to get you?" Braids said, as she started her moped.

"I'll be fine. I can hide." I backed away.

Braids smiled. "Thank you. You saved my life."

"You're welcome." I watched her drive away. I screamed when a hand clamped down on my shoulder.

"Sapphire, you promised me you wouldn't try and save her," Gavin said. Turning, I flinched at the sight of his clenched jaw.

I took a deep breath. All the adults I've dealt with hated to be corrected, and they hated it even more when I used the 'letter of the law' instead of the 'you knew what I meant.'

"No, I promised that I wouldn't put myself or anyone else in danger."

Gavin's green eyes hardened. "You knew what I meant," he hissed.

"I couldn't let her get killed." Crossing my arms, I looked out over the parking lot. The crowd broke up, and Shin walked back to the school auditorium with some of the other performers. I didn't see the walk-in anywhere.

"Sapphire, you're important. There are thousands of magical beings in the world waiting for you to send them home. You can't destroy their chance to go home by impulsive and reckless action."

I stared at my feet. "It wasn't a risk. Shin helped, and I stayed out of sight."

Gavin sighed. "Let's go. We need to go back inside the damping field. I sent the others on ahead. We can shower and change at the house."

I planned on following behind Gavin, but he did that adult thing where they wave you in front of them to 'keep an eye on you'. *Ouch, I guess he is seriously pissed.* I shuffled forward keeping my head down.

Tense silence filled the car on the ride home. No one broke it, not even Anali. I scrambled out of the car, up the stairs, and into one of the showers. I hoped Anali would talk to Gavin and calm him down.

I scrubbed the stage make-up off, and managed to get the mass of gel out of my hair. I wanted to stay in the shower until the hot water turned cold, but the others were waiting for their turn.

"Are you okay?" Kayin asked, as I stepped out of the bathroom.

Kayin hadn't showered yet, and silver glitter still highlighted his cheekbones. "Yeah, I'm fine. Is Gavin still mad?"

"He seemed more scared than mad to me. Right now he's in the shower."

"Cool, I'm going to put my stuff away and then go and sit on the front stairs."

Kayin shook his head. "You can't hide from your uncle."

"I'm not hiding. I'm staying out of the way." There's a big difference between the two. For one thing, they're spelled differently.

Kayin snorted as he shut the bathroom door.

Luck was on my side. I managed to avoid everyone else in the house, and I slid out the front door, shutting it quietly. The warmth of the stone steps seeped through my jeans. A few stars shone through the glow of the city lights. Ten o'clock and the city wasn't slowing down. Buenos Aires never seemed to slow down. The air carried the Argentinian night life: tango music, the scent of food, and the laughter of friends.

I wanted to run out into the night and get lost in the city. I wanted to surround myself with people who didn't know me, people who didn't want anything from me. A group of teenagers walked down the street, laughing, bumping into each other. Closing my eyes, I held myself back from running after them.

"Hey, Sapphire."

My eyes popped open, and I plastered on a smile. "Hi Shin, thanks for your help earlier."

Shin's long bangs covered half his face and fell below his jaw, the blue streaks glowing against his natural black. Shin shrugged. "No problem, my mom and grandma both get 'feelings.' I've learned to trust them. I made dinner and we're going to watch a movie, do you want to join us?"

"That would be great." I stood up. "Let me tell someone and I'll come over."

"Cool, I'll put a plate together for you," Shin said.

I opened the door peeking around the edge breathing a sigh of relief when I saw a turquoise sari. "Anali, I'm going to hang out with Shin and the others and watch a movie okay?"

Anali's disapproval scratched against my empathic bubble. "You and Gavin need to talk."

"I know, but don't you think it would be better to talk tomorrow when he's not so upset?"

"Maybe, or maybe waiting will make everything worse."

I winced at her sharp voice. I wasn't sure what to do. I didn't want to talk to Gavin. I didn't see the point, we weren't going to agree. I would get lectured and have to sit there and listen.

"Are you saying I'm not allowed to go?" I asked. Anali hadn't done the firm-rule-setting-parenting thing yet. I was pushing my luck, but I bet that she wasn't going to do it now.

Anali sighed. "No, I'm not saying you can't go. All I'm saying is you need to talk to your uncle."

"And I will, but not tonight. If you need me, I'll be with Shin." I walked away, trying to shake off her frustration and disappointment. I hoped Gavin and Anali would talk and work it out. Then I wouldn't have to deal with it at all.

Opening the door to the house, I smelled the spicy red bean paste used in Korean food, along with soy sauce, garlic, and sesame oil. I loved it when Shin cooked. I followed the laughter and found at least half of the circus sprawled across the living room.

"Come and sit." Shin held up a bowl of noodles.

"Dinner smells great." I stepped over a pile of acrobats and sat next to him on the love seat. "How did you get the love seat?"

Shin grinned. "Cook gets the first choice."

"Very nice. What're we watching?" I adjusted the chopsticks and dug in. The translucent orange sweet potato noodles were tossed with a rich spicy sauce, tofu, and lots of fresh vegetables. "Dinner is amazing."

Shin chuckled and hit play on the remote. "I'm glad you like it. My mom sent *The Good, The Bad, and The Weird* for us to watch."

"It's a Sushi Western," Nyota said, sitting on the floor with her back tucked between my and Shin's legs.

"Sounds like fun."

I was choking on kim-chi because I had laughed with food

in my mouth when Kayin knocked and poked his head into the room. "Do you mind if I join you?"

"Come on in," Shin said.

"What's up, Big Brother?"

Kayin walked between people sprawled out on the floor and sat on the arm of the loveseat. "Not much. The others are going to a tango bar, but I thought it would be more fun to hang out over here."

"You're always welcome," Shin said.

"Come on," I scooted closer to Shin allowing Kayin to squeeze onto the small couch. Determination, protectiveness, embarrassment, and an emotion that felt hot and filled with longing hit my shield all at once. *Perfect, my safe place to hide from the crazy just became crazy.* I considered trying to sort out the wave of emotions, but they faded and I didn't want to know. *My new rule: I'm only dealing with my crazy, everyone else will have to sort things out on their own.*

Chapter Seven

"A quick temper will make a fool of you soon enough."
—Bruce Lee

I sipped mango juice hoping the sweetness would help wake me up. It was almost eleven; I should be awake and functional by now. I enjoyed the movie, but hadn't gotten to bed until after one. Today we needed to pack up, and tomorrow we would drive to our next stop, somewhere in northwestern Argentina.

"Gavin, please wait. Let's talk about this," Anali said, as they came down the stairs.

"No, I'm putting my foot down."

Looking around the kitchen, I tried to decide the best way to leave the room without being seen.

The door slammed open. Gavin swept in, his flame red hair as wild as the emotions coming off of him. "You are grounded!"

"What?" *What is he talking about? I haven't broken any rules—there are no rules to break.*

Gavin paced across the hard tile, his bare feet slapping with each angry step. "I received your grades. You have a D in history."

"So why am I grounded?"

"Why? After the stunt you pulled yesterday, and now this. Of course you're in trouble."

Anger flushed through my body, I was too tired to stuff my

emotions down and act like the 'good girl' I had trained myself to be.

I stood up so fast my chair fell back with a crash. "Why? I did exactly as I promised, and you didn't make any rules that if my grades drop I get grounded. You can't make up some rule whenever you feel like it."

Gavin's glared at me. "Don't talk to me like that. I'm in charge and I say you're grounded. No computer except for homework, no going out unless you're with me or Anali, and when we're at the house you stay in your room except for meals. Get up to your room right now."

"Whatever." I stormed up the stairs I slammed my door and changed out of my pajamas. I stuffed some essentials - my mom's journal, my scrap book, and money - into my backpack. He might be able to make me go to my room, but he damn well couldn't keep me there. And how dare he try! Months of no rules at all, and now suddenly I'm grounded. Rules, fine. Consequences, fine. But sudden punishment for pissing him off? No way.

"What's happening?" Miu asked.

"Gavin's being an ass." I added a hat, sunglasses, and a change of clothes to my backpack.

Miu twisted her hair around her finger. "What're you doing?"

"I'm going out for the day." I zipped up my bag and slung it over my shoulders. "I'll come back later."

Miu handed me my cell phone. I hadn't planned on taking it with me. It's why I'd left my phone on the night stand. "Take this, in case you need it. You can always turn it off if you want to."

I saw the worry in Miu's pale green eyes and felt it against my half-formed empathic shields. I needed to calm down in order to raise and maintain my shields. "Okay." I shoved the phone in my pocket.

Miu smiled. "I'll peek out the door and let you know if it's safe to go."

That was a surprise. I didn't expect her to help me. "Thanks."

"I don't see anyone," she whispered, "and their voices sound like they're coming from the kitchen."

"Thanks, Miu. I'll see you later."

It wasn't hard to creep down the stairs, into the living room, and slide out the window. Gavin could hear the front door. Avoiding the thorny, pink bougainvillea growing in front of the house almost ended my escape in a face plant on the sidewalk. However, after some careful footwork and a somersault lacking in grace with a painful landing on concrete, I kept moving. I walked about five blocks before I realized tears were running down my cheeks. I began rethinking my plan.

Looking around, I didn't recognize anything. The street seemed to go on forever. I went to the nearest cafe and ordered a media luna—a delicious breakfast pastry popular in Buenos Aries—and a cup of tea.

What was I going to do now? Getting back to the house would be easy enough, but I still didn't want to deal with Gavin. Despite his current opinion, I had never disobeyed him. Until now.

What a mess. I should have gone up to my room and pouted until Gavin felt bad and calmed down enough to talk to me. How was I going to cope with this?

When feelings get hurt and tempers flare it's easy to say or do something that you'll later regret. Do your best to keep your anger under control. Don't allow thoughts of how right you are, how badly they've wronged you, or why it needs to be done your way keep you from listening and thinking about what the other person is saying. Keep in mind your goals. Do you need to finish a project, heal a friendship, or set boundaries with someone? Having nothing to do with the person or situation might be the best choice. But make that choice calmly. Examine your feelings and thoughts without an out-of-control temper clouding your judgment.

Okay, my mom's advice has always helped before, so the goal is for Gavin to not be angry. The easiest way: go home, let him yell at me, and accept whatever consequence he gives me.

But why should I? Gavin and Anali have never set any rules.

I argued with myself over and over as I tore my breakfast to shreds not eating any of it. Looking at the plate of mangled pastry, I sighed. Should I get a new one or mush this mess together and eat it? The idea of eating anything made me gag. I pushed my plate away and sat back in the wooden chair.

I watched life go by. Couples in trendy outfits. Families out for a walk. Men hitting on pretty woman. They all walked by as I sat there trying to figure out what to do next.

My phone rang, the happy ring tone making me jump. I pulled it out of my pocket and saw the dark purple case framed a picture of Kayin. I couldn't ignore my big brother.

"Hey," I said.

"Little sister, are you okay?" Kayin asked.

"I'm all right, I guess."

"Have you been crying?"

My eyes filled again. "You know me too well."

"I wish you had told me—I would have left with you. I don't like the idea of you being out there all alone, especially since there was a walk-in last night." Kayin sighed. "Will you come back?"

"Yes, but not right now. I need some time to figure things out." I took a sip of my tea. Yuck—it was cold. "I'll be fine, big brother, don't worry. I have money and my phone."

"Okay, call me later," Kayin said.

"I will." I paused for a moment. "Is Gavin totally pissed?"

"He doesn't know. Anali took him to their room. We can hear them arguing."

"Oh ... wow ... okay then." *Good job at being coherent, Sapphire.*

"I'll let him know you're all right."

"If you need to. But I won't answer my phone after this." I was not going to spend my day arguing.

"I'll tell him. Bye, little sister, and take care of yourself."

"Bye." I tucked my phone in my bag and walked down the street. Trees and tall stone buildings lined the busy avenue. Black wrought iron balconies and carved stone decorated the buildings. They reminded me of the pictures Melanie took in Paris.

I still didn't have a plan, but I couldn't sit still any longer. Window shopping as I walked kept my mind focused, but I didn't buy anything. It didn't seem like a good idea to go back to the house with shopping bags as if I'd hung out with friends for the day instead of taking off.

A side street opened up into a large plaza filled with stalls and people. The steady thrum of hip hop music layered with a distinctive tango rhythm moved the crowd as they shopped. I bought a limeade and sipped on it while I looked over the booths.

A small stage sat at the far end of the plaza. A group of kids danced to Latin hip-hop music, their bodies flowing and popping to the fast beat. I found a place to stand and watch from under the shade of a tree. The energy they kept up song after song amazed me.

"It is you," said a sweet voice as cool hand grabbed my arm.

I started to pull away until I recognized Braids. "Hello."

"I can't believe I found you. I hoped I would. My family wants to thank you for saving me. I'm Alanna by the way," she said in one breath as she tugged me away from the crowd.

"Sapphire, and I didn't do all that much," I said, walking with her. "There's no need to do anything."

"You obviously don't know what you saved me from." Alanna turned to look at me and stopped. Her hands dropped, and I felt this muddled wave of emotion: embarrassment, excitement, and awe. "I'm sorry. Please, will you come with me?"

"Wait? What? You haven't done anything wrong." *I had hoped for a normal teenage day, window shopping, eating out, noticing a cute boy here and there, and then getting yelled at back at home. Do other people have crazy pop up all the time or is it me? Maybe attracting crazy is one of my Phoenix gifts.*

"It'll be so much fun." Her hands twitched as if she wanted to grab me again. "My family owns a restaurant outside of town on the beach. We can have lunch, and go swimming. Please."

Her round aqua eyes held mine, begging me to come with her. I felt myself caving in, but going off with a stranger would make Gavin flip out. Hadn't I done enough damage already? But the beach sounded much more fun than window shopping.

My phone buzzed. *"Gavin found out you're gone. He's asking everyone to start searching for you,"* Miu texted.

"Thanks," I texted back. *"Tell him not to bother. I'm headed off with a friend for the day. And I'm turning my phone off."*

"So how are we getting there?"

Thirty minutes later my butt was numb. I clung to Alanna on the back of her silver moped. I kept my eyes closed as Alanna tore through the city. She darted in-between cars and zipped through yellow lights with terror-inducing speed.

I dared to open my eyes once we left the city. The clear blue-green ocean sparkled in the sun. Maybe the nerve-shattering ride was worth the chance to swim in the warm water without the crowds that covered the city beaches.

We rounded a corner and a white, two-story building with dark blue trim came into view. Alanna slowed down, and the noise level dropped. All I heard through the helmet was rushing air, a constant loud whoosh which vibrated in my bones.

Alanna pulled into the driveway. People filled every table on the porch. Through the large windows the inside looked as busy. How did they get here? Only a few cars sat in the parking lot.

Alanna stopped the scooter, and I slid off. My sore butt headed for the hard ground, as my legs, too numb to hold me, gave out. Luck was on my side, and someone grabbed my arms and steadied me.

"Thank you," I said, taking off the helmet.

The guy smiled and took the helmet from me. "I'm Alanna's brother, Namor." His brown hair was done in small braids decorated with beads like his sisters, and he had the same aqua eyes, high cheek bones, and round jaw.

"Hello."

"This is Sapphire. She's the girl who saved me yesterday," Alanna said, taking the helmet from her brother.

Namor raised a thin eyebrow. "I can't believe you found her. It must be fate." He turned to me and held out his arm. "Let me escort you inside. I know how Alanna drives, I'm not surprised you had trouble standing."

"Hey. I drive just fine."

I took his arm for fun and so I wouldn't fall, again. "Thank you."

"Did you see her eyes?" Alanna said, her words more high-pitched and my head ached as I instinctively translated what they were saying. What language were they speaking? Would a normal human even hear anything that high-pitched?

"Yes, they're a very pretty green," Namor replied.

"That's not all—look again," Alanna said, her voice smug even in the other language. "Sapphire, make sure my brother gets you something cold to drink. I'll meet up with you as soon as I put my bike away," she said in English.

"Sure." What about my eyes? I knew she was some kind of magical creature because of the walk-in hunting her and the fact that I could translate what she was saying, a gift that only worked with magical beings. Did she know what Shamash's children looked like? And if she did, why are my eyes the clue and not my hair. My hair! I reached up with my free hand and began to comb through the wild tangled black and red mess. Why must I be around attractive people all the time and always look such a wreck?

"Mom," Namor called out. A plump woman with a bright smile and hair like her children's turned from where she waited a table. "This is Sapphire, the girl who saved Alanna."

Before I could blink she swept me up in a hug. The scent of lemons and the ocean surrounded her. "It's so nice to meet you, Sapphire. I'm Dorma," she said, ignoring her son. "You must sit. My husband will make his finest meal to thank you for saving our daughter."

"You don't need to. I didn't do much." I twisted the hem of

my shirt. People began to stare.

"Vulko! Come here and meet the girl who saved our Alanna," Dorma called.

I looked up, way up, to see him. "Hello."

Vulko smiled, his skin puckering around vicious looking scars. One eye a dark aqua the other white. I felt his happiness and kindness, which is the reason I didn't run.

"It's very nice to meet you." Then he froze. "Fire," he whispered.

"Vulko?"

"Dad?"

"She has fire in her eyes," he said changing to their language. His voice higher than when he spoke English. "Sapphire is Phoenix royalty."

The news of who I am swept over the restaurant. What I thought were people were magical beings, and they all began to talk in their native tongues.

"Phoenix royalty, how exciting," chirped a man in a squeaky fast language.

In a deep melodic language a woman asked, "Do you think she'll send us to Akasha?"

"I don't want to go."

"Is that why the gateway called to us?"

I covered my ears, my eyes watering as sharp pain exploded in my head. Too many people were speaking in too many different languages. "Stop. Please stop talking."

"Sapphire," Alanna said, "are you okay?"

"It's too much. Too many people talking. My head feels like it's going to explode."

Alanna turned her braids hitting me in the face. "Dad, you need to make everyone quiet down."

"Quiet!" Vulko commanded.

Everyone stopped talking. The stabbing in my head dulled enough for me to think again. "Okay, one thing at a time please. How do you know who I am?"

"We tell our children stories about the Phoenix Children and the fire which dances in their eyes," Dorma said.

Shit. I'd forgotten my contacts when I took off this morning. Okay, I would accept punishment for this, too. I majorly messed up. "Okay, next, someone said something about the gateway calling out."

"My grandfather built this house over one of the ancient portal stones," Vulko explained. "Three weeks ago it began to call out to magical beings. The call has gotten stronger every day."

"Except," said Namor, "last week when it quieted down for four days then picked back up again yesterday."

Was this because of me? If my being here awakened the gateway stone and called out to all of these magical beings, has it also called to the Sons of Belial? Have I put all of these people in danger? "What time is it?"

Alanna looked at her watch. "Almost three. Why?"

"The walk-in thing that tried to grab you last night, doesn't like the sun. We need to get you out of here before they come."

"So you are going to open the portal and send us home to Akasha?" asked a woman with silver gray hair and dark eyes. Her voice stirred within me the desire to obey her. I touched my fire pendant and opened myself to the energy of Akasha. The pull of her voice faded.

"Yes, with help I can open the portal."

"And those who don't want to go?" Her voice slithered around me, as if trying to find a way to entrance me.

"I won't make anyone go." I said keeping hold of my necklace. "I never have."

"How will you protect those of us who stay behind?" asked a man with a thick accent I hadn't heard before.

I twisted my ring. "I don't know. I haven't ever protected anyone from the Sons of Belial. I open the portal, that's it."

I'd never thought about what happens to the magical being still in the area after I open the portal. Had those left behind been hunted down, captured, and killed?

"There are some dark creatures hiding in the woods and in

the water," Vulko said. "We have kept them at bay, but they will want to go through the portal, can you protect us from them?"

"I can't, but my friends can." I pulled my phone out of my back pack and turned it on. It began beeping and chiming at me letting me know I had multiple voice mail and text messages. "I'll need to call and have the others come here, I can't do this on my own."

"Do whatever you need to," Dorma said, giving me a motherly pat on the hand. "We trust you."

"Thank you." I dialed the phone.

"Sapphire," Gavin said, anger and relief heavy in his voice. "Where are you? Are you all right? Come home right now. Do I need to come and get you?"

"Gavin, I know you're upset, but right now I need you and the others. We need to open a portal."

"Excuse me?"

Chapter Eight

"The strongest principle of growth lies in human choice."
—George Eliot

"Well," I said, drawing out every sound in order to delay having to explain.

"Sapphire," Gavin said his voice clipped. "I'm a red-head. I have a temper which I am holding onto as tightly as I can because I love you, but if you don't tell me what's going on. . ."

Gavin didn't need to finish, I understood. "So, remember the girl with the braids last night? She kind of found me at this market, and I went home with her, because her family wanted to thank me for saving her." I heard Gavin's sharp intake of breath, but kept talking before he could say anything. *I'm a rip the Band-Aid off person, when I'm forced to confess things.* "And people, who are actually magical beings, are hanging out here wanting to know if I can open a portal for them."

Gavin took several deep breaths. "You and I need to have a long talk when you get home. Where are you?"

"I'm not sure, hold on." I passed the phone to Alanna. "Can you please tell my uncle how to get here?"

"Of course," she said, and took the phone. I cringed with every new step she gave him, I could feel him getting angrier through the phone. She hung up and smiled at me. "It'll take them at least an hour to get here," Alanna said handing me the phone. "Let's have some lunch."

"Yes," Vulko said. "I will make a lunch fit for . . . " He looked me over. "I guess you are a princess. Yes?"

I shrugged. "I've never thought about it."

"Such modesty." Dorma led me to a table far away from the other guests. "Sit down and rest. Alanna and Namor will sit with you in a bit."

Butterflies danced in my belly as I sat in the warm sun and tried to relax. The salty ocean breeze caressed my skin and soothed my nerves. Iridescent blue and green fairies flew over and began to braid my hair. Had they done Namor and Alanna's hair?

My phone chirped at me reminding me of the messages I needed to answer. Careful to keep my head still, so I wouldn't get pinched by a faerie's sharp nails, I scrolled through the messages. I deleted everything from Gavin, we already talked. That left four other voice mails, which I deleted, Gavin would have told them what was happening by now.

Scrolling through my text messages, I rolled my eyes at all the ones asking if I was okay. *Seriously, I was gone for a few hours. It's not like I needed a keeper.*

I tucked the phone in my pocket as Alanna came over with a tray of drinks. The tall clear glasses held ice and a cloudy pale green liquid. "What's this?" I asked picking up the glass.

"Cucumber lemonade," Alanna said sitting next to me.

Taking a small sip, I let the tart, crisp drink slide over my tongue. "This is so good." I drank some more. A sharp pinch on my ear let me know I moved my head too much.

"Thanks, it's a family recipe. It keeps us hydrated out of the water."

"Alanna, may I ask what you are?" Miss Manners didn't have guidelines for introducing yourself to magical creatures.

Alana smiled. "We're merfolk. Most of the time the beings who come here are from the ocean. Sirens, nymphs, encantados, selkies, and other creatures who can turn into human forms for a while. But since the gateway stone began to call, we have gotten all sorts of creatures swimming about. Several types of sea serpents, ceetka, some merfolk who don't have a human form, and of course tons of sea horses."

"Sea horses? And what are encantados and ceetka?"

"You didn't think sea horses were from Earth did you?" Alanna asked. "Sea horses are an underwater cousin to faeries. Encantados are underwater shape shifting fae, they live in fresh water rivers and lakes. Ceetka are devas who watch after sea creatures, and humans say they are the face of god."

"How will they go through the portal? Isn't the gateway stone on dry land?"

"The stone is long," Namor said, as he set down plates of pasta covered in a garlic cream sauce. "It starts under the porch of the restaurant and goes out into the ocean."

"We've never seen the portal open. Namor is only two hundred and three, and I'm one hundred and twenty-seven. But the old ones say the portal would open out far enough that the largest sea serpent could pass through." Alanna tucked a braid behind her ear.

Something hit my cheek, reaching up I felt a thin braid. The fairies must have finished another one. "Thank you for braiding my hair, but I think we need to take a break. I won't be able to keep my head still while I eat."

They sighed, a sound like a spring breeze fluttering through leaves, and flew off.

"I didn't realize you were so old. You both look like teenagers."

"Well, I'm not. After one hundred and fifty you are considered an adult." Namor looked at my untouched plate. "Eat, we can explain everything later. Dad makes the pasta himself."

I wasn't sure I could eat. My stomach fluttered with nerves about Gavin coming, all the creatures waiting for me to send them home, and the possibility of the Sons of Belial coming. Not wanting to act rude I took a small bite. At the first taste of the creamy garlic sauce, any nervousness I felt faded away.

One drawback, or in this case benefit, to being empathic is that you can feel what the cook felt when they made the dish. Their emotions soak into food, and I have no idea how to block that. Most places the staff feel kind of numb, cooking is their job, their routine. Sometimes I feel something stronger, but this felt intense. Dorma and Vulko loved to cook. Their joy and excitement swept away my own feelings. I wonder if this is what being high feels like?

"This is delicious," I said, trying to stay focused.

"Thanks," said Alanna. "Mom and Dad make everything by hand."

Another wave of love and happiness swept through me, burying my own emotions even deeper. "I can tell. I've never eaten anything this amazing before."

I ate another bite. Not the best idea, but today didn't seem to be the day for good ideas. And this felt much better than how I felt before. We ate in silence for a while, which worked for me as I couldn't keep a thought in my head let alone make a sentence. *Sadness, my food is all gone.* I set my fork down and leaned back in my chair letting the sun warm my face.

"Sapphire, are you okay?"

I turned my head in Namor's direction. Opening my eyes, I blinked several times before I could focus on him. "I feel fine."

"Sapphire," he asked, his nervousness tickled my skin. I think I giggled. "Sapphire, focus, are you empathic?"

I stared at Namor, focusing on him. "Yes." I closed my eyes again.

"Crap," he said, then cussed in merfolkese.

Why do people always cuss in their native language?

Namor pulled my chair out and scooped me up. "Alanna, get some towels and find some clothes for her to change into."

"Okay, I'll meet you down at the beach."

The beach, we were going swimming? "I can't swim," I mumbled. Why didn't my mouth work right?

"Don't worry I'm not letting go of you, and we're going to sit in the water."

"Why?"

Someone took off my shoes and socks. Namor shifted, then walked again, his feet splashing in the ocean waves. "It will help pull the emotions out of you."

"This has never happened before." My head flopped against his arm as I made an attempt to move.

Namor snorted. "I'm sure it hasn't. The stories of mermaids and sirens calling sailors to their doom are true. We can call out to people, to influence their thoughts, and emotions." Namor sat down. I squealed as the water washed over my legs. "It's okay, wait until this fades, and you'll be able to think again."

I hummed in agreement. I liked the way it felt, so I began to hum an odd little tune.

Namor chuckled. "You are so stoned."

"You still have legs."

"Only the very young can't control the change."

I nodded against his chest and went back to humming.

I don't know how long I laid there. My first clear thought was I was being held on a stranger's lap. I moved.

"Hey, calm down. It's me, Namor, remember?" His arms tightened around me, which was good because I didn't have control of my muscles. "As soon as you can sit up on your own, I'll move you."

"Hey, Sapphire, it's Alanna. Everything's fine. The water will fix this soon."

"Did you tell Mom and Dad?"

Alanna sighed. "I didn't have a choice once they saw you carrying her into the water. They thought, you were trying to steal her as your bride."

"What? Are they crazy, I'm too young for that, and anyway she's a baby."

"Rude," I muttered before squealing, again, as a wave crashed over my shoulders.

"She's amusing. If we weren't going to Akasha, I might try and find her again in ten years," Namor said.

"Are you going?" Alanna asked.

"Sure—hasn't that been the plan all along?"

"Mom and Dad are talking about it. They want to go, but they will also miss their life here." I felt Alanna move next to us. "All of the elders are going, but the others feel torn. Families are arguing, some wanting to stay other wanting to go."

"It's not safe to stay," I said, doing my best to maintain focus. I opened my eyes blinking at the reflection on the water. "What tried to grab you yesterday was a walk-in. They work for the Sons of Belial. They will kill anyone they can get their hands on. When I open the portal, it will help them hone in on this location."

"Hold still and I'll move you," Namor said, picking me up and setting me between him and Alanna. "Some are willing to risk it."

"Do you know what their leader does to magical beings?" My voice high as fear filled my belly. "Cartazonon drains them of their magic and life-force. It's painful and slow. Please, everyone needs to be safe, they all need to go."

Alanna reached up and wiped tears off my cheek. I didn't even realize I was crying. "We'll let them know the risks, I promise. But they're going to make their own decisions."

They have their own paths and their own lives to live. Even as we see the pain and suffering they choose, we must let them choose their own way. We can offer advice, support, and love, but in the end we must let others live their own lives and make their own choices. The only thing you have control over is how you react and whether you decide to be a part of their choice. I know it's hard to see someone you care about suffer, but we can't force others to live as we think is best.

Thinking about my mom's words and how it applied to what was happening, I turned to look down at my feet stretched out in front of me. I let my tears fall as I watched sea horses swim around my toes. I could only hope I wouldn't dream of Cartazonon performing his ghastly ritual on anyone I met.

Chapter Nine

"There is always a solution to every human problem—neat, plausible, and wrong."
—H.L. Mencken

When the RV pulled into the parking lot I was dressed in Alanna's clothes with a headache so painful I felt nauseated. Gavin wasn't going to be happy when he saw me with my pale skin and bloodshot eyes. I felt like crap, and I tried to stop the trembling in my hands. I hadn't gotten my empathic shield up and everyone's emotions were on high.

Walking to the parking lot I saw Gavin sitting in the RV, his hands gripped the steering wheel and he stared straight ahead. Anali's hand rested on his arm as she talked to him. This didn't look good. I kept walking, no more hiding.

Once Gavin saw me he jumped out of the RV and rushed to my side. He tried to block his emotions behind a wall of determination and anger, but I could feel his fear and hurt.

I blinked back my tears.

"Are you okay?"

How he could talk with his jaw clenched tight? "Uncle Gavin?"

He became more rigid. Running a hand through his hair, he took a deep breath and forced himself to calm down. "I can't do this right now. I'm pissed as hell. We will talk later. Right now I need to know if you're okay and then we need to open the portal before the Sons of Belial come."

I wrapped my arms around myself. "I'm fine."

"How did she find you? Did you tell her who you are?"

The others gathered around us. "I think Alanna found me by accident. As for knowing who I am, it's possible that I might have forgotten to put my contacts in before I left." And now for the interesting fact, which I hope will distract Gavin enough to get me out of trouble. "Did you know I make the portal stones hum? Or maybe it's all of us that make them hum. For the past three weeks the stones marking the ancient gateway have hummed and called out to magical beings. That's why the Sons of Belial showed up, and why we have to open the portal today."

"Wait, what? They're being called to the portal? How do you know it's because of you?" Gavin said.

"They have felt it for the past three weeks, then while we traveled to Patagonia the stones stopped and started up again yesterday. Uncle Gavin, it's my fault that the walk-in came. I've put all these people in danger. We have to help them."

Gavin reached out a hand towards me, then clenched it and let it drop to his side. "Who do I need to talk to?"

Looking behind me I pointed. "Dorma and Vulko own the cafe. It was their daughter Alanna last night."

"Put these on." Gavin handed me my contact case and walked off.

Anali squeezed my shoulder and I felt her concern and disappointment. I wanted to say something, but she followed Gavin.

"Sapphire, you look like crap." Ice blue eyes looked at me with concern.

I sighed grateful he didn't seem angry at me, too. "Thanks, Taliesin, I feel like crap."

"What do you need?"

"Something for a headache."

"I'll be right back."

"Little sister," Kayin said, hugging me.

I relaxed, now I felt safe. Tears filled my eyes. I wrapped my arms around him. "Hey, big brother."

He pulled back, his brown eyes shone with disappointment. Kayin never looked at me like this before. "If you ever do something this stupid again I will chain you to me. You affected everyone's safety and you know better than to go out alone."

"I'm sorry."

Kayin stepped away and crossed his arms over his chest.

Miu held up a compact mirror, and I put the contacts in to mask the fire dancing in my eyes. "Was it worth it?" I could feel her nervousness and sense of responsibility. Oh, I bet no one else knew she'd helped me leave.

"If she hadn't run off we wouldn't be here. We wouldn't know about all these beings waiting. Things happen for a reason. Here," Taliesin handed me a bottle of water and two pills.

"So what are we going to do?" Miu asked.

"Open portal," Sasha said, before I could answer. "We do not have choice. We open portal and hope everyone gets through before Sons of Belial find us." Sasha's displeasure made his accent stronger and his voice clipped and hard.

Wincing, I looked out over the ocean where magical creatures were waiting for us. "It will be light for a while yet, and most of the time the Sons of Belial wait until dark, or at least dusk,"

"Sapphire, look at me," Kayin said, waiting until our eyes met before he continued. "We are not saying no, but this is very risky."

"I know, but we have to try. Look at all of them waiting, and there are more in the water and in the forest."

"Some of them are night creatures and they won't want to come out during the day." Taliesin said.

"Can you use your unicorn psychic stuff and explain it to them? Talk them into coming out early?" Miu asked, as she twirled a braid around her finger.

"I'll try, but it might not work." Taliesin looked at me. "You'll have to decide when to close the portal. You can feel the Sons of Belial stronger than anyone else, and you might have to leave some beings here if they don't cross through quickly enough."

Oh, great the whole leadership thing again. At least this is an easy decision and not one that will break my heart or put anyone in danger. My mom's words echoed in my head.

Frequently in life there are no easy answers. Someone will get hurt, something won't get done, you must give something up. The best you can do is look at all sides of the problem, ask for advice and do your best. You can't solve every problem, some you have to live through. Trust yourself, follow your heart, and do your best, my darling.

Miu bounced closer to me. "I trust you. I know you'll do your best to get as many creatures through the portal as fast as possible. And I know you will do what you need to do to keep all of us safe."

How in the world could she trust me with that after the mess I have made today? I hadn't done anything to earn that level of trust.

"Let's talk to Gavin and see what he thinks is best." There's no way I'm doing anything without his okay.

"He's headed this way," Kayin said.

I turned and watched Gavin's red hair flutter around his face as if moved by his anger. Anali was still talking to Vulko and Dorma.

"Okay, there are several hundred beings here. Some want to go, some followed the call from the gateway stone. I told them we're going to open the portal in thirty minutes and we'd keep it open for an hour at the most." Gavin rubbed his hands over his face. "This is a huge risk and we'll feel exhausted after, but there are so many beings here."

"Will it be dark by then?" I asked, my voice soft. "Taliesin says there are a bunch of night creatures here and he might not be able to convince them to come out before dark."

"The sun should start setting at that point. It will have to be enough."

I bit my lip and looked up at Gavin. I didn't want him even madder at me, but this was important. How to do this without making this worse? "Umm, Uncle Gavin, do you . . . could we talk for a minute before everything starts?"

Gavin's jaw clenched, his anger flared.

"Please, just for a minute."

Gavin nodded and walked to the beach.

Kayin squeezed my hand for luck before I took off after him.

Gavin stopped at the edge of the waves. He stared over the water and everything about him screamed leave me alone, but I couldn't do that.

"We were talking about the night creatures, and it was suggested that because I'm more sensitive to the Sons of Belial I could say when to close the portal."

It was a long painful silence before Gavin spoke. "Can you tell how far away they are?"

"No, but I can tell if they are moving closer."

"If you can't tell how far away they are, how will you be able to say when they're too close?" Gavin didn't give me a chance to answer. "And since you were stoned earlier today, do you trust yourself to stay clear and focused?"

"I didn't," I stopped and cleared my throat. "I didn't know. I didn't do it on purpose. The medicine is already taking away my headache. Uncle Gavin, please, I know you're mad at me and I messed up, but I need you to help me. I can't do this on my own. I don't want anyone to get hurt or worse, but these creatures have waited for me, for us, some of them for centuries and I can't abandon them. What are we going to do?"

Gavin put his arm around my shoulders giving me half a hug. His anger faded some, his protectiveness stronger. "I need you to be honest with me. After everything you've been through today and how you're feeling now, will you be able to keep the portal open *and* focus on the Sons of Belial?"

"Yes."

"Will you be able to tell when they are too close and shut the portal down even if beings are still waiting to get through?"

Good question. Could I? "I don't know. I want to say yes so I have the chance keep the portal open as long as possible, but how do I decide that?"

Gavin dropped his arm and turned towards me. "I don't know. But I won't risk any of you. If you can't be sure, then we are keeping it open for one hour."

Relief swept through me. I didn't want to make such choices and now I didn't have to. I nodded. "Okay, you're right, I'm not sure I can keep everyone safe. We'll keep the portal open for an hour."

Gavin raised an eyebrow. "I expected more of a fight."

"I'm not happy about leaving the night creatures behind, but this isn't a choice I want to make. I don't want to be responsible for people's lives." I scrunched the sand between my toes waiting for Gavin to say something.

"You've needed this for a while haven't you?" Gavin asked.

I looked up at him confused.

"Boundaries and rules," he clarified.

I shrugged.

Gavin sighed. "We don't have time to talk about this right now. We need to get back to the others and start setting up for the ritual, but we will talk. About today, last night, and what we both want out of becoming a family."

"I'm sorry," I blurted out.

"I know. Me, too." He dropped my hands. "Come on, let's go. We have a lot we need to get done."

Twisting my mother's ring on my finger, I watched as everyone moved into place. The gold and silver bracelets chimed as they shifted with my movements. I wonder how many of the magical creatures carved into them would go through the portal tonight.

Gavin and Anali insisted from the beginning that I wear all of the jewelry from Akasha that my mother passed down to me when we open a portal. It helps open the connection between the two worlds.

Tonight I also wore the silver and red armband and the beaten gold wrist cuff Lichuen gave to us. The armband from Shamash felt similar to the other jewelry. Quetzalcoatl's cuff connected me to Akasha, but its energy felt more wild and young.

"Are we ready?" Anali asked. She stood next to Kayin in the East position of the medicine wheel. We agreed to use the ritual we all knew this time. There simply wasn't room for error, although I wasn't sure it would work. We needed seven Children of Fire and only had six. Taliesin agreed to fill in.

Until now, Taliesin had stayed with the magical creatures keeping them calm and making sure they didn't eat each other or us. Tonight he would help open the portal, if he could.

Anali sprinkled blue cornmeal on the ground surrounding us in a circle of protection. When she completed the circle she began to call in the spirits at each direction. "Spirits of the East, I invite you into our circle. Please bless us with your knowledge and strength."

Fire surrounded Kayin. He spread his arms running the flames along the cornmeal circle.

Anali walked to the South where Gavin waited. "Spirits of the South, I invite you into our circle. Please bless us with your knowledge and strength."

Vines sprouted around Gavin's feet. He raised his arms sending the vines out to create a second circle.

"Spirits of the West, I invited you into our circle. Please bless us with your knowledge and strength," Anali chanted.

Water swirled around Miu. She threw her head back and her arms out wide. Water flowed, creating the third circle.

"Spirits of the North, I invite you into our circle. Please bless us with your knowledge and strength."

Sasha's hair whipped around his face as wind blew around him. His arms raised, and the wind howled, creating the final circle.

Anali walked back to Kayin and entered the circle. She

moved to stand between me and Gavin. Taliesin stood behind me, his nervousness prickled against my shield. Anali raised her arms up then knelt on the ground placing her palms on the Earth. "Mother Earth, we invite you into our circle and ask that you bless us with your nurturing and love."

An image of Aya fluttered over Anali. "You have my nurturing and love," Aya said, her voice faint and wispy.

I turned to look at Taliesin, hoping this would work. He raised his hands to the sky, fingers spread open. "Father Sky, we invite you into our circle and ask that you bless us with your protection and love."

Endless seconds passed before Shamash's image appeared over Taliesin's. "You have my protection and love."

The air crackled with power. Taking a deep breath, I pulled it all in. Under my feet the gateway stone sang with energy. Holding my hands out in front of me, I released the power. Phoenix fire shot from my hands, and the portal burst open. A bright white-and-purple doorway appeared in the sea.

The sea horses went through first. Their fins seemed to wave at us as they went home to Akasha. We watched as hundreds of beings crossed over. The water was so clear and bright I could see massive sea serpents from the nightmares of sailors swimming through the deep water and into the portal. Their joy and excitement energized us, making it easier to keep the connection to Akasha open.

"Ten minutes," Vulko called out. "The portal will be open for ten more minutes."

Sorrowful howls filled the air as the night creatures watched their chance at going home being taken away from them. They couldn't come out into the sun light. I blinked back tears. It wouldn't be fair to Gavin for me to cry. He didn't want this either, there was no choice. I heard an engine, maybe an airplane? Great. The papers would spot us and write UFO stories, again. I looked up as four parachutes opened against the sunset.

"They're here. The Sons of Belial are here," I yelled.

"Arm yourselves!" Vulko called out. Merfolk surrounded us, silver tridents gleaming in the fading light.

Not good, so not good. My stomach gurgled and my skin itched as the unnatural evil came closer to us. Those beings staying behind screamed and began to run or surrounded us ready to fight. I recognized General Saran from the first time they attacked us, now there shone a lock of white hair in the brown. Could that be from when I had hit him with Phoenix fire?

"What are we going to do?" Miu cried out.

"Shut down the portal and run like hell." Gavin pulled a gun out from the back of his jeans firing at the parachutes as he moved.

The circle dropped and the portal closed. The cry of fear and anger hurt my ears.

"I have a plan," Taliesin whispered in my ear. "Open the portal again in one hour."

"Taliesin," Sasha said. "Why are you naked?"

I stepped away. Naked is not part of the ritual.

"One hour, I'll be back."

I turned as Taliesin shifted into a unicorn.

"What are you doing?" I asked. "You're too young to change on your own. How will we get you back?"

He snorted and took off to the forest standing at the tree line for everyone to see.

"Stop!" yelled General Saran. "There's a unicorn. Ignore the others. Mr. Cartazonon has strict orders. The unicorn is top priority."

Taliesin pranced off while Saran and the three walk-ins ran after him.

Chapter Ten

"The needs of the many outweigh the needs of the few or the one."
~Gene Roddenberry

Gavin looked at me, his peridot eyes blazing with fury. I held my hands up. "I had nothing to do with this. All he told me is to open the circle again in one hour."

"I can't believe this is happening again!" Gavin tugged on his hair. I feared he would rip it out.

"Uncle Gavin, this isn't the same thing." I pulled my phone out of my pocket to check the time.

"No, it's worse. Taliesin showed himself on purpose to lure the Sons of Belial after him."

"And away from us," Kayin pointed out.

Gavin growled under his breath and began to pace.

"Taliesin was channeling Shamash. That's how he changed into a unicorn. It must have been Shamash's idea," I said. Gavin stopped pacing and looked at me. "How else could Taliesin know they would go after him? I didn't know the Sons of Belial would go after a unicorn over any other being, did you?"

Gavin shook his head. "No, I didn't. Well I guess we wait and open the gate again in an hour."

"We need someone in father sky position." Sasha asked.

Gavin shook his head. "I don't think so. I'd assume

Shamash has a plan."

"Okay we'll go with that." Anali shrugged. "So what now?"

After the slowest hour of my life, I rushed to my spot and rocked on my feet, my eyes never leaving the forest. *Taliesin, where are you?*

Anali began casting the circle and calling in the directions as before. She called in the spirits of the West when Taliesin burst through the forest. His white coat glowed silver in the moonlight, and his crystal-clear horn shone.

"They're far behind me," Taliesin said telepathically, and I repeated to the group. *"We have at least one hour, maybe longer, before they come back."*

Taliesin moved into place next to his clothes.

"One hour and then we leave," Gavin said, his voice firm.

I focused on my connection to Akasha. "One hour will be enough." Phoenix fire leaped from my hands and the large portal opened. Shadow figures, hissing serpents, and snarling beasts rushed through the doorway anxious to get back home.

My arms began to tremble halfway through the ritual. We had never opened a doorway twice in one day. I looked at the others. They held their arms open but they kept shifting trying to ease the strain on their muscles. A low haunting screech echoed as a group of sea serpents surfaced and swam through the doorway, their gray-green scales larger than my head. Dragons did live in the deep ocean waters; I guess the old map makers told the truth.

My shoulders and arms burned with fatigue. I dropped to my knees as my vision swam. I wasn't sure how much longer I could keep this up.

"A few more minutes, my Jewel," Shamash said. "A few more of our people need to come home."

I nodded and kept my focus.

"It's been an hour." Gavin's voice tight.

"Let me change Taliesin back then you can drop the circle," Shamash said.

Miu squeaked, and I assume that meant Taliesin was human

and naked. I wasn't going to turn around to find out.

"Thank you, my children," Aya whispered as the circle fell.

I flopped onto the grass. "Oh, man, I hurt."

"Other than having Jell-O for arms, is every one all right?" Gavin asked, getting a chorus of 'yes'. "Good, then get in the RV. None of us can handle the Sons of Belial right now."

I pushed myself up and looked around at the empty beach. It felt dead without the thrum of magic from all of the creatures.

Taliesin waved a hand in front of my face. "Sapphire! Stop zoning out, we need to go."

"Yeah, I'm coming. Don't get your panties in a bunch."

"So, how mad was Gavin?" he asked.

"If Shamash hadn't helped you, Gavin would have forgotten about me running away, he was so pissed."

Taliesin flinched. "Well hopefully the lecture won't be too bad."

"Please, I think we are all going to have a discussion once we're safe."

Taliesin tugged on one of the braids the fairies had made in my hair. "Well at least mine won't be as bad as what's going to happen to you."

I swatted at his arm, well, I tried to swat his arm. It looked more like a muscle spasm. "Whatever." Worry twitched through my body.

* * *

We drove for hours in painful brooding silence. The others twitched and darted looks between them in silent communication. I had dealt with this before back when I lived in group homes, although this was the first time I was the cause of such angst.

The others shifted the furniture into beds and slept. I sat on the passenger seat facing the door listening to music and doing a word search, even though it made me queasy. It didn't matter.

I had no intention of sleeping tonight if I could help it.

An hour later I was nodding off, so I turned up the music. I needed to stay awake. I couldn't move around or roll down the window, and I didn't have anything else to do so my only choice involved blasting my eardrums.

A hand tapped my arm making me jump. I pulled out my ear buds and turned enough to not be rude. "Yes," I whispered not wanting to wake up anyone who was sleeping.

Gavin sighed. "If I can hear the lyrics to your music it's too loud."

"I'll turn it down."

"You should get some sleep."

"Whenever we have run into the Sons of Belial I've had nightmares."

Gavin grunted. He was quiet for a minute, so I moved to put my ear bud back in.

"We need to talk about what you did. You can't break rules whenever you feel like it."

"There are no rules," I said.

"Of course there are rules. The other kids all follow them."

"Follow what? The only rules you and Anali have told us is to be on time for shows and to wear our contacts. That's it. Nothing else."

"The basic simple household rules that every normal child learns growing up," Gavin said.

I froze for a second, my face becoming an emotionless mask, my voice clipped and cold. "I'm not a normal child. I'm an institution freak. Every time I was moved into a new place I was sat down while dozens of rules were given to me. Then I was made to sign a paper saying I understood them and would follow them. You had nothing, you gave me nothing."

"An institution freak?"

"Well, institutionalized, it's what they call kids who have spent the majority of their early childhood in group homes." I stared out the window. "It means we don't react like normal kids and it's harder for us to adapt to normal family environments."

Gavin's voice was so soft I barely heard his question. "Who told you that?"

"No one. I read it in my file when a counselor stepped out of his office. It also said that I'm unlikely to form normal healthy attachments to anyone."

"I don't believe that," Gavin said. "We have a bond from when you were little. I held you moments after you were born, you looked right at me and smiled, I don't care what the books say, you smiled at me. Yes, we were separated for years, but the foundation is still there. You were loved and nurtured as a baby until you were five years old. It might be harder for you to trust, but in your early years you were taught how to trust. It will come back. I believe that."

I hadn't thought about it like that before. Not knowing what my life was like before the group homes, I assumed I was broken and planned to live my life alone. But now I had Gavin who was trying, who wanted us to be family. I bit my lip trying not to cry.

"If you didn't understand the rules why didn't you come to me and ask for help?"

I hunched my shoulders. "I was doing fine guessing. I never got in trouble. None of us ever got in trouble, so I tried to stay inside what I knew was working."

"Until the other night. Then you did whatever you wanted." Anger and fear flared around him.

My hands shook as a clenched them into fists. "I *did* come to you. I begged you for help. Alanna needed us, and you refused to help me."

"It was too dangerous," he snapped.

"Obviously not. Shin and I got her out of there safely."

"So that gives you right to run off whenever you feel like it?"

"No, what gave me the right to run off was when you decided to punish me for nothing," I hissed not wanting to wake the others, but my anger made it hard to keep quiet.

"You got a 'D' in history."

"And you never set a standard as to grades, so why did it matter?"

"Of course grades matter."

"And I know that how, exactly?"

Gavin's chest rose with his breaths, his eyes flashing between guilt and anger. I knew how he felt, I didn't like this, either. Part of me wanted to apologize and stop this; however, self-righteous anger continued to wash through me.

I should have kept my mouth shut. I was so stupid. Was he going to get rid of me now? No, he couldn't, could he? I was the Jewel and that made me needed and important. I swallowed a sob that threatened to escape.

"Anali said I should try and work towards solving the problem and not yelling at you and punishing you for your behavior." Gavin sighed. "Sapphire, I'm not looking for you to swear you won't do it again, or you'll always listen to me. I want us to have a clear plan of action, something we both agree to. Let's start with the other night and you disobeying me."

"Okay, I'm not sure what to do next time. It's my job to save them."

"Yes, it is *our* job to save magical beings. But *we* can't do that if they capture you." Gavin's hands tightened on the steering wheel. "So how do we decide if something is too dangerous?"

"Well, the other night you wouldn't even consider saving her. So, if we try to come up with a plan and can't?" I offered. It sounded like a weak idea to me, but if Gavin was going to try than I should too.

"That sounds fair. Okay so we will decide what needs to be done, and how we can do it. But what happens if we can't find a safe way to help the creature?"

I stared out the window at the stars in the sky. "How do we determine that?"

"Well, if you wouldn't let Kayin do it because you're afraid he'd get caught then it's not safe enough for me to let any of you try."

"That's not fair, using Kayin against me."

"Have you heard the saying, 'The needs of the many outweigh the needs of the few or the one'?"

I nodded.

"The point is all of you are important to thousands of magical creatures. It isn't right to ruin the chance of so many to go home to save just one." Gavin cleared his throat. "I know it may seem cruel, but from a logical view it's the truth. From an emotional standpoint, I care for all of you, and the thought of losing any of you to the Sons of Belial scares the crap out of me. I lost you once, along with your mom and dad. I've finally found you, and I can't lose you again. Not to those monsters."

I blinked back tears. "I don't like it."

"I don't like it either, Sapphire. I wish we could save them all," Gavin said. "The question is will you respect the decision and walk away if needed?"

Could I walk away from someone who needed my help? Could I put my friends and family in danger to save one being? "I might not do it happily, but I will walk away if we can't find a plan to save them that is safe enough for us."

Gavin reached over and patted my shoulder. "I can deal with unhappy. Hell, I'll be unhappy too. What about the running away?"

I slid down in the seat. "Well, that was kind of stupid, but you go for walks when you get upset."

Gavin nodded. "True, I do go for walks. I'm also an adult, trained to deal with the Sons of Belial, and I make sure I'm always wearing my contacts."

All valid points. "Hey, shouldn't I learn how to protect myself from them too?"

Gavin looked at me before focusing on the road. "I suppose. Let me think about it. I would prefer it if you ran away from them."

We were quiet for a minute and I hoped that the conversation was over.

"So the running away?"

"I've never done it before." I shrugged. "I guess I felt like you were being unfair, and I wanted to show you that you couldn't ground me."

"Did you have a plan?"

"No. I was in a market watching a dancing group when Alanna found me." I twisted my mom's ring and the band of blue stone set in silver sparkled like the night sky. "I guess I would have shopped and walked around until I got bored and was ready to face you back at the house."

"I don't like the idea of your being scared of me," Gavin said frowning.

"I wasn't scared, like worried you would beat the crap out of me the way some parents do. But I also knew going back meant accepting whatever consequences you chose."

"I will never hit you," Gavin said firmly. "My parents didn't even spank your mom or me when we were little."

"What would they have done if you had run off?" I covered my mouth as I yawned.

Gavin's face turned as red as his hair and he slid down in his seat a bit.

"You ran away," I said. "Oh, my god, you're on my case for something you did, too."

"It was different," Gavin muttered, defending himself. "There weren't Sons of Belial around, and I wasn't in a foreign country."

I grinned, he was so busted. "So why did you take off, and what was your punishment?"

Gavin shook his head and smiled at me. "I snuck out with some friends to see a Metallica concert. My parents wouldn't let me go because I had a final the next day."

"And?"

"And, they grounded me for a month and lost my car for three months. It sucked," Gavin said.

I imagined an angry pouting teenage Gavin sitting in his room blasting music.

"So what's my punishment?"

"I don't know. On one hand you did do something wrong,

but on the other hand I feel like I did the wrong thing too." Gavin looked over at me. "We could chalk this up to a learning experience for both of us? If you promise not to run away again."

I looked at Gavin, his worry and hope sliding against my shields. He wasn't a professional caregiver, trained in how to parent, he was totally new to this family thing just like me. But he wanted to learn, he wanted to make us a family. "I promise, I won't run off again." Once was exciting enough.

"And I promise to try and be clear about the rules, expectations, and the consequences. If you're unsure you need to ask me or Anali." Gavin paused for a moment. "So, what's up with your history grade? I have a degree in history. I can help."

I groaned and thumped my head against the seat and yawned. "This class is so boring."

Gavin laughed. "Maybe I can help, tell me what's going on."

"I have to memorize dates and battles. Who cares about stuff like that?"

"It's important," Gavin began. He rambled on about why it's important to know when things happened and how battles changed who ruled and how people lived. I made the appropriate humming noises in the right places, but my eyes wouldn't stay open. Maybe listening to Gavin talk would keep me grounded in the here and now and I wouldn't have a freaky dream. I held onto the sound of his voice as I drifted into sleep.

"General Saran. I expect you have good news for me?" Cartazonon cleaned the oval table with a soft cloth, making sure to polish the thin web of Akashic metal embedded in the black stone.

"I'm sorry Mr. Cartazonon. We weren't able to capture any of the magical creatures."

He adjusted the ear bud and switched rags to oil the leather restraints. "My sources said there were thousands of magical creatures there. How did you and your team fail to capture even one?"

"There was a unicorn, sir. And per your instructions we stopped and focused on trying to capture him," General Saran explained.

"Are you sure you saw a unicorn?" Mr. Cartazonon set the rag down,

and waved to Lee. "There haven't been any signs of unicorns on Earth for two thousand years."

"He looked as you described. White coat with a silver sheen and a crystal horn."

Mr. Cartazonon held a small, red-brown arm in his long fingers. "Hush, don't struggle. There is no need for this to be any more painful than necessary. General Saran, how old was he?"

General Saran cleared his throat. "If it had been a horse I would say between one and two years of age."

He gently took a thin leg and strapped it down, patting the struggling creature. "That makes him between fifteen and twenty years old. Quite young. Where did he come from?"

"He was with the group that keeps opening the portals."

"Interesting. Where are you now?" Cartazonon finished binding the small being and took off his Armani jacket and vest, setting them on the back of his chair, then he rolled up his shirt sleeves.

"In Buenos Aries, sir."

"They are long gone, probably off to the next portal." Cartazonon straightened a framed photograph of himself on the cover of Time. "We need to know where these portals are."

"Yes, sir. What about the unicorn?"

"I'll have to figure that out. None of you can get close to him." Cartazonon ran a hand through his dark hair. "Unicorns can see the worth of your heart, the value of your word, and the purity of your soul. It's difficult enough for them to be around normal humans, to know all their corruption and lies. He will never let any of my people close enough to catch him."

"We could use tranquilizer darts."

"No! I have no idea what that will do to him. No, I will think of something. Next time let him go, stay focused on those you can capture."

"Yes, sir."

Cartazonon studied the Time photograph. His face looked as it had ten years ago. Aristocratic thin features, dark eyes and hair, full lips. He was handsome and dangerous; his picture gave some people the shivers. "I'm going to have to get a wife and age myself again. It's been too long. People will start getting curious."

"Of course, sir. I will have the folders brought to you. I have three make-up artists I think will work well with you, and five woman who look wholesome and will behave properly while being power hungry enough to do what is needed."

Mr. Cartazonon sighed. "Do you remember that pretty little blond woman in Paris in 1623? I should have made her one of us. I liked her. She was so bloodthirsty."

"Renee was good," General Saran said. "But she wouldn't have been able to have children."

He shrugged. "It's not like any of them are mine anyway. I'm sure we could have faked it."

"Maybe you will find someone special in this batch, sir."

Cartazonon sighed, "Perhaps. I want you to stay where you are for now. I doubt they will leave South America any time soon. You might get another chance."

"Yes, sir. I'll let you know if anything happens."

"Good." Cartazonon hung up the phone and walked to the head of the oval table. He took off his necklace and placed it in the hollow carved into the top of the table. The dark crystal, set in metal from Akasha, sparkled up from the depths of the depression in the wood. Reaching out, he ran his fingers through the wild brown hair of the sprite.

"This will hurt, but it's for a good cause," he said before putting his hands on the bowl. The sprite fought against the leather straps holding him down. Cartazonon took a deep breath and began to pull the life and magic out of the small being. The sprite screamed.

Chapter Eleven

"Were we fully to understand the reasons for other people's behavior, it would all make sense."
~Sigmund Freud

A little girl tumbled down the mat of Señora Santiago's dance studio. She reminded me of Shante as she squealed and hugged me when she came to the end.

"Good job, you've worked hard this week." I said.

"Thank you," she said before joining the others.

Little kids speaking English with heavy Spanish accents might be the cutest thing ever.

"Okay," Anali said. "It's almost time for lunch, so let's practice handstands before we go."

I moved into position ready to spot the kids. Hearing a squeal, I turned. One of the kids with Taliesin at the silks hung upside down. I wasn't sure that had been the goal of the lesson. Taliesin explained how to get down. Agustin, Señora Santiago's son, translated for him. Agustin saw me and smiled.

Blushing, I looked away just in time as dirty little feet came flying at me. I caught them and helped the little boy balance into a handstand. I enjoyed helping the little kids; it was fun and relaxed. Not being a teacher, just a helper, sometimes I switched between the five other camps Michael organized. The ones for the teens and adults, while still fun, tended to be more serious and a lot more work, because the students wanted to learn as much as possible.

"We'll see everyone in two hours," Anali said.

I love Argentina: two-hour lunches give enough time for food and siesta. Siestas rock.

"Ready?" Kayin asked once all the kids left.

"Yep." I shouldered my bag.

Taliesin slid on his sunglasses. "Let's go."

We walked down the block to 9 de Julio Park. We'd found the park not long after we arrived in San Miguel de Tucuman, Argentina. The city reminded me of Buenos Aries, a busy modern place with a lot of European-style buildings. San Miguel de Tucuman is an old city and fun to explore. Our favorite part, so far, was this park.

Birds fluttered about, landing on marble statues and bathing in the fountains. Children flew kites on the grass. Couples picnicked in the cool shade provided by large leafy trees. Delicate flowers perfumed the air. I loved the park from the first moment I stepped into it. The park was filled with life and happiness, and I always felt refreshed after being here.

"Hey, there's my lovely lady," Gavin said, waving to Anali. It was interesting to watch people as they walked by us. Some would stare openly, others tried to peek at us without being caught, men were frequently smacked on the arm by girlfriends and wives, and some looked like the stick up their butt had given them a splinter. In fairness we were an interesting looking bunch, with a variety of hair styles, ethnic backgrounds, and well-worn workout clothes. Friends grouped together laughing and talking as they ate. Except for Taliesin. He would find a shady spot and sit by himself.

A week passed since my vision of Cartazonon. To distract myself from worrying, I spied on Taliesin. After what Cartazonon said about unicorns, I wanted to try and figure out if Taliesin held back because he was trying to protect himself or if he simply didn't like people. I shifted my book so I could see Taliesin over the top of it. He sat alone, as he frequently did at lunch. As soon as he finished eating, he would take out his sketch book and draw.

"Here you go, Sapphire," Gavin said, handing me a salad.

"Thanks Gavin."

"How's your book? Is that the one for your history project?" Gavin sat down opening the lid on his salad, and began to eat.

I sighed and gave up watching Taliesin to assure my uncle I was doing my homework.

After Gavin ate and interrogated me about the book, he went to lie down with Anali. Most of the circus performers stretched out on blankets and dozed in the shade. I glanced at the tree where Taliesin sat earlier, and it was empty. *Crap. Where did he go? Okay let's calm down, try to look casual.* I ran my fingers through my hair, irritated at how curly the humidity made it, and scanned the park. Kayin snoozed next to Shin and Sasha, but no Taliesin. With his snow-white hair he's hard to miss.

"Looking for me?" Taliesin asked.

I whirled around, almost knocking over my water. "You scared the crap out of me!"

Taliesin hummed and sat down. "Why, exactly, have you watched me all week?"

"What?" No way could he know that for sure. I was careful and sneaky.

"Sapphire," he said, blue eyes staring into mine. "Since we opened the portal you have watched me from over the tops of books and computers, in mirrors, around corners. Do I need to go on?"

I picked at the grass choosing not to look at Taliesin. "I watch everyone; you're all very entertaining."

Taliesin sighed and lay down. "Wouldn't it be easier to tell me what's on your mind?"

I bit my lip, should I tell him the truth? I didn't want to upset him, but I also didn't want to lie to him. But I would want to know the truth. I took a deep breath, the truth it was. "In my dream, Cartazonon talked about unicorns. He said they didn't like being around people because they knew the purity of their heart and soul."

Taliesin said nothing. I could feel the nervousness rolling off of him.

"I guess it's like your empathy," he said after a while. "It isn't pleasant knowing how damaged people are."

"Can you block it?"

"I try to, but it doesn't work that well."

"I can teach you what I do. I still know what people feel, but it doesn't affect me. Like there's a window between me and them."

"Thanks." Taliesin folded his hands on his stomach. "What were you looking for?"

Blushing, I focused on the grass again. "It was stupid. I wanted to figure out if you were protecting yourself or being a brat."

"And?" Taliesin said, his voice teasing.

"You stand away from people even when you're talking to them and move off on your own. You tend to avoid certain people, but you relax around small children."

"Very observant. Young kids haven't done as much in their lives. I'm not saying they aren't trouble makers or difficult, but most of them don't realize that what they are doing hurts others. The ignorance of youth keeps their hearts and souls pure," Taliesin explained.

"What do you see or feel? Do you know what the person has done? Or does it look like a black mark on them?"

Taliesin rolled onto his stomach and laid his head on his arms. "Well, it's a mix of seeing and feeling their aura. I can't tell what they've done, but I can tell how dangerous or nasty they are, or at least how they were. The colors in their aura gives me clues, but thankfully, I don't know the details."

"Can a person change? Can the good they do in their lives wash away the wrong?"

"I don't know."

"Who do you feel comfortable around?" Are any of us innocent enough, pure enough, to not bother Taliesin?

"Sasha and Miu are fine. If I had to guess I would say they lied, got into arguments, said things they regret. Small things like that, things that everyone does."

"You don't," I interrupted. "You always tell the truth."

"Even a unicorn can go bad. It's easy to think of survival or wanting more power and safety. I have to do my best to stay pure."

"Does that mean you can't have sex? Oh God, I'm so sorry, don't answer that."

"Calm down, Sapphire. Yes, I can have sex, but it needs to be from a place of love and trust. People lying, using and hurting others, and being untrue to themselves—things like that cause darkness in a person, not love."

"Oh," New topic. "What about me and Kayin?"

"You want me to have sex with you and Kayin, together?"

I blushed and smacked him on the arm. "No! Gross. You said how Miu and Sasha felt, what about me and Kayin."

Taliesin chuckled. "I know what you meant. Kayin's easy to be around, he doesn't lie and does his best to be kind."

"And me?" I whispered. I wasn't sure I wanted to know.

"You're odd. The more you accept your Phoenix powers, the cleaner your soul and heart become."

Interesting. "Does it fluctuate? Did running off make it harder to be around me?"

"No, you didn't run to hurt Gavin. Intention is everything."

Yawning, I lay back on the blanket. "I thought I was done with afternoon naps."

Taliesin closed his eyes. "I like naps."

"They are pretty awesome." All around us people napped on colorful blankets. "It's like we're back in kindergarten."

"Might as well be with the way some people act," Taliesin said.

"I'm sure you're not talking about me."

"Of course not."

"Taliesin?"

"Yes," he mumbled.

"You can hide behind me or Kayin if it gets to be too much."

"Thanks, but most people think I'm an ass and leave me alone. It's not so bad."

"But you're not like that. Are you?"

Taliesin snuffled in his sleep. I guess I would have to find out for myself. The one thing I had learned, my mom was right.

When we understand what drives our actions, we can accept ourselves for who we are. Once we can look at our own behavior and see the fear, anger, love, sadness, etc. which motivates us we can look at others and understand that they too are ruled by the same emotions. Then we realize that a person's actions reflect who they are and we can find compassion for ourselves and others.

The shrill ringing of my phone woke me up. Who would be calling me? Almost everyone I knew was sleeping here at the park. "Hello?"

"Hey, Sapphire, it's Philip. Is Gavin nearby? I tried calling him but he didn't answer."

"Yes. Hold on, let me find him." I stood up, blinking in the sun, and made my way towards Gavin and Anali. "How are things in Frisco?"

"Good, but I miss all of you. My new teachers need some work but I'll get them sorted out. How is my baby brother?"

I rolled my eyes, Michael was two years younger than Philip. "He's a great manager, I feel as safe with him as I did when I was taking classes at your school."

"Sapphire, that's so sweet and I'm glad Michael is taking such good care of you." I heard the smile in his voice. "I obviously have taught him well."

As I got closer I noticed Gavin's arms lying in the sun had turned bright pink. "Gavin, wake up," I said. "And you need to start wearing sunscreen."

"What?" Gavin asked. He rubbed his hands over his face. "What's up? Everyone all right?"

"Philip's on the phone." I pressed the speaker button. "What did you learn about the gateway stones?"

"Well," Philip began, "not a whole lot. We can't find a map or key to where they're located, but several of the dreamers are focusing on locations and trying to find them. Has Sasha said anything?"

Gavin looked at me. I shook my head. "Sasha hasn't said anything to me, but he doesn't talk to me about his dreams."

"Okay, will you please ask him?" Philip said. "Historians have started searching through the archives. I'll call you as soon as we know anything."

"Do you have any idea of how far away I need to stay before they activate?" I asked.

"We think you need to be more than fifty miles away," Philip said. "We're not sure how long it takes before your presence starts to activate the portals.

"Sapphire, did they say how long the gateway stone had been humming?" Gavin asked.

"No, not that I remember."

"Well, you were in Buenos Aires for four weeks before the Sons of Belial felt the pull," Philip said. I imagined Philip rubbing his head as he thought, moving his salt and pepper Mohawk.

"But now they're searching for it and us," Gavin said frowning.

"Yes, but we are too," Philip replied. "Everyone is in battle mode. We knew some day the Sons of Belial would actively hunt us and we're ready."

"Wait," I said, "haven't they been a threat all along?"

Gavin sighed. "Yes, but only if we run into them by accident. They haven't bothered to search for us like they search for magical creatures."

So my parents' deaths were flukes, accidental meetings? "Why not?"

"There are hundreds of thousands of descendants of Shamash and Aya," Philip said. "Most with no gifts or even knowledge of their heritage. A few of us have a little bit of power, we can do one maybe two things, it is the rare few with strong gifts. Hunting us down normally isn't worth their time."

So most Children of Fire can walk past the Sons of Belial except my parents. It was worth their time to hunt my parents. If the walk-in hadn't accidently seen the fire in their eyes, if my parents had been weaker would I have grown up with them? My whole life would've been better. Gavin squeezed my shoulder. I felt his sadness. We must be thinking the same thing.

"I need to go. I'll call when I find out more. I emailed my research on Quetzalcoatl to you."

"Thanks, Philip," Gavin said.

"No problem, take care," he said then hung up.

"Are you okay?"

I shrugged—it's the teenage answer to everything.

"If you need to talk, or have questions I'm here," Gavin said.

"I know, thanks."

* * *

I dried my hair, eager to get downstairs to dinner. Sitting on my bed I started to braid my hair. Something bumped into me. "What ..." Had Miu started leaving her stuff on my side of the room? I picked up the small music box and an old, beat-up book with a black feather sticking out of it.

Wait, this is my stuff. My old caseworker Five gave me this music box. A Russian firebird shone on top of the small gold lacquered box. Opening it, I heard a fast happy tune. When he'd given it to me for Christmas last year I'd about had a heart-attack, wondering how he knew about me. But the next time I saw Five, he told me about finding the box while shopping. It sounded like a coincidence at the time. But why was it on my bed? I'd brought it with me, but it stayed in the RV packed and stored under the bus. I wasn't even sure why I'd brought it in the first place.

Looking through the book, a memory came back to me. Five had given me this book the day I left San Francisco. *What the hell? Where has it been? And how can I have forgotten about it?* I opened the book. The feather glowed iridescent black against the creamy paper, the edges of the feather soft and wispy. I felt a faint magical hum to it, something similar to the jewelry from Shamash and Quetzalcoatl.

Under the feather was a thick piece of paper.

It's amazing what these dreamers see, isn't it?

It's time for you to read this journal. There's a ritual in here that will save your brother's life. If your mother hadn't been betrayed, it would have saved hers.

Good luck and don't worry too much. I'm keeping an eye on you. I always have.

Because my life wasn't crazy enough, this had to be added to it. I thought about throwing everything out, but rational thought won out this time. I gathered everything up and took it downstairs to show Gavin and the others.

Gavin and Sasha sat at a large wooden table. Parrot-green bowls filled with steaming groundnut stew and small plates with sadza, a thick cornmeal paste, waited. I'd never eaten peanut butter like this, but the rich spicy scent made me want to try it. "It looks and smells wonderful, thank you for cooking, Kayin."

"I hope you like it. I tried not to make it too spicy," he said, handing Gavin another bowl to set on the table. "Sit and eat."

I took a piece of sadza and shaped it into a tiny bowl so I could scoop up the stew. Kayin's groundnut stew tasted rich and spicy, the flavor of peanuts mixed with the chunks of vegetables and seasonings to make a delicious whole. My favorite were the bright orange yams. "It's so good."

The others agreed and praised his cooking. I saw a faint blush on Kayin's ebony cheeks. It's a good thing I worked out as much as I did, with all the good food people kept feeding me.

"What do you have there?" Gavin asked, pushing his empty bowl away.

"I found these on my bed." I put the stuff on the table.

Sasha looked over them. "Box looks Russian."

"It is. Five gave it to me last Christmas."

"Someone names a child Five?" Sasha said, wrinkling his nose. He picked up the box and opened it. "Is Firebird Suite by

Stravinsky."

"What?" Gavin asked coming over.

"No they didn't name him Five, his real name is David."

"Wait," Gavin said taking the box from Sasha. "Last Christmas, days after you came into your Phoenix Gifts, your caseworker gives you a music box with a phoenix on it and playing music from a symphony about a phoenix and you didn't tell me?"

Well, if you say it like that it sounds bad. "Gavin, he told me about going shopping in an antique store and liking that piece of music. It's a coincidence. Do you remember Five? Baby face, big blue eyes, brown curls, always wearing sweater vests or tee shirts with comic cook superheroes on them?"

"Underestimating people can get you killed," Gavin said setting the box down. "Why was it on your bed?"

"I don't know, but this book was with it, along with this feather, and note."

"Where did this journal come from?" Gavin asked, after reading the note he passed it to Anali who sat down next to him.

"I remember Five giving it to me the day we left."

Gavin flipped through the yellowed pages. "Why didn't you tell me about it?"

I looked up at Gavin. "I'd forgotten about it until I saw it today."

"How is possible you forget something so important?" Sasha asked.

"I have no idea, but until I saw the book I hadn't remembered it."

"This is what your parents went looking for." Gavin said looking over the first page. "Padre Miguel Carrillo was a priest in Florida in 1742. Your dad, Keagan, studied the genealogy of several Children of Fire and found Padre Carrillo. Local legends said that God spoke to him in his dreams, which he wrote down in this diary."

"What about the note saying my mom used a ritual in it?" I

asked. My hand itched to grab the diary from Gavin. *He wouldn't keep it would he?*

"The last letter I received from your mom said she found a ritual that should break the walk-in's trace on her. Gabriella said as soon as she was free she'd come home." Gavin lowered his head his hair covering his face as his hands ran over the worn cover of the diary.

"What's with the feather?" Taliesin asked leaning over me to pick up the magical feather.

Anali cleared her throat. "According to the information Philip sent on Quetzalcoatl, there are four brothers, and they are associated with colors. Quetzalcoatl, the feathered serpent who presides over the world, he's the blue one. Camaxtli is the red. We think they mean Shamash. Huitzilopochtli is the god of war and the sun who dies at night and is reborn every morning. His color is white. The last brother, Tezcatlipoca a shapeshifter, is black. He and Quetzalcoatl fought for power over the world. Worshipers of both deities sacrificed many people to strengthen their God so he would win. They knocked the sun from the sky during their fiercest battle. Quetzalcoatl won, but Tezcatlipoca was still around punishing wrongdoers and hiding as a jaguar, ocelot, or a turkey."

Miu picked up the large black feather twirling it in her fingers the soft edges fluttering. "So this is from Tezcatlipoca?"

"Maybe," said Anali.

Why hadn't Aya and Shamash told me about the other brothers? "How did it get in my room? Is he Shamash's brother? Is this an old feather or is he still here?"

"Let me see the feather," Kayin said. I placed it on his hand. He pinched the quill. "It's a new feather the quill is white and flexible."

Gavin nodded. "Okay, I guess this means he's here, someone wants us to think the feather is from him, or they are saying they're one of his descendants."

"Why wouldn't Shamash mention him if he is still here?" *I don't need another mystery to solve. Isn't finding Quetzalcoatl enough?* "And what about the fighting? Is Tez—whatever—a bad guy? Is that why Shamash didn't mention him?"

Gavin shrugged.

"So what do we do now?" Miu asked.

"I guess I read the book and translate the rituals," I said, hoping Gavin would give it back to me.

"I'm not sure it's safe," Gavin said with a frown. "We don't know who put these things on your bed."

"Well, it looks like Five, or possibly Tezcatlipoca." Anali pointed to the music box. "It's the only logical explanation."

"Five couldn't have given it to me. He's a normal person, I never felt any energy from him." When I touched other Children of Fire, I always felt a spark of warmth.

"Sapphire, did you ever touch Five's skin? Shake his hand or something?" Gavin asked. "You're not a very touchy person."

"Um, when I first met him it was before I changed." I touched my black and red hair which was brown before my fifteenth birthday. "What about you or Anali—did you feel anything from him?"

Anali shook her head. "That's your gift, as the Jewel. I can't feel the difference between shaking hands with you or someone in the grocery store."

"Really?" *Oh, good, I needed another difference today, life was getting boring and too easy.*

"I don't feel anything different," Miu said.

"I don't either," said Sasha between bites of stew.

I looked at Kayin, he shook his head.

"I can," Taliesin said. "But I don't remember meeting anyone named Five."

"His real name is David," Gavin explained. "And I think he only came to the circus center once."

"Sasha, can you dream tonight and ask Shamash and Aya?" Miu asked. One of her braids fell and almost landed in her bowl.

"I don't dream like that," he grumbled, his Russian accent heavy. "I don't talk to Phoenix King and Queen. I don't ask;

they give."

Miu muttered in Japanese. I was thankful no one else understood her. For a girl who covered herself in Hello Kitty and sparkly pink she had a foul mouth.

"So you wake up just knowing things?" I asked.

"Da, I see map, or know where is thing. Is in my head." Sasha shrugged. "I try remember, write down, when I wake up."

"Can you focus on something specific before you go to sleep and control the information given to you?" Anali asked.

"I try tonight."

"I think I should read the diary, especially if it will help Kayin." I said, looking at the worn book still in Gavin's possession.

"How do you know the note refers to Kayin?" Taliesin asked.

"Kayin's the only one I call big brother."

Taliesin snorted.

"Did you feel anything bad when you handled the diary?" Gavin asked.

I shook my head. "No, I wasn't looking for anything."

"And you can translate it?" Anali asked.

"I should be able to, as long as Padre Carrillo was a Child of Fire." Unlike my mom who could translate anything, my gift was limited to magical beings.

Gavin stared at the book. "Okay, but you write everything down and don't perform any ritual without checking with me or Anali first."

"Of course," I said taking the journal that Gavin slid across the table. I ran a finger over the leather cover. The Sons of Belial killed my parents for this journal. I hoped this time it wouldn't kill anyone else.

Chapter Twelve

"Tact teaches you when to be silent."
~Benjamin Disraeli

Woo-hoo, a day off! I flew down the stairs and into the kitchen. No classes to teach, no performing, no big work outs, just a day of fun!

"You seem excited," Anali said.

"The boys and I are going out for the day." I scooped some yogurt into a bowl, adding granola and sliced banana.

"The boys?" Gavin asked putting down some work papers.

"Kayin, Shin, Sasha, and Taliesin." Who did he think I meant?

"Oh, what's Miu doing today?" Anali asked.

"She's going out with the girls who do the contortion act, some girls' day out thing."

"And you're going out with the boys?" I stared at Gavin with my mouth open and spoon halfway to my mouth—a movie perfect shocked look.

"Um, I don't wear make-up. I have enough clothes. And the only jewelry I wear is my mom's." I held up a hand showing the night sky ring.

Gavin reached up and touched his fire pendant which was hidden under his shirt. "Well, what are you and the boys doing that is so much better?"

Anything else. "Well, I need to get some post cards, and I want to go through the open air market."

"Sapphire," Anali began. "What money do you spend? You never ask me or Gavin for money."

I stared at them for moment as my mouth was full. They had a lot of questions this morning, which didn't bode well. "Why would I ask you for money? I get paid for the circus work."

"Well you don't get paid a lot," Gavin said.

Not a lot in Gavin's world of the rich and famous. "So, I save half and spend the rest. I don't buy a lot of stuff—food every once in a while and gifts for people." I shrugged.

"Well, we think you should get an allowance," Anali said.

"Oh, okay. Well, that would be nice." Like I would turn down money. "What are the rules?"

"Well, you already keep your space clean and help with chores without being asked. So as long as you keep helping out that will be enough." Gavin looked to Anali. She nodded. Okay, this was her idea. Why? He pulled out his wallet. "Here you go."

I took the money - a hundred dollars, was he kidding? "This is a lot. How long is this for?"

"The week."

"No, Gavin," Anali crossed her arms her brow furrowing around her red bindi. "That is for the month, so you have enough to buy the extra things you want."

"Oh, cool." I'd have to change it into pesos, easy enough.

"I also want to give you this." Gavin handed me a gold credit card.

I twisted it amused by how it sparkled in the light. "What is this for?"

"Emergencies."

What do they define as an emergency? Did they expect me to go all teen movie girl and charge up a storm to teach me about responsibility?

"When you ran away and went with Alanna, I didn't know if you had money on you. What if your phone had gotten lost or broken and you couldn't get help? So at the beginning of every month you'll get allowance, and I want you to keep the card on you in case we get separated," Gavin explained.

"Okay," I shoved the money and card in my messenger bag.

"If you need more money, let me know," Gavin said. Anali huffed. I guess they didn't agree on this point. "Depending on what you need the money for, I may give it to you."

"Okay, but I'm sure this will be more than enough."

"You will need to do extra chores to earn extra money," Anali said.

"Sure." That's fair, and I wanted to avoid the argument I felt building.

"No, you don't have to do more work," Gavin said to me. His pale green eyes focused on Anali. "I have more than enough. In fact, you have more than enough." Gavin turned to me. "You inherited all your parent's money and property. It's in trust, but I could help you get an allowance from that, too."

"Gavin, can we talk privately for a moment please?" Anali held the door open. Gavin's jaw clenched as he walked into the hallway.

I watched the door swing shut. Now what I supposed to do?

"Gavin, we talked about this. There is nothing wrong with working to get what you want."

"I know that, but she already works hard. And I gave in to a hundred dollars a month instead of a week like I wanted."

I heard footstep and hoped they would go somewhere else, I didn't want to hear this argument.

"Gavin, we don't want to spoil her. Sapphire isn't used to this kind of money. If you shower her with things, how will she learn the value of hard work, or money well earned?"

"Are you saying I don't know those things?" Gavin asked.

They didn't argue often, most of the time just playful bickering about something silly. Their sharp anger hit my shields. Could I stop the argument? What if I gave the money back? Or offered to do more chores? Would that help? Maybe if I let Gavin sneak me money when Anali wasn't looking, then made sure to save it so when she found out—which she would—I could show that I was responsible? I threw away the rest of my breakfast. I wasn't going to be able to eat any more.

"Gavin, you've had things easy, but you also saw what your parents did to earn the money. And even then, while it could be stressful, your family businesses have been established for generations, it would take work to destroy them."

"I work hard. I do what I need to and show up for practice and performances on time."

"Please, the circus is playing to you, not real work."

My stomach churned. I didn't want to be here. My breath sped up, and I tried to stay quiet and small. I picked up my bag, tiptoed to the door, and pushed it open.

"Sapphire, you're leaving?" Gavin asked.

"Yes, to meet up with the guys?" I said. It sounded a lot like a question.

"I would like to know where you're planning on going and when you plan on being back."

"Sure, of course. Um, we're going to go to the market, and then the Casa Historica de Tucuman. I think the plan is to come back after lunch for a siesta. Is that okay?"

Gavin nodded. "That's fine, call me of you're going to be later than one."

"Yes, absolutely." I forced myself to walk down the hallway when I wanted to run. Kayin and Taliesin stood on the stairs. Taliesin arched a white eyebrow.

Kayin grabbed my arm and lead me out of the house. "Are you okay?"

His deep voice wrapped around me, as did his arms, letting me know I was safe. I shook my head. Tears ran down my cheeks.

"Don't worry, Sapphire, adults fight sometimes." Taliesin pulled out his phone, his thumb skimming across the screen.

"I guess." But what if they broke up? What if it was all my fault? I mean Gavin is attached to me because of knowing me as a baby and I'm his dead sister's kid. But to Anali, maybe I'm just baggage that came with Gavin? She's always nice to me, but maybe it wasn't working. Maybe loving a child that's not yours isn't possible.

"Ready?" Shin asked as he came out his house, Sasha following behind him. "What happened?"

"Gavin and Anali are arguing," Kayin said.

"About me, they're arguing about me," I whispered.

Sasha grunted. "I hate that. Worst fight my parents got into I was nine years and wanted to join soccer team at school. Mama was going to sign me up, but Papa forbade it. Mama wanted me to be kid. Papa said I was to be ballet dancer. If I got hurt playing soccer, it could ruin life."

Wow, this fight wasn't *that* bad. "What happened?"

Sasha's gray eyes hardened. "Papa won, he always wins."

Shin bumped his shoulder into Sasha's. "My mom always wins. I think it's because she starts screeching in Korean and my dad gives in."

Shin began talking in a high pitched rapid voice and switching between his hands on his hips and wagging a finger at us. I laughed and shifted so I stood next to Kayin instead of hiding against his chest.

"Come on, let's go," Taliesin said. "Kayin and I missed breakfast."

"Do you want to eat something first?" Shin asked.

"No, they're fighting in the kitchen." Kayin draped his arm over my shoulders I relaxed, feeling safe with my big brother. "We can get some fruit and pastries at the market."

"Sounds good to me." Shin rubbed his belly, his yellow tee shirt bunching under his hand.

"Pig," said Sasha. "You already ate."

Shin shrugged and began to walk down the flower-lined street.

Open air markets are better than a mall any day! They have live music, bags of spices, piles of fruits and vegetables, people calling out showing off their hand-made clothes, jewelry and freshly cooked treats. Munching on warm apple empanadas, we browsed the stalls.

Kayin's dark brown eyes lingered on dolls and toys.

"Kayin, how many siblings do you have?" I asked, handing him my empanada. This had gone on long enough. Things might never be okay with his family, but I was damn well going to try.

"Two little sisters, and one brother. Why?"

I ran my hands over the dolls. Their soft cloth bodies came in a range of browns from pale tan to chocolate brown. Each wore a fancy party dress and their black yarn hair done in braids. "I'm going to get this one for Shante." I held up a doll in a pink dress. "Which ones should we get for your sisters?"

Kayin sighed. "I don't know where to send them or if my mom would even let the girls have them."

"Well, we're going to try. Wouldn't you feel better if you tried?"

Kayin's eyes became shiny with tears which he blinked away. "Yes. Yes, I would. Anashe liked blue, Chidiwa orange."

I picked out two dark skinned dolls and handed the grandmotherly woman some money. She wrapped them in brown paper to keep them safe, at least I assume that was the goal with the gentle way she patted the wrapped packages. I held them and looked around the market. "My bag isn't big enough, we need a basket."

"Over there." Taliesin pointed to the end of the row where a man holding up woven shopping baskets called out to people.

"Perfect." I was on a mission. Anali and Gavin would sort themselves out. Kayin needed my help. I bought two deep baskets woven from flexible grass. Who knew grass could be so strong?

"Now we need gifts for the rest of your family."

"I should get something for my family too," Shin said. "It's been a while since I sent anything home."

"I would like to get something for Shante," Taliesin said. "She spends so much time with my mom it would be rude to ignore her."

I smiled. "What about you, Sasha? Anyone you need to shop for?"

He tilted his head forward, and his golden blond hair streaked with red covered his eyes. "Da, I could get something for parents, and I have cousins I'm close to. It would be nice to have presents in time to ship home for Hanukkah."

"When does it start?" I suck as a friend. I should know something this important.

"In six weeks."

"Do you need anything for it?" Kayin asked.

"I need menorah and candles, but should be easy. Is large Jewish community in Argentina," Sasha said.

I pulled a small notepad out of my bag and began writing everything down. I like lists—they help me pretend my world is neat and tidy when in truth it's different levels of chaos.

We came back from the market with baskets and bags full of presents. For the first time, the white door glowing against the pale blue house didn't look cheery or inviting. What would I find inside? Gavin and Anali still arguing? How bad had the argument become? Had they decided I was the problem? Did they not want me around anymore?

"Go on," Taliesin said poking me in the back.

I walked up the steps and opened the front door. The house was silent. Is this good or bad?

"Let's sort everything in the living room," Shin said, pointing to the cream and mint green room.

Gavin walked in the house to find the glossy wood floor covered in brown paper, string, toys, jewelry, alpaca wool shawls, candles and other treasures. "I thought you were going to the market, not bringing it home." Gavin smiled, but I could still feel his sadness.

"We were home before one," I blurted out. *Good, Sapphire, let's show everyone how uncomfortable you are. Very nice, very smooth.*

"Is it after one?" Gavin checked his watch and shook his head. "What's all this?"

"Well," began Shin. "We have Christmas presents, some

Hanukkah presents, birthday presents, just because presents, and since I'm Buddhist, mine are kindness presents."

"It looks like you got enough that your shopping should be done. I think finishing holiday shopping in October will set a new world record."

"Gavin, do you know where we can send gifts to Kayin's family?" I asked.

Gavin tilted his head to the side. "We could send it to the lodge. I remember people picking up mail from there right?"

"You were there?" I didn't know this. Why hadn't anyone told me?

"Yes. Anali stayed in New York, and I went down and met up with a group of others." Gavin turned to Kayin. "We hoped to stay until your dad got back, but there were Sons of Belial close by."

"Your dad didn't know about the changes before you left? I thought you were thrown out of the village?"

Kayin nodded. "I was, by my mom and some of the other women. My father was leading a film crew on a safari."

"Why didn't you try to explain?" I asked Gavin. Didn't he know how hurt Kayin was?

"I tried. I did. But once they saw that my hair matched the red curls Kayin woke up with, they began throwing rocks and shouting about evil spirits." Gavin knelt on the floor next to us. "Kayin, I know your dad went to college right?"

Kayin picked up the doll in the blue dress. "Yes, after I was born, that's why there is such a big gap between me and my sister."

"Your dad will listen to you. I'll write him a letter, too. We'll do our best to fix this." Gavin touched the blue doll. "I'm sure your sisters will love these. Do you need a box? There's a UPS store not far from here; I can go and get some."

"We do need boxes. I'll come with you." I put my pile of presents into two baskets, tucking Gavin's knife with the stone inlay handle and a turquoise shawl and several pairs of earrings for Anali at the bottom.

"Okay." Gavin shrugged.

I didn't have anything important to talk about, but if he and Anali came to some big decision I wanted to be told without everyone else around.

"Did you have a fun day?" Gavin asked as we stepped out onto the side walk.

"Yes, we had a ton of fun. I didn't know a lot about their families, and now after helping find the 'perfect' gift for each of them I feel like I know them better."

"That's cool." Gavin tucked his hand in the pockets of his jeans.

My stomach fluttered as I decided how badly I wanted to know what was going on. "What did you do today?"

"Michael and I went to a pub and played darts." Gavin chuckled and shook his head. "Don't ever bet that man while playing darts. I lost fifty bucks!"

"I'll keep that in mind, but I don't think I've ever played darts."

"It's fun, we could go there later and play."

"They won't let me into a bar," I said.

"Pubs are different—they serve food. I saw some kids in there," Gavin said. While we walked, I hoped Gavin would say something about the fight earlier. Maybe there was nothing to say. Did kids ask their parents about their fights? Or did they wait to see if anything would affect them? There were tons of books on how to parent, but what about on how to be a child?

"Here we go," Gavin said, opening the glass door for me.

The small store looked almost exactly like the one I went to in San Francisco. Flat boxes, large envelopes, bubble wrap, and tape lined one wall. I went over and began picking out boxes for everyone.

"Do you need bubble wrap?"

We didn't 'need' it, but it could help, and it was fun. "Yes, and tape."

Gavin got some of each. "I'll grab a packet of address labels too."

"Thanks. Okay, I'm ready." The flat boxes weren't heavy but awkward, my arms weren't long enough to balance them.

Gavin smiled. "I'll carry the boxes home."

We walked home in uncomfortable silence. What should I do, if anything?

Sometimes we want to know something desperately. We catch a piece of a conversation. See a paper half covered by another on a desk. Watch two people arguing. And we want to know the rest. What does the letter say? Who started that conversation? How did the argument end? But it isn't any of our business. Before you ask someone a personal question, especially about something you were not a part of, think for a moment. If your safety or immediate future isn't affected, then keep your questions to yourself. The person might willingly talk to you later if they don't feel like you have pushed or violated their privacy. Or they might not. But tact and knowing when to be quiet is always a good thing.

Should I keep quiet? Did I have the right to ask about their argument? They were arguing about me, so wasn't I involved? Or was I? Was this an adult issue? We all had very little privacy as it was and Gavin and Anali deserved to have theirs. If they needed me to know something they would tell me, right? This sounded reasonable, too bad my curiosity bounced inside of me like a super ball.

Chapter Thirteen

Cartazonon sank deeper into meditation and reached along the energetic thread which connected him to General Saran. Born with some psychic ability, Saran was one of the few of Cartazonon's people who didn't mind when Cartazonon spoke to him mind to mind.

—*Saran, how are things going?*

—*Very well.*

Cartazonon could see his dark brown hand, missing his first finger, rhythmically sharpening his kukri.

—*We have a dive team digging up the gateway stone. It's huge and hums with power.*

—*Excellent, send it to my home.*

Cartazonon might have houses all over the world, but only one home. One place he had kept for the past three thousand years.

—*What about the magical creatures, or those who were opening the gateway?*

—*The walk-ins couldn't find anything. But there was a small water dragon hanging around the gateway stone that we were able to capture, plus a small herd of sea horses.*

—*I knew I could count on you. Can you remember anything about the ones who opened the portal?*

—*No. It's like the memory of them is blurred in my head.*

—*Yes, of course. Shamash and Aya always protect their descendants from those who would harm them.*

Saran snorted.

—Even the pictures I took are blurry. Of course the bright light from the gateway didn't help.

—Send out more walk-ins through Argentina and into neighboring countries, in case they haven't left the area. I think Melusine and General Senach are both free to help.

Cartazonon felt Saran shudder as he rubbed his chest where a thick knife scar was.

—Not Melusine, but Senach could help.

—I'll send him right away with some more men. I want to know what is going on. Nothing this interesting has happened for centuries.

Cartazonon took a deep breath and opened his eyes, which watered as light reflected off of his white glass-and-chrome office. Why in the world he let that modern decorator do this to his St. Petersburg office he had no idea. It must have been the vodka. He'd hire someone to fix it right away. He looked over his schedule. There was no easy way to get to South America and help search. He'd have to trust his generals to take of things for him.

Chapter Fourteen

"A harmful truth is better than a useful lie."
~Thomas Mann

I was French braiding my hair in preparation for tonight's performance when Anali stepped into the room.

"Your door is open, is it all right if I come in?"

"Sure," I said, staring into the mirror while I separated my hair into thin sections and braided it in. It took a lot of concentration to make the braid tight enough so it wouldn't unravel while performing.

"I wanted to let you know that everything is fine. Gavin and I worked it out, and while we started arguing about you, it wasn't really about you, at least not from my side." Anali sighed and sat down on my bed. "Normally parents don't explain their arguments to kids, but this is new to you, and you've felt nervous since the argument Gavin and I had a few days ago."

I looked up, our eyes meeting in the mirror. "Okay."

"I don't mind you having money, and I realize that you know how to work hard, save money, and wouldn't become lazy and expect Gavin to support you." Anali stood up and began to pace. "In the village where I grew up most of us are related, so when looking for a suitable husband, we would check out men from other villages during large celebrations."

"I thought parents arranged marriages in India."

"Some do, and most have final say, but we were allowed to meet and tell our parents who we liked. One of the things we would look for were signs of good fathers. Did the young man play with the children, spoil them, or ignore them altogether? These were important clues as to what kind of father he would be."

I turned as I finished my braid, securing the end. "So you don't think Gavin will make a good father?"

"I don't know. In my village he always made sure the kids were following the rules when he played with them. But I don't want our children to become spoiled and pampered." Anali looked up at me her golden eyes pleading with me to understand. "What if something happens and they have to work for a living? I want them to know how, and to feel good about a hard day's work. I've seen kids throwing fits at the mall until their parents buy them something. Will that be our child one day?"

I was way out of my depth. I knew nothing about raising children, not in the normal world. It never occurred to me that Anali would want kids. I did my best to ignore the worry that crept up at the thought of how their having kids would affect me. "Have you talked to Gavin about this? I doubt he wants a spoiled brat for a child either. When he sees kids throwing fits, his nose wrinkles, and he walks away."

Anali nodded. "True. And he doesn't let the kids in camp get away with poor behavior. Thank you, Sapphire. I came in here to comfort you and instead you have helped me."

Blushing, I looked down grabbing my shoes as if I'd been looking for them. "It's no big deal. I'm glad you told me. I wasn't sure how that worked, parents fighting and if kids find out how it ends."

"Most kids don't, and we shouldn't have fought where you could hear us." Anali placed a hand on my shoulder.

I smiled. "Thanks, Anali."

"Sapphire, how would you like to start training to do statue? Your strength and flexibility have grown." Anali asked.

"That would be great. I'd love to do statue."

"Good, start joining us for conditioning after yoga. I'd better go and get ready." Anali left a tickle of a happiness skating across my shields as she walked away.

* * *

"I hate to be pulled on," Sasha said once we were backstage. He kicked some stray popcorn out of his way.

We had finished working at the sales booth showing people how to use the poi and juggling balls that were for sale. Little kids would come up and tug on our clothes to get our attention and ask for help. Sasha did not like his personal space being invaded like that. My shirt had a pink sticky spot from where a toddler with a handful of cotton candy had grabbed me.

"You're such a grump. The kids were so cute," cooed Miu.

Wanting to avoid an argument I changed the subject. "I've read over both of your rituals for opening the portal. They're very different." Miu's Shinto-based ritual was short and everyone sat close together. Sasha ritual had more steps, and we would need a larger space.

"Which one are you going to pick to use?" Sasha asked.

"Well, like I said they're very different and I can see both being powerful and helpful in different situations. So I'm not picking one, until I know where we'll need to open a portal next time." I hoped they accepted this and didn't think I was copping out. "I can see Miu's ritual being good for smaller spaces. It works with our group because we know each other and can connect easily. Sasha's ritual is better for a larger space. And because of the prayers and meditation beforehand, it will be useful when we have other Children of Fire helping us."

"I'm sure once you have tried them both, you'll realize mine is superior and we'll do it from then on. I can wait." Miu walked off, her layered petticoat skirt bouncing in time with her high pony tails.

"Six," I said.

Sasha shook his head. "No eight different shades of pink. You missed ring and watch."

"Damn. I always miss her jewelry. Come on, let's change." Hanging curtains made changing areas. Most of my modesty was gone now, but I was thankful the curtain separated the men from the woman.

"You seem happier today," Sasha said from the other side of the curtain.

"Yes." I struggled into the Lycra top covered in black and white swirls. "Anali said I had improved enough to start learning statue. She asked me to join the advanced conditioning group."

Sasha was silent but the bitter envy that scratched against my empathic shield spoke loud and clear. "I am sure you can join. You are stronger and more flexible than I am."

"I-have-to-be-careful-I-must-not-get-hurt-my-future-is-with-the-ballet," Sasha said in a bitter singsong voice.

The weight of the words he must have forced himself to say hundreds of times pushed the breath from my lungs. I gathered up my long skirt and my make-up kit and sat in front of the bank of mirrors. I began to paint my lips and cheeks cherry red. The smell of the make-up and popcorn grounded me as much as the familiar routine of painting my face.

Sasha sat next to me, his aristocratic face blank and cold as he began doing his make-up.

"We don't know how long this will take," I said, as I put on thick dark mascara. "It could be years before any of us goes home."

"So," Sasha said as he painted his cheeks a dusty pink.

"And you rarely have time to practice ballet. I see you sometimes finding space and time, but it isn't often." Thick green glitter eye shadow went on next.

"What is point?" Sasha snapped as he painted his own eyes with silver eye shadow.

"My point is you should live for today and for yourself, instead of for tomorrow and your father." I pinned the tiny black satin top hat into place. "No one will tell him. He doesn't need to know."

Sasha sat his body stiff, the muscles in his jaw bunching. I walked away to watch the others perform. The excitement and awe of the crowd swirled around me like a purring cat as Taliesin began to climb the silk.

Sasha cleared his throat. "I could do that."

"Yes, I'm sure you could. You and Taliesin could choreograph a beautiful routine." I kept my eyes on Taliesin. Sasha's anxiety scratched against my shield.

Sasha turned away from the stage. "We will see. Time to get stilts on."

I strapped myself into the aluminum stilts.

Sasha leaned over. "I have been dreaming."

"That's good, isn't it?"

"I know not everyone trusts my dreams after what happened with the werewolf and Taliesin."

"Sasha, we don't expect you to see everything. We're all getting used to our powers." I said, redoing the straps on the left stilt. "So what have you dreamed?"

"I see a sign and then we travel on river. There is village of fairies and dwarves. I see us run on jungle trails and find ancient temple." Sasha's fists clenched. "It was not clear. I do not know everything that is going to happen."

I thought about saying something mushy and sweet, full of goodness, hope, and empty promises, then I remembered an entry in my mother's journal.

The truth can hurt, but not as much as a lie. Sometimes we are tempted to tell someone what they want to hear. "Everything will be okay." "That dress looks great on you." Some mindless comment to make others feel good. But what happens when it's not okay? Or your friend gets teased about the dress she's wearing? Why can't you be honest and offer hope at the same time? "I don't know what will happen but we'll deal with it together." "I think you look much better in the blue dress; it brings out your eyes." The truth doesn't mean vicious or blunt, it can be kind and it can offer hope. One thing it will do much better than any lie, is build trust.

"No one ever gets to know the future entirely. But we'll be together when we find out what waits for us." I held out my hands. "Help me up?"

Sasha put his feet against the bottom of my stilts and pulled. I took a couple of steps before I found my balance and let go of his hands.

"You need to have jewelry on you, the silver armband and Quetzalcoatl's bracelet that we got from Lichuen, and diary. I do not know everything that will happen, but I know those are important."

"Okay, I will make sure I have them at all times." I bent down and patted the top of Sasha's head, his red streaked blond hair crunched from all the hair-spray. "I trust you."

Sasha snorted, but I could feel his happiness.

* * *

They wanted me to wear a dress. I glared at Gavin and Miu. "Sapphire, the owners from the different studios we've held our workshops at want to throw us a going-away party. Everyone is dressing up." Gavin waved a hand over himself. I wasn't sure if a midnight blue silk shirt and black cotton slacks counted as dressing up enough to warrant my wearing a dress.

"It'll be fun." Miu wore a pale lavender dress, with a silver belt. A rhinestone Hello Kitty buckle matched her earrings, necklace, and ring. She teetered on strappy thin high-heels, and her hair was down and decorated with hair clips in various shades of pink. "I can help you pick something out."

My eyes narrowed. No way was I going out in whatever Miu chose for me.

"Sapphire," Anali said, joining the conversation. I blinked when I saw her. Her top was a simple white blouse with lace edging. The skirt started out a dark pumpkin orange fading through ten different shades of orange until reaching a soft pale orange at the hem. I don't think I'd ever seen her in a western style skirt. "How about you come with me, and we'll try and find something. If nothing works, you can go as you are. You look fine."

I nodded and followed her, mesmerized by the way the thin cotton flowed around her copper brown legs. It barely came to her knees, which was short for Anali. Her heels clicked against the hardwood floor. My own white Keds made almost no noise. "I don't see what the big deal is." I was wearing a nice clean pair of denim capris and the tee shirt I'd gotten from Philip at the San Francisco Center for the Circus Arts.

"Sometimes it's fun to get dressed up and go out," Anali said, bypassing my room and heading to hers. It made sense, I didn't have any dresses. "Plus they have a dance floor, which means tango, and that needs a dress or skirt."

"I'm not planning on dancing."

"Agustin will be there. You might want to dance with him." Anali dug through her closet.

Agustin had attended the summer camp I taught at. He was nice, and cute, but we were leaving tomorrow. What was the point of dancing with him tonight? "I'm sure there will be plenty of other girls there for him to dance with."

Anali pulled a bag out from the back of her closet. "I'm sure there will be. But, Sapphire, if Agustin gets up the courage to ask you to dance, please say yes, unless you have a bad feeling about him. It takes guts to risk being rejected."

Crap, I hadn't thought about it like that. "Okay, if he asks, I'll dance with him."

Anali smiled and held out the bag. "I bought this for you a while ago, it will be perfect for tonight."

I opened the bag and pulled out black silk shirt, silver strappy sandals, and a wrap-around skirt of three sheer layers of fabric with thin silver threads running through them. The colors reminded me of a peacock feather, the bottom layer a deep blue, the middle a dark green, and the top a rich purple. I wasn't thrilled about wearing a skirt, but this was very nice. If I'd seen it in the store I would have reached out to touch it.

"So?"

I nodded. "Okay, I'll wear it."

Anali clapped her hands. "Go change and then I'll fix your hair."

I raised an eyebrow but did as she asked. The shirt had a low V-neck exposing my necklace and pale copper brown cleavage. I think it's enough to be called cleavage. The skirt fell above my knees and swayed as I moved. The silky material felt soft against my legs. I buckled the sandals, and the thin leather straps felt weird but not uncomfortable.

"Sapphire you look lovely," Anali said as I stepped out of the bathroom, already armed with a brush. "Let me fix your hair."

I sat on the edge of the bed. Anali undid my braid then brushed my hair. My eyes fluttered closed. It had been a long time since someone older than five had brushed my hair. This was not the hurried brushing of an adult trying to get a child ready for school. Anali brushed my hair in slow soft stokes, holding my hair as she came to the ends as she brushed out the tangles so it wouldn't hurt. She began to hum under her breath. Once my hair was brushed to her satisfaction she pulled the sides back.

"Is this okay?" Anali asked, holding a clip out for me to see. It was a simple silver rose.

"Yes, thank you."

Anali clipped my hair, brushed it some more then led me to the mirror.

For the first time my hair didn't look like a punk wannabe. The black was glossy and rich and the red streaks shone in the light. I looked nice. I might even go so far as to say pretty.

"A few more things." Anali handed me silver earrings, a warm pink lip gloss, and a bottle of perfume. "These were also going to be presents. I guess now I'll have to do more shopping. Oh, well, that's what I get for shopping so early."

I put the earrings in—the silver roses matched the one on the hair clip. The lip gloss was subtle and a few shades darker than my own color. I looked different but not clownish, so I was happy. I opened the perfume afraid it would smell sweet. Instead, there was a light crisp floral scent.

"It's neroli, orange blossoms."

"I love orange blossoms," I said, spraying some perfume in a cloud, then walking through it.

"I know. Well, what do you think?" Anali asked her hands still on my shoulders. Her skin several shades darker than my own, almost the same shade as Aya's.

I thought it was a toned down version of a teen movie makeover where the plain girl suddenly has boys drooling. I wasn't sure I was comfortable with the change, but I wasn't embarrassed. "I like it. Thanks Anali."

Anali squeezed my shoulders. "You look beautiful. Come on, I bet everyone's waiting."

I twisted my mother's ring as we walked down the stairs. What would the others think? I hope they wouldn't laugh, or expect me to dress like this all the time. Tomorrow, I'm wearing yoga pants and a baggy tee shirt.

"Finally," Sasha said, as we reached the bottom of the stairs.

"Hush," Miu said. "You look so great."

"You look like a girl," Taliesin said.

Gavin smiled at first, then once he saw all of me he began to frown. "Isn't that top too low? We should go buy a different one."

Anali patted his arm. "It's fine, Gavin. Come on let's go."

Kayin slipped his arm through mine. I relaxed. "You look very nice, little sister."

"Thanks, so do you." I tugged on the cream silk shirt.

"Gavin bought it for me. Sasha and Taliesin already owned dress clothes. It's odd to think this shirt use to be a bunch of cocoons."

The party was held at the house of one of the dance teachers. I was told who it was, but wasn't paying attention. Paper lanterns and *luminarias* lit the backyard, where people gathered into small groups. A band played tango music for the dancers. Beyond the party, moonlight reflected off a lake.

"Do we know all these people?" I asked Kayin.

"I believe they are students and teachers from all the different schools where we held classes, and of course, the rest of the circus. So we know a few people." Kayin answered leading me down to the crowd of people.

"I don't like being around strangers."

"Yes, I know, you poor thing." He patted my hand in fake sympathy.

Huffing, I let Kayin lead me through the crowd. We stopped and chatted with people who took the workshops with us. Blushing, I thanked people as they gushed over our show, and sipped sweet tea, careful to avoid anything alcoholic.

"Kayin, I'm done being nice to strangers." There were too many people for me to shield against, and my empathic bubble was wearing down.

Kayin headed straight for a bench away from the crowd. "I'll get us some food, okay?"

"That would be great."

Kayin left, slipping through the crowd to the line of tables covered with food.

"I thought he would never leave you alone," Agustin said, sitting down next to me. His mocha skin and dark brown hair glowed against his white shirt. "I'm glad you're here."

Chapter Fifteen

"One who asks a question is a fool for five minutes; one who
does not ask a question remains a fool forever."
~Chinese proverb

Agustin ducked his head, his cheeks flushing as he looked
up at me through thick lashes. "Are you enjoying the party?"

"Yes, but there are a lot of people here."

"Aren't you used to crowds?" His r's rolled in a way that
made my tummy flutter.

"Not really. At shows we're separated and people want to
talk about the performance. Here I have to be social." I
shuddered.

Agustin smiled. "My papa doesn't like big parties, either. He
finds a place to sit and waits for his friends to come and talk to
him."

Smart man. "I like that. I'll try that next time."

Agustin looked out over the crowd. "Do you tango?"

I shook my head. "No, sorry, I don't know how."

He opened his mouth to reply then snapped it closed as his
dark eyes looked over my shoulder.

"Hello Agustin," Kayin said, handing me a plate of food.

"Thanks Kayin. It looks great." He had brought me a
tropical fruit salad, empanadas, and a dark green leafy vegetable
cooked with onions and garlic.

"What kind of empanadas did you get?" Agustin asked, shifting a little closer to me. "My *abuela* made a bunch."

"Cheese and vegetable," Kayin said.

"Those are the ones she made. I told her that many of you are vegetarians."

"Thank you." I picked up one of the golden half-moons and took a bite. It seemed like the polite thing to do. The crisp buttery pastry cracked, revealing warm melted cheese, sweet corn, tomatoes and onions. "It's delicious," I mumbled around my mouthful.

Agustin beamed.

"Yes, please thank your *abuela*," Kayin said, his African accent making the Spanish word hard to understand.

"She'll be pleased you're enjoying her cooking." Agustin fidgeted while Kayin and I ate. I could feel his nervousness and hope. I understood why Anali made me promise I would dance with him if he asked.

"Kayin, do you know how to tango?" Agustin asked.

Kayin shook his head. "No. Is that the dance they are doing over there?" he asked, pointing to the dance floor where couples moved together. Some moved in clean lines and sharp turns while other couples seemed locked together shifting between hating each other and wanting to rip each other's clothes off.

"Yes. I'll have my cousin Solana come over, and when you're done eating we'll teach you." Agustin pulled out his phone and waited for a response.

Kayin nodded towards me. "As long as she's willing to risk her toes, I'd be happy to learn to tango."

Agustin flushed and texted his cousin.

I followed Agustin to the dance floor hoping my body could dance as well as my nerves seemed to be. I willed myself to calm down. He and Solana led us to an empty spot at the back. I had never danced before and the longer I watched people tango, the more complicated it seemed.

Turning, Agustin held out his left hand. I placed my hand in his hoping it didn't feel all sweaty and gross.

He placed his right hand under my shoulder blade. "Your other hand goes on top of my shoulder. Make sure to keep your arms up and strong and look at me, not your feet."

I nodded. *Arms strong and look at Agustin I can do this.*

"We'll start with a basic step; trust me to guide you."

"Okay." I took a deep breath.

Agustin taught me a basic eight count step, and I stared at my feet the whole time. One might think I would pick up a dance easily, but they don't know me.

"I'm sorry." I said, stepping back and letting go of Agustin's hand. "Your poor toes."

Agustin laughed. "My toes are fine. Relax, look in my eyes and let me lead you. You're overthinking the dance. It's simple, you have it."

Agustin held his arms up and I stepped back into dance position. If he wanted to risk broken toes that was his problem.

Kayin and Solana danced around us. *His grace comes naturally.*

"Look at me," Agustin said, as he began to move. "Relax, you're doing fine."

Exhaling, I tried to relax. I felt the gentle pressure of Agustin leading me. He felt calm and confident. *Agustin knows what he's doing*, I thought and relaxed. I stopped counting beats and steps and danced.

He smiled and began moving a little faster and changed direction as we moved. I held my breath for a second, then followed. I doubted I looked graceful, but I was having fun.

"Ready?" Agustin asked.

"Ready for what?"

"We're going to spin. No, don't tense up."

I relaxed. It hurts less when you fall if you're relaxed.

We spun in a tight circle and I giggled at the sensation. Agustin looked down at me, his brown eyes warm and soft. The energy shifted between us. Feelings of hope and happiness flowed over me along with something intense, hot, and tingly. I couldn't look away, my heart sped up. He dipped his head a little and his gaze moved to my mouth.

Oh, my God! Is he going to kiss me? My heart pounded in my chest and I felt dizzy. *Do I want him to kiss me? Am I sending kissing signals?* When I didn't move away, Agustin moved a little closer, still dancing. Then the music stopped, and everyone clapped. We stepped away from each other, and I felt my face flush hot.

The guitarist said something in Spanish, as the rest of the band put away their instruments.

Agustin placed his hand on my arm and ran it down until he held my hand. I shivered. "Would you like to go down by the lake?"

"Hey, little sister," Kayin said, as he wrapped an arm around my shoulder, ignoring Agustin. "Did you have fun?"

"Yes. You?" Turning I saw Solana next to Kayin, her arm wrapped through his.

"I like the tango; it is very fun." Kayin looked at Agustin. "So what are we doing now?"

Cold disappointment slid over my shields. "I suggested to Sapphire that we could go down by the lake."

"That sounds like fun." Solana hugged Kayin's arm.

"I need to ask Gavin." What exactly was I agreeing to? I didn't mind going to the lake, but was he really asking for something more? Like in the movies when the boy asked if she wants to go look at the stars, but he wants to make out? Was it okay to ask what he expected? Or was I supposed to play dumb? I didn't want to be rude, but I also didn't want to agree to something I wasn't ready for.

Sometimes we find ourselves in a situation where we need to ask a question. We simply don't know the answer, and no matter how stupid it may seem or how foolish you feel asking, ask. As long as you do so with sincerity and respect the other person should respond kindly, and if not you've learned something valuable about that person. My second grade teacher had a sign in her class room that said "There are no stupid questions, only stupid mistakes." So remember my darling, gather your courage and ask away, it will be probably less embarrassing than you think.

The four of us went to find Gavin. We found him talking with Agustin's mother, Señora Santiago, and drinking a glass of wine.

"Gavin, we were wondering if it was okay to hang out at the lake?" I asked.

Gavin looked at Agustin. "Is it just the four of you?"

This sounded like a question, but it wasn't, and it would help me avoid having to ask mine. I guess parent-type people are good for something.

"Of course not, if it's okay with both of you we'll go ask the others if they want to come." Agustin looked at his mother.

"It's fine with me. You can make a fire if you like," said Señora Santiago.

"If a group is going and you come back in two hours." Gavin looked at his watch. "That will be midnight."

Señora Santiago tutted. "So early?"

"I'm sorry, but we are leaving in the morning," Gavin said.

"Midnight." I set the alarm on my phone to remind me. "Thanks."

"Agustin, why don't you and Solana pack a basket while Sapphire and Kayin get the other kids?"

"Have fun; be careful," Gavin said.

"I'll keep an eye on her." Kayin took my arm and looked at Agustin as he went towards the house. "Come on, let's find the others."

Fire lit the dancing teens as pop music played on the radio. I took off my shoes and let my toes sink into the warm sand. *Is this what normal teens do? Dance on the beach with friends? Does anyone else here scan the shadows for hidden creatures?* My skirt fluttered against my thighs with the breeze.

"Would you like to go for a walk?" Agustin held out his hand.

I felt hope and nervousness coming from him. "Sure, but I can't go too far."

He wrapped his warm hand around mine. "I heard Kayin

say he would look out for you. Don't worry, we won't go far."

"Where are you going next?" Agustin asked, once we were away from the noise of the party.

"Peru. We're going to see Cuzco and Machu Picchu."

"I've visited there. It is very beautiful." Agustin stopped and looked out over the water. "I wish you weren't going."

Looking down, I dug my toes into the sand. I didn't realize he liked me that much. "I've had a lot of fun here. Tucuman is a lovely city."

"Can we stay in touch?"

"Sure, I have a Facebook page."

"Me too." Agustin turned to me. "Maybe someday you'll come back."

"Maybe." If there were magical creatures still left here.

"I hope so." Strong hands cupped my face and Agustin pressed his mouth to mine. His felt lips soft, probably softer than mine. Reaching up, I held onto his arms and did my best to kiss back. My first kiss on the beach under a starry sky.

Then something wet touched my lip. I squeaked, but didn't pull away. It was his tongue. What was I supposed to do? I felt his lips part as his tongue ran across my bottom lip. I opened my mouth slightly and his tongue slid inside. It wasn't unpleasant, just odd, and wet.

"Sapphire," Kayin called out.

I pulled away and sank back down into the sand. I hadn't realized that I had been standing on my toes.

"He takes his job protecting you very seriously," Agustin said, then kissed me lightly. "Come on, I don't want him and the others after me."

I took his hand and walked back to the party. That was a nice first kiss, even if it was a little wet.

Kayin didn't let me out of his sight for the rest of the evening. Did he know that we had kissed? I looked in the direction we had been and I couldn't see much past the firelight. Could he tell by looking at me? I blushed. Well, if I stop blushing every few minutes it wouldn't be so obvious. Agustin squeezed my hand and smiled at me, as he had done every time I blushed. I'm such a girl! I'm never wearing a skirt again, all of this must have happened because of the skirt. If I'd worn jeans he never would have kissed me. I ran a hand over the soft silky material, maybe it wasn't such a bad thing.

I jumped when my phone buzzed. "We have to go."

Agustin held onto my hand. "Do you have to? Can't you stay a few minutes longer?"

"I'm sorry. I told Gavin I'd be back at midnight." I stood up and slipped my shoes back on.

"Can I walk you back?"

"Sure."

"We'll all go." Kayin stood up and offered a hand to help Solana up. "Hey, guys we need to get back."

Groans and protests were heard as we walked away. Miu, Sasha, and Taliesin joined us as we walked back to the house. Miu's lipstick was smeared a little. Had she been kissing someone too?

"Agustin, thanks for having this party for us," Sasha said.

"You're welcome. The classes were great and so was meeting all of you. I do hope you'll come back sometime." His thumb rubbed over the back of my hand.

"I'm sure we would all like that." Taliesin's voice was cold and controlled.

"Gavin, we're back," I said.

"Thank you for being back on time." Gavin and Anali stood up. "Is everyone ready to go?"

We all nodded and followed him out to the driveway. Agustin walked with us. He slowed down, keeping a firm hold on my hand. Sasha smirked as he walked by and Miu grinned. I knew we'd have a 'girl talk' later. Kayin who walked ahead of us looked back, his round eyes narrowing at Agustin, but Anali took his arm and lead him to the RV.

"Here." Agustin handed me a piece of paper. "It's my email and Facebook information."

"Thanks." I looked down, unsure of what to do.

Agustin touched my chin and tilted my face up. "I wish we had more time." Then he kissed me, soft and sweet and no tongue this time.

"Goodbye." I gave him a quick kiss then went to the RV. The others watched out the windows. I didn't bother trying to hide my blush.

Anali smiled at me, it's that odd happy and sad smile adults get when you do something new that takes you a step closer to being an adult. "Did you have a nice evening?"

"Yes." I moved to an empty seat.

"He seems nice," Miu said moving to sit closer to me. "Is he a good kisser?"

"I don't like him." Gavin turned onto the road.

"Sapphire, you need someone to watch over you," Kayin said.

Sasha laughed and Taliesin stared out the window.

"Agustin was a gentleman."

Gavin huffed. "I think we have different opinions of what makes a gentleman."

Miu poked me in the side with her elbow. "So, is he a good kisser?"

I fiddled with the piece of paper in my hand. "Yes, I guess so. I don't really know."

"Was this your first kiss?" she whispered into my ear.

I nodded, not willing to have anyone else overhear.

She squealed and hugged me. "That is so sweet."

"Did you have fun tonight?" I asked, before she could ask any more questions.

"Yes." Miu proceeded to tell me every detail of her evening as we drove back to the house. I made the appropriate noises of interest in the right places, even though I was thinking about Agustin. I allowed myself a moment to wish I could stay here, date, go to school, and have a normal life.

Looking out the window, I saw small flickering lights in the flowering bushes lining the road. As the RV stopped, one of the lights came closer. A small faerie waved to me through the glass.

I waved back. Maybe being normal was overrated. I could always date later.

Chapter Sixteen

Cartazonon guided the ambassador's wife around the parquet ballroom floor. "I am so glad we were able to save the nature preserve today. Siberian tigers are too majestic to not protect."

She smiled, the wrinkles in her dark skin framing her mouth. "They are stunning creatures, but I must admit I'm surprised that a businessman such as yourself cares so much."

He chuckled. "I am sure my shareholders will chastise me, but how can I make money knowing what I'm doing is killing such amazing creatures?"

"I am glad you feel that way. I should introduce you to the ambassador of Kenya, he could also use a strong ally." Her white curls bounced around her face as they spun in time to the music.

"I am honored that you have such regard for me, and I would love to help. What good is wealth when the planet you live on is dying? We must all fight to protect and preserve our home."

"Well said, Mr. Cartazonon, well said indeed."

After hours of dancing even handmade Italian shoes hurt your feet. Cartazonon climbed the stairs to his room and began to remove his tuxedo. He'd had to play the charming environmental humanitarian all night, but it was worth it. He now had full access to several large preserves where he suspected magical creatures were hiding, and he had some great tax write-offs.

Turning on his Jacuzzi, he slid into the hot bubbling water. He preferred natural hot springs, but one shouldn't be too picky. Looking out the window he watched the snow fall down onto St. Petersburg. A cool breeze caught his attention.

—*Yes?* he asked, mentally connecting with the walk-in.

—*We have checked through Argentina and haven't found anything. Should we move up into Peru? You have several people there who owe you favors.*

—*Yes, all right go to Peru, but if you don't find them in a day, then leave. I won't use all my resources there for this one thing."*

—*Yes, Cartazonon, we'll be careful.*

—*And use low-level people. No one with any real power, there is more to my empire than feeding off magical creatures,* he reminded the walk-in.

—*Of course, sir.*

The walk-in broke the connection and Cartazonon relaxed into the water. No, he wouldn't risk everything for a bunch of fire chickens playing games they didn't understand. He would act with patience and care. They would mess up eventually. And then he would find out about the unicorn.

Chapter Seventeen

"Worry never robs tomorrow of its sorrow, it only saps today of its joy."
~Leo Buscaglia

Driving from 3,000 to over 11,000 feet above sea level in one day would make anyone feel off. Add translating Padre Carrillo's journal from Spanish into English and you get a migraine, and the desire to throw up everything you have ever eaten.

The RV shook as we drove over potholes, my stomach churning in protest at the rough Peruvian road. The city of Cuzco had better be worth all of this suffering. Right now we were passing yet another dusty potato field with people bent over tossing potatoes into baskets on their backs.

"Have some more tea," Miu said, her yellow and pink lace outfit causing pain to explode behind my eyes.

"Why do you keep pushing this stuff?" I said through clenched teeth. In Puno, Miu had taken off to the market and bought bags of green leaves. She'd made gallons of tea for each RV and told the others they had to drink it—all of it. The fierce gleam in her eye had the other performers promising they would drink it all. I sipped it.

"It's made from coca leaves, which will help prevent altitude sickness and the mint will help sooth your tummy on the bumpy, winding roads. My gift of healing extends beyond being able to magically heal." She held out the glass.

I took a drink. At first my gut rebelled against having anything in it, but the fresh mint was crisp and soothing. I should listen to Miu, not that I would tell her that. "Thanks for making the tea."

"Can I heal your headache?"

I looked into eyes the same shade of peridot green as my own, but without the flecks of gold. "That would be great. I always get a headache translating spoken languages, but this..." I pointed at the tight neat script which filled the journal's yellowed parchment pages. "This sucks."

Miu ran her fingers through my hair. Warmth flowed from her fingers and melted into my pounding head. "Have you found what you're looking for yet?"

"No. He wrote about dreams of events that have already happened, like 'black slaves rising up against their masters for freedom.' And he complains a lot about a Padre Francisco, who drinks too much of the wine and causes problems." He also mentioned a woman whose blue eyes and lush curves tempted him almost to the point of madness, but it seemed rude to tell others about something so private and difficult for him to overcome. If he had overcome it. "I don't know how my mom got through this book while on the run with me." I shivered as Miu's gift washed away the pain behind my eyes.

"Well, maybe she didn't translate everything. Maybe she read it until she found what she needed."

I looked down at my notebook and the journal. I had been translating everything, but I could do that later. Right now I needed to find the spell or ritual or whatever to help Kayin, if the cryptic note I had found was true. "Miu, thank you. You saved me a lot of time, and pain."

"Good, because you need to lie down. You've pushed yourself too hard. With the altitude change, you need to rest and let my magic work. After you drink the rest of your tea." Miu waited until I had drunk it all before leading me into the back of the RV where there was a fold-down bed. She sat down next to me stroking my hair and humming until I feel asleep.

"Sapphire, time to wake up," Anali shook my shoulder. "How are you feeling?"

"Much better." Miu hadn't used her gifts on me before and while I had seen her help others, I was surprised at how good I felt. "Where are we?"

"We're pulling into Cuzco." Anali smiled. "It's beautiful. Come and see."

Gavin drove down the cobblestone street. Small adobe buildings stood next to large colonial residences, testaments to Spanish occupation. Gawking tourists, calm locals, and natives wearing colorful woven clothes and hats walked the streets together, their smiles infectious. I couldn't wait to get off the RV and explore.

Gavin parked in front of a yellow and white hotel. Two of the other three RV's were already there. "Where's the other one?" We were always the last ones in because Gavin was the only driver and he liked to stop a lot.

"Michael called. Shin got altitude sickness, so they stopped and bought some oxygen." Gavin got out and opened the storage door under the bus and began to cough. "The hotel has a laundry service. Please make sure all our dirty laundry gets done. This reeks. They also have Wi-Fi, so send in all your school work and download anything else you need." Gavin set our luggage on the ground.

I sent Shin a quick text: *I hope you're okay.*

My phone chirped. *Doing better, should be there in an hour.*

Are you drinking the tea?

I hate mint.

Trust me you want to drink the tea, it will help a lot.

OK :) see you soon.

"Are you sure this is a good hotel?" Sasha asked, looking around. "I do not see any other cars here."

"We booked the entire hotel. It's not very big, only sixteen rooms." Gavin swept Anali up into his arms. "I got us one of the suites, it has a Jacuzzi tub."

Anali giggled.

Ew, gross. I grabbed my bags and headed to the lobby.

"How about we meet back here in an hour?" Gavin asked, passing out room keys and laundry bags. "That will give everyone time to shower and rest before we go explore the city. Señora Mendoza says to put your dirty clothes in the bag, then set them outside your room, and she'll take care of the rest."

It must have smelled awful. I don't think Gavin's ever asked about laundry before.

Miu and I were on the third floor. It was a beautiful room with high ceilings, large windows, mottled cream colored walls, and two twin beds. Chocolate brown and dusty pink dominated the decorating scheme, giving the room a warm cheerful look. Our window overlooked the center of town. What was once the main plaza for the Incan empire today held tourists and an outdoor market.

"You shower first. You're faster." Miu opened her suitcase and began putting her dirty clothes into the cloth bags.

I grabbed some khaki cargo pants and a black shirt with a white Asian style dragon on the front. "Okay."

After I showered, sorted my clothes, and took care of my school work, I pulled out Padre Carrillo's journal. I had just started working when someone knocked on the door.

"What's up, Sasha?" I asked gesturing for him to come in.

"I have same dream many times." Sasha unfolded a map and laid it on my bed, as Miu's was already strewn with debris. "We need to go to jungle."

I looked at the green area to the west of where we are. "Do you know where, exactly?"

"No, but I find out." Sasha took off his fire pendant and held it over the map moving it slowly over the jungle area. "It will spin when is over the area. My babushka taught me this."

Well, we certainly wouldn't want to limit our crazy. "Okay," I said and watched the pendant.

He was a quarter of the way into the jungle when it began to spin. *Wow, that's cool.*

I read the map. "It's over the Manu Wildlife Center."

Sasha put his necklace back on and folded the map. "Do you think others will be disappointed? This is time off. We planned to spend two weeks here before we go to Lima and work again."

I shoved down my own pouty feeling about our vacation being cut short. "This is what we do, why we're here in the first place. Maybe it won't take very long and I've never seen a rain forest. It should be fun."

Sasha handed me the map and opened the door. "I hope others feel same way."

"Hey, you're coming with us right?"

"Da. I see you downstairs soon."

Looking at the map I thought about going to see Gavin, but then I remembered the Jacuzzi comment and decided I'd talk to him later. Pulling out my phone, I updated my Facebook and checked in with Shante, but she always asks for pictures of where I am, so I wanted to wait and take some first. I blushed at the thought of checking in with Agustin, but wasn't even sure what to say. I'd wait until I had pictures to post, that's always a conversation starter. I put the phone back until later.

Miu stepped out of the bathroom followed by a cloud of steam, which seemed thicker because of the white outfit she wore. "How much time do I have?"

"Fifteen minutes."

"Okay," Miu began braiding her hair into two braids which started at the very top of her head.

"Do you have any more of the tea leaves?"

"Sure, are you feeling bad again?" She looked at me in the mirror.

"No, but Shin hasn't been drinking the tea because he doesn't like mint."

Miu reflection changed into a glare. "Stupid boy. I have leaves, but check the room service menu they might make some for him, then it'll be hot and fresh."

"I'm sure if he'd known, he would have drunk it anyway," I said looking over the small menu. There it was—hot coca tea. "They have it. I'll ask them to send some to his room as soon as he checks in."

Miu tied silver ribbons in her black hair. "Do you know where we're going?"

I shrugged. "Nope, but there's seems to be a lot going on outside, so I guess we'll just walk around."

"I hope we go to the market." Miu slipped on silver wedge sandals. "Are you ready?"

Miu asked me this every time we had to go somewhere, I don't think she has ever gotten ready before me. "Of course." I picked up my bag.

"You've left your hair down." She tugged on a black and red curl.

"Yeah, I didn't feel like pulling it back."

"It looks nice. Now I have to get you into some skinny jeans."

I watched Miu walk down the hall. Her white skinny jeans looking painted on. No way was I ever wearing anything that tight.

* * *

"What do you think, Sapphire?" Kayin asked, placing a light gray fedora on his head. It was a very popular hat in Peru.

"I like it but maybe another color?"

Gavin walked over. "Try the charcoal gray." Switching hats he nodded. "Much better color for you."

Kayin ginned. "You should try one." And plunked a black fedora on Gavin's head.

"No, he's too pale for black that close to his face," Anali said and switched it for a brown hat. Gavin posed. One of the benefits of always traveling—when your adults are embarrassing, it doesn't matter because no one knows you.

"What about you, Taliesin?" I said, trying to draw him into the fun. He'd brooded since the party. At first I thought I had done something, but he'd avoided everyone equally. "The first one Kayin had on would look nice on you." I'd seen him wear that shade of gray before, so I knew it would look nice.

"I don't usually wear hats."

I nudged him towards the booth. "Try one on. It'll be fun."

Taliesin raised an eyebrow. He resisted until the others had moved on. I grabbed a random hat and set it on his head. The bowl hat looked awful on him, unless he wanted to start clowning for the troupe.

Taliesin switched it for another before I could take a picture. The soft kitten gray fedora style hat made his eyes look darker. "What do you think?" he asked.

"I like it, you look like a hero in an old black and white movie. Very dashing," I said.

"I'm not sure."

While Taliesin looked in the mirror trying to decide if he liked it, I paid for the hat.

"So what's going on with you lately?" Subtle hints are so not my style.

Taliesin huffed and crossed his arms over his chest. "I just. . . " He paused taking a deep breath, "I didn't do something I was supposed to. You're not the only one with a job to do."

"What are you talking about?"

"Look can we leave it? I messed up, I feel guilty, and I won't do it again. It doesn't affect anyone on this trip or your destiny so I don't see how it's any of your business." Taliesin walked ahead his braid snapping.

What did he mean about a job to do? Did it have something to do with him being a unicorn? I had the book on royal magical creatures back in the RV. I had skipped over the chapter on unicorns. It seemed rude to find out information about Taliesin that way, but maybe I should read it?

Careful not to touch the Incan stone walls, I followed the others. My bubble kept most of the emotions out, but the memories of the ancient city flashed before me like ghosts. If the images showed a consistent story I wouldn't have had a problem, but the stones seems to hold little flashes of many memories.

Young lovers stealing a kiss. A child falling down. A man in a linen wrap and bright feathers in his hair gasping for breath as he ran. Metal clad Spanish soldiers leaving a trail of blood as they rode through the city. Excited white men in poufy tan pants and black riding boots, discussing an old brown skull one of them held.

Peering through the translucent images, I kept on eye on my friends and trusted that following them was a good idea. Stepping out into the courtyard, I realized it wasn't a good idea. In fact, it turned out to be a very bad idea. A huge stone platform stood at one end, ghostly blood dripping down it and covering the stone floor. The last emotions of those sacrificed to the Incan gods swirled around me. Terror, hopelessness, pain, betrayal, and the fanatical love of the devout giving themselves to their gods swirled around me.

Stumbling, I manage to regain my balance before I touched the stones, but I didn't feel sure not touching them would protect me. I had been pulled into emotionally charged antiques before. While interesting, it wasn't something I wanted to do around a bunch of tourists. Hopefully, people would assume I had altitude sickness instead of having a weird psychic episode.

"Gavin," I said, my voice echoing in my ears. I hope I spoke loud enough.

"Sapphire." I blinked trying to focus on Gavin's face. "Let's get you out of here, okay? Anali, I'm going to find a cafe or something over that way, call when you guys are done and we'll meet up."

A strong arm went around my shoulder leading and supporting me. "Let's get you something to drink."

"Okay," I said, as we walked through the ghosts of an Incan crowd watching the ritual sacrifice of a young girl. Their cheers and prayers almost drowned out her screams.

I tripped. Gavin held me up. "We're almost out of here. Hold on."

I did my best to walk but Gavin carried me at least half of the time. The images faded and soon I could see the buildings and tourists around me.

"Sit here." Gavin pulled out a metal chair on the patio of a small cafe. "I'll get us something to drink."

Nodding, I sat down and closed my eyes, letting the crisp mountain breeze wash over me. I imagined it taking the ghosts of the past with it. My head ached so bad, I felt nauseated. Clouds moved in blocking the sun, which helped my headache, but took away the warmth. Shivering, I wrapped my arms around my chest.

I jumped when someone tapped me on the shoulder. A small, elderly woman smiled at me and spoke in rapid Spanish. I shook my head, which ached from the sudden movement. Unless someone magical spoke, my gift for knowing languages didn't work.

She looked me over, her small, dark eyes analyzing me for something. Her gnarled red-brown fingers sorted through the fabric in her arms. Grinning, she pulled one out and held it out to me. It was a beautiful shawl, the long rectangle of woven alpaca wool, black with bright fire colors woven through it. Reaching out a shaking hand, I touched the soft wool.

Nodding, I pulled out some money from my wallet. She placed the shawl on my shoulders then counted the money. She frowned and tried to give me some back. I wrapped myself up in the warm wool and shook my head. She gave me the 'firm parent' look. I pointed to the scarves which she carried on a basket slung over her shoulder.

"Here you go, Sapphire," Gavin said, setting a mug of hot chocolate down in front of me.

"Thank you."

The old woman smiled and dug through her basket pulling out an alpaca wool scarf in blues and handed it to Gavin. She patted my cheek and walked up the hill.

"What was that about?" Gavin asked, holding up the scarf.

"The clouds moved in and I was shivering. She picked the colors."

Gavin frowned, and turned to look for her, but she couldn't be found. "Quite a gift she has picking out colors, blue is my favorite." Gavin wrapped the soft scarf around his neck. "That is better. It's amazing how quickly the temperature drops at this altitude."

I hummed in agreement and sipped the hot drink. The hot chocolate tasted more bitter than sweet, but very good, and it must have had some chili in it. I felt heat in my mouth after I had swallowed.

"So what happened back there?"

"Do you remember when we went to the museum in San Francisco and I saw the life—for lack of a better word—of the perfume bottle?" I waited for Gavin to nod, he should remember he had to carry me out of the museum. "It felt like that. Walking down the street, I saw the images of past memories. But they were faint, and I could ignore those. But there used to be human sacrifices in the court yard, and I couldn't block that emotion out." I tried to sound casual because if I guessed right, the rest of this conversation wasn't going to be very pleasant.

"Okay, we'll have to find out how we can block more of your empathic abilities. I wonder why this hasn't happened before?" Gavin sat back. I waited for him to take a sip of coffee and set the cup down before speaking again.

"It happens all the time," I said.

Gavin blinked then leaned towards me. "Excuse me?"

"I see the images of the past all the time." I shrugged. "Stone seems to hold important moments better than wood does, which is interesting."

"Why haven't you said anything?"

"It didn't bother me. After the perfume bottle I understood what was happening, and I ignored it. I mean the images are see-through, sometimes barely there. They're not like ghosts trying to talk to me or something. Just a moment in time profound enough to have left an imprint on a place." I drank more. Chocolate is magic. I could feel my headache fading with every sip.

Gavin frowned. "Sapphire, this is serious. Why didn't you tell someone?"

"I don't know, it wasn't bothering me until today. Anyway, I assumed it was part of the whole empathetic thing, you know, like still knowing what emotions people are feeling without feeling them myself. That's what my protective bubble does, puts a thin barrier around me, but doesn't shut everything down."

Gavin ran a hand through his hair, disrupting the forgotten hat, he caught it before it hit the ground. "Sapphire, we need to do something about this. What happens when we go to Machu Picchu? Or stay in a castle? The house in New York is full of antiques and itself is old and has its own history."

"I hadn't thought about it."

"Which is why you need to tell me about things. I can help or at least I'll try to help."

Gavin looked frustrated. I could sense a lecture coming. "I do have something I want to talk to you about."

Gavin raised an eyebrow and picked up his cup. "Oh really?"

Rude, just because I have good timing to distract him doesn't mean I'm not genuine. "Sasha told me he's having dreams about the jungle, specifically the Manu Wildlife Center."

"Did he say if there was a time factor?" Gavin asked, his voice monotone. "Did he see any danger?"

"He didn't say anything to me about that."

"Oh well, we couldn't have gone to Machu Picchu anyway."

Excuse me, but I want to go. "Why not?"

"Well, with you seeing ghosts and such . . . " Gavin waved his hand at me as if it would finish the rest of his sentence.

"I'll be fine. I've dealt with it fine, well until today. But that caught me off guard, next time I'll breathe or something."

Gavin arched an eyebrow, his peridot green eyes unblinking.

159

"You'll breathe or something? Are you sure that will work?"

Double rude. "What did you have in mind?" I sat back and sipped my hot chocolate, waiting for some brilliant piece of grown-up advice.

Gavin coughed, looked away, and shrugged.

What-ifs are insidious little devils that will bounce around your mind and try to chain your heart. Don't let them. Yes, be prepared for things that could happen. Yes, pack what you might need, but don't stay home because something might happen. Don't let worrying and what-ifs win. Sort through them, prepare properly then cast out all the silly things and the ones you can't control. Enjoy life and don't allow fear of what could happen rule you.

"So, let's not plan around what I might see or experience, we can't determine what crazy will pop up."

"We need to find something that can help. It's not okay for you to be bombarded by strange, possibly dangerous emotions." I shrugged. I wasn't worried.

Chapter Eighteen

"Doubt is not a pleasant condition, but certainty is an absurd one."
~Voltaire

My ears popped three times on the train ride to Machu Picchu. I'd never ridden on a train before. The rocking motion and the steady clacking of the wheels on the track soothed me. Out the window I saw perfect green squares of farmland covering the valley below as we rode through steep, shrub-covered hills.

"Soda?" Taliesin asked, handing me a gold can as he sat down.

"Thanks." Inca Cola, the most popular soda in Peru, tasted a lot like cream soda. "How are you doing?"

Taliesin shrugged. His furrowed brow and tense shoulders gave him away.

That morning Taliesin had found one of the hotel staff dead in the hallway.

"It's okay to feel upset after finding a dead body."

Taliesin turned to look at me, and the pain and sadness in his eyes made my heart stop.

"I didn't find him dead. I don't want to talk about this."

What had happened? I wanted to pry and insist that he tell me everything, but no one likes to be pushed and nagged.

"That's fine; we don't have to talk about it."

I placed my hand on top of his and squeezed letting him know I'm here for him.

Taliesin turned his hand over and laced our fingers together. His pale white fingers next to my copper ones reminded me of Shamash and Aya.

"Thank you."

He closed his eyes, but his body still looked tense. I bit my lip, looked at our hands, and began to hum. My pendant warmed as I drew on the Phoenix power from Akasha and let it flow into my voice. Once I used the power of my voice to protect Taliesin, now I used it to soothe him. I didn't like using this gift; the ability to influence someone's emotions wasn't as much fun as one would think.

Taliesin sighed as his body relaxed. I hummed until he fell asleep. He never let go of my hand.

I jumped when my phone vibrated in my pocket. I set my copy of *The Red Badge of Courage* on my leg, rubbing my hand against my jeans to get rid of the image of Henry's burnt hands, and fished for my phone one handed, trying to not wake Taliesin.

"Hello."

"Sapphire," Shante sniffed.

"Shante, honey what's wrong?"

Shante began to explain in loud tear-filled wails. I had no idea what she was saying, but I made cooing noises trying to calm her down.

"Hum," Taliesin mumbled next to me.

"What?"

Blinking as he woke up. "Hum, like you did for me, otherwise she's not going to calm down."

Did this means he felt okay with what I had done? "Will that even work over the phone?"

"I don't know. It's worth a try."

I hummed into the phone feeling very stupid, but Shante's sobs became sniffles, and after a few minutes only the sound of her breathing. There had to be a way to calm someone without putting them to sleep. I'd have to work on that.

"Sapphire?"

"Cordelia? What's going on?" I relaxed, knowing Cordelia would take care of Shante. I realized I had been gripping Taliesin's hand. I whispered sorry and pulled my hand away, my cheeks flushing.

"Shante went to court today. Sophia, her mom, isn't doing what she needs to do. The judge was going to give her three more months. Sophia said she loved Shante but was sick of CPS being in her business and chose instead to give up her parental rights."

"Oh, crap." Sophia had been my guardian angel when I first went into the system, and now she was just another druggie dragging her kid through hell. "What happens now?"

"Well," said Cordelia, "Shante gets to stay with me tonight, and tomorrow I have an appointment with her casework to switch from mentor to foster adoption. I've taken all the classes."

"Thank you, I'm so glad you're taking care of her."

"I adore Shante, I can't wait until she can live with me. Where are you now?" Cordelia asked.

I looked out the window seeing the tops of mountains and ancient stone walls. "I'm in Peru, we're on a train to Machu Picchu. In few days we're going into the jungle, so I don't know if I'll get service there."

"I'm surprised you have service now. Make sure to send pictures, include some of you this time. I better go, tell Taliesin I'll call him later." Cordelia said.

"Sure, I'll let him know." I hung up. I put my phone away and pulled out my iPod. Without looking at Taliesin I said, "Sophia gave Shante up. Shante's upset. Your mom will call you later."

"I'm sorry," Taliesin said. "I know how much they both mean to you."

I shrugged and put on my headphones.

"You know my mom will want to adopt her?" Taliesin asked.

I made a vague noise of agreement and lay back closing my eyes and turning on my music. I knew I wouldn't sleep but hoped I would be left alone. I heard Gavin muttering behind me to Anali. Had they heard us? I thought about turning my music up loud enough to drown out even the faint sound of their voices when Taliesin took my hand lacing our fingers together. I held onto his hand and turned to face the window as tears ran down my cheeks.

* * *

I'm never leaving this hotel with its lush tropical gardens filled with orchids and bright birds overlooking Machu Picchu and the cloud-covered mountains. Sitting on a bench, looking at the main ruins of Machu Picchu, I contemplated how I could stay here forever.

"Hey, little sister."

Kayin sat next to me and wrapped an arm around my shoulders.

I leaned into him, letting feelings of safety and love envelope me.

"Hey, big brother."

"Do you want to talk about Shante?"

I shrugged.

"I heard Taliesin say his mom would want to adopt her. Doesn't that make you happy?"

"If she really wants her." I watched a bird with a black body and odd shaped red head eat some berries.

"Cordelia has been her mentor for almost six months, why wouldn't she want her?" Kayin asked.

"Living with someone as damaged as Shante is a lot different than hanging out with her on occasion." I touched the eye Shante had blackened once when she threw a fit because her mom couldn't see her on Christmas. "We would get kids being 'given back' by adoptive parents because they're too much trouble, especially when they become teenagers."

Kayin stayed silent for a moment. When he spoke, his rich voice was soft. I felt his concern. "Are you afraid Cordelia will give Shante back, or are you afraid that Gavin will give you back?"

I sucked in a breath, it sounded even more painful out loud than in my head. Thankfully, my mom's words helped.

Self-doubt, what-ifs, and fearful thoughts can eat away at you. Most of the time these are caused by not knowing. Not knowing how others think or feel, not knowing what to do next, or not knowing what is coming. Try to calm your thoughts, make a plan, be brave enough to ask others— whatever will help you ease your self-doubt and toxic thoughts.

"Sapphire, what could he say to convince you? What could Gavin do that would let you know how much he cares and that he won't get rid of you?"

"I don't know." Nothing was permanent. Forever isn't real. I scooted closer to Kayin, my hand grasping his tee shirt. "What would you want from your parents to know they wouldn't cast you out of your village again?"

"You're right. There isn't much my mom could do in one grand gesture. They would need to be there and accept me every day, and one day the fear of being rejected again would be gone."

Kayin squeezed me tight.

"There is a lot of worry bouncing around in your head."

"We'll stick together, won't we, big brother?"

"Yes, little sister. We'll stick together."

The soft click of the door made me turn. Gavin walked over to us smiling. "I got off the phone with Cordelia. She's already called her lawyer and the caseworker so she can start the adoption process for Shante."

"Do you think she'll adopt her? And keep her forever, not giving her back even when things get tough?" I asked.

Gavin stopped, his forehead wrinkling as he frowned. "Why would she give her up? Cordelia loves Shante."

"Sometimes love isn't enough. Sometime things become too difficult. Sophia, her mom, loves Shante and gave her up."

Gavin's pale green eyes stared into mine, confusion turned to determination as he knelt beside me. "I am never giving you up."

I looked at the ground. "I know. I mean, you need me for the whole portal thing."

Gavin reached out lifting my chin and turned me to face him. He spoke each word slowly and clearly. "I am not giving you up. You. My niece, whom I held minutes after you were born. Sapphire Aya Rayner, I am never leaving you."

I tried to blink back the tears. "But what if I ..."

"Then we'll figure it out."

Gavin wiped away the tears from my cheeks.

"We're family. We were separated, not destroyed. While I hope you don't wind up with multiple baby daddies and prison tattoos, I won't ever leave you."

I shoved down the 'what ifs' and the worrying and allowed myself to believe my uncle's words for a little while.

* * *

My plate held one of the most colorful breakfasts I'd ever seen: slices of boiled purple potatoes, sautéed onions, and green bell peppers covered in a spicy yellow cheese sauce topped with black olives and hard boiled eggs. Potatoes are one of my favorite foods. Purple potatoes look so pretty and taste a little sweeter than a regular potato.

"The woman at the desk said we should get in line early to beat the crowds into Machu Picchu but this is so early." Gavin gripped a cup of coffee like he held a holy object.

"I'm so glad everything worked out so we could come." Anali's smiling face made a sharp contrast to Gavin's somber mood. "I'm so excited."

"I'm looking forward to it. Looking down at the ruins from the garden has been amazing." I said, trying to cheer up Gavin.

He yawned. Maybe he would feel better after another cup of coffee.

"I hope you don't go all funny," Sasha teased.

"I'll be fine. I didn't read anything about the Inca doing human sacrifices here, the rest I can ignore."

"Will we see the sunrise from Machu Picchu?" Miu asked. She liked to take pictures of the sunrise from different places for her collection.

"Why do you like seeing the sunrise so much?" Kayin asked.

"My family has been the guardians and caretakers of Mount Fuji since before the samurai trained at the base of the mountain. Mount Fuji is known for being the most amazing place to see the sunrise." Miu did a little shrug. "My grandparents asked me to send them pictures of sunrises wherever I go." The little bit of energy she had gathered faded, and Miu rested her head on her hand as she ate.

* * *

Reverence surrounded me. The strong, powerful, and uplifting emotions intensified as the sun rose between the mountain peaks to illuminate the sky. Miu snapped photos, bouncing around from place to place in order to get the best shots.

Mingling with the tourists were modern and ancient sun worshipers. One woman kowtowed next to the transparent image of an Incan woman. Together they moved raising themselves to the sun then bowing to rest their forehead on the ground. The Incan woman held a bowl of food in her hands, the tourist a quartz crystal necklace. Could she feel the memory of her ancient counterpart as she prayed?

The bands of pinks and yellows faded from the sky as the sun rose higher. People began to walk around the ruins, and those praying to the sun faded into history or joined their friends. The woman put on the necklace, tears sliding down her plump cheeks. "I feel so connected now. I always felt like I lived in Machu Picchu, and now I know it. My heart is so full with the feeling of home."

Past lives? I've never thought about reincarnation, but how cool would it be if the tourist had been the Incan woman?

"Are you okay?" Gavin asked.

"I'm fine." Was he going to ask me that all day? It would get old quickly.

"Are you seeing anything?"

I shrugged. "Yes, but nothing out of the ordinary."

"I will find something to help you." Gavin's jaw tight as he's eyes held mine.

"I believe you. It's okay. I'm okay. Sometimes it's fun to see the images of the past."

Gavin stiffened. "Yesterday was not fun."

"I'm fine, Uncle Gavin, it's okay."

Anali took Gavin's hand. "Come on. I want to see everything!"

Gavin smiled at his wife. "Okay, love. Come on guys."

I watched Kayin's dark fingers run over the ancient stone walls, envy settling in my body. The stones were smooth and fit together with a perfection that modern man couldn't duplicate. I wish I could touch the walls without being sucked into the past.

"Archeologists believe that this was the summer palace for the emperor and his people," Gavin read from the guide book.

"It's quite the vacation house," Taliesin said.

"I wonder why they came up here," Sasha asked, as he looked over the cliff. "Was it just to party?"

Miu backed away from the edge. "Maybe the teens came to get away from the adults."

"More like the adults getting away from the kids," Anali grinned.

Looking into an open room I saw the transparent image of a couple having sex. Eeewww, gross! I turned away, my face hot. After seeing three more couples together I stopped looking inside the houses. The Inca were a frisky people, and I did not want to see that!

An hour later I walked around on my own. The others wanted to investigate every building. I stayed in the courtyards and the fields, where there were no—oh gross—make that fewer naked people. The flat steps the Inca carved out of the mountain side to grow crops were beautiful. The steep top of the neighboring mountains gave me an idea of the work they must have done to create Machu Picchu.

I walked along a narrow path, at least I thought it was a path. The ancient emotions were getting to me and the terror and fear of the people they had sacrificed started to make me queasy. I breathed deeply as I left the aura of the ruins, and the crisp mountain air swirled around me.

Sitting, I focused on my breath. Five counts in, hold for five, exhale for five, hold for five, and repeat. I began to relax as my shield strengthened and the emotional gunk clinging to me vanished.

My bubble blocked people's emotions, but I still knew what they felt. Like the difference between tasting food and smelling it. The 'smell' triggered my empathic abilities, and I still had a sense of what they felt. Okay, good, except when I was someplace with so much ancient emotional residue. I hoped to have my abilities strong enough soon that knowing what people felt would be more like looking at a picture, more detached.

Well, I wasn't doing anything else right now was I? Wearing my mother's jewelry, originally given to one of his children from Shamash four thousand years ago, did help connect me to Akasha. I would open that connection, just a bit, in order to strengthen my shields. The question was, could I maintain the connection, focus the energy on my shields, walk, and interact with people as needed? One thing was for sure, I wasn't going to try chewing gum, too.

My ring, which looked like a thin band of the evening sky set in silver, hummed and began to warm as the connection opened. My fire pendant, with its red, orange, and yellow flames surrounding flames of purple, green, and blue set in a circle of gold, vibrated against my throat. My eyes fluttered at the increase in energy and power.

I focused on strengthening my shield. In my mind's eye, I could see the thin translucent soap bubble surrounding me become thicker, but still soft and flexible and with more layers. Time to test it out.

Hoping my divided attention wouldn't cause me to trip, I headed back to the ruins. I walked slowly, passing by my first group of people. I could see their happiness as it swirled over my shield in warm bright colors. Small sparks, like mini fireworks, showed me they were also excited.

Yes! Success! While I couldn't read them at a deeper level, I didn't need to. Anyway, it always felt rude to know that much about someone without their permission.

Walking around the edge of the ruins I enjoyed the freedom of feeling only my own emotions. The colors that swirled against my bubble would take some getting used to, but were easier to deal with than the emotions.

Once I had circled the edge I began to walk into the ruins. The images from the past still played, but I felt nothing from them, only a faded glimpse of a life. Smiling, I explored Machu Picchu without fear. I found it difficult to keep the connection open, walk, and look around, but as long as I moved slowly I could do it. I would be tired, but I could sleep on the train. The more I practiced, the better I would get. I couldn't walk on stilts and spin poi at the same time without practice either.

Walking down the path, I faced the ultimate test. I reached the place where they offered human sacrifices to their gods. The visions from the past were shadows so faint I could barely make them out. My hand shook with effort as I walked closer. The emotions embedded in the stones slithered against my shields. Sickly reds, gray, and yellow stuck to my shields.

My jewelry warmed as took in more power from Akasha. The painful emotions began to drip off like melting wax, a transparent body thrown to the earth, landing in front of me. I stepped away. I could protect myself, but it still wasn't fun being around it.

"Sapphire, are you okay?" Kayin asked.

I jumped, where did he come from? "Yes, why?"

"I felt you calling me."

"What?"

"Da," Sasha said coming from behind Kayin. "It feels like portal."

My palms became clammy. What had I done? Looking up I saw the others walking towards me. "I didn't know. Do you think the Sons of Belial felt it too?"

Gavin stood in front of me. "What are you doing?"

"I opened up my connection to Akasha to strengthen my shields."

"Did it work?" Anali asked.

"Yes, it helps a lot, but at what price?" Closing my eyes, I took a deep breath and exhaled, closing the connection to Akasha. I swayed from the rush of emotions.

Gavin wrapped an arm around me and led me towards to edge of the ruins. "You should have waited until you were further away from where they sacrificed people."

Yes, that would have been smarter.

"How long have you had the connection open?" Taliesin asked.

"Um, thirty, maybe forty minutes?"

"That's a long time," Miu said biting on her thumb nail. "Do you think they know where we are?"

Gavin's energy was calm and strong. "We need to stick together, keep our eyes open, and wait. Make sure your necklaces are hidden." We all tucked our fire pendants away. "Does everyone have their contacts in?"

"Nyet," Sasha said. "One of mine fell down sink this morning. My other pairs are back in Cuzco."

"Does anyone have an extra pair?" Anali looked at each of us, the hope in her eyes fading as we shook our heads.

Another foolish mistake. How many were we going to make today? And how much trouble would these mistakes cause us?

Taliesin took off his sunglasses. "Here Sasha wear these."

"Thanks." Sasha slid on the black Ray-Bans. Sasha always looked striking but now his GQ level rose.

Gavin checked his watch. "Our train leaves in two hours. Let's keep touring the ruins. It's a sunny day, and the walk-ins don't function well in the sun. We don't know if they were able to pinpoint where we are. We won't borrow trouble. Water?"

Gavin took off his backpack and passed Anali and me our water bottles. While the others were distracted getting their own water, I saw Gavin slide a knife into his belt. As he stood up he un-tucked his shirt to cover the matte black folding knife. Gavin smiled as he stood up, but his peridot green eyes were hard as they scanned the crowd behind us.

Kayin moved next to me. "Everything will be all right."

"Of course." My gut clenched as a group walked by. The train would drop us off in Cuzco at dusk, and any one of these people could become a host for a walk-in. It was going to be a long day.

Chapter Nineteen

"A single rose can be my garden . . . a single friend, my world."
~Leo Buscaglia

My bottom lip ached from where I had bitten it during the long trip back to Cuzco. I screamed and jumped as a train passed us headed up to Machu Picchu.

"It's okay." Kayin rubbed my arms and didn't push me off his lap. "Little sister, calm down."

I kept my eyes on the passing train, it was a blur of motion but I couldn't look away. For a second, an itchy slimy feeling passed over me. I stiffened and moved away from the window squishing Kayin. "It's a walk-in, there's a walk-in on the train."

"Are you sure?" Kayin asked.

Gavin knelt next to Kayin's chair. "Sapphire, what was it?"

"One of the Sons of Belial, a walk-in I think."

Gavin stood and looked at Sasha, who slept on the other side of the train. "Okay. I doubt it felt us. They aren't that sensitive and the moment was too brief, but we should expect to find more in Cuzco." Gavin looked at me. "You can't react like this. Walk-ins have trouble pinpointing Children of Fire. They find us because we use our gifts, they see the fire in our eyes, or because we react to them."

I twisted my fingers together. "I don't know if I can ignore them. I feel so sick when they're around, like something is

173

crawling on me."

"How can we help you?" Gavin asked. "What can we do?"

I wanted to scream that I didn't know, but the whole point of the conversation was to not draw attention to us. "Could you knock me unconscious?"

Gavin rolled his eyes. "What if you held someone's hand?"

"That might slow my movements."

"What if you drop your shields?" Kayin rubbed my arm. "Wait—before you get upset, listen. If I have my arm around you, and your empathic bubble is down, then you will feel my emotions strongly and it might drown out the walk-ins."

"That might work, but we need to know if there are walk-ins around. And do you want to do that? I have no idea how much I'll find out about you." This sounded about as much fun as the walk-ins.

"What if there are two of us?" Taliesin turned in his seat. "I can walk on the other side of you and help block everything else out."

"I'm willing to try it. Even if it slows my reactions, it will help." *Fun. I love being overwhelmed by other people's emotions.*

"Okay, everyone, grab your stuff." Gavin said as we pulled into the station. Standing, he tugged his shirt down over where he'd tucked the knife. "Sasha, I know the sun is setting but you're going to need to keep the glasses on."

Sasha adjusted the sun glasses with a frown.

The itchy feeling began as soon as the train stopped. I closed my eyes and bit by bit released my bubble. A swirling mass of emotions hit me making me gasp. I swayed under the confusion of hundreds of different feelings. Strong hands slid into mine. Even with my eyes closed, I knew who was who. Kayin's brotherly love and warmth flowed up my right hand while Taliesin's cool restraint, sorrow, and kindness surrounded my left hand. For a fleeting moment I was distracted. *Why does Taliesin feel so sad?* The swirling emotions flooded over me again.

"Let's go," Gavin said.

I opened my eyes and held onto Kayin and Taliesin as we

walked off the train and into the crowd.

"Should we try to get a cab?" Miu pointed to the congested area where the cabs stopped.

"We're not that far from the hotel. We can walk." Anali looked to me, and I nodded. I could walk the few blocks to the hotel. Anali slid her arm through Sasha's to help guide him down the dim streets.

"How are you doing?" Taliesin asked.

"Okay. I know how the two of you feel about every little thing, which is disturbing. And I know there are at least two walk-ins nearby, but I don't feel panicked."

"Good," Kayin said, before I felt a flush of desire then embarrassment as a group of teens walked by. A second later I felt the same from Taliesin. Too bad I couldn't figure out which one caught their attention. And I supposed it would be rude to tease the boys while they were helping me.

I kept my eyes on the ground so I wouldn't trip and trusted the boys to lead me safely through the streets. My head ached, and I desperately wanted to put my shield back up. The constant onslaught of emotions was becoming too much. I tugged my hand wanting to rub my head and get a break from the constant emotion.

Taliesin's fingers tightened around mine. "We're almost there. I can see the hotel at the end of the street."

"Good." One foot in front of the other, I trudged up the street. I sighed as we entered the damping field and safety. Nyota is my hero, I would need to buy her something nice. She has tried to explain how it works, but I couldn't understand it all. It worked, and that was good enough for me.

"Hey everyone," Shin called waving from the front door of the hotel. "Where did you go?"

I listened as the others talked, letting go of Taliesin and Kayin and began to rebuild my empathic bubble. I needed a shower to wash off the residue of everyone's emotions.

"Are you okay?" Shin asked, his kind, dark eyes looked through his blue bangs.

"Yes, I have a bad headache. How are you feeling?"

Shin smiled. "Great. Miu's tea and the oxygen helped a lot. I'm bummed we couldn't go with you to Machu Picchu; it would have been fun. Are you going to tour Cuzco for the rest of our vacation?"

"No, we're going into the jungle for a few days." My bubble felt weak. Shin's disappointment slid against my skin. I didn't want him to feel left out. "Orchids," I blurted out. Smooth, Sapphire, very smooth. "Anali read about how at this time of year there are some very rare orchids blooming, and so we're going to fly out spend a day or two traipsing through the jungle."

Shin's lips twitched. "Traipsing?"

I shrugged it sounded good at the time.

Shin's eyes darted over Kayin then back to me. "Maybe we can hang out when you get back?"

"Of course. I'll tell you all about the traipsing."

"Shin, sorry we made you wait." The other men who performed Chinese Pole stepped out into the parking lot.

"We're going to dinner and a club," Shin explained.

"Have fun, we're going to get room service and rest. We have an early flight." Gavin tugged on my arm.

"Bye Shin, I'll see you in a few days." I gave him a weak smile.

"See you when you get back. Bye, Kayin. Bye, everyone." Shin waved as he walked off with his friends.

Kayin paused for moment. "Good-bye, Shin." His deep voice softer than the others, but I could tell Shin heard him. He smiled before turning away. I filed that reaction away to think about when my head wasn't pounding and I wasn't in fear for my life.

* * *

I learned something new. I hate tiny planes. The whine of the engine didn't sound much different than a lawn-mower and the whole plane vibrated and bounced—yes, it bounced—through the air. The pilot cheerfully explained something about cold air pockets and how everything was fine. I glared at the back of the greasy head of our pilot, then I turned my glare to Gavin, but he glared back. He'd already explained that this was the only pilot he could get at six in the morning.

"I like Shin," Kayin said.

Okay. Random, but distracting. "He seems to like you too."

"Do you think he wants to be my friend?" Kayin asked, his voice rough with emotion.

The sadness and hope I felt from Kayin let me know being a friend meant something more to him than the word did to me.

There are different types of friendship: acquaintances, casual friends, work friends, and then you have the friends who you can call at four in the morning because you had a bad dream and were afraid to go back to sleep. Friendships take trust, time, and commitment but it's worth it. When you find someone who is a true friend, cherish them. Good friends can become lifelong family.

"Big brother, what do you mean by a friend? Taliesin, Sasha, Miu, and I are all your friends."

Kayin grabbed my hand. "Little sister, you are a dear friend, but you are also a girl. In my tribe, men and women stay separated. I like being able to sit and talk and eat with everyone, but it would be nice to have a male best friend to do things with."

"Well, I don't know what Shin wants. I thought you two were already friends. You hang out and talk."

"Yes, but always in a group and we don't talk about deep meaningful things. In my tribe a best friend stands by you when you hunt, try and get jobs, get married, stuff like that." Kayin sighed.

My heart broke at all that had been taken from Kayin. *I should stop whining about my own life.* "I don't know if Shin wants to be friends like that, I don't know how he views friendships, but you can ask him. He's very nice, and he seems to like you. Why don't you start hanging out and see what happens from there?"

It sounded like dating advice.

"Will you be there?"

"If you want me . . .Oh!" I screamed as the plane dropped several feet.

"It's okay, it's all good, cold air." The pilot chanted in heavily accented English.

I brought my foot up to kick the back of his seat. Kayin's dark hand landed on my knee and pushed my leg down. "No, Sapphire, please do not kick the person flying the plane."

"You need to learn to fly a plane," I pouted.

Kayin chuckled. "As soon as we're done traveling the world and saving magical beings, I will take flying lessons."

Kayin thought I was kidding, but Gavin said I had a lot of money. I would make Kayin go to flight school.

"We're going to land now," the pilot called out as the plane began to fall towards the ground towards a tiny black strip surrounded by lush green. "Lining us up."

I buried my face in Kayin's shoulder and held onto him. If we lived through this, I was going to kick the pilot. Thank goodness I'd worn my hiking boots.

When we stepped off the plane Kayin grabbed me around the middle and took me away from the pilot. Rude. I wasn't going to kick him that hard.

"Look at the birds." Kayin turned me so I could see the bright parrots sitting in the trees.

They squawked at me in greeting. I trilled. They seemed happy, so I guess I said something nice.

"I can't believe you said that to them," Taliesin said his cheeks pink. "I mean really, Sapphire."

"What? What did I say? I don't speak bird."

"That's obvious. I didn't think you could be that crude especially with how freaked out you were when I woke up naked." Taliesin shook his head, his white hair fluttered around his head. "I'm kind of creeped out right now." He walked away.

"What did I say?" I screeched.

Kayin shook his hand over his mouth, his eyes bright. Was

he laughing at me? My eyes narrowed. Kayin couldn't hold it in anymore, and I couldn't stay mad when I heard his deep rumbling laughter.

"What so funny?" Gavin asked.

"Sapphire is saying nasty things to the birds."

"What?" Gavin frowned. "Anyway, the van is here to take us to the preserve."

"I hope it isn't a long drive. My stomach is about done with all of the excitement," I said groaning as it bubbled in agreement.

The smooth road and lush jungle made the long drive to the Manu Wildlife Preserve bearable. We had driven through many forests, but nothing compared to the vibrancy of the Amazon jungle. Humid, flower-perfumed air filled the van and a constant symphony of bird calls echoed through the open windows. The jungle glowed with life. Every puff of air, every speck of ground burst with life.

The preserve had wood and grass huts which stood in a clearing built up on platforms several feet off the ground. This began to look a lot like camping. Tall trees and vines surrounded the clearing, blocking out light, hiding a multitude of unknown creatures.

"Welcome, my name is Alvaro. I run the visitors' camp and give guided tours of the preserve." Bright turquoise eyes glowed from a reddish-brown face. His lean body moved quickly as he showed us around the clean, simple buildings. "This is what a village of any of the jungle tribes looks like—including my own. Except for the beds. We always sleep in hammocks. Go ahead and get settled, then meet me over at the big lodge for breakfast."

"Thank you for your help," I said, holding out a hand for him to shake. The spark of warmth when we touched confirmed my suspicions—Alvaro was one of Quetzalcoatl's descendants.

He looked at his hand, and his brow crinkled with confusion. I started to tell him about us and what we wanted, but remembered that I promised Gavin I would talk to him first. My teeth clicked together as I shut my mouth. "Thank you," I mumbled for lack of anything better to say and went into the hut.

"What was that about?" Miu asked, as she sprayed insect repellent all over herself.

"He's one of Quetzalcoatl's line." I answered.

"Good to know," Gavin said. I jumped, not realizing he'd come in. "Does he know who you are?"

I shook my head wisps of hair fluttering around my face. I undid my hair, and fixed the crazy curls into a tighter braid. "I don't think so, he seemed confused. Who knows what stories have survived."

"Okay, I'll talk to him at breakfast. Do we know what kind of magical creatures we're looking for?" Gavin grabbed the bug spray creating a noxious cloud as he covered himself.

"Sasha didn't say; you'll have to ask him."

Gavin handed me the can as he left. "Put some on. We'll see you in a bit."

I frowned at the can in my hand. It reeked of chemicals and fake flowers and I didn't like things on my skin that smelled and felt sticky, but I hadn't bothered to research insects of the Amazon, and I don't like bugs. I held my breath, closed my eyes, and sprayed.

"Breakfast is ready," Alvaro called out.

Miu and I clumped down the stairs. "It smells good," Miu said.

I humphed. Bug spray was all I smelled.

"Hello again. I have hard boiled eggs, bread, and local fruits for you this morning. We'll use these for plates." Alvaro held up large glossy leaves.

I filled my leaf and sat on the ground. I love fruit, especially mango.

"So. It will take us until mid-day to get to the village," Alvaro said. "I don't know how long it will take you to open the doorway to Xilbalba, but after that if we walk quickly we should be back before nightfall. My wife will have dinner ready for us."

Gavin sat up straight. "How did you know where we wanted to go?"

"The shaman told me. He also said you need to hurry, that a nightmare follows you. I'll get your lunches and extra water." Alvaro walked away before anyone could speak.

"He doesn't seem very happy." Miu twirled her finger in her hair.

"He cares for the dwarfs and fairies that live in the village," Sasha said. "I saw him in my dream, and he looked so sad."

"Are you sure that's all there is?" Miu demanded.

Sasha's eyes narrowed. "That's all I saw in my dream."

"We're not listening to this fight again." Anali held up her hands. "Does everyone have their backpack with them?" We all nodded. "Okay, check them. Everyone should have water, snacks, extra socks, a shirt, and any other gear you chose."

"You have the book with you right? And the jewelry?" Sasha reached out as if he wanted to check my bag.

"Yes, I've kept them with me since you told me about your dream." He knew something, or felt something. "Did you have another dream?"

"I didn't see anything, but I woke up with a bad feeling." Sasha ran a hand through his honey blond and red locks, which fell back into its perfect GQ hair style.

"If anything comes to you speak up, okay? Even if it's only to me." I hoped Sasha would trust himself and his dreams again soon.

"Okay, everyone gets one bottle, one packed lunch, and a flashlight in case we're out later than I'm planning." Alvaro passed out liter bottles, small flashlights, and stacked metal containers that locked together.

"Tiffin tins." Anali smiled as she held the metal container. "My mom would pack my dad's lunch in these."

"They keep the food nice." Alvaro said. "Also I have plastic baggies. You can use as many as you need to keep your things dry, but each one you take, you must bring back. Do not leave anything in the jungle."

I grabbed three of the gallon bags and put the journal in one, the socks, tee, and jewelry in another and toilet paper in the last one. I don't go to places without toilet paper.

Alvaro looked over our stuff. "Someone has bug spray and a basic first aid kit?"

"Yes," Gavin said his hair curling around his shoulders from the humidity. "I have both."

"I have bug spray." Miu held up the can.

"Okay, good job not over packing." Alvaro strapped a knife around his waist, and put on his backpack, which looked very light. Weren't hiking guides supposed to carry everything you might need? "Let's go."

I watched him walk towards a path in the dense jungle, his bare feet silent. I looked at Gavin. Were we going to follow a man who would go into the jungle without shoes on?

Gavin secured his pack. "Come on, we don't want to get left behind."

Okay, then. I guess we are.

Chapter Twenty

"If you want to be respected by others the great thing is to respect yourself. Only by that, only by self-respect will you compel others to respect you."
~Fyodor Dostoyevsky

Cries, chirps, barks, screeches, and chatter from animals and birds surrounded us, yet the dense jungle plants kept them from view. I could see about ten feet into the trees and even then some creature could sit in a bush, hang onto a branch, or slither up a vine, and I wouldn't see them until they moved. Do prey animals feel like this? Weary of what watched them or hunted them all the time?

We walked on the trail, a four foot wide hard dirt path with small wooden bridges over the valleys and streams. Who knew there were so many hills in the jungle?

"This is amazing." Anali touched Gavin's arm and pointed up. "Look at the orchids."

I followed her finger, and hanging from a tree branch, grew a group of pale pink and yellow orchids. A slick, cold, predatory feeling slid over me. It reminded me of the Sons of Belial. I jumped as what I thought was a vine slithered along the branch hanging over the trail. I kept my eyes on the snake as I walked under the branch. Visions from movies of vicious super-fast snakes flashed in my mind.

"Relax," Kayin said take my hand. "You're too big to be food for most animals. As long as you're not a threat, there's no reason to attack you."

Most animals? "Was that supposed to be comforting?"

Kayin shrugged. "It just is."

Alvaro pointed out interesting plants and wildlife as we walked over the worn trail. How he spotted anything at the speed he walked, I had no idea.

After an hour Alvaro stopped. Where we there? Looking around for magical creatures, I saw nothing.

"We need to leave the tourist trail. The hiking will get harder, there are no bridges and the path becomes smaller. Be careful of wait-a-minute-vines and stay close to each other. It's very easy to get lost."

"What is this wait-a-minute-vine?" Sasha asked.

Alvaro smiled. "It a vine that reaches out and grabs your foot saying 'wait a minute.'"

I looked at my feet. Was he joking or were vines going to grab me?

"Come on."

Single file, we followed Alvaro.

The path narrowed to little more than an animal trail. After a few minutes I gave up trying to tuck my arms in and accepted leaves and branches hitting my arms with every step.

I could sense the jungle all around me. I didn't mean the plants which blocked out most of the sky, the bugs that buzzed in my ear, or the heavy wet air that made my clothes stick to my skin. I felt the energy of the jungle dancing around my protective bubble. An awareness of life, and contentment that felt one dimensional, not specific thoughts or even an awareness of self, simply a *we live, we grow, we feed* kind of group consciousness. The jungle herself knew we walked through her.

The constant animal calls faded as we headed deeper into the jungle.

"Why is it so quiet?" I whispered. I don't know why I whispered, it seemed the thing to do.

"The animals near the tourist area are used to people, so they ignore us. Out here the animals don't like people so close and stay quiet or leave the area," Alvaro explained.

I liked the idea of the animals leaving the area.

Something, most likely a huge, fang-toothed hungry something, screeched in the canopy of leaves. Looking up, I hoped to see whatever evil beast stalked us. Something grabbed my foot. I fell to the ground with a cry.

"Sapphire, are you all right?" Gavin asked, picking me up from the forest floor.

"Yes, I think so." I brushed the dust from my hands and knees.

Alvaro walked over. "I told you to watch out for the wait-a-minute-vines."

A small brown vine lay over the path, smooth except for a small bump which had caught my foot. No one else had tripped. Staring at the vine I narrowed my eyes. Had the vine moved? Or had the others seen the blasted thing and stepped over it?

"Come on. No lunch until we get there." Alvaro turned on his bare feet, stepping over vines even as he pointed out a purple and white orchid hiding in the hollow of a tree.

"Do you need to rest?" Gavin asked.

I wiggled my legs, the muscles felt tired but warm. "No, if I stop my muscles will get stiff and then it'll be worse."

My fingers twitched as I tried and failed to block the life surrounding me. I wasn't willing to open up to Akasha again, even though panic bubbled inside of me and slick, cold, hunting emotions came and went. I was sure some of the feelings came from snakes, and I didn't want to think about what other animals lurked close enough for me to feel. My stomach clenched as we passed something hungry.

Kayin ran a bandanna over his face. A useless gesture—he'd get soaked again in a minute. "I don't like this. I want to see the sky. I don't know what time it is, or what is hiding in all these trees. I don't like this jungle; it's too much."

I took Kayin's hand. "It's okay, big brother. We're just here for the day. This evening we'll sleep in the huts by the river, and tomorrow we'll be back in Cuzco. There's lots of sky there."

"Thanks." Kayin squeezed my hand. "I feel silly getting so upset."

That was upset? "It's fine. I'm sure we'll arrive at the village soon, hopefully that's in a more open place."

Soon isn't how I would describe the rest of our trip. All of us were breathing hard as we climbed yet another hill and saw the village. Layers of rope bridges decorated with flowers and bright feathers connected the trees with intricately carved doors and windows in them.

"These are the dwarves' homes," Alvaro said, pointing to a door about three feet off the ground. "The fairies live up there."

My eyes followed his finger pointing into the canopy. At first I saw nothing but leaves and branches, but as a breeze blew by I saw groups of leaves sewn together making little covered hammocks. The trees were full of the little faerie beds. "Where are they?"

Alvaro took off his bag and sat on the path. "Around. Let's eat, that usually tempts them."

"What do they eat?" Gavin asked, pulling at his soaking wet shirt with a grimace as he sat.

"The dwarves will eat anything, but the fairies eat fruit, vegetables, and sweets." Alvaro unpacked his lunch setting a container of cut up fruit on the ground.

I hadn't expected them to act shy. So far all the magical creatures had been happy to see us. I pulled out my sandwich, grateful the container had kept the bread dry. I took a bite, letting the flavors roll over my tongue. Cashew butter instead of peanut combined with jam made from mangos resulted in an exotic PB&J. Taking another bite, I pulled apart the other containers. One container was full of potato salad made from whole small yellow potatoes. Lunch also meant an apple, and a pastry filled with vanilla custard.

"Lunch is wonderful. Please thank your wife for us," Anali

said, all of us mumbling our agreement through full mouths.

Alvaro smiled. "You're most welcome. It took several tries to find something vegetarian, ethnic enough for tourists, yet familiar enough they would eat it."

"Well, it's lovely," Anali said.

We ate in silence, too hungry and tired to talk. Then something flew by. A small faerie landed next to the container of fruit. He was thin and about four or five inches tall. His hair stuck up in wild black clumps. His wrap made from snake skin, and his pale green chest shone bare. The faerie grabbed a piece of papaya and flew over to Alvaro. His wings reminded me of a dragonfly.

"Hello. These are the people I told you about. The ones who can send you home to Xilbalba." Alvaro's voice soft and full of love and sorrow.

The faerie patted Alvaro's leg with a stick like fingers and whistled - a shrill and much louder sound than I thought a person that size could make. I guess that was the magic signal because we were now overrun with fairies and dwarfs. The other fairies also had pale green skin and black hair. The women wore skirts made from bird feathers and the children flew around us naked.

The dwarves dressed in the same fashion. However, they wore their black hair long and in braids, and their skin looked like tree bark. The older dwarves had thin, wispy beards.

A dwarf, wearing a crown of feathers in his gray hair, walked out of the crowd. "Who is the Jewel?"

"I am."

He looked me over and sniffed. "You have enough power to send us home?"

Rude! "I don't open the portals alone. We all work together."

The old man huffed. "We will need some time to get ready."

"That's fine. We're still eating and could use a rest after the long hike."

He sniffed again and walked away. "I will summon you

when it's time."

Summon me? He was going to summon me? Okay, that was uncalled for. "Excuse me. I am not here at your command. I have done nothing rude or disrespectful that I know of. I will not be treated like this and neither will my friends. If you don't want us here, then we'll leave."

The old dwarf smirked. "Maybe you *are* strong enough to send us home. Everyone get packed and meet at the shrine."

"What did he say?" Miu asked, blushing as a group of female dwarves walked by.

"That they need to pack and meet at the shrine." I felt silly for arguing with a man a foot tall.

Sasha set his water bottle down. "He said more than that."

"It's not important."

"Itzli wasn't impressed with her." Alvaro cut some of the fruit into smaller pieces for the children.

"Oh, well, she's not looking her best right now," Taliesin said.

Rude! Yes, my clothes are sticking to me, and somehow hair kept escaping my braid and curling around my face, but still I doubted I looked that bad.

"How long before they're ready?" Gavin asked, his hair messy waves of red. *See, everyone is effected by the humidity!*

Alvaro shrugged. "An hour or so."

"Will that leave us enough time to get back before dark?" Gavin asked.

Alvaro lay down and closed his eyes. "Hopefully."

Gavin stared at our guide, his peridot eyes hard. "Everyone finish eating and then get some rest. We're going to need it."

Oh, good. Here I feared that the day would be boring and not a life or death test of my endurance. I didn't want to be in the jungle at night. Using my backpack as a pillow, I closed my eyes. The energy of the jungle buzzed against my skin, and I couldn't sleep.

Focusing on my breathing, I let go of the tension in my muscles one by one. Relaxing into the ground I found myself drifting off. Maybe I could sleep after all. Dreams had begun to form on the edge of my consciousness, when a prickly energy hit my skin. It felt like ants crawling up my arm. I opened my eyes and checked to make sure I wasn't under attack.

Looking around I saw Itzli, his small dark eyes focused on me.

"What?" I said.

"There's a group who don't wish to leave."

"Okay, that's fine. They don't have to go."

Itzli shifted. "I don't want to separate my people. I want you to tell them they have to go, that they don't have a choice."

What? "No."

His eyes narrowed. "I don't think you understand. Humans invade more of our space every day. This group, they are children. Four hundred years is hardly enough time to make good choices. They need guidance."

"I am sure you and their families have given them lots of guidance." Images of long stern lectures with twig like fingers wagging popped into my mind. I shoved down my laugher. "We can always come back and check on them in a few years and I can send them to Akasha then, if they wish to leave."

"Not acceptable!" Itzli cheeks reddened with anger. "They must come now! I demand that you force them to go. I will not have my daughter stay behind with these fools."

I might not know much about being part of a family, but I know enough not to get involved in a family feud. "No. That is not my job. I open the portal. I won't force anyone to go through the portal, nor will I open it if people are being forced to go through. The most I am willing to do is come back and check on them in a few years."

Itzli growled, showing sharp white teeth. "You will ask your male leader," he said, pointing at Gavin.

Self-respect comes from hard work, doing what you know is right, and standing up for yourself. No one will respect you if you don't respect yourself. You need to set your boundaries—no one will do it for you. You teach people how to treat you, how to talk to you, and how they can act around you. I know it can be intimidating to stand up for yourself, but you have the right to insist people treat you well. And if you want to be treated with respect, first you must respect yourself.

Well now, this was a problem. Gavin would want to know, but I didn't want to argue about it. I mean, what if he had a different opinion? Then what? And Itzli demanded I do things his way. My mom was right, I need to stand up for myself. "No. The decision is mine, and I have told you what I'm willing to do."

"Alvaro," he said, stomping over to our guide. "You tell him."

Alvaro glanced at me his turquoise eyes blank but I felt his confusion, hope, and loyalty. "Itzli, you know I have great respect for you and your family. Many times I have sought your council and always followed your advice. I am not sure how this group works. Sapphire could be the one to make the decisions."

"Babies should not make such important decisions. If this child of a man is in charge than there is nothing I can do, but I ask you please, Alvaro, help me try and save my daughter."

Alvaro nodded and turned to Gavin who had sat up. I guess he'd watched the conversation. "Itzli would like you to tell his people that they all must go through the portal, that they do not have a choice," Alvaro said.

Gavin's brow furrowed. "Sapphire?"

With a deep sigh of teen age annoyance, I told Gavin about Itzli's daughter and the deal I made him.

"Well, this is quite the pickle isn't it," Anali said.

Gavin frowned. "Sapphire's idea is a good one, but I can also understand Itzli's desire to protect his daughter. Is there anything else we can do?"

"If they contacted us we could come back sooner," Anali said.

"I could call you," Alvaro offered. "Leave me your information."

"I'll see if that helps." I turned to Itzli. "We can leave a way for Alvaro to contact us if the ones who stay behind want to leave and we can come back."

"No! That is not good enough. You are too stupid to understand the dangers. They must go now."

"That's all there is." I opened my bag and put on my mother's bracelets and ring. My connection to Akasha increased and hummed around me. "We'll open the portal in a few minutes, get your people ready."

Itzli opened his mouth, but Alvaro spoke up. "Sapphire and her family might not understand, but your daughter and the others do. They grew up here and have survived for hundreds of years. You have raised strong children. You should feel proud."

His anger faded, and Itzli's shoulder slumped as the fight went out of him. "You're right, Alvaro, my friend. They will be fine and I know you will look after them." He turned to me. "We will be ready."

"Our rest is done, da?" Sasha said.

"Yes, let's go and check out the space." The bracelets chimed as I moved.

"This way." Alvaro stood and walked into the jungle.

Off the trail we stepped carefully to avoid being tripped by wait-a-minute-vines and falling into holes. The village was bigger than I had thought. We had to walk almost thirty minutes to reach the far end.

The fairies flew around with packages wrapped in leaves. The dwarves had wooden carts and trunks which they pushed up a hill to the gateway stone. I felt the welcoming hum of Akasha long before I saw the stone.

The gateway stone gleamed in the sunlight. Veins of gold ran through translucent white. The trees had been trimmed so nothing blocked the stone from the sky. The hill was neatly kept, with plants growing in tidy square sections. At the base of the gateway stone lay offerings: flowers, food, polished rocks, and leaves with writing on them.

"All the herbs growing on the hill are medicinal," Miu said. "They must be using the energy from the stone to make their potency stronger. I've never seen any of these before, but their healing essence calls out to me. I could tell you what each one is used for."

"That's amazing." I watched as groups lined up in front of the stone, ready to go through to Akasha. Tears of happiness and sorrow filled their eyes, and the anguish of the families being separated cut coldly against my shield.

"How are we going to do this?" Kayin asked. "There isn't a lot of space."

"Good question." On one side of the hill, I found a small space that didn't seem to be growing any crops. "I think we can do Miu's ritual here. There is enough room if we sit close together."

"It's fitting," Alvaro said. "That's where they hold many of their ceremonies and rituals."

"Okay. Miu, I remember a little bit about your ritual, but you'll need to talk us through it. There was quite a bit of prep work as I recall."

Miu beamed and her humidity-ravaged hair bounced as she inspected the area.

"Is no room for my ritual here," Sasha said.

"No, your ritual needs more space than this."

"Da, it is much bigger ritual." Sasha walked towards the clearing, his perfect posture and GQ hair the picture of aristocracy. Okay, well he wasn't mad, but his feelings were a bit hurt. He goes all princely when he wants to cover up some emotions.

Taliesin sat on a fallen log, his hair being attacked by fairies. I counted ten different braids before he caught me looking. Eep, he's not a happy camper. "Miu, how can I help?" I asked leaving Taliesin to his fate.

Miu pulled a large plastic baggie from her pack. "We'll need some water to wash with." She lit a stick of incense. Starting in the center of the space, she walked in a tight spiral, chanting under her breath. The smoke from the incense curled around her.

"There is a stream not far from here," Kayin said, pointing.

"It's over there."

I began looking around. "Thanks, now we need something to carry the water in."

"Do you need something? You look a little lost," asked a dwarf wearing a skirt made from many shades of blue feathers. While it was hard to tell from with her bark-like skin, she seemed young.

"Yes, thank you. We need water for the ritual, and I don't have anything large enough to carry it in."

"There are canoes by the river."

I have no idea how big a dwarf's canoe is, but it might work. "Would you show us?"

"Yes. I'm Yaretzi, Chief Itzli's daughter," she said walking down a narrow path.

"Gavin, we'll be back in a minute," I yelled following the quick dwarf.

"Are you going to force us to go to Akasha?" Her voice, hard and demanding, resembled her father's harsh tones.

"No."

"Oh. My father said we didn't have any choice—that we had to go."

"I didn't say that." I stumbled over a vine hoping the conversation was over. There was no way I could talk and walk at the same time right now.

"Oh," she said, "I'm sorry I spoke rudely to you."

"It's fine," I said, stopping to let a thin green snake slither by.

"Is everything all right?" Kayin asked, watching the snake disappear behind a tree.

"Yes."

"You're not very talkative."

"I can't talk and focus on walking at the same time."

Kayin laughed as I tugged my foot loose from another vine.

"The jungle needs us," Yaretzi said. I hummed and focused on walking. "We protect, help things grow, and add enough magic that when people visit, they feel connected to our jungle and want to help keep it safe. We don't know what will happen if we all leave."

What was I supposed to say to that? My goal: do not get in the middle of this fight. "It's not my job to make anyone go to Akasha. Each person has to make their own choice. If you need us to come back and open the portal, ask Alvaro. He'll be able to contact us."

Yaretzi sighed. "Thank you."

"You're welcome." We stepped out of the trees and a blue river sparkled before us.

Kayin took a deep breath and looked up, his eyes watering at the brightness of the sky. I reached out and took his hand. "This is much bigger than I expected. The trees muffle so much of the noise."

"The canoes are here," Yaretzi said.

Dark brown wood canoes lined the bank. They weren't very deep, but they should work. The smallest stretched about four feet long. "What about this one?"

Kayin looked it over. "It'll be heavy filled with water. I'll need Taliesin and Gavin to help carry it."

What? I'm buff. I can help. "Hey, I can help carry it."

Kayin smiled at me as if I were small child and walked up to me and looked down to meet my eyes. "You would get very wet. This will be easier to carry on our shoulders. Taliesin and Gavin are the closest to my height."

"Oh," Well, he had a point. "Okay, I'll go get them."

Kayin pursed his lips. "By yourself?"

"Yes, we only walked a few minutes, even I can hear the noise of the village."

"All right."

"Yaretzi, I'm going to get some of my friends to help with the canoe. I'll be right back." I squeezed Kayin's hand and headed back to the village. Something screeched, and the sounds sent shivers down my spine. *Why do sounds always seem louder, closer, and more menacing when you're alone?* I sped up as another something screeched in the trees.

Chapter Twenty-One

"It takes courage to grow up and become who you really are."
~e.e. cummings

I managed to fall twice during my rush through the jungle.

"Sapphire, is everything okay?" Gavin asked as I burst into the clearing near the village.

"Yes. Why?"

"I think, dear, it's because you are without Kayin and covered in mud." Anali pulled out a cloth and wiped off the side of my face.

"I fell. I'm not hurt. We found a canoe that will work to carry the water, and Kayin needs help moving it."

"Why did you not help?" Sasha asked, with more attitude than I thought necessary.

I rolled my eyes, as if I hadn't had the same question. "Because once it's full of water it will be hard to carry with me being so much shorter than him. Kayin hoped Gavin and Taliesin would go and help."

"Yes," Taliesin shouted, walking away from the pouting fairies.

"Of course. We simply follow the trail?" Gavin said pointing to the six inch wide path.

"Yep, have fun." My grin must have looked evil because Gavin raised an eyebrow at me. I changed to a more innocent smile. He shook his head and they headed down the trail. Guess I didn't pull off innocent.

"Does Miu need any help?" I asked Anali.

"No, she's still doing prayers to bless the area. Apparently, it's quite interesting." Sitting on a log, the small naked village children and a few adults who finished their work watched.

Miu had several sticks of incense burning in the center of the clearing, which she walked around ringing a bell between each step, and chanting prayers. Her turquoise top with a glitter rainbow on the front was soaked and clung to her body and her yellow shorts stuck to her legs. Combine that with her crazy hair and I could see the appeal in watching her.

Miu finished blessing the clearing when the guys came out of the jungle.

Miu clapped her hands and bounced on the balls of her feet. "This is perfect thank you so much."

Gavin managed to say, "You're welcome." Taliesin and Kayin grunted and grabbed their water bottles.

"We'll rest for a bit then get started. Don't worry—the ritual is very simple and I'll talk you through each piece." Miu sat by the canoe. She took off her socks and shoes. Using a scoop, she washed her feet, face, and hands.

Anali patted my leg. "Come on, let's get started and let them rest."

"Sure." We took off our socks and shoes and followed Miu's example and washed. Sasha sat and joined us.

"The purpose of washing off is to come into the sacred space as pure as possible." Miu sounded very formal. She spoke slowly and her voice had a mystical quality to it. A giggle bubbled up at watching Miu act in such an 'I'm in charge' way, then I remembered one of my mom's journal entry.

Allow people to grow and become more than what they have shown you. Too often we take the day-to-day mask people wear as the truth. Then when someone opens up and expands beyond that image we have for them, we can get uncomfortable. In our discomfort we might tease the person and put them down. We do this because we're afraid of showing our true and vulnerable selves. Allow others to be who they are, allow them to shine, allow them to be great, and it will inspire others.

Focusing on Miu, I let go of my idea of who she was. Miu had trained for this. Just because I hadn't seen this side of her before didn't mean it wasn't genuine.

Miu pointed to the middle of the clearing. "Sapphire, I'd like you to sit here please and face the stone."

I folded into a cross legged position trying to create Miu's calmness within myself. I took slow deep breaths and let my eyes become unfocused and relaxed.

One by one, Miu positioned the others. Gavin sat to my right with Anali behind him. Sasha and Kayin sat behind me, and to my left Taliesin with Miu sitting behind him.

"Those of us on the outside will connect to Akasha." Miu placed her hand on her fire pendant. "Once we feel connected we'll touch the person in front of us allowing the energy to flow from us and into them. They will then establish their own connection and then touch Sapphire."

Taliesin turned. "I've been part of a circle, but I haven't connected to Akasha on my own before."

Miu nodded. "Yes, you need to use my energy and my connection to help establish your own. If you can't connect allow my energy to flow from you and into Sapphire."

Taliesin nodded, his flower-decorated braids swaying around his face.

I closed my eyes and focused on my breath as the others began to connect to Akasha. I could feel them one by one channeling in the warm welcoming energy of my many-times-great-grandparents' kingdom. My jewelry heated up as I opened the connection between the worlds.

Sasha placed his hands below my neck. The rush of power felt intense, and my body shook. Gavin placed his hands on my shoulder. My eyes flew open. I glowed with energy.

At first Taliesin touched my arm with the tips of his fingers, then bit by bit wrapped his hands around my upper arm. The glow around me turned into Phoenix fire. The others gasped.

Their hands tightened for a second but didn't move. I opened my mouth to scream when Taliesin's moonlight cool power flowed into me soothing the heat enough so I could focus.

I held up my arms and sent the energy into the gateway stone. A purple-blue light burst from the stone, opening the portal.

"Let's go," Alvaro said. "Fairies fly high enough so the dwarfs can walk under you."

Calls of thanks preceded each group as they entered the portal. They were going home to a world many of them had never seen. The chief stood by the opening encouraging his people and helping push carts and trunks up the hill.

The Phoenix fire didn't sputter or hiss as cold, fat drops of rain began to fall from the sky. Soon a steady torrent of rain began to flow. Each drop hit multiple leaves on the way down causing a symphony of splatting noises.

"Hold on, please hold on. We have almost everyone through," Alvaro shouted, as my arms began to shake.

"Father, you must go," Yaretzi said hugging him.

"Please," he choked, "please come with us."

"I can't. Not yet."

Water began to flow around us, as the low ground became a river. "I need to close the portal," I said, my body couldn't handle much more of being caught between hot fire and cold water.

Itzli pulled away. "I don't like it, but I'm proud of you." He walked into the portal, turning to wave good bye in time to see his worst nightmare burst out of the forest.

"Grab them! Get as many as you can," ordered a man in camo. "Stun guns and tranquilizers only. No live ammo."

"Yes, General Senach," said a huge man dressed in camo with face paint and leaves stuck in their hats and clothes. Four others followed him into the small clearing.

"Yaretzi," Itzli yelled as I closed the portal, and he went to Akasha. Power snapped and crackled around us, forcing the breath out of me.

"Get up," Gavin yelled grabbing me and Anali by the arm and hauling us up. "Run."

One of the men headed for us. I sent a ball of fire at him. He screamed and fell to the ground rolling in the water with a hiss, his eyebrows gone. "I will get you."

Someone grabbed my arm. We ran down a path. I didn't know who was with me. When I turned to look, Kayin pushed my shoulder. "Don't look back—run."

"They're shooting us with arrows," one of the soldiers yelled.

"Capture them," General Senach ordered, the strength of the evil I felt coming off of him told me he belonged to Cartazonon. I forced my fear down and ran faster.

"They're over there." Boots stomped towards us.

Yaretzi burst out in front of me. "Follow me."

"Got you."

Miu screamed.

The thick sound of flesh hitting flesh rang through the jungle.

"Run," Gavin ordered.

"Follow me," Alvaro shouted. "There are more. We'll find them later. Come."

"Sapphire, keep running. I'll find you later," Gavin shouted as the angry grunts and sharp yelps of pain from the soldiers came closer.

"We're not going to make it," I screamed.

Yaretzi turned and smiled. A dwarf pulled a vine across the path. We ran over it and seconds later there were shouts of surprise.

"They did it," Sasha said. "They tripped them all."

"Here are your bags," said a faerie popping out from behind a tree. "Quick, quick, hurry, hurry."

Shouts and screams from the soldiers mixed with high-pitched war cries.

"Take the left trail," Yaretzi said pointing to a trail flowing with water that led uphill. "We'll stop them here and hold them off as best as we can. Keep running. Once you cross the bridge, cut it down. You'll be safe on the other side."

"What about Gavin and Anali?" I asked.

"I'll tell Alvaro I've sent you into the Father's mountains." Yaretzi waved. "Go, everything will be fine."

Kayin pushed me. "Run. We must keep running."

I nodded and took a deep breath before running up the hill. All the frustration I had felt for the jungle disappeared as the rain stopped, the path smoothed out, and the vines moved out of the way as we ran. I heard shouts behind us, but Kayin kept me moving.

I followed the path until it opened out to a gorge. "What the hell? What now?"

"The bridge," Taliesin pointed to a rope bridge, the kind from Indian Jones with rotten boards that break and sends you into the river thousands of feet below.

"Oh, hell, no." I backed up.

Kayin grabbed my hand. "We won't be safe until we're on the other side."

"One at a time. Who's first?" Kayin said standing to the side.

"I'll go." Taliesin stepped onto the wet wood and held onto the sun bleached ropes. None of the boards broke, and the ropes held.

A gun shot cracked through the air.

"I'm next," Miu almost ran across the bridge on her tip toes, as if she'd put less weight on the swaying bridge.

Sasha followed her moving slower but just as determined.

"You go next," I said, my eyes still on the deep gorge below.

"No, little sister. You will go next, and then me." Kayin squeezed my hand.

My hands shook as I stepped onto the bridge. I wish I hadn't watched so many action adventure movies.

"Look, see Taliesin? Focus on him." I nodded and walked out onto the bridge. I might have whimpered a bit when it swayed, but I won't put that bit into the story I would tell Gavin later. Holding my breath, I crossed. A few terrifying minutes later I grabbed Taliesin's hand and let him pull me onto solid ground.

I turned to watch Kayin cross. He waved to me and stepped onto the first plank. Two soldiers burst from the trees and yanked him off the bridge.

"Kayin," I screamed.

The soldier held a knife to Kayin's throat. "Cross, one by one."

"What do we do?" Miu asked.

"The one guy said stun guns and dart guns," Sasha reminded us.

"That means they want us alive," Taliesin said.

"I can't risk Kayin." I stepped out onto the bridge, my eyes locked with Kayin's letting him know he wasn't alone.

Kayin shook his head cutting his skin on the knife and held up his hands. Flames burst from his fingers setting the bridge on fire. The wet wood and rope hissed and smoked as it burned.

The soldier dropped Kayin with a curse. Another stepped forward and stunned him. Kayin's body convulsed as the weapon forced electricity into his body.

Miu cried out.

Taliesin's finger dug into my shoulder. "Sapphire, come on. Don't look. We need to keep going."

I stood there watching a soldier grab Kayin's arms and dragged him into the jungle.

"What do we do now?" Miu sniffed.

"Maybe there's another bridge," Taliesin said "We can walk along the gorge until we find one."

Their voices faded, my chest tightened, and I couldn't breathe. I felt tears run down my checks but I couldn't move to wipe them away. My knees buckled and my vision grayed. Kayin. They had taken Kayin.

Hands grabbed me and helped me to the ground. "Sapphire, take a breath. Nice and slow. Breathe with me." Taliesin began slow deep breaths.

"What's happening?" Sasha asked.

"Panic attack," Taliesin said. "It's been a long time since she's had one."

Miu began to rub my back, like one does for an upset child. "Why don't we rest here for a minute and we'll figure everything out."

My vision cleared. I focused on Taliesin pale blue eyes. "I'm sorry, but ..."

"It's fine." His rough fingers wiped the tears from my cheeks. "Are you okay?"

I took a shaking breath. My chest ached but I could breathe again. "Yeah, I'll be okay give me a moment."

"We can all rest." Sasha sat and drank some water.

We sat in uncomfortable silence. It's not good for morale when the supposed leader freaks out.

"Okay, any ideas of what to do?" I asked once I felt able to focus on solving the problem instead of wallowing in fear.

Taliesin cleared his throat. "I bet that wasn't the only bridge to cross this gorge. We could walk along it until we find another one."

"That makes sense," Miu said. "But which way do we go? And how long do we walk hoping there is a bridge?"

I looked down the gorge both ways. I couldn't see anything promising on either side. "We could flip a coin."

Taliesin rolled his eyes.

I shrugged. "Any other ideas?"

Shrieks made us all jump and turn. A huge flock of black and orange birds flew from the trees on the mountain behind us.

"We need to go that way," Sasha said.

"That takes us further from the village," Taliesin pointed out.

Sasha blushed.

"Did you dream about this?" I asked.

Sasha shook his head. "Not being attacked or the bridge, but I did dream of the birds."

"Okay." I stood up and brushed the dirt off my butt. "Let's try and find a path."

Taliesin stood, his face blank, but I felt his worry. Miu huffed and glared at Sasha.

"There is trail on other side of boulder." Sasha pointed to a large gray rock.

"You should lead the way," I said. "You seem to recognize things from your dreams."

Sasha nodded and walked in front of me. "This way."

We walked over trails made by animals, twisted through trees, and traveled up and down hills. I felt numb. My muscles had stopped burning and my heart no longer broke with each step we took away from Kayin, Gavin, and Anali. My thoughts shifting between desperately trying to think of how we would survive and how I could find everyone later.

"Are you sure we should be doing this?" Taliesin whispered.

I swallowed so I could speak over the lump in my throat. "We have to do something. I'm hoping the dreams Shamash sent Sasha will help us."

"Okay."

I waited for Taliesin to argue with me. To tell me how following a dream when we didn't know the outcome was foolish and we should go back. Try to find the others. Try to fight. He didn't say anything.

Loneliness washed over me with such force it brought tears to my eyes. I didn't want to lead, to be the one making these decisions. Itzli was right—I was a baby. What did I know?

I wiped at my eyes and looked ahead hoping to see something that gave me a clue as to what we were headed for. But I got the same view I had seen all day - tree trunks, leaves, vine, and dirt. No horizon. No mountain. Nothing to let us know where we were or how far we had come. I stifled the urge to scream and trudged along.

"I can't go any further." Miu stopped. Her legs trembled as she stood on the muddy slope. We had been hiking uphill for a while, and we were all happy to stop. I wondered if I'd be able to start walking again if we rested for too long.

Taliesin looked around. "We can't stay here, and it's getting dark. We need to find a place for the night."

"I do not think it is much further," Sasha said, wringing his hands together.

I'd never seen him looking this nervous. It didn't help my confidence. "What isn't too much further?"

"There is entrance into mountain. We need to get inside the mountain." Sasha looked up the trail. "It is not far. I can feel it."

Miu drank some water. "I'm almost out of water. Is there water in this cave?"

"I am not sure," Sasha said. "I cannot remember. I remember feeling safe."

Safe. Safe works. "Okay, let's take a minute and rest and then we'll walk again. While Sasha looks for the entrance, the rest of us will try to find a good place to sleep for the night."

"What about food?" Taliesin asked. "Do you think there's any chance of us finding something out here?"

"I still have the snacks Anali had us pack." Miu said holding up a plastic baggie of trail mix.

"I forgot about those," I dug through my bag and found it at the bottom. "Do you guys have any?"

"I let the kids in the village have mine," Taliesin said.

Sasha shrugged. "I ate mine at lunch."

"Miu and I can share. What about water does anyone have any extra?"

Everyone shook their heads. "Water is a top priority, then shelter and food."

An animal growled.

"Let's get going," Miu said, putting on her pack.

We walked uphill panting with each step. Even though the sun lit the sky to dusky blue, the jungle floor was already dark. The yellow beams of our flashlights lit the trail but threw the jungle around us into darker shadows. It was horror movie creepy. Miu and I huddled together and jumped at every sound.

I shone the flashlight into the jungle hoping to find a place to rest. The light caught the glowing yellow eyes of something in the forest and I screamed, clutching at Miu even tighter.

"It's okay, she's only curious about us." Taliesin said. "She has kits nearby and wanted to know who were are."

"Ask her if she knows where the entrance is," Sasha said, his voice high with excitement.

Taliesin sighed. "She says this path isn't the right way. She says she'll take us there, but only if we don't scream again. It frightened her kits."

"Tell her I'm sorry, and I'll do my best," I said and released my grip on Miu.

An ocelot stepped out of the darkness, a little bigger than a house cat. Her golden coat decorated with small black spots and swirls, and two small kittens stayed close to her side.

She growled, then turned and walked slow enough for us to keep up. There was no real trail, so we had to walk with great caution.

"She says the entrance to Father's mountain is up ahead."

"There." Sasha pointed to a large gray boulder. "There. Is like from my dream." Sasha ran his hands over the stone tracing the weather-worn carving with shaking fingers.

Miu and I sat in an ungraceful collapsing sort of way. The ocelot kittens came up to us sniffing and pushing on us with tiny paws.

"Can we pet them?" Miu asked.

Taliesin looked at their mom. She huffed and lay down. "She said yes, but don't pick them up. Let them move on their own."

I reached out letting the kitten sniff my fingers. Once satisfied, he began sniffing my leg again. I scratched behind his ears. He began to purr a deep rumble that vibrated into my hand.

"Sapphire, I need Quetzalcoatl's cuff." Sasha said, turning and walking over. His movement so sudden it startled the kittens who hissed, their little backs arching, and their fur stood on end. It looked cute for a second until needle sharp claws dug into my leg.

If they had been normal kittens I would have tossed it off my leg. However, I didn't want to get in trouble with mom, so I whimpered in pain and froze waiting for the kitten to calm down. Their mom chirped at them and both kittens scampered to her side. Blood welled from the small puncture wounds on my leg.

Sasha shoved his hand in my face, cupped fingers wiggling as he demanded the cuff. A wisp of anger flickered then faded due to exhaustion. I dug through my bag and pulled out the beaten gold wrist cuff.

Sasha went back to the rock tracing—a carving of Quetzalcoatl in serpent form. Sasha blew on the eye, then slid the cuff into the carving. Energy pulsed and yellow-orange flames ran along the carvings, stones ground, locks clicked, and dust filled the air as the door opened.

"Yes!" Sasha jumped in the air "Come on." He pulled open the door and removed the cuff out of the eye, revealing a large dark cave.

Oh, yes, very inviting. Let's rush right in.

Taliesin shone his flashlight into the cave. Cobwebs, jagged rocks, dirt, and bugs. Big bugs. This is a serial killer's cave. No way. I wasn't going in there. A drop of rain hit the top of my head. The mom ocelot meowed, and the kittens left as it began to pour. Miu yelped and forced herself up and into the cave. Taliesin and Sasha were already inside. Lightening flashed and thunder boomed through the sky. *Fine. Serial killer death cave it is.*

"So what now?"

Sasha shut the door. "We need to go further."

Miu moaned. "Let's stop and eat something first. We can share the trail mix and the last of our water."

Sasha looked like he wanted to argue, fuelled by the excitement of seeing his dream unfold. The rest of us were tired enough to cry.

I sat, and the dust that puffed around me stuck to my wet clothes. Gross. "We're resting," I said trying out a firm 'leader voice'. They sat, so either it worked or they choose to humor me.

Everyone received a handful of trail mix and a few mouthfuls of water. My body wasn't the only one to rumble in protest at the lack for food and water.

As soon as we were done Sasha was ready to go.

"No, Sasha. I know you're excited, but we are going to sit and rest for a while."

Sasha pressed his lips together ready to argue with me this time.

"We need to take inventory of what we have." Oh, good one, Sapphire, good plan.

Sasha sighed but began to unpack his bag. Soon a pile of plastic bags and empty water bottles sat in front of us. Not a lot of stuff. Miu had her ritual items, and she had a box of matches. Oh, wait. This was good. "Does everyone have dry socks and tee shirt?" I pulled mine out of the pile. The others did the same. Thank you, Anali! "Okay. Let's change."

I took off my socks, wincing as a few blisters protested the movement.

"Give me your feet," Miu said holding out her hand.

I shook my head. "No, I'm fine besides, you're tired and healing drains you." I pulled on the soft, dry cotton socks. I sighed in pleasure as my feet relaxed into the dry warmth. I went to grab my shoes, but wanted to wait before I put on the wet boots.

Scooting around so my back faced the others I changed my shirt, wishing I had a spare bra.

"What else do we have," I asked turning around. "I brought toilet paper, and I have the journal and jewelry." I went to take off the bangles and my mom's ring. I didn't wear them all the time.

"No," Sasha said. "You need to wear them, don't forget armband and cuff." He handed me the beaten gold wrist cuff.

Oh, well. I secured the red and silver armband to my upper right arm. Moving the all bangles to my right wrist, I wore the cuff on my left. Solid and heavy, the hum of energy had a different feel to it than what I felt from Shamash's jewelry. More playful and wild. I also felt love, strength, and power in the connection. I could feel Akasha, but it was like I had taken a different path to get there.

I ran my hand over the journal. I would have to find the spell to help Kayin. When we got him back, we'd have to break the connection the walk-in had to him. I would do it. I could fix this. I sealed up the bag and put it back into my pack.

"Don't pack your wet things," Taliesin said. "We can hang them on the outside of our bags and let them dry."

Great idea. "Thanks, Taliesin. I wouldn't have thought about it."

He shrugged. "I saw it on one of those survival shows. I also have a magnesium block for starting fires, a small first aid kit, and a survival knife."

"I have bug spray," Miu said holding up a bag with several cans. "I also have hand sanitizer and glitter strawberry body spray."

"I have deck of cards, pocket knife, cell phone and tallit, my prayer shawl." Sasha held up a baggie containing a white and blue stripped silk shawl with fringe pooling around the edges.

"Does anyone have a signal?" I said holding my phone up in different positions, as if I could catch a signal inside a cave in the middle of the rainforest.

"No, we didn't even have a signal when we landed." Miu said. "That's why I put in it my bag and not my pocket."

"Okay, let's pack up, and then we'll walk a little ways into the cave. At some point soon we should find a place to sleep."

Miu wrinkled her nose at the dirty cave floor. "Gross."

I agreed. I didn't want to sleep on the dirty floor, but what other choice did we have?

Our footsteps echoed as we walked deeper into the musty darkness. Unseen things scurried away from our lights, leaving behind creepy shadows and fear. Sasha walked ahead. I felt his anxiety rising as he hunted for the next image from his dreams.

As the cave curved we found ourselves facing a pile of

rocks. There were a few gaps, some big enough for us to squeeze through, but I wasn't tempted to try.

"We must get to other side," Sasha said, peering into an opening.

"I'm done." Miu lay on the cave floor using her bag as a pillow. "I'm not going to risk my life climbing through a cave-in to get to what you dreamed is on the other side."

Taliesin sighed and sat against the wall.

Sasha turned to argue with Miu, I ignored them. Now that there wasn't any light shining on the rocks, I thought I could see something.

"Hey, guys, turn your flashlights off," I said.

"What?" Miu asked.

"I think I see something. Turn off your flashlights."

At first I saw nothing, but as my eyes adjusted to the dark I could see it. Light flickered through the cracks between the rocks.

Chapter Twenty-Two

"If you understand—things are what they are. If you don't
understand—things are what they are."
~Zen quote

"What do we do?" Miu asked, her eyes never leaving the
glowing light.

The entrancing light promised warmth and possibly people.
With luck, people with food and water.

"We must get to other side." Sasha started to climb the pile
of rocks.

"What if we get stuck? What if over there sucks worse than
this?" Miu asked, her voice a mixture of whining and
demanding.

"I will go first." Sasha shone his flashlight into a gap below
the ceiling. "This looks like is all the way through."

Sasha squirmed into the narrow space. I held my breath, all
we heard were muffled grunts and the occasional Russian curse
word.

"I made it," Sasha called. "Light is coming from another
room. This room is empty, but clean."

Miu stood up. "Clean is good." She climbed up the rocks
and slid into the gap. A few seconds later she called to us. "It's
easy—come on."

"Ladies first." Taliesin waved to the rock pile.

"Nope, you're the biggest of us. If you get stuck you might need a push." Taliesin ran his hands over his abs. I rolled my eyes. "Your shoulders are broader."

"Oh, good point. Let's send the bags through first. Those two were so excited they forgot theirs."

"Guys, we're going to send the back packs through." Taliesin climbed up and shoved a bag into the gap.

"Got it," Miu chirped.

It must have looked much better over there. I tossed bags up to Taliesin. When we finished, he took a deep breath and scooted inside the gap. It took longer for him to get in than it had Sasha. I held my breath. What would we do if he got stuck? This was a bad idea. I began to pace to keep myself from climbing up and checking on him. What if my extra weight shifted the rocks?

I heard muffled cursing. I wonder if that's where Sasha got stuck and cursed too. Sasha said something that I couldn't make out, but the cussing stopped. A few grunts and the echoing clink of small rocks falling broke the tense silence.

Forget this. I began to climb. I wasn't waiting any longer.

"I'm through," Taliesin said, his voice tense with pain.

I pulled myself up to the gap. "Are you okay?"

"He's got a cut," Sasha said. "Miu's looking at it. Come on."

I climbed into the narrow space and began to scoot over the rough rocks. I bumped my head on the ceiling. "Damn it."

"You can do it," Sasha said.

I moved forward, pushing with my toes and pulling with my forearms. About halfway through a coppery smell filled the air, dark spots marked the rocks. Flecks of blood decorated the rest of the rocks.

I moved faster. Blinking, I came out into the light.

Taliesin lay against the wall, blood running down his arm while Miu bandaged his shoulder.

"What now?" I asked letting Sasha help me down.

"There is statue in big room. I felt safe there." Sasha looked at Taliesin, his gray eyes filled with guilt.

"Okay, Miu stay here with Taliesin. Sasha and I will go and search the area."

"I can't do much," Miu said. "There's too much dirt in the wound."

Okay, water jumped in importance. "Is there anything in the first aid kit?" I asked.

Miu shook her head. "No, there's anti-bacterial stuff which we can use to prevent infection, but I still need to clean the wound before I can heal him. And some rest and food to have the energy to do it safely."

Okay, I was the one who led the others into following Sasha's dream. Now I needed to shove down the desire to curl in a ball and cry, and instead find a way to make this work. "We'll come back soon. We won't walk for more than fifteen minutes before turning and coming back."

"Be careful," Taliesin said. I nodded and followed Sasha.

"This way," Sasha said following the lit torches.

The floor of the cave was smooth and free from dust. The walls were covered with beautiful carved images: woman working in green fields, children playing, men hunting, and their god Quetzalcoatl—a powerful being flying above all of them and protecting them.

"Someone takes care of this place. Torches don't burn for centuries," I whispered.

"Da."

The hall opened up into a huge chamber, and in the center sat Quetzalcoatl.

"This is statue from dream," Sasha ran over to it. "Look—is table full of offerings. Food and pitchers of wine and water."

Sasha lifted the lids on baskets and handmade pots. I ignored him and focused instead on the statue. The wrist cuff hummed as I got closer. Reaching out, I placed my left hand on the brown stone.

Energy exploded from the cuff. Shamash's jewelry heated up with power as I became a conduit between Akasha and Quetzalcoatl.

"What's happening?" Sasha asked.

"This is Quetzalcoatl, not a statue."

"Sapphire, come on. That cannot be real."

Stone cracked as Quetzalcoatl took a breath.

"What do we do?"

"Go get the others. Take them some water and help them here. I'm fine."

"Sapphire?"

"Go. They need to be here. He needs our combined energy to heal." I turned and placed my other hand on his side. Every few minutes he would breathe again, the stone cracking a little more each time. Energy flowed through me and I swayed from the intensity.

"Sapphire, step away and let us all help out." Taliesin said. "You need food and rest, and then we'll do more, okay?"

I'm fine is what I meant to say but something unintelligible is what came out of my mouth. Flames filled my vision, and my body felt heavy.

Hands pulled me away and laid me on the floor as I fell asleep.

The turquoise sky of Akasha loomed above me. A large, warm hand held mine. I saw Shamash as he sat swaying to the tune he hummed. Gold eyes opened and my many times great-grandfather smiled.

"You found my brother. You found Quetzalcoatl. Thank you."

"He's buried under stone. I don't understand what happened."

"He's been sleeping. He was injured, so he went to sleep. The little magic he had protected him by turning the dust that gathered on him into stone. He hasn't connected to Akasha until you touched him." Shamash closed his eyes. "Even now, with your help, only the tiniest trickle of energy is reaching him."

"How can we help him?" I asked sitting up.

"Do the ritual for opening a portal. Once Quetzalcoatl has enough energy and is healing, he'll be able to keep the connection open on his own."

"What about Kayin—is he okay?"

Shamash's face softened, and he began to pat my hand. "They are keeping him drugged so he can't use his powers. He's not that far from you.

I'll make sure Sasha can find him. He's becoming a powerful dreamer."

"How do I keep Kayin safe? By now the walk-ins must have seen the fire in his eyes." *Tears filled my eyes.*

"Hush, little one. You have everything you need. Help Quetzalcoatl, then go and save Kayin. Aya is guiding Gavin and Anali towards him right now." *Shamash's eyes became unfocused. "You have to go now."*

I felt something sharp poke me in the neck. *What the hell?* I was about to ask but Miu screamed, and my eyes flew open.

A small man stood over me. His dagger pressed against my throat. I felt blood dripping down my neck.

"Why are you here?" he demanded. His reddish brown face twisted into a snarl and his bright turquoise eyes shone hard as glass.

I held up my hands. "We are here to awaken Quetzalcoatl."

An older man came over, his face painted with thick black stripes. A headdress of feathers and stones showed his importance. "Wait, son, wait. Child, let me see your wrist."

I held out my arm, and he examined Quetzalcoatl's cuff.

"She speaks the truth! This is from our Father! Let them up, they are honored guests." His wrinkled face beamed with happiness, and tears fell down his face. "This is what generations of our people have prayed and worked for. They will awaken our Father, and we will walk with him into the light of Xilbalba!"

The men released us whooping and dancing.

I scooted away and began to move towards the others.

Miu's fingers bit into my arm as she pressed her other hand to my neck healing the wound there. "What in the hell is going on?" Miu asked.

"They have cared for Quetzalcoatl for centuries, well not these people, but their people. Look they all have turquoise eyes, they're all his descendants, and they think they will go back to Xilbalba with him." I relaxed as the pain of my wounds faded.

"Sapphire," Taliesin moaned.

"What? I didn't do this on purpose. And why is it my fault?"

The old man came over grasping my hand. "Come, come. We must share the news with the others. And we would be honored to have you as our guests. Let us care for you."

"That is very kind of you, but Quetzalcoatl needs our help. And one of our friends, one we need to open the doorway to Xilbalba has been captured by dark forces we need to get him back."

"We will help you, but you can't do any of that without food in your bellies." He tugged on my hand and I followed. "Come men, we'll share the joyous news with our families!"

The warriors cheered again.

Okay, we are the guests of a freaky Quetzalcoatl cult, Kayin is being held captive, and Gavin and Anali are in the jungle somewhere. It's one way to start a day.

The sun made my eyes water as we stepped out of the cave. The large opening sat high at the edge of a lush valley. Gleaming white houses and roads paved with stone lay below us. Farther off, fields of deep green shimmered in the sun on the other side of a clear blue river. It was paradise.

"It looks like something from a movie," Miu whispered as we followed the men along the trail to the village.

A look-out spotted us. "What's going on?"

The old man smiled, his joy almost knocking me over. "Run, run and ring the bell. Call everyone to the square. These honored guests are here to awaken Quetzalcoatl."

He turned, running down the steep slope and within seconds the deep gong of a bell echoed through the valley. Cries and shouts followed. We saw people rushing from their homes and fields to the village square.

When we got there a regal looking man stood on a stone dais wearing a cape of iridescent black feathers. His forehead lined with deep frown lines and his skin shone as if it had been oiled. "Chan Bahlum, what is going on?"

"Yax Pac, I come with wonderful news. It is time for our Father Quetzalcoatl to awaken and for us to join him in Xilbalba."

215

For a moment there was dead silence, and then everyone began to talk. A wave of fear, hope, joy, despair, and anger hit me. I stumbled and reached out. Taliesin caught my hand, holding onto me.

"Thanks." I turned to the others. "I'm going to speak and see if I can't get things sorted somewhat. Shamash told me we need to find Kayin this afternoon and that Gavin and Anali would be there."

"I know the way," Sasha said. "I can see it clearly in my head."

I nodded and stepped forward. The people quieted and a sea of turquoise eyes stared up at me. My stomach dropped, and my skin became cold and clammy. *Crap. Sapphire now is not the time to get stage fright. You don't have time for this.* I took a deep breath and prayed I wouldn't throw up on anyone.

"Hello. My name is Sapphire, and I am a descendant of Camaxtli, Quetzalcoatl's brother. My friends and I need to open a connection to Xilbalba to give Quetzalcoatl enough energy to heal and awaken. Then we need to get our friend who was captured by dark forces."

The people began to murmur to each other.

"We need to get him back or we won't be able to open the doorway to Xilbalba." More frantic whispering and the same mix of emotion. Like with the dwarves, not everyone wanted to move on. "We are not here to force anyone to go to Xilbalba." Okay, that was the wrong thing to say. I didn't even know if they would be allowed to go to Akasha and now some of them were yelling at me. I guess that didn't go with their myths.

"What have you done?" Sasha hissed.

"I told them they didn't have to go to Akasha if they didn't want to. How was I supposed to know they would freak out?"

The old man stepped forward raising his arms high above his head. Everyone stopped talking. "These children are the blessed ones, family of our father, and the ones who can awaken him." The villagers nodded their heads their emotions calming. "Once the great Quetzalcoatl has woken he will be the one to decide who goes to Xilbalba."

The anger left, but the fear remained. It would have been wise to keep my mouth shut, but I didn't want anyone to fear me.

"I am sorry if I upset anyone. I can feel your emotions and I can feel some of you are afraid, and I want you to know nothing bad is going to happen. It doesn't hurt, walking through the doorway to Xilbalba. I spoke to Camaxtli and he is very kind, he speaks with great love for Quetzalcoatl." There was some confusion, more hope and less fear. Okay, I could work with that. "Please, let us celebrate meeting each other and Quetzalcoatl's awakening."

Strong hands touched my shoulders and the old man and the chief stood next to me.

"Yes, my people," said the chief. "This is a time for celebration. Chan Bahlum, may I offer my daughters to bathe and prepare our guests so your priests and priestess can help our people prepare for this great day?"

"Of course," Chan Bahlum said bowing his head. "We should all prepare for this great day. We shall feast and then go to our Father's cave and pray for his awakening!"

The villagers cheered. Four young women stepped forward, their black hair twisted into elaborate patterns and their red-brown skin oiled and shining in the sun. "This is my daughter Ichika," said the chief. "She'll be in charge of your comfort."

"What is happening now?" Sasha snapped, as we followed the chief's daughters.

"We're going to be prepared for the ceremony," I said. "This is a holy day for them."

"Sapphire," Taliesin said, his teeth clenched as he smiled. "What does that mean?"

"It means we're going to be bathed and dressed in ceremonial clothes."

"We have to take a bath? That's fine. Why not say so?" Miu asked.

I took a deep breath. "No, we are going to be bathed."

"By girls?" Taliesin squeaked.

"Yes." I shoved down my own discomfort.

"Will we all be in the same room or tub?" Sasha asked.

Flushing I asked, "Excuse me will we all bathe in the same room as the boys? In our culture we always bathe separately."

"Oh, we can put you in separate tubs and draw a curtain," Ichika said.

"Thank you." I switched back to English. "We'll be in the same room, but with a curtain between the tubs."

"What are they going to do?" Miu asked.

"I have no idea."

We walked through the bath house where families were sliding into tubs preparing for the return of their god. The stone tile floor felt slick, and the walls were painted with scenes from their mythology. Quetzalcoatl was shown in many of the murals. Blushing, as a naked woman walked by, I stared at the floor. What was protocol in a place like this, not looking, trying to look at people's face, or do you look and that's fine?

I breathed a sigh of relief as we entered a private room in the back. The murals on the walls were accented with gold and silver. The tubs steamed, and the sulfur smell from the hot water mixed with a heady floral scent. Two of the sisters set up a fibrous white curtain between the tubs allowing us some privacy.

"Please get undressed," Ichika said.

"Woman, I can undress myself," Taliesin squeaked for the other side of the curtain.

"Be calm," I said. "They don't mean anything by it."

I moved to get into the tub. "No, no. Washing first." I let her lead me to a corner where she dumped a bucket of water on me and washed, rather scrubbed, me clean. She was very thorough, much to my dismay. Judging by the squeaks of protests, the boys agreed with me.

"You seem comfortable," I said.

Miu shrugged. "In Japan we have bathhouses, and families bath together."

"Now, into the tub," Ichika said after dumping a bucket of cold water on me.

Grateful, I slid into the water feeling less exposed. My feet stung as I slipped into the mineral scented water. "Hot springs?"

Miu nodded. "I think so. It feels wonderful."

I agreed, the heat soothed any lingering soreness, and despite my discomfort I was happy to get clean.

The chief's daughters sat behind us and began to massage us. I moaned in pleasure as strong fingers rubbed my scalp. She poured some warm flower scented oil into her palm and worked it into scalp and then my hair.

"This is the best thing ever," I sighed, unsure of what language I spoke until Ichika laughed.

"I'm very glad you're enjoying it. You have beautiful hair, and the pale boys are so interesting looking."

How am I supposed to respond to that? "Thank you. Have you ever seen anyone white before?"

"Once when my aunt and I were gathering herbs that grew outside of the valley." Ichika combed my hair. "There were two men, they had all sorts of weird things with them. One of the river people saw us and led them away. They were loud and big.

"A while later there was a loud bang, and the birds cried out in fright and took to the skies. We left after that." Ichika set the comb down. "We'll go and get ceremonial clothes and some refreshments, please relax and do any prayers you need to prepare. Come, sisters."

"What's going to happen now?" Taliesin asked.

"They're getting us ceremonial robes, and something to drink. We hang out and enjoy the water."

"Then what?" Sasha asked his Russian accent thicker in his agitation. I guess being washed by pretty girls wasn't all that relaxing for the guys.

"We aren't leaving here until we do the ceremony, and we need to awaken Quetzalcoatl anyway. Once that is done, we go and free Kayin." See, I had it all figured out.

"How?" Miu asked.

"Well Shamash told me Sasha would know the way, and that Aya was guiding Gavin and Anali to him. Shamash said everything would be fine, and it's either believe him, or go crazy, because right now we have no power over this situation."

Acceptance of what is will make your life so much easier. There are always things beyond our control. We can resist these things or we can understand it's not in our power to change them, take a deep breath, and do your best. You might accept it and deal with it, you might find a way to change your response and therefore, change the situation, or you might leave all together. They key is acceptance of what is, and being wise enough to know what you can change and what you cannot.

"Yax Pac and Chan Bahlum both know we have a friend in trouble, and we can't open the doorway to Xilbalba without him. They will help us." I paused and looked at Miu, hoping she would understand. "This moment is proof that the god their people have worshiped for centuries is real. They're going to know that the being they pray to loves them and will fulfill his promises. I can't rush them through this, I can't."

Miu reached a wrinkled hand out of the water and held mine, her peridot green eyes soft with compassion and understanding.

"Will he?" Taliesin asked. "Will he take them to Akasha?"

Images of kids in the group home flashed through my mind, the hollow dead look that would come into their eyes as promises were yet again broken and a child's hopes, dreams, and prayers shattered. "He has to. I can't destroy this many people's hopes."

The chief's daughters came back in before they asked more questions.

"Here it's a ceremonial drink made from corn and fruit," Ichika said, handing me a wooden cup.

I took a sip. It tasted sweet with a sharp warmth at the end. Alcohol, they gave us alcohol. I was going to refuse to drink more, but I felt the prayers and devotion that went into making this drink. I took another sip and my eyes fluttered. I saw the priest as he stood for hours stirring the drink in a large cauldron. The moon shone through a hole in the roof making the surface of the liquid glow. The priest looked up at the moon. Another took over the duty of stirring as the priest changed into a panther.

"This is alcoholic," Sasha said.

"Yes, it's a ceremonial drink." Wow, my voice sounded far away.

"Sapphire, are you okay?" Miu asked.

"A lot of prayers went into this drink. It's supposed to help us open up to the spirit world and connect at a deeper level."

Miu sighed. "Do you remember Sapphire telling us how doped up she was at the mermaid's house?"

"Oh, crap," Taliesin muttered. "And that didn't involve alcohol, just the emotions of another magical being."

Ichika smiled at me. Her teeth are so white and shiny. "As soon as you're done, we'll get you ready."

"Ichika says we need to finish our drinks and then they will get us ready." I drank the rest of mine, it made me feel all warm inside.

I stood up, and the world swayed. Warm hands guided me out of the tub, and Ichika dried me off. I should feel embarrassed and maybe I was blushing, but I couldn't feel my face.

"Sapphire drank it all. Come on guys, we don't want to be separated." Miu downed her drink and got out of the tub.

I heard muttering and a few squeaks as we were dried then rubbed with oils and something rough like one of those exfoliating face scrubs. Ichika brushed the gritty bits off me with a clean cloth. I held up my hand turning it back and forth. My skin glowed.

Ichika dressed me in a turquoise dress decorated with gold beads and a rainbow of feathers at the hem, which tickled my calves, and sandals made from rope. I wish I had a mirror. I bet I looked all fancy.

"Come." Ichika held out her hand, and her warm fingers clasped mine her excitement, hope, and faith flowed into me.

We walked through the bath house into a small courtyard with a sweet little fountain and flowers everywhere. "Sit."

"Sapphire," Taliesin said. I blinked in surprise. I didn't know he would come along, too.

His hair glowed silvery white as it fell around his shoulders. He wore a turquoise skirt decorated with gold beads and feathers, which fell above his knees. "You look amazing, but you feel very unhappy." My eyes filled with tears. I didn't want my friends to be unhappy.

"Hush, I'm fine, just confused. Do you know what's going to happen now?"

"No, I'm sorry." I looked at Miu and Sasha who were dressed in the same outfits we were wearing. "You all look so amazing and shiny."

"As soon as you're done, the royal family and the priests will accompany you to the temple." Ichika set a large box on a table of dark polished wood. "The rest of the villagers will follow on the path, saying prayers. Then we'll feast." She pulled out a pot and a small paint brush. "Now close your eyes."

I closed my eyes as I told the others the master plan. Something cold touched my eyelid, and I jumped. Ichika shushed me and continued.

A solid necklace was placed around my neck, my fire pendant carefully placed on top of it, rings added to my fingers, and fine chains fastened around my ankles.

Ichika rubbed my earlobes. "You don't have holes in your ears."

"Nope."

"Could I pierce them? I have earrings for you to wear."

"Hold on," I said then switched to English. "Miu, do you feel able to do a healing?"

"I guess so, Why?" she asked as round earrings with black stones were placed in her ears.

"Ichika wants to pierce my ears for the ceremony."

"And you're okay with that?" Taliesin asked.

I blinked. His sky blue eyes were lined with black. "Um,

everything seems fine to me." Were his eyes that big before?

Sasha snorted. "You are stoned." Only one of his gray eyes was lined in black so far, and looking at him made me dizzy.

I turned to Ichika. "It's fine, go ahead."

She cleaned a sharp bone needle and held onto my earlobe as she pushed it through in one swift move.

I hissed. Damn that hurt! She slid an earring in, and then moved to the other ear. My earlobe burned, and the earring hung heavy pulling at the tender lobe. Not good, it needed to heal. "Miu." Thin warm fingers touched my ears, and the pain disappeared. "You rock, thank you."

Miu giggled. "You're welcome."

"It's a miracle," Ichika whispered.

I waved my hand, the sun reflecting off the rings catching my attention. "It's something she does."

"Are we ready?" Chan Bahlum asked. He wore a cloak of feathers over a white skirt. "The sun will be in the proper position to illuminate the cave soon."

"Yes," Ichika said. "They are prepared."

"Come, let's go."

I stood to follow Chan Bahlum, and the world swayed again. Sasha grabbed my arm. "You are lightweight."

"Your accent is pretty."

Sasha raised an eyebrow and helped me down the worn stone stairs. In the court yard villagers surrounded several chairs with poles underneath them. The dark wood shone in the sun, and thin white fabric draped over the top. As we passed people they bowed their heads. From what I could see everyone wore their best clothes, and their black hair shone in the sun. Sasha helped me sit then wrapped my hands tight around the arms of the chair. "Do not let go."

"Will she be okay?" Miu asked.

"We could tie her down?" Taliesin suggested.

"I won't let go, I promise." Like I couldn't stay in a chair. Two men stood in front of me and two behind me. They knelt and picked up the chair. I squealed and tried to get off.

"No," Taliesin yelled. "Sit. Sapphire, sit down. They're going to take us to the cave."

"Okay, okay. Sorry, I wasn't expecting that."

We walked up the path single file passing large stone buildings, small houses, and sparkling aqueducts. Priests and priestess surrounded us tossing flowers and chanting prayers. They began to glow golden white and my jewelry began to warm as the connection to Akasha opened up.

They had covered the cave floor in blankets. A priest led me to the blanket closest to Quetzalcoatl. I sat with the others close behind me.

"How are we going to do this?" Taliesin asked. His muted voice sounded far away. "Sapphire's already buzzing and I'm not even close to being open and connected."

"What if we touch her back? Let her connection draw us in," Sasha said.

"That could work." Miu placed a hand on my back. "Kind of the reverse of my ritual."

Two hands touched my shoulders. I sent my energy into them. Their fingers tightened. The villagers chanted prayers, and their voices echoed through the cave. I closed my eyes and floated on the power. Reaching into each of them I found their center, the place all their power originates from. I pushed a little more energy into them and watched their center open and accept energy from Akasha.

Chapter Twenty-Three

"Courage is doing what you're afraid to do. There can be no
courage unless you're scared."
~Edward Vernon Rickenbacker

"Sapphire, stop. I don't want to shift," Taliesin said, his
voice low and tight.

Oops, I pulled back, the power from the others following
me, Taliesin's cool power once again making the intensity
bearable.

Their power joined the power from the priest and priestess.
The warmth of Akasha flowed in their energy, but I felt
something more. Something wild and fierce like the energy of a
thunderstorm.

My body shook. Raising my hands, I sent the energy into
Quetzalcoatl. Chunks of rock fell, exposing dull lifeless feathers
as he stretched and groaned. His children cheered and their
chanting became joyous.

I kept focused on holding open the connection to Akasha
and sending my many times great-uncle the energy he needed.
Some of the holy people dropped the chant and began to
whisper the name "Camaxtli." I opened my eyes. The ghostly
image of Shamash in Phoenix form hovered over his brother
and sang.

Flames burst from my hands as Shamash's power flowed

through us. All three hands tightened on my back, fingers digging into my skin.

"Sapphire?" Miu said.

"It's okay. He's here to help. It won't be much longer."

Quetzalcoatl rolled over, showing a belly of flaky pale lime green serpent scales. He began to hum along to Shamash's song. His voice deep and in tune even though he still slept.

My hands shook as energy poured out of me and into Quetzalcoatl. The tune of Shamash's song changed. Old feathers and scales dropped away revealing vibrant new ones.

Quetzalcoatl rolled back onto his belly, snorted, and stretched his wings, the tip brushed against my forehead.

Shamash stopped singing, and the energy slowed. "Thank you. Eat, then go and save Kayin."

Shamash vanished. I lowered my hands. We had done all we could for Quetzalcoatl, who snored and sprawled over the cave floor stretching his arms and legs as far apart as possible. What a bed hog!

I stood up, still fuzzy from the alcohol and lack of food, but the energy from the panther shape-shifter was gone.

"He has been released from his dead sleep and now rests peacefully, his body adjusting to the new life. He will awaken soon, but my friends and I need to eat and rescue the others so we can open the portal to Xilbalba." I blinked, wow that sounded formal. It must be Shamash's influence.

"Yes," Chan Bahlum said, standing up. "We must get prepared for when our Father awakens. Come we must tell the others and allow them to come and see the miracle that has occurred."

"Better now?" Sasha teased.

"Much, but if I don't eat something soon I might throw-up."

"Quetzalcoatl has awoken from his death sleep," Chan Bahlum announced his arms spread wide. "He now rests adjusting to his renewed life. Go and see him my people. Go and bask in his glory."

The chief and his family stepped forward, all dressed in deep red robes with large collars that framed their faces in feathers. Gold jewelry adorned every possible part of their red brown skin. "We have prepared a feast. Please feel free to eat while we greet our Father."

I bowed my head, but maintained eye contact. I wanted to show respect not subservience. And again my connecting with Akasha resulted in weird knowledge about customs popping into my head. "Thank you. After we eat we will need to leave and rescue our friend."

Yax Pac gestured to the five young men behind me. "Three of my sons will accompany you."

"Thank you. I am certain they will assure that we will return safely to open the doorway to Xilbalba."

Pride made the chief's eyes glow. "We shall join you shortly." His family got into their own chairs and were carried to the cave.

"It is so creepy when you fall into the whole polite diplomat thing," Taliesin hissed.

"I agree, it's like it's not even me talking. But would you rather have me channeling Aya and Shamash or talk like I normally do to these people?"

I smiled as the villagers passed us. Tears ran down the face of many. They bowed to us on their way to the cave muttering their thanks and gratitude.

An old woman reached out a hand to us. I knelt and took her hand.

"May you be blessed with goodness, prosperity, and many children," she said before letting go and holding her hand out to Taliesin. One by one, she blessed us all.

"What did she say?"

I cleared my throat. "She was blessing us. Hoping we had a happy life."

Sasha snorted. "If she is like my grandmother she also said many children."

I blushed and focused on the next person who decided to stop and offer blessings. By the time the villagers passed us we had been blessed with so much good fortune, fertile fields, true weapons, easy hunting, and children, I was a little worried about what my future held.

"Come," Chan Bahlum said leading us to a gleaming wood table covered in bowls and platters full of food. "Please, help yourselves."

"Are you sure?" I said looking at all the empty places. A clean banana leaf set in front of most, but we were directed to places with wooden dishes inlaid with gold and silver along the edges. It reminded me of the china plates Gavin had. I closed my eyes hoping the others were safe.

"Yes, yes. You need to eat after what you have done."

I nodded and turned to the others. "He said to eat."

Using manners so polite it would have made Anali glow with pride, we served ourselves. The flat bread, fruits, and bowls of steamed quinoa were passed among us.

"What are the other dishes?" Taliesin asked.

"This one looks like greens of some kind," Miu said spooning some bright green leaves onto her wooden plate. "I don't smell any meat."

Taliesin held his hand out for the bowl.

"Are these plantains?" Sasha asked picking up a platter of mixed vegetables.

"I'll ask." I switched languages. "Chan Bahlum, what's in this dish?"

"That one is plantains, fish, and other vegetables."

"Thanks. Sasha, it has fish in it."

Sasha nodded and took some, so did Miu. Taliesin declined.

"Do you not eat fish?" Chan Bahlum asked as I passed him dish without taking any.

"Sasha and Miu eat fish, and none of us eat meat."

Chan Bahlum nodded to a servant, and a bowl from further down the table was brought to us. "This is dried corn and beans cooked in spices."

"Thank you," I spooned some of the stew onto my plate and passed it to Taliesin. "There's no meat in this one."

Taliesin smiled and took some.

I hadn't realized how hungry I was. In fact, since I downed that drink I hadn't realized much of what was going on. Careful to eat slowly, I didn't want to get sick, I finished about half of my food when the chief and his family came back. The others were getting seconds.

I felt shock and joy. I guess even the devout hadn't fully believed that the statue was Quetzalcoatl.

They stopped in front of us. "Thank you. My people owe you a great debt. As soon as they are finished eating, my sons will accompany you to save your friends. My people will prepare to leave to Xilbalba."

The children of Quetzalcoatl came back in small groups. Tear tracks marked cheeks spread wide in beaming smiles. People hugged, danced, and trembled as they entered the courtyard and sat at their tables. I closed my eyes and focused on strengthening my empathetic shields as waves of emotions hit me. Apparently seeing your god come to life is a very emotional and confusing time for people.

"Are you all right?" Taliesin asked.

"Yes, it's a lot of emotion."

"Are we going to able to leave soon?" Miu asked.

I looked over at the chief's sons. Their plates were empty. "I hope so. Are you guys ready to go?"

"Yes, but can we get our clothes back?" Sasha asked.

I turned to the priest. "Chan Bahlum, we need to leave soon. Is it possible to get our clothes and bags?"

"Do you not like these?"

My eyes widened, crap. *Quick, Sapphire, quick! Channel some of that diplomatic doubletalk.* "These are beautiful and obviously very special. We want to keep them nice for later when we open the doorway to Xilbalba. Rescuing our friend might not be safe for such fine clothes."

He reached out a weathered hand and patted my cheek. "You're such a good girl and so right. We'll save them here for you. Your clothes are clean, but probably still damp. Don't worry about your bags, the chief's sons can take care of everything."

He wanted to make sure we came back. I wasn't up to fighting for it right now. "Damp is fine. We're very grateful for them being cleaned," I said and my head twinged a bit. The numbing effects of the alcohol wearing off.

"Are you ready?"

"Yes, we are very anxious to get our friend back." Poor Kayin.

Chan Bahlum waved a hand, and a young boy came over. "Take the blessed ones to get their clothes. It is time for them to retrieve the rest of their group so they can open the doorway to Xilbalba."

The people applauded as we stood. I blushed and followed the young man back to the bath house. Wet clothes are hard to get on, they stick and pull. It took forever to get my shirt to lie flat. I wrinkled my nose as I put on the cold wet socks.

When we walked back to the courtyard, three of the chief's sons waited for us. They each held a spear and a blow gun tucked into their wrap. Their faces and bodies were painted with black lines. They stood straight with eyes forward as if at attention.

The chief looked at his sons, his turquoise eyes shining and his chest puffed up with pride. "My sons Muhuizoh, Nelli, and Yaotl will take you to save your friend."

Sasha nudged me. "I think they are waiting for you to say something."

"What?"

"Say something about his sons," Taliesin said. "About how awesome and manly they look."

"Oh." I looked over the three young men. "Thank you chief for allowing three of your strongest warriors to accompany us. I have no doubt that we will return soon with all of my people so we can open the portal."

The chief puffed up even more, and I feared he would tip over. Their mother smiled and held onto her daughter's arm.

Muhuizoh stepped forward. "Where do you need to go?"

"Back on the other side of the gorge," I translated for Sasha. "Then a large clearing with a lot of monkeys."

Muhuizoh nodded. "Yes, we can get you there very quickly."

The children of Quetzalcoatl cheered and called out wishes for our safe return as we followed the warriors out of the village. We walked in silence through a labyrinth of tunnels coming out in the middle of the gorge. The gorge ran for miles on both sides, but the opening was in the middle of the wall. Running from the opening to the other side hung the scariest rope bridge ever. Thin ropes draped across the massive drop. Small, oddly-shaped pieces of wood were placed every few feet. No way in hell I was crossing that thing.

One of the men stepped out and crossed the swaying tiny bridge. He didn't look worried at all.

"Are you okay?" Muhuizoh asked.

"It's very high." I didn't want to insult their bridge that would be rude.

His brow wrinkled. "Our children use this bridge, it's very safe."

He shooed me onto the bridge, even though his brother wasn't half way across.

I nodded, thought of Kayin, and stepped onto the first board. I was going to die. I tried not to look into the gaps between the boards. My fingers held onto the ropes as the bridge began to sway. Below us the river curved and bubbled around rocks taunting me, mocking my pathetic attempts to cross the gorge.

Enough of this drama! Kayin needs help and I've already crossed one of these stupid things. Boards that touch adds extra weight; this is probably safer. I began to walk, holding my breath as long as I could. My stomach rolled as the bridge swayed with the wind. I kept walking. If I stopped I would never get started again.

Movies often portray heroes and heroines as being fearless, but if there is no fear there is no courage. Being brave is accepting that you're scared, taking a deep breath, and doing it anyway. Bravery doesn't have to be a big flashy thing. It can be something as simple as taking a test instead of hiding in the bathroom. However it comes, know that I believe in you. Take a deep breath, accept that you're scared, and act courageous one terrifying step at a time.

I recited my mother's words in my head over and over again as I walked across the bride. I was doing fine until a red brown hand appeared in front of my face. Screaming, I jumped back one of my feet meeting nothing but air. Nelli grabbed me and hauled me into the cave.

He looked at me, his eyes full of concern.

I gave him a pathetic, shaky smile as I did my best to not kiss the ground in happiness.

Nelli laughed. His eyes sparkled behind his black war paint.

The others did much better crossing the bridge. No screaming or pale faces.

We walked through the jungle. If there was a trail, we weren't taking it. I did my best not to trip on roots or fall into holes, but I wasn't very successful. After the third time, Yaotl took my arm and guided me through the jungle.

We walked for several hours. I felt more and more sick as we got closer to the Sons of Belial. I heard the chattering of monkeys and turned to Sasha. "You said Kayin is being kept near monkeys, right?"

He nodded. "Da, we are close."

"Come," said Muhuizoh.

A small monkey jumped from the trees. It swung from a branch in front of Taliesin. I guessed they were talking, as the monkey stayed focused on him. The monkey's odd little face kept changing expression. The top of its head was dark gray at the widow's peak, around its mouth and down its back, but the rest of its face and belly were white. The golden color of its arms shone in bright contrast to the gray of the rest of its body.

"She's willing to help us," Taliesin said. "Apparently some of the fairies have kept an eye on Kayin for us."

"I'm for any help we can get," Miu said.

"I agree. Does she know where Kayin is?"

Taliesin held out his arm and the little monkey jumped to his shoulder. "She says we need to be quiet because we're close and the men are always listening."

I told the brothers what was happening.

As we began to walk again they were silent and kept low to the ground. The rest of us tried, but weren't close to silent.

Muhuizoh held up his hand, and we all stopped. He crawled forward. A moment later he came back. "Come as quietly as you can." The look he gave us made me think he wasn't impressed with our sneaky jungle skills.

The monkey screeched, and the trees came to life with monkey's playing and chattering.

"They're covering for us," Taliesin said walking. "Move quickly."

I forced myself to ignore the unnatural feeling of the Sons of Belial sliding against my skin and followed them.

Two tents stood at the far side of the clearing. They had Kayin tied to a post in front of them. His head drooped onto his chest. My heart clenched, he was so still. Near the middle sat three of the mercenaries, their gear piled on a table, and they laughed as they played cards. Two walk-ins huddled inside the clearing trying to keep out of the sun. General Senach stood over a table looking at some maps. His bright ginger hair braided keeping it away from his flushed face.

He rubbed his square jaw. "Boys, I think we need to call back the others and re-group. We have the boy and a few other creatures," he said in a thick Irish accent. One of the men kicked at a cage under the table I hadn't seen. The three dwarves and four fairies trapped inside screeched. "I want to get these to Cartazaonon before something happens. We can't keep the kid sedated too much longer."

That bastard! I began to stand when strong hands grabbed me and pulled me into a sweaty, stinky chest. Gross.

"Sapphire, are you okay?" Gavin whispered, hugging me tight.

My eyes filled with tears, and if anyone asks later, it was

from the smell. I nodded, afraid of being heard. A small hand patted mine. Looking over Gavin's shoulder I saw Anali. She was a mess but healthy and here.

The monkeys started acting up again and Muhuizoh lead us away from the camp, and Kayin. "We need to make a plan," he said once we were far enough away.

Yaotl drew a map of the camp in the dirt while I translated.

"I need to get to Kayin," Miu said. "Hopefully, I can help him recover from whatever they gave him."

"Okay, Nelli will go with the healer." Muhuizoh pointed to one of his brothers. "Can anyone else fight?"

I asked the others. Gavin drew a knife out of his pack. "Yes, I know how to fight."

"I'm going," said Anali.

"Me too."

Taliesin and Sasha nodded their heads.

"We're all going."

Muhuizoh looked like he wanted to protest, but wasn't sure he could argue with me.

The monkey on Taliesin's shoulder squeaked and pointed to the map. I guess she was going too.

We waited in our positions until the men holding Kayin started eating lunch. Perfect.

Three little monkeys came out of the trees and begged for food. General Senach looked up to see what the commotion was then went back to his maps.

"Here you go," said one of the mercenaries holding out a grape.

The little monkey went over to him a little at a time, careful to keep out of arms reach then jumped, grabbed the grape and went back to his friends, hunched over his prize. Round black eyes turned to the other men who responded and began handing out fruit.

Taliesin's monkey led a group to the weapons. I held my breath as they climbed up on the table and picked up the stun guns, tranquilizer guns, and knifes. They stole about half of them before a monkey dropped something.

The mercenaries turned yelling as they saw their weapons being dragged into the jungle. One fell over as he lunged for the table covered in thieving monkeys. The mercenaries turned to run after them, most of the weapons scattered on the ground as the monkeys leapt into the trees.

"Stop," General Senach said. "It's a diversion. The others are here for their friend."

The monkeys threw fruit and poop at the mercenaries. Apparently, that was the signal for the insanity to start.

My heart beat so fast I feared it would explode. Anali held my hand as we watched. Muhuizoh and Yaotl attacked the mercenaries. Sasha and Taliesin went after the walk-ins. Gavin ran from the trees right at General Senach.

Senach smirked and pulled a knife from his belt. Gavin shifted his own knife. Instead of a mini-sword fight like I had seen in movie knife fights, Gavin and Senach held their knives so the blade hung along their forearms. They lunged at each other their whole bodies providing vicious force behind their attack. Their movements became a blur. Metal blades clashed. Grunts sounded as lines of red blood stood out of white skin. I didn't know Gavin could fight like that. Anali grabbed my hand. "Gavin will be okay, and we can't help him anyway. We need to help the others."

I stared at Gavin trying to see if I could help, but Anali was right. We ran for the cage. The dwarves and fairies jumped up and down calling to be let out.

"It's locked," Anali said and pulled on the padlock. "You see if there is another way to open it I'll look for a key." She crawled over the table which had been knocked to the ground and searched through the debris.

The cage looked solid, but I poked and pulled at it. One of the hinges wiggled. I grabbed a butter knife and tried to pull up the screw. My hands shook as I worked. My friends were fighting for their lives while I wrestled with a stupid screw. Someone screamed. I worked harder. One of the fairies stuck his hand through the cage, pushing on the bottom of the screw.

A mercenary fell in the dirt next to me. We both froze. My heart stopped. He lunged at me. Muhuizoh jumped on top of him, sticking an obsidian knife in his back. I will never forget the mercenary's scream or coppery smell of his blood.

I looked for the others. Anali still searched for a set of keys. Nelli guarded Miu while she healed Kayin. A flash of white hair in the trees let me know where Taliesin was.

I turned and saw Gavin panting as sweat and blood dripped down his arm. The General lashed out. Gavin danced out of the way. The knife cut his shirt. He tripped, falling hard. His knife was knocked out of his hand from the impact, and General Senach stood over him.

Screaming, I ran towards them. Anali jumped on the General's back pulling on his braid and hitting him. He reached back, pulled Anali off, and threw her to the ground. Gavin scooted, placing his body over hers.

"No!" I yelled, my power building. I threw power from Akasha at him. "Get up! Run!"

Gavin and Anali scrambled to their feet.

Deep wrinkles cut into Senach's face, his pasty skin hung loose. I focused the energy on him. He wasn't going to kill my family. He fell to his knees.

A roar filled the sky as Quetzalcoatl flew over us. Blue flames came at me. I ducked, losing my connection to Akasha. One of the mercenaries screamed as he fell right behind me, a knife in his hand.

Quetzalcoatl landed. The Sons of Belial dashed into the jungle, scattering in all directions.

"We can track them, my lord," Muhuizoh said, falling to one knee.

Quetzalcoatl changed into his human form. A handsome young man with pale skin, bright green hair and turquoise eyes. Thankfully, he also wore a linin skirt. "No my son. They're gone. I do not wish to have any more fighting on this glorious day."

"Is everyone okay?" I said, looking around. Sure Quetzalcoatl seemed cool and all, but I had seen magical beings before. I needed to know if my friends were all right.

"We got crap beat out of us," Sasha said, limping out of the trees. His lip was split and bleeding, and one of his eyes was swollen shut.

Taliesin followed, not looking any better and holding his arm. "My arm—I think it's broken."

I ran over and helped him into a chair. "We'll get Miu to fix it okay?"

He nodded, his face tight with pain.

"I'm cut up, but nothing I can't heal on my own." Gavin said as he helped Anali up. "Are you okay?"

"I'm fine, nothing worse than a practice session gone bad." She smiled and stroked his face. "I was so scared."

Gavin wrapped his arms around his wife. "You saved my life."

"I had to. I can't live without you."

I turned away letting them have their sappy moment and brushed sweat from my eyes.

"I'm fine," Miu said. She didn't look fine. Her skin pale and her hands shook. "But Kayin needs help."

Chapter Twenty-Four

"You can't stop the waves, but you can learn to surf."
~Jon Kabat-Zinn

I ran. Kayin lay on the ground. His skin gray and clammy, and his breathing slow and raspy.

"They kept him drugged," Miu said, her hands shaking. "We need to get food and water into him before I can heal him fully."

"Here," Anali said rummaging through a cooler. "They have water and Recharge."

"Recharge," Miu said. "He needs electrolytes, I don't think they gave him any water at all."

"I'll do it," I sat and pulled Kayin up so he rested against me. "You need to rest and take care of yourself before you heal anyone else."

Miu nodded and headed for Gavin. Anali handed me the bottle. "Do you want some help?"

"I'm not sure what I'm doing," I said. I knew I needed to do something, it was my fault he'd been taken in the first place. I should have made him go first, or walked across the bridge faster.

Anali opened the bottle. "Try talking to him, maybe give him some energy. If we can get him to wake up enough to drink on his own this will be easier."

"Big brother, I'm sorry we took so long. But we're here now and it's time to wake up. We have something for you to drink." Kayin shifted a little but didn't wake. After what happened to General Senach I felt nervous about sending energy into Kayin. I looked up as a shadow fell over me.

"Hello, niece. Muhuizoh, Yaotl and Nelli told me all about you while I healed them," Quetzalcoatl said, kneeling next to me. He reminded me of Shamash. Quetzalcoatl's jaw was rounder and his eyes, while wise, held a sadness that was not in Shamash's eyes. "Will you let me help your friend?"

I tightened my grip on Kayin but nodded.

Quetzalcoatl placed his hands on Kayin's forehead and stomach. They began to glow a pale blue. The blue light covered Kayin more with each breath he took. His eyes fluttered opened, bloodshot and dry.

"Kayin, it's Sapphire. You're safe now. Relax, this is Quetzalcoatl." His eyes held mine, flames dancing in the brown iris. They had taken his contacts out. The walk-ins could track him. I needed to read that damn journal, which I'd left back at the village.

Kayin nodded. "Water?"

"Not yet," Quetzalcoatl said. "In a moment you're going to throw up all that poison they put in your body. Then you can have some water."

Kayin groaned, his breathing became shallow, and sweat beaded on his forehead.

"Help him turn over."

"Okay." I shifted to a better position.

Kayin brought a hand to his mouth. Quetzalcoatl moved and I gave a push. Kayin threw up some nasty smelling clear liquid. His body shook as he purged the poison. When he finished, Anali gave him some water, which he swished in his mouth then spat onto the ground.

"Let me carry him into the shade." Quetzalcoatl held out his arms. I tightened mine. "I promise he'll be safe."

"It's fine," Kayin said, his hand limply patting my leg.

Quetzalcoatl scooped him up and carried him to a shady spot, both of them covered in blue light.

Anali handed me the bottle of Recharge. "Get him to drink this. I'm going to help the others."

My stomach churned with guilt. I looked over to see Miu working on Taliesin, cradling his broken arm, his pale skin clammy. Had she rested at all?

"It's okay, go help Kayin," Anali said pushing me.

Kayin sat against a tree, his eyes half open. "I have some Recharge for you. You need to sip it." I held the bottle to his mouth, and he took some, groaning when I took the bottle away. "A little at a time."

Kayin nodded and closed his eyes.

I turned to my, what, extremely great uncle? "Thank you for helping him."

"You're welcome, thank you for healing me and waking me up. They said you're able to open the doorway to Akasha."

"Yes, well we can, it takes all of us. I don't know where there is a gateway stone nearby. I know of a piece of one but the portal it opened is only big enough for the dwarves and fairies to get through."

"I was lying on one." Quetzalcoatl grinned and ran a hand through his blue green hair, reminding me of Gavin. "I wasn't thinking clearly. We all knew the portals were losing power, but then something went wrong and they began to die like candles at the end of their wicks. I used all the magic I had trying to force that one open and lost consciousness when it exploded. When I left the cave, the gateway stone was humming. It will open."

"If it's humming, it will attract the Sons of Belial." Crap, we couldn't fight more of them.

"Who?"

"They're a group who use the life, power, and magic of others to extend their life. They'll find the village."

Quetzalcoatl's face hardened. "I can protect the village. I can block the energy from being detected. We need to leave."

"Taliesin, Sasha, and Kayin must be healed first, and Miu is going to need to rest. There is no way they can walk to the village right now."

He smiled. "I'll help heal them, and none of you will need to walk."

That didn't sound good, not good at all! I turned to Kayin and gave him some more to drink and tried to ignore the butterflies in my body. "Come on big brother, the fun is not over yet."

Once everyone was healed and rested, we sat waiting for the Master Plan to be revealed. The chief's sons stood at attention, ready to serve Quetzalcoatl at a moment's notice. It was a little creepy.

"The easiest way to get all of you back to the village is to fly."

"We'd fly on your back?" I squeaked.

Quetzalcoatl shook his head. "No, my back is too broad and I couldn't move my wings without hitting you. I'll have to carry you in my claws."

"How will that work?" Gavin asked, walking over to us.

He curled his hand into talon shapes. "I'll scoop you up. I can carry two of you that way."

Quetzalcoatl large feathered serpent form, was big but not big enough for being clasped in his claws to be comfortable.

"What if we were secured in ropes?" Gavin asked. "Could you hold on to the ropes?"

"Sure then I could carry three of you."

"I'll see if I can find some rope," Gavin said.

Wow, who would have thought the scary rope bridge would ever look good. I looked over the group imagining them dangling from ropes as they flew through the sky. "Wait. Where's Alvaro? And did the fairies and dwarfs ever get free?"

"Oh," gasped Anali. She found the keys and opened the cage while Miu brought over some fruit for them.

"Alvaro went back to the village. He wanted to help heal

those who'd gotten hurt and repair the damage," Gavin explained, as he emptied the mercenaries' backpacks. "Okay, I've found a bunch of rope and some harnesses. We'll need to reuse them but I can make this work."

"So who's first?" asked Quetzalcoatl.

"The blessed ones should go first," said Muhuizoh.

"No, we'll need to bathe again to cleanse ourselves from battle, and I would hate to surprise your sisters. Please go ahead and tell them of what we'll need to prepare to open the portal." There that sounded proper and logical.

Taliesin raised an eyebrow. Okay, so I didn't fool everyone.

"Are you sure? We do not wish to leave you unprotected," Yaotl said.

A wave of power washed over us. "They will be safe, and once I'm at the village I can protect it, too."

The brothers nodded. Quetzalcoatl shifted—a smooth, effortless transformation from man into a huge feathered dragon. Gavin strapped the brothers into the harnesses and then attached ropes to the harnesses, they looked like the safety harnesses he made for rigging the circus. Gavin braided the ropes together and handed them to Quetzalcoatl who gathered them up in his lime green talons. With a huff he stood and flew into the air. His flapping wings made the trees bend, and leaves filled the air. The brothers screamed as they lifted into the air.

"Sapphire," Gavin said in his newly acquired 'calm parent' voice. "What exactly is going on?"

"It's not my fault," I said before explaining what happened and what was to come.

"So we will be ritually bathed, given an alcoholic drink which will turn you loopy, and then we'll open the portal?" Gavin crossed his arms and raised an eyebrow.

"Um, yes?" I answered.

"I don't like it."

As if I couldn't tell that from his body language.

"I don't want you drinking it," Gavin said.

"It's harmless," Miu said. "It hardly affected me."

"I, too, was fine," said Sasha.

"I felt a buzz but nothing more," Taliesin admitted.

Gavin groaned and rubbed his hands over his face. "Could we change the ritual? Tell them that we have our own way of doing it?"

"No," I said. Everyone stared at me. That might have come out a bit harsher than I'd intended. "For generations these people have guarded Quetzalcoatl. They have devoted their lives to him, and prayed for this day. The day he wakes and takes them all to Akasha. We can't ruin this."

Gavin paced for a moment. "I don't like it. Do you feel that all of us will be safe?"

I nodded. "Yes. If Quetzalcoatl can block the energy so the Sons of Belial can't feel us opening the portal, then I think we will be safe."

Gavin sighed, then searched the camp and brought back some bread and peanut butter. "Everyone eat some of this. The food will help with the alcohol." He passed out peanut butter sandwiches.

Anali held up a hand, the tips of her fingers sticky with peanut butter. "Did you say the whole village is going to Akasha?"

"Yes."

"Does Quetzalcoatl know about this?" she asked.

I shrugged. "I have no idea."

"Little sister, we should discuss this with him when he returns."

I looked at Kayin, glad he felt well enough to talk. His eyes were still a bit pink, but overall he looked much better. "Okay, but they're going."

"Aren't they like you guys," Taliesin said. "Just descendants of a magical creature? Can they even survive in Akasha?"

"I suppose so, but we'll need to talk to Quetzalcoatl about it when he returns." Gavin looked up into the sky. "Which seems to be now."

In his feathered serpent form, Quetzalcoatl was a bright

streak in the sky. I wonder what others thought they saw. Would stories or photographs show up on the internet? Did the Children of Fire even have a cover-up team to fix sightings and such? How many National Enquirer stories are true?

Quetzalcoatl landed and shifted into human form. "I need to take a break. I'm not fully healed yet."

"Do you want some water?" I asked rummaging through the cooler.

"Yes, please." I handed him a bottle of water. He turned it back and forth in his hands, the tip of his tongue sticking out as he puzzled over the new item.

"Let me open it." I twisted off the top and handed it back.

He drank and made a face. "This tastes bad."

"It's the plastic, the container the water is in, it tastes like it."

"Okay who's next?" Quetzalcoatl said, setting the offensive bottle down.

Gavin stepped forward. "Before we go we need to speak with you. Are you aware that the villagers are planning on going with you to Akasha?"

Quetzalcoatl sighed. "Yes, I know, and I'll figure out how to tell them they can't come, don't worry."

"Well," Gavin began.

"They're going." I interrupted. "These people have protected you and worshiped you. Their entire way of life is all about this day and they will go to Akasha or Xilbalba with you."

His eyes became hard. "I don't know who you think you are ... "

Seriously that line is thousands of years old. Dude, adults need to update their spiel. "I know who I am. I am the most powerful descendant of Shamash and Aya. I am the Jewel. And I am the only one who can open the portal to Akasha." I clenched my hands into fists trying to stop them from shaking. My cheeks flushed hot with anger and fear. It's never easy standing up for yourself, and I didn't even know the full extent of Quetzalcoatl's powers. "Your Children will go with you, or follow behind you. I don't care which. But I will hold the portal open long enough so they all make it through."

Wind whipped around us. Quetzalcoatl's face stretched tight, his lips pressed together, and he took a step towards me. Gavin placed a hand on my shoulder. The others surrounded us.

"You will calm down and take a step back," Gavin said, his voice firm.

Quetzalcoatl paced as the wind responded to his mood, and the trees swayed with his movement. The monkeys who helped us earlier fled, screeching their outrage.

"They're humans. They belong here."

"They want to go with you," Anali said her voice soft. "They see themselves as your children. Going with you is their reward."

"They don't understand what it's like over there."

"Then you'll have to help them," Gavin said.

The wind picked up. I huffed, he seemed bit old to be having such a temper tantrum.

Quetzalcoatl stopped pacing, and the wind died down. "You have to get Shamash's permission."

I felt his satisfaction. He thought he'd won. Foolish man, um, god.

"That won't be a problem," I said.

We stared at each other for a moment before Gavin jumped in. "Kayin, Sasha, and Anali are next. Kayin needs help and the longer he rests the better, and there needs to be an adult with them."

Anali nodded and walked over the pile of harnesses and ropes.

Quetzalcoatl changed back into his dragon form and lay down while they got into the harnesses. Kayin was placed in the middle so they could support him.

Kayin's dark eyes widened with fear as Quetzalcoatl's electric green and yellow wings spread out. "It's okay, big brother, I'll see you soon. And the people in the village will take good care of you."

Kayin gave me a shaky smile, then tightened his grip on Sasha and Anali's hands and closed his eyes as they lifted off the ground.

Gavin put an arm around my shoulders. "He's a holy person to them. He'll be taken care of."

I nodded. "So how mad do you think I just made a god?"

Miu laughed. "Let's sit and rest, and not wonder how much trouble you've caused this time."

Rude. It wasn't always my fault. I sat against a tree. One of the small monkeys dropped into my lap. Its little masked face and big dark eyes looked all sweet and soft. I hoped he didn't have fleas.

Miu braided her sweaty hair ignoring the monkey sitting on her leg. "Taliesin, how's your arm?"

A few more monkeys dropped from the trees looking for attention.

"You aren't doing any more healing." Taliesin scratched one of the monkeys behind the ears. "You're pale and shaking as it is. Plus I can feel how little energy you have."

"I need to work on channeling energy from Akasha and not using my own, but that takes time and focus and I did not have either." Miu stood, getting a screech from the displaced monkey, who ran over to Taliesin. "Quetzalcoatl helped heal the others, but I didn't see him work on you."

"No one is blaming you, and my arm is good enough," Taliesin said.

Gavin play wrestled with a small monkey like one would with a puppy. "We all need to work on our gifts, so relax. It sounds like you'll need your energy soon."

"Yes, I'm so looking forward to the rest of the day."

I rolled my eyes at Taliesin. He's always so pessimistic. One would think petting a monkey would make a person happier.

The monkey squeaked as I scratched under its chin. I couldn't help but smile. *See why is he such a grump?*

The monkeys ran off when Quetzalcoatl landed. He didn't change form this time, his impatience to get going rolled off him strong enough for Gavin to feel it.

"So who goes next?" he asked.

"My arm still aches so I'd like to wait a rest a bit." Taliesin said, pulling his newly healed arm to his chest.

"I would prefer to stay," I said hurrying to explain as Gavin's eyes narrowed. "Their emotions are intense even with my shields up. If I stay I can get a break from all the emotions and strengthen my shield, not that it will matter much once they give me the drink."

"Maybe I should stay with the two of you?" Gavin said.

Miu squeaked. I guess she didn't like the idea of flying through the air alone.

"We'll be fine, Quetzalcoatl said he put some sort of magical force field up." I reminded him.

"Okay we'll go," Gavin strapped Miu into the harness. "You both know how to work this?"

"Yes," we chimed, we used them all the time for setting up rigging in the circus.

"Stay safe we'll see you soon." As soon as Miu and Gavin hooked into the harnesses Quetzalcoatl took off.

I grinned, it felt a little evil. "I guess he didn't want to talk to me again."

"You should try to avoid pissing off powerful magical beings."

I looked at Taliesin, he didn't seem that worried. "He needs to go home—what is he going to do?"

"Well, that's kind of the point. You don't know what he can do."

Whatever. I doubt he would want to face Shamash if he hurt me. "How's your arm?"

"Tender but okay." Taliesin leaned against a tree. "How are we going to do this? None of us is strong enough right now. Even Miu's ritual was tiring and needed a lot of focus."

"Sasha's ritual. His takes longer, but we can relax and allow him to guide us into opening to the energy and letting it flow through us. At least that's how it seemed on paper."

"Aren't you worried at all?"

I looked up in shock. "Are you insane? I'm terrified. Everything could go wrong. We might not be able to open the portal. I didn't feel the gateway stone. Is it dead or did we activate it when we woke Quetzalcoatl? And if we did activate it are Sons of Belial on their way?"

Taking a deep breath, I continued. "If we can get the portal open, can we keep it open long enough to let everyone through? And if we get everyone safely through what will we do then? Can we find our way through the cave? And what about the rope bridge?"

Taliesin knelt in front of me, his long fingers cupping my face. "It's okay. We'll all be together at least." He pressed his forehead to mine. "Look at me."

His sky blue eyes filled my vision. I began to match my breathing to his. One of the worst things about all these stupid Phoenix gifts: the overload of emotions which makes me cry all the time.

Balance is a tricky thing. Most people feel it's finding a perfect place where everything is neutral. But it's more than that. Balance is learning to flow with life's ups and downs. It's more about learning to surf life than it is walking a tight rope. You're going to be amazing and have special gifts, and with these gifts will come difficulties. A good nurse has compassion. Because of that compassion, it can be difficult to detach from her patients, and her heart will break as they suffer. An excellent chef might have difficulty with his weight. A strong cop might find it hard to be calm and gentle when his own children break the rules. Within our gifts and strengths lies our own weakness and undoing. We have the vices of our virtues. Learn to surf the tide instead of trying to balance on a wire as life crashes over you.

"I'm sorry," I muttered even as my hands tightened around his wrists not ready for him to move.

"It's fine. Breathe with me."

As my panic receded I felt Taliesin's fear and pain. Wait. I hurt him. I released my grip on him. "Taliesin I'm so sorry! Your poor arm!" My shield allowed him in. I was flooded with emotions and my heart ached for him. I gasped for breath as he revealed his fear and pain. It wasn't just his arm. Something weighed on his soul.

I saw Taliesin standing in front of a man, the man he'd found dead in the hotel, but the man was still alive. Taliesin held out his hand. The star on his forehead, where his horn would be, glowed silvery blue as the man touched him and began to convulse. The glow faded as the man's breath left him. Taliesin waited for a moment knowing he had gone, but needing to be sure. When the man stopped moving, Taliesin sighed, shoved down his self-loathing and regret, and went to tell the hotel manager.

I didn't understand what had happened, but I knew Taliesin had done what his instincts as a unicorn told him to do.

I needed to help him understand and heal. Overwhelmed with emotions, I couldn't speak. I touched his cheek with trembling fingers. My breath came in short gasps as I tried to deal with the intensity of emotion.

"Sapphire, what's happening?" He sat back and held up a finger. On the tip sat a tear. One of my tears, with an opalescent sheen to it, sparkled with the faintest image of a rainbow reflected on the surface. It looked like a watered down version of one of Shamash's pearly luminescent tears. "Did you cry a Phoenix tear?"

"Kind of, I guess. A real Phoenix tear is more pearly and larger." I sniffed and wiped my eyes checking to see if there were any more. "It's for you," I said without thinking. Wow, that sounded bright.

Taliesin raised an eyebrow. "What do I do with it?"

I shrugged and shook my head.

He looked at the tear then gasped as it sank into his finger. He stretched out his arm. Small orange and yellow flames flickered on his skin. "Sapphire?"

"Does it hurt?" I reached for his arm.

"No, but it's warm." We stared at his arm as the flames faded. "It feels better. Stronger. And the pain is gone."

He sat rolling his wrist and staring at his arm, a soft smile on his face. The smile faded, and he clutched his chest as

it began to glow.

Chapter Twenty-Five

"The world is full of people who have never, since childhood,
met an open doorway with an open mind."
~E.B. White

"Taliesin." I placed my hand over his. I felt the warmth of
the Phoenix fire in his chest. "Does it hurt?"

Taliesin panted and shook his head. "No, it feels like
something is shifting." Taliesin took a deep breath his eyes wide.
He blinked and took another slow deep breath. The warmth
faded as I felt his chest expand under my hand. "I haven't been
able to take a deep breath in ages."

"You held a lot of sadness and regret in your heart—
something to do with the man who died at the hotel." Taliesin
stiffened. "I'm not sure what happened, but I know it wasn't
your fault. It's your unicorn side, and unicorns aren't evil or
mean."

Taliesin relaxed. "I guess so. I don't pick them. I can see
their soul crying out for help. The people don't always die." He
turned away.

I pulled my hand back. "What else happens?"

I wasn't sure if Taliesin would choose to answer. He stared
off into the jungle unmoving. He started to turn towards me
when Quetzalcoatl landed in the clearing.

Taliesin sighed and bowed his head, worry radiating from

him.

"It doesn't matter," I told him. "I know you're a good person, and I know whatever happened isn't evil or cruel." I stood up brushing the dirt off my shorts. "Come on, we have to save the day."

I stepped into the harness, making sure all the straps were done up tight. Taliesin nodded to me. "We're ready."

Quetzalcoatl snorted and took off, the pressure from his wings making me close my eyes.

"I don't like this, I don't like this," I chanted as I watched the trees become smaller.

"Remember you're a bird, they like the air," Taliesin said.

One crucial fact he forgot. "I don't transform into a bird."

"Not yet."

Was I going to change into a Phoenix someday? I'd have to ask Shamash the next time I saw him. My thoughts were interrupted by Quetzalcoatl swooping up over the mountainside. My stomach dropped and twisted. I felt utterly helpless dangling from massive talons on what now seemed like insanely thin rope. I wished I hadn't made Quetzalcoatl angry. *Maybe I need to think about what I say and when I say it.*

We skimmed over the tip of the mountain. I pulled my feet up which caused us to swing.

"Sapphire, calm down." Taliesin squeezed my hands. I'd forgotten he hung in the air beside me, his pale skin tinged green. "It won't be much longer."

Quetzalcoatl dropped, skimming the massive trees which lined the valley. I couldn't see the village. Being small and so deep in a valley had kept them safe, sheltered from the outside world. And now they would get to leave before the modern world ruined their lives.

The scream, which lodged in my throat when Quetzalcoatl lifted off the ground, came out now in little squeaks as the damned dragon 'enjoyed' flying. His mischievous and malicious happiness grated on my skin as he shifted direction and flowed like a wave. *Rude! I might have pissed him off but I didn't do it to hurt him. And, hello, I'm a kid and he's supposedly some ancient powerful being, yet he's the one acting like a child.*

For a while, the ropes he held in his talons kept my tongue firmly between my teeth. Until Taliesin spoke up. "I think I might be sick. Do you think he treated the others this way or is he doing this for you?"

Okay, you can mess with me, but no one messes with my friends. "One would think Quetzalcoatl learned his lesson about acting childish and irresponsible when thousands were sacrificed in order to get his help. I guess his nap didn't help his disposition."

Quetzalcoatl hovered, his wings moving enough to keep us up yet not going anywhere. *"You know about that?"* he sent telepathically.

He sounded lost and sad. If I were a better person I would have taken pity on him, but I was mad, and both Taliesin and I were scared. "Yes, I know about your granddaughter."

I could hear him suck in a breath over the beating of his wings and the wind whipping around us. "You don't hold back do you?"

"Do you think you deserve better right now? You have our lives in your hands and instead of treating this as a sign of monumental trust, you act like a child."

"I won't hurt you," he said his voice pouty.

"I don't know you well enough to know that to be the truth."

"I wouldn't. How could you think that about me?"

A little bit of guilt wiggled inside me. I knew enough to ignore it. "Words are useless. Prove it. Get us to the village unharmed and feeling safe."

Quetzalcoatl huffed and began flying more smoothly. He wasn't sending me his thoughts, but he hadn't closed off the connection between us and his mutters echoed in my head.

Taliesin squeezed my hands. "Thank you."

I grinned. "Hey, I'm the only one allowed to drive you crazy."

He raised an eyebrow. I blushed and turned to watch the deep velvet green jungle pass beneath us.

We landed in the village courtyard to cheers.

"Welcome back," Chan Bahlum said. "Come. You must join the others and prepare for the ceremony. Will you be coming with us to Xilbalba?"

"No. There are other magical beings that need to be sent home." I took off the Swiss seat and began helping Taliesin out of his. If I translated too much I would get a massive headache.

"Then I shall make sure there is food and drinks waiting for you after the ceremony."

I smiled at the old shaman as I took Taliesin's hand and began walking towards the bath house. "Thank you so much. I am sure we will be very hungry afterwards."

"Stupid people," Quetzalcoatl sneered as the villagers brought him offerings of food and drink while others kowtowed and cried out for his blessing.

"Suck it up!" I shouted through the telepathic connection. *"Grow up and behave. These people have devoted their lives to you. Maybe you could pretend that the lives they are offering to you mean something."*

I stormed off, leaving Chun Bahlum behind. Taliesin kept hold of my hand and walked with me, his long legs matching my angry stride.

"Do you know where you're going?"

"Yes, it's that building there."

"I guess it looks familiar." He didn't sound convinced.

I peeked in the open doorways looking for the hall Ichika had taken us down, but catching glimpses of naked villagers instead. My cheeks burned by the time I found the right entrance.

We walked down the hall and into the private bathing chamber. All of the chief's daughters were there, helping to bathe, dress, and primp for the ceremony. I averted my eyes from the boys' side of the room as Sasha was helped out of the tub.

"Come, come," Ichika said, as Taliesin and I were led to opposite sides of the room.

As soon as I was naked, they washed me then took me to the bath and gave me the ceremonial drink. I guess they were excited to get going, or simply had a lot to do. This happened much faster than last time.

"Sapphire, are you all right?" Gavin asked, his voice echoing in the stone room.

"Yes, just mad, but don't worry I'll be all stoned out of my mind in a minute." I sipped the drink, the same wild passionate devotion from the brewer seeped into me, bypassing all of my empathetic shields. "How are you, Kayin?"

"Much better. But tired. How are we going to do this?"

I hummed as my scalp was massaged. "Sasha. We're going to do Sasha's ritual."

"What? But I'm not prepared."

"That's what they're doing right now; they're preparing us." I let Ichika shift me so she could gather up my hair.

"Sasha, do you have everything you need?" Anali asked.

I turned to see her being dried off. I closed my eyes. Yes, much better. I took another sip of the fruity drink.

"I don't need anything," Sasha answered.

The others talked, reassuring Sasha and helping him plan, while I floated on a wave of spiritual devotion and pampering. Could I get a massage while not stoned? Because this felt good. I moaned and let myself sink into the tub.

"Sapphire?"

"Yes, Uncle Gavin," I cooed.

"She's fine," Anali said. "Just blissed out."

I smiled, still not opening my eyes. I wanted everyone to be dressed before I looked at them again.

My skin was dried and polished with the rough oil, then put into the same turquoise dress decorated with feathers and gold beads.

"Come," Ichika said.

"What's happening now?" Gavin asked.

"Last time they put make-up and jewelry on us," Taliesin answered his voice tight in his discomfort. He needed more of the special drink.

I jumped again as the sticky liquid was painted onto my eyelids. The gold jewelry felt cool against my skin at first, and it warmed as I connected it to Akasha.

I looked at the others and their fire pendants lying lifeless below their throats. Again, I was the only one open and buzzing. Oh, well, Sasha's ritual would fix that.

We were walked back to the courtyard and placed in another chair. *Oh, yippee, skippy.*

"Sapphire, hold onto the arms," Gavin said. "Will she be all right?"

Taliesin snorted. "She managed to stay in the chair last time."

Quetzalcoatl walked over, and the cape of fathers hung from his shoulders and trailed on the ground behind him. "Are we ready?"

"Yep."

He arched an eyebrow over a turquoise eye. "What's wrong with you?"

"Nothing. Come on let's go and ask Shamash about your children."

He shook his head and sat on one of the fancy chairs. I squeaked as the chair rose and held on while they carried us up to the cave. The villagers trailed behind us, carrying their most precious possessions ready to follow their god into the next world.

Gavin helped me off the chair once they set me down. The world spun as we walked into the cave.

"Are you sure you're okay?" Gavin said.

I patted my uncle's hand and felt his worry, cold and prickly. "It's all good, relax."

"Last time she was all right afterwards," Miu said. Her voice sounded far away.

"Everyone sit on rugs," Sasha said. He led me to bright

colors lying on the cave floor. He reached up and turned his fire pendant around to show the engraving of the word 'Shaddai' on the back. "First, I will sing family niggunim. These are wordless songs, one I will sing is for connecting to Akasha. Then I will give blessing before people start going through portal." Sasha cleared his throat. "It's customary for people to close their eyes during blessing." I watched him fling a white shawl with blue stripes over his head and around his shoulders. He began to rock back and forth and the fringe on the shawl fluttered as he moved. Sasha muttered under his breath. I knew he was praying, but couldn't catch the words.

I translated for the priest so he would know what was going to happen and could tell his people. I wasn't sure how listening to a wordless song would connect us together so we could open the portal, but I was willing to go with it.

It's great to have an idea of what might happen, to be prepared, but when you get to whatever new thing you're going to try, a restaurant, performance or ceremony, do your best to release your expectations. Let it be what it is, enjoy it, hate it, fall asleep, let it happen. You'll get a lot more out of life experiencing it than you will measuring it to your expectations.

Quetzalcoatl sat in a stone throne against the wall. His presence was as regal and powerful as the people deserved their god to be.

The villagers quieted, sitting as close to each other as possible, everyone wanted to see the doorway to Xilbalba open.

Sasha looked at me, and I smiled. I aimed for reassuring but judging from the eye roll he did, I failed. His lips parted and a burst of joyful, energetic notes spilled forth. One after another wordless sounds came from Sasha. Some sounded improvised, all made me dance inside. I closed my eyes and allowed the sounds to move through me, much like I had with the drum the guardians used.

The blessing felt reverent and hopeful. I could sense the others relaxing, but their connection didn't open. I thought about sending out my energy to spark their connection, but decided against it. I would respect Sasha and his ritual and allow it to be exactly what it is.

It happened in a breath, one last prolonged note, and then power flowed through Sasha's voice. He connected to Akasha and the gift of Phoenix song was bestowed on him. Our jewelry vibrated, and the others took deep breaths as the power of Sasha's song began to open the connection.

The villagers must have felt the power rise, because they murmured prayers of thanks and blessings.

Sasha's song turned joyous as our power built and connected. It wasn't an explosion like with Miu's ritual, or a force like the Guardian's. This was a gentle opening. Their energy flowed into me. I placed my hands palm up on my knees and Phoenix fire danced from me to the gateway stone.

At first the stone glowed with a purple and white light. The light grew moment by moment, until the portal fully opened.

I opened my eyes. Sasha stood facing us with his hands upraised, his fingers spread in what looked like a Vulcan greeting. His shawl was over his head and spread wide with his hands like a shield over us. *"Y'bhārēkh-khā Adhōnāy weyishmerēkhā..."* Eep, I wasn't supposed to have my eyes open. *"May the Lord bless you and keep you ..."*

I felt Shamash step through the doorway, his presence making the power expand and solidify. I waited for Sasha to be done.

"Brother," Shamash said as Sasha's voice faded. "It has been too long."

"Camaxtli," the villagers whispered.

Quetzalcoatl stood. Translucent blue tears filled his eyes and fell to the ground. Small plants began to grow where the tears fell. "I'm so sorry. I should have listened to you."

Shamash held out his arms. Quetzalcoatl walked into them clutching at his older brother as his shoulders shook. "You're home now. That is all that matters."

Aya stood beside them, running her hand through Quetzalcoatl's green hair. "Welcome home." She looked up, her peridot eyes sparkling with happiness. "Hello, Sapphire, it looks like you have an audience."

"Hello, grandmother. These are Quetzalcoatl's children. They're coming with him."

Shamash raised a thin red eyebrow. "What?"

"I told her no. But she pitched a fit and insisted, so I said she needed to get your permission first," Quetzalcoatl ratted me out.

I glared at Quetzalcoatl. *Pitched a fit, he thought that was fit? I could show him a fit.*

"Sapphire, my Jewel. Tell me what's happening," Shamash said, his voice calming me. If I hadn't felt loopy from the drink, that would have irritated me.

"For generations his children have watched over him, prayed to him, kept his body safe, and all for the reward of going with him when he leaves. Grandfather, please. This is their dream. Their whole life they have worked, prayed, and hoped for this moment."

He knelt before me kissing my forehead, which helped clear away some of the fog. "Don't worry I'll take care of it." He stood and opened his arms. "My nieces and nephews, welcome home."

Cries of joy echoed in the cave as the villagers held each other crying.

"Shamash, what are you thinking? What will they do? How will they survive?" Quetzalcoatl demanded.

"They are children, and their father will show them the way." The two brothers stared at each other until Quetzalcoatl bowed his head.

"What if I make a mistake?"

Shamash laughed. "We all make mistakes. We will help you. Won't we, my heart?"

Aya moved to Shamash's side. "Of course we will."

Quetzalcoatl took a deep breath and stood at the side of the doorway. "Come, my children, it's time to go home."

The priests stood first, they bowed and stepped through the portal. Waiting behind them, the royal family came next. Ichika looked at me, excitement and fear in her eyes.

"Everything will be fine. It doesn't hurt," I said.

She smiled and held her head high as she walked towards her people's future.

As they approached the doorway, they bowed and offered thanks to their gods. Shamash walked to the opening of the cave. I heard him call out to any magical beings nearby. As he walked back he stopped in front of Kayin. "Hello, my treasure. It looks like one of those shadow spirits is tracking you." A large pearly tear formed in the corner of his eye. Shamash took the tear and put it on Kayin's forehead where it vanished. "There, that's better."

"Thank you," Kayin said.

"Of course." Shamash smiled and moved to stand next to his wife and brother as they welcomed the villagers to Akasha.

By the time the last of Quetzalcoatl's children went through the doorway, my butt felt numb. One of the nice things about this ritual was how gently the energy flowed, allowing for small movements for comfort, but at this point the rug-over-rock seating was uncomfortable in any position.

"I know you're all tired," Shamash said, "but there are some of my people waiting to come through. Can you hang on a little longer?"

We all nodded yes.

Quetzalcoatl stepped forward. "They left a feast for you in the courtyard. And I have put a protection around the village. You will be safe."

"Are the Sons of Belial waiting for us in the jungle?" I asked as a group of small furry creatures with sharp yellow teeth passed by us. They hissed and jumped at a woman and child who both shifted into panthers.

"Stop!" Shamash commanded. "I don't know how you keep them in line without Taliesin's help. Try and find other Children of Fire to be in the ritual with you. Taliesin can help, but his true gifts lie elsewhere."

I turned to Taliesin to see the silvery-blue star on his

forehead glowing.

"To answer your question, yes, they're still in the jungle. They came back to the camp and are calling their leader Cartazonon." Shamash closed his eyes. "I can't get a read on the leader. He's too far away and whatever he's done to himself he's gone against his nature so completely that I can't connect to him."

"If you can't reach Cartazonon, how can you reach his followers?" I asked.

Shamash smiled. "I can't. Some of the fairies are watching them. It's time for me to go. Thank you for finding Quetzalcoatl for me."

"You're welcome."

Shamash stood in the portal his flame-red hair fluttering from the energy. "Sapphire, there are two more still in your world."

"Two more what?"

"Brothers."

Chapter Twenty-Six

"There are some kind of men who are so busy worrying about
the next life, they've never learned to live in this one.
~Harper Lee

"Did he say there are two more brothers?" I asked staring
where the portal had been seconds ago. "I had hoped they were
in Akasha. I guess this means the black feather on my bed was
real."

Gavin placed a hand on my shoulder. "Yep."

"I hope they're not as much trouble as this one," Anali said,
moving to stand next to her husband.

"Now what?" Sasha asked looking around the empty cave.

They turned at me, but I turned to look at Gavin.

"Let's go back to the village, eat, and get back into our
clothes." He pulled at the turquoise skirt wrapped around his
hips.

Anali pouted. "But you look so sexy in this."

Gavin grinned and grabbed her waist. "I didn't say I'd get rid
of it. I know I look amazing, but the other boys—well, this isn't
a look they can work."

"Hey," Sasha said. "I look very sexy."

Taliesin glanced at me and shrugged. "I don't know if I
should argue with that or not."

Kayin said, "I don't care if Gavin sees me as sexy."

Gavin gasped placing a hand over his heart. "Kayin, I'm hurt."

"Chan Bahlum said he would leave food for us," I said hoping to stop this silly conversation before it got worse. "Let's go eat before the bugs and animals get it all."

We left the cave. The sky shone radiant with color as the sun set. The village below us glowed in the low light. It looked like paradise to me.

As we got closer to the village, the quiet became creepy. Ghost towns didn't have to be haunted, the expectation of noise, people, and movement played tricks with your mind. I kept waiting for someone to come around a corner, or to hear the laughter of a child.

Shooing monkeys and birds off the long wooden table, we sat. I explained the different dishes, smiling because Chun Bahlum remembered that we didn't eat meat. I filled my plate with roasted potatoes, fruit, and spicy greens.

"We should explore the village. I want to make sure nothing from Akasha is left behind," Gavin said.

"What about items like this?" Taliesin asked holding up the beautiful beaten gold cup.

Gavin sighed and touched his own cup, his fingers tracing a stone set into the side. "We can't carry everything out of here, and it would be wrong to take artifacts out of the country. I can contact people and let them know about this valley."

"What about the items from Akasha?" Miu asked.

"We need them. I don't like taking away these people's history, but for our own protection and theirs, we need to take them with us."

"How should we do this?" Anali asked as she pushed her empty plate away.

"In a bad horror movie this is where we would break into small teams to be picked off one by one," I said.

Anali laughed. "I think I'll take my chances. Let's go explore over there." Anali pulled Gavin towards the bath house and chief's home.

"We should go this way," Sasha said, wrinkling his nose at Anali and Gavin.

What is that about? I watched my aunt and uncle walking away with their arms wrapped around each other. Sure it was a little embarrassing but there wasn't anyone else here.

Kayin took my hand. "Come on, let's explore."

We didn't find anything from Akasha in the homes, however, they left behind beautiful pottery, jewelry, blankets, and furniture. It felt weird going into people's homes and looking through their things, but they had moved on, and all of this was unwanted.

At the end of the village, next to a waterfall, rose a small flat-topped pyramid. I hesitated, but couldn't feel anything bad. At the top of the stairs stood a shrine to Quetzalcoatl.

"This must be the priest's quarters." Miu walked into the room. "Look at these."

The left-over emotion in the room made my skin crawl. They had prepared the ceremonial drink here. I saw a large stone bowl with the inside stained red. "I can't stay in here for long."

Kayin squeezed my hand. "We can leave whenever you need to, little sister."

"Sapphire, check these first." Miu held up a silver comb. "I think it's from Akasha."

I let go of Kayin's hand. Touching the comb I felt a warm pulse of Akashic energy. "Yes, this is one." The dais held many pieces: combs, small bowls, cups, and a variety of jewelry. Some pieces were old but normal. I felt the hum of power letting me know which were from Akasha: a beaten gold cup, a dark wooden comb inlaid with a red-gold stone that sparkled, a silver wrist cuff, and a silver ring with a black stone reflecting rainbows on the surface.

"What about the others?" Taliesin asked. He picked up a necklace with chunky silver beads and a silver jaguar pendant. "Do we leave these here?"

I touched the necklace, not from Akasha but the power

from the priest thrummed in the stones. "Let's take them to Gavin. He'll know what to do with them."

"Here," Kayin held out a woven basket with a sturdy handle. We placed the other items in the basket and headed back to the court yard.

"Did you find anything?" Miu asked once we had all gathered back together.

"A few things," Anali said holding up a basket.

"We found several things too." I placed our basket in front of Gavin so he could look through it.

"What now?" Miu asked. "It's too late to go anywhere."

"There are plenty of bedrooms in the chief's house. We'll stay here tonight," Anali said as she walked towards the large stone home.

I sat alone on a firm bed. The soft sheets were a rich shade of pink that reminded me of one of the berries we'd eaten at dinner. Cries from the jungle echoed through the empty stone house. The noise seemed worse than camping. Lying down I tried to calm my racing mind. The general and his men could be anywhere; what if they found us? Would I have a nightmare tonight? What creepy crawly would decide to come and share the bed with me?

I glanced at the wooden door and thought about finding someone else to sleep with. *Wait, before you go and bother someone else, try breathing. Good advice.* I settled into bed and began my five count breathing. As my anxiety lessened, I felt the protection Quetzalcoatl cast over the valley. It hummed happily, and I knew we would be safe, at least for tonight. I slipped into sleep.

* * *

Cold thin air filled my lungs as I sat in the garden of our hotel in Cuzco. Everyone else had gone up to bed, exhausted after our trek out of the jungle, but I didn't want to sleep. The protections Quetzalcoatl put over the village kept me from dreaming of Cartazonon, but I wasn't sure if I had been away from the Sons of Belial long enough to escape dreams of their leader. Maybe being in Shamash's presence would have cleared the energy, but that seemed like wishful thinking. I sensed this odd connection like a strand of spider web vibrating with the frantic struggles of a dying fly.

"Sapphire, are you all right?" Gavin asked, sitting down next to me.

He wore sleep pants and a sweat shirt. "What are you doing up?"

"I saw you from our window." Gavin pointed to the third floor. Anali stood in the window in a bright pink nightgown.

"I don't want to go to sleep."

"Did you have a bad dream last night?"

I shook my head. "No, but I will tonight."

"Sleep in our suite, the living room couch is long enough for you."

I raised an eyebrow. "I don't want to keep you and Anali up."

Gavin shook his head. "You won't. Anyway, you'll sleep in another room. And with how badly the dreams affect you, I would prefer you close to me."

I wanted to argue. I wasn't that tired, and I'd be fine. Then I yawned. *Damn it.* "All right."

I followed Gavin up the stairs and into the suite. Anali guided me to the couch which she made up for me and tucked me in. The door to their room closed with a click. I planned on lying there and forcing myself to stay awake, but the couch was soft and warm, and soon I fell into a dream.

Cartazonon clicked on the thumbnail photos, gasping as the image of Quetzalcoatl appeared. "A god, they found a god." Greed showed in his black eyes as he clicked on the other photos. "I could keep my empire safe and protected forever with the life force and magic from a god."

Picking up his phone he dialed General Senach. "Tell me what happened."

Cartazonon nodded as Senach told him. Long pale fingers caressed the screen as the picture of a group of teenagers came up. He couldn't see their faces as they were blurred and overexposed. One of the boys had a silvery halo surrounding him. "The unicorn."

"Sir?"

"I want to know what's going on. For centuries I've ignored these Children of Fire unless they got in my way. But now I want them." Cartazonon stood up and walked to the window staring blindly out. He didn't even notice the Eiffel Tower or the colorful swirl of tourists. "I want to know what they're doing. Are they sending beings to Akasha?" An image of his mother flashed in his head. He squashed it down.

"I want them," Cartazonon snarled.

"Then you shall have them, my lord."

He snapped his phone shut and sat back down in his chair looking through the pictures again. His whole body stiffened, his eyes unfocused.

"Who's there? I can feel you."

He stood. Reaching out, he gasped.

"I can sense Akashaic enery."

I screamed, and my arm burned with cold as his hand grasped me.

I fell off the couch and scooted until my back hit a wall. Where the hell was I?

"Sapphire," Gavin said, kneeling down in front of me. "You're safe. The dream is over, you're safe now."

Hot tears ran down my face and I cradled my arm to my chest. "He's coming after us. Cartazonon said he'd ignored us unless we got in his way, but now he wants to know all about the Children of Fire."

"Why, what changed?" Anali asked, handing me a glass of water.

I took a sip. "He saw a picture of Quetzalcoatl. He wants a god."

"You're shaking," Gavin rubbed my arm. I cried out. He held his hands up. "What happened?"

I pulled back the sleeve of my shirt. Four pale blue lines crossed my forearm.

"What the hell," Gavin reached out and held my arm in his hands.

"He touched me. He could tell I was there, and he reached

out and touched me."

"I'll get Miu," Anali said throwing a robe over her nightgown.

"The others?"

"I'll call Phillip as soon as Miu gets here. We knew this would happen eventually. For so long we've been insignificant, but we all knew that would change some day." Gavin sighed and handed me a tissue. "We'll figure it out, you should talk to Sasha. But for now don't worry."

Don't worry? This madman is focused on us—the man who killed my parents—and I'm supposed to not worry. My arm throbbed. There was no way I wasn't going to worry.

"What happened?" Miu asked, her hair a wild, black mess.

"Cartazonon touched me in a dream."

Miu shooed Gavin away and sat in front of me cradling my arm. Breathing slowly she let her gift of healing flow into my arm. "The skin is frozen."

I gasped as the heat of her Phoenix powers began to heal the frozen marks.

Gavin grabbed my free hand. His eyes locked onto mine. "Breathe honey, it'll feel better soon."

Needle-sharp prickles of heat covered the marks as the damage healed.

"Sorry," Miu whispered as I hissed in pain. "I've never healed anything like this before."

New rule: don't let someone who has warped their nature touch me.

It seemed to take forever, but finally Miu finished. "I'm sorry, Sapphire, that's the best I can do."

Four smooth white scars marked my arm. "It's okay. It doesn't hurt anymore."

"Do you think you can go back to sleep?" Anali asked.

I looked at the clock, two-thirty in the morning, no way could I go back to sleep. "Sure, I feel better now." Standing up, I moved back onto the couch and let Gavin tuck me in.

"I'll walk Miu back to her room," Anali said.

"Are you going to be able to sleep?" Gavin asked.

"No, but I can lie here quietly."

Gavin sighed and sat on the edge of the couch. "Are you afraid you'll have another dream?"

"No. In the past I've only had one."

Gavin stood. "Do you want me to leave a light on so you can read?"

I saw my backpack on the floor. "That would be great." I dug through my pack and pulled out Padre Carrillo's journal. I needed to find the ritual to break a walk-in's trace, then I would go through page by page and translate the whole thing in case something else in here was important. With great care, I turned the brittle yellow pages and began scanning the archaic Spanish.

When the sun rose, my eyes were dry and my head pounded, but I had found the ritual. Someone being tracked by a walk-in had two options: they could sit in meditation for three days, keeping a connection to Akasha open to allow the energy to break up the trace, or they could step into a portal. They didn't have to stay in Akasha or even walk all the way through. Being surrounded by the energy was enough.

I set the book down and rubbed my eyes. Both options sucked. Both put me and others at risk. And we still don't know where all the gateway stones were located. Maybe the answers lay in the journal. I wouldn't give up. People were counting on me, and while I might not be even close to the leader they wanted, I was going to try my best.

I watched the sky turn into ribbons of color. Hope and fear warred in my heart. I wanted to believe that I could keep everyone safe, but Cartazonon was ruthless and determined. I wrapped my arms across myself hoping to ease the queasiness.

"Sapphire, are you okay?" Gavin asked, kneeling in front of me. "Did you rest at all?"

I shook my head. "I found the rituals to break a walk-in's tracking spells, but they're not safe. One you have to step into a portal, the other the one my mom probably did is meditating for three days and staying open to Akasha."

"Shamash was able to take the spell off of Kayin with a

tear," Gavin said.

"I cried a tear for Taliesin but it was weak, a glimmer of what Shamash's tear looked like." My hands flailed as I tried to find an answer. "I don't know what I need to do to make the tear stronger, me stronger. And how do I cry them? Can they be bottled to protect others?"

Gavin wrapped his hands around mine to stop the frantic movement. "Sapphire, honey, calm down. Don't do this to yourself. You can't save everyone. You aren't responsible for this." I blinked trying to force back the tears filling my eyes, stupid regular tears that were of no use to anyone. "We are in this together, and there are more Children of Fire in the world than you know about. We will all work together to keep each other safe."

"But the journal, there could be more, there could be something else that could help." I tried to tug my hands free, but Gavin held on. "Uncle Gavin, shouldn't we try to find more journals? How did my father do it?"

"Keagan studied the genealogy of Children of Fire tracing back their ancestry." Gavin shrugged. "Padre Carrillo is from Phillip's and Michael's family tree. I don't know if anyone has continued his work, but I can ask Phillip to find out. But we need to continue to live and have fun. If you let this consume you, you'll become miserable."

It can be easy to become overwhelmed by your emotions, especially when things are difficult. Don't let your fear and your preparations for a time when something goes wrong consume you. Do what you need to, take a deep breath, and then look for the good. Find something joyful to focus on, keep living your life, and always look forward to your future. The bad times will pass, and then you'll have all of these wonderful memories.

"How? How do I forget that we're being hunted?" I asked.

"You don't forget. We'll train and take precautions. But the Sons of Belial aren't everywhere. They don't know much about us, and so far they don't know who we are. So we keep going as we have been."

Worry and hope warred in me. I looked into Gavin's eyes.

He felt strong—no fear or worry came from him. I closed my eyes. If I couldn't believe in myself, than I would believe in Gavin.

"Okay, Uncle Gavin, what are we going to do today?"

THE END

Heirs of Avalon

Book Three in the Children of Fire Series

CHAPTER ONE

"Experience: that most brutal of teachers. But you learn, my
God do you learn."
~ C.S. Lewis

Never, ever, offer to help a leprechaun pick up its spilled
gold. Groaning, I stretched. My hand protested as the scabbed-
over teeth marks pulled, and my stiff muscles resisted the
movement. Blinking, I looked around the room wondering
where I was. Rich cream-on-cream striped walls gave away no
secrets, and the mirrored sliding door leading to what I assumed
was the closet didn't look familiar either. Sitting up I watched
the cream cotton sheets and black satin comforter pool around
my waist. Swanky, yet still unfamiliar.

Scooting to the edge of the bed, I let my toes hover over the
polished oak floors, where a pair of white slippers waited for
me. I slid my feet into them and stood, my knees wobbling.
What in the world was wrong with me? I shuffled towards a
door, but the locks on it marked it as an exit and not the
bathroom I desperately needed. I looked around me. In the
center of the room stood a cream love seat with black throw
pillows, facing a flat screen TV set on the wall a few feet from
the front door. Black drapes covered one wall. An ornately
carved desk and chair sat against the far wall, and next to it

another door. Opening the door, I gasped seeing the largest hotel bathroom ever. The sink, counters, and bathtub were carved out of some pale tan stone, flecked with white. Glass encased a separate shower stall, and finally I found the toilet. Ooh, thank goodness.

Okay, time to figure out where I am. On the desk sat a full sized pad of stationery with Royal Garden Hotel, London, England, embossed across the top. I pulled open the thick satin black drapes, and revealed sheer cream curtains underneath. Beyond both of them I saw a park. Gray branches reached into the foggy December sky. I placed my hand on the cool glass, red scabs marring my light copper skin. Stupid leprechaun. I remember opening a portal in Ireland, getting bitten, the walk-ins, and then rushing to the hotel. The rest of the Cirque du Feu Magique performers had gone ahead to Belfast. Most of the troupe have no idea who we really are or why we travel with them, except Michael the ringmaster and his daughter Nyota, our tech wizard.

Belfast had crashed through my empathic shields. I was too tired and weak to protect myself, and the pain trapped in the stones of the city overwhelmed me. The last thing I can remember was being stuffed onto a small plane with images of bombings and the screams of its victims flashing in my head.

I heard a soft knock on the door, and it opened. "I'm checking on her now, Gavin," said Anali. Her shoulder-length hair looked mussed from sleep, and her purple nightgown and robe was bright against the neutral colors of the room. She held a cell phone in her hand. "Oh. Good morning, Sapphire. Feeling better? Yes, Gavin, she's up. Well, I don't know how she feels; she hasn't answered yet. Well, perhaps if you spoke to her." Anali handed me the phone.

"Hi, Uncle Gavin," I said, my voice raspy.

"Sapphire, are you okay?," I held the phone away from my ear. "I am so sorry. I should have known."

Anali looked me over as she placed her hand on my forehead, then handed me a glass of water. "Are you okay?" she whispered.

I nodded then guzzled the water.

"Good. I'll go get changed and then come back and help you get ready," she said.

I nodded again and waited for a chance to speak. "Uncle Gavin, calm down, I'm okay now."

"You sound fine," he said his voice soft.

"I am fine. Ireland was lovely, except for the damn leprechaun. I had no idea I would react so strongly to Belfast."

"I should have known. You were tired, and we were all drained from opening that portal and running from walk-ins. My only thought was to catch up to the circus and Nyota. I knew she would have the dampening field set up in the hotel and we'd be safe, but then ..." Gavin's voice cracked.

"'Experience: that most brutal of teachers. But you learn, my God, do you learn.' C.S. Lewis said that."

Gavin chuckled. "One of the quotes from your mom's journal. So what did she have to say about experience?"

"'We can do our best to read and prepare, but life will always be our greatest teacher. We will make mistakes, flounder, and sometimes fail. But as long as we learn from each experience, then it isn't bad or wasted. Try not to stress out about being prepared for everything—that is impossible. Just do your best and learn,'" I recited from memory.

"True," he sighed. "But still ..."

"Uncle Gavin, none of us thought I would tap into the tragedies that had happened in Belfast. It was too much and too new. I was unprepared to deal with it. Anyway, you got me out of there."

"I worried when you didn't wake up right away. Anali said you were fine."

"And she was right; isn't she always right?" I teased.

Gavin huffed. "Yes, she is, but still you were asleep for over twenty-four hours. How do you feel now? What do you feel now?"

"My body's a bit stiff, but if I slept that long, I know why.

My empathy isn't picking up on anything specific right now. But this hotel seems modern, and we are pretty high up."

"I thought that would help," Gavin sighed. "After the trouble you've had, I didn't want to put you in an older building. I hoped being higher up might help buffer anything that had seeped into the ground."

I blushed. Gavin did this for me? We stayed in nice places, but this was insane, and I couldn't imagine how expensive. I ran my fingers over the silky drapes. He chose this place to help me?

"Can you feel anything at all?" he asked.

I closed my eyes and reached out to open up my empathy to the area. A gentle hum of old magic came from the garden. "If I open up, I can feel an ancient magic."

"You said the same thing about Ireland."

"Yes, but Ireland felt more mischievous. Not that the magic here is all serious, just a calmer playfulness. It's like magical beings have lived here for so long their powers are soaked into everything." I laughed. "I wouldn't be surprised if there was pixie dust in the soil, and fairies' tears in the water. It's everywhere."

"But it all feels safe?"

I took a deep breath allowing my empathy to stretch out. "There are dark beings here just as they are everywhere. Nothing feels overwhelming or sinister, and from my room I have to focus to feel even a faint shadow of magic. Thank you, Uncle Gavin."

"I'm glad I was able to make things easier for you." Gavin sighed, and I imagined him running a hand through his wild flame- red hair. "I have to go. Have fun with Anali. We'll be there tomorrow morning; tonight's the last show."

"Tell everyone I said hi. Hey, what did you tell the circus people?"

"I told them you had a severe migraine that sometimes can last for days, so I sent you and Anali ahead for the peace and quiet."

"They bought that?" I'd seen some of the circus performers rolling their eyes at the lame excuses we gave over the seven months. Of course, if we came right out and said, "Hey—we are descendants of a Phoenix King and Queen. We'll be gone for a week while we open a portal to Akasha, return magical creatures to their home, and battle an ancient evil," I doubt that would go over very well either.

"As much as ever." Gavin answered. "They know they are paid well and given better food and lodging than most circuses, so they put up with my eccentric ways. I need to go. Michael wants everyone at the gym in an half an hour."

"All right. Have a good day."

"Bye, Sapphire, and stay safe."

"You too, Uncle Gavin."

Guilt trickled into my stomach, I felt bad for not being there for the show tonight, and for keeping Anali away. Even though we needed to disappear now and then, we did our best to make it to performances. Sighing, I opened the closet door. My clothes had been hung up or folded onto the shelves on the side. Anali must have gotten bored. I grabbed some clean underwear, socks, jeans, a tee shirt, and sweater and headed for the shower.

After trying all the different settings on the shower—rain being my favorite—I felt ready to face the day. Anali sat at the desk flipping through a guide book. "Feeling better?"

"Much," my stomach growled. "Well, except for being hungry."

Anali smiled, her brow crinkling around her red bindi. "That we can fix."

Luxury surrounded us. The décor was subtle and simple, but even I knew it was the best quality. The brass railings on the elevator didn't even have smudges or fingerprints on them. Anali's footsteps echoed on the black marble floor of the lobby. Her pink cotton pants and tunic trimmed with silver leaves and vines were reflected in the marble's polished surface. Note to self: be careful when walking across this floor in a skirt.

My stomach growled again as we reached the restaurant. The gentleman seating us wore a crisp, dark gray suit. A moment later a woman in a white blouse and straight black skirt filled our glasses with water. "What can I get you this morning?"

"A pot of Oolong tea to share, and I think we'll have the continental breakfast," said Anali.

"Very good. I'll bring that right out."

Anali patted my hand. "You stay here. I'll bring you something."

"Okay." I sipped my water and watched the other guests, feeling very conspicuous in my simple outfit. I felt like I was sitting in a movie or fashion magazine. Well-groomed people ate with impeccable manners. Silk ties and scarves were in no danger of having anything spilled on them. Hair stayed put, possibly from gel and hairspray, but I suspected it was force of will that kept many locks in their stylish dos. I ran my hand through my damp curls, and my fingers caught on a tangle.

Almost a year ago—had it only been a year? On the morning of my fifteenth birthday I woke up to find my brown hair had turned black with fire-red streaks. My dull gray green eyes had become pale peridot green with golden flecks, and my light brown skin had become a soft copper brown. I went from being another unwanted group home kid to Gavin's niece and the Jewel of Shamash and Aya, the Phoenix King and Queen, my direct ancestors. Here I sat in London, days away from my sixteenth birthday, and I still felt lost in a faerie tale. Of course today it seemed more like an episode of *Doctor Who* because of all the lovely British accents.

"Here you go." Anali handed me a plate filled with several pastries, a bowl of yogurt topped with muesli, and fresh fruit. "There is also a selection of cheese and rolls if you want something more savory."

"Thanks, Anali, this looks great." I picked up a pastry and moaned when I tasted the filling of bittersweet chocolate and almonds. Instantly I felt better.

"Pardon me," said the server setting down a white tea set with hand-painted periwinkles and poured us each a cup of tea. "Can I get you anything else?"

"No thank you," said Anali. She turned to me. "It's been two days since you've eaten, so make sure you eat slowly."

Stuffing the last bite of chocolate almond awesomeness into my mouth, I nodded and added honey to my tea. She was right. As much as I wanted to try my first scone, I needed to slow down before my stomach cramped. Instead I watched as Anali covered her scone with clotted cream and lemon curd.

"So what should we do today?"

I shrugged and sipped my tea.

"Well, we can stay in and watch TV or read if you're tired. Or do touristy things. Or you could finally admit that you've grown, and your clothes are too small, and go shopping."

I reached up to adjust my bra. Was I spilling out of it again?

Anali raised an eyebrow and took a sip of tea.

I sighed. "Okay, we can go shopping."

"Wonderful. I was looking in the guide book the hotel provided, and Knightsbridge isn't far. It has a lot of stores, including Harrods and Harvey Nichols, which are department stores. We also need to get you several formal outfits," Anali said stirring her yogurt and muesli.

"What, why? And what do you mean by formal?" Images of lacy frills and pinching shoes filled my mind.

"Well," Anali said, "Gavin received an invitation to a charity gala, your birthday is coming up, and my cousin is getting married while we are here."

"Oh. But why do I need something fancy to wear on my birthday?"

"Miu is making plans," Anali said.

I hoped that Anali was helping with those plans. I guess, I could, in theory, find a nice outfit and wear it to all the different events, right? Then I wouldn't need more than one uncomfortable outfit. I bit into the scone—it tasted like a lemon meringue pie only better.

"My cousin is having a traditional Indian wedding, and I was wondering if you wanted to wear a sari," Anali asked. "Most of the women there will be wearing one."

My forehead crinkled. Anali always looked so elegant when she wore a sari. I wasn't sure I could pull it off. I certainly didn't feel elegant. "The saris you wear are very pretty, and they look more comfortable than a lot of dresses. At least there won't be any ruffles."

"Okay, we'll find a sari shop, and I am sure we can find several dressy outfits for you without any ruffles."

We stood in front of the hotel while the doorman got us a cab. The air felt cold and the gray sky threatened rain. Frowning, I wrapped my scarf around my neck.

Anali bumped me with her shoulder. "Come on, it'll be fun. I never get you all to myself. And I promise we'll only buy things you like and that look good on you."

I smiled. "It does sound like a lot of fun. And I do need new clothes," I admitted as we got into the cab.

I kept my eyes closed while Anali talked about all the clothes I needed. Riding on the left side of the road freaked me out.

"Here we are, ladies," the cabbie said. I strained to understand his accent, a mix of Cockney and Turkish.

Anali paid him, and we scooted out of the cab. Our shoes squeaked on the damp cobblestones. Red brick buildings loomed above us with, the bottom floors trimmed in bright white paint trying to break through the fog.

"Where do we start?"

Anali smiled and linked our arms together. "Let's start walking and see what catches our eye."

A lot caught Anali's eye, and soon I had bags from several stores with jeans, blouses, sweaters, and even a denim skirt.

"Oh, perfect." Anali grabbed my hand, jostling the bags I carried, and pulled me towards a bright pink shop. In the windows hung bras, panties, and lacy things that didn't look practical or comfortable at all.

"Why are we both going in there? I can wait out here."

Anali stopped and turned to look at me, her light brown eyes warm. "Sapphire, you're almost sixteen now, a young woman, and it's time you had beautiful things. When I was your age my mom took me shopping for adult clothes like this." Anali bit her lip. "Not that I'm your mom, or trying to be your mom."

I grabbed Anali's hand. "I know. It's fine. I guess I could look inside."

She smiled and began walking again. "You're a beautiful young woman, and while no boy should be seeing your underwear, you should feel sexy while wearing it."

I wasn't sure how underwear made you feel sexy but I followed along.

"Good morning ladies, how can I help you?" asked an elderly woman. Her gray hair was pulled up into a neat bun.

"My niece needs to be measured for new bras, she's grown quite a bit."

I blushed and looked down where I was yet again escaping my current bra.

"Ah yes, blossoming into womanhood are we? Come here, and we'll get started," she said pulling out a tape measure.

She hummed then sent me to the dressing room. "I'll bring you several different styles in your size, then we can look at colors and fabrics."

I undressed and groaned at the stack of bras she passed over the door. The first one barely covered anything, the second pushed what I had up like an offering, the third wasn't bad but didn't have enough support. "I like this one." I lifted my arms up above my head and the fourth bra didn't shift. It covered everything, and I didn't look like I was advertising.

"Pass it over, dearie, and we'll get some more in that style for you to try on."

"Can't I just pick them out since I know it will fit?" I asked passing the bra over.

"Goodness no, you need to see the colors against your skin and feel the fabrics."

"Are you doing okay?" Anali whispered.

"Yes, but I'm not sure I understand the point."

"I didn't either at first. I'll set aside a white, black, and beige in cotton. It's always good to have the basics."

"Thanks Anali."

A mass of color was handed to me over the door. I was supposed to try all of these on? Picking up a pick cotton bra with little pink hearts, I set it in the 'no' pile.

I fastened the hooks on a navy- blue satin bra with white lace on the edge of the cup. The color shone against my light copper skin. Was this what Anali meant? I blushed and picked another bra to try on.

Opening the door with a bunch of bras draped over my arm, I sighed, grateful to be done.

"Are these the ones you want?" The sales lady asked taking the pile from me.

"Yes, there's a bunch more in the dressing room."

She waved her hand. "You leave those; I'll get them later. Now the matching panties are over here. We have each style in several cuts. I'll put these up front while you're looking."

In the past I wore plain cotton underwear, but looking at the display, I found the ones that matched the bras I chose. Sticking to boy shorts and low cut briefs, I matched each bra. My blush wasn't going away anytime soon.

"Those are so cute," Anali said pointing to the dark purple boy shorts with light purple polka dots. "You should change into a new bra so you don't have to keep fiddling with yours the rest of the day."

"Here." The sales lady popped up holding out a white lace bra with dark green leaves embroidered on the straps. "I've already cut off the tags. We also have some lovely nightgowns and pajamas if you're interested. Can I take those?"

"Oh, thanks." Anali handed over a sheer nightgown and some lacy thing. I turned back to the dressing room to change, not interested in my aunt's choice of lingerie.

When I came out, I searched through the sheer gowns and

little lace whatevers until I found some simple satin camisoles and shorts, and several sets of cotton tank tops and soft pajama bottoms.

"All done?" The woman asked folding each piece into crinkling pink tissue paper.

"Yes. Thank you for all your help."

"You're most welcome, dearie." She handed me two large shiny pink bags with the store's name in metallic silver across both sides.

Anali handed her a credit card as the sales woman told her the best way to wash her delicate things.

"I'm going to wait outside."

Anali smiled at me and nodded.

I stepped onto the street. The crisp air refreshed and cooled my poor cheeks. The sun had burnt off the fog. I looked down the ancient street lined with tall red brick buildings with white trim. Their pointed spires reached for the sky. A small group of brownies slipped between two stones into a bakery while faeries danced along the evergreen wreaths and garlands hung on the store fronts. I thought about going over and saying hello when I felt someone staring at me. Turning, I saw a young man, who looked like a poster boy for traveling to England. He was at least six feet tall with short brown hair and bright blue eyes. A long scarf knotted around his neck and hung down his chest. He glanced at the bag in my hands, gave me a cheeky grin, winked, and walked away.

And I am blushing again.

"Ready?" Anali asked, making me jump. "Lost in thought?" she giggled.

"I'm ready." I tucked the pink bags closest to me and placed others on the outside of them.

"Are you getting tired or hungry?"

My stomach was still full from breakfast. "I'm not hungry, but I could sit and get something to drink."

"Let's keep walking. I'm sure we'll find a tea shop."

"Sounds good." We paused to look at the window displays

which caught our eye, enjoying the holiday themes.

"Sapphire," Anali squealed. "Look at this. Isn't it the cutest thing you've ever seen?"

I walked over to the store front window and saw the smallest cable knit sweater ever. "It's very cute."

Anali sighed. "I have to have it."

I followed her into the shop, feeling her emotions bouncing against my shields. Anali is normally calm, but right now longing, hope, happiness, and nervousness all bounced against me. What in the world was going on?

"Oh, look they have a bunch." Anali sorted through a rack of tiny sweaters, pulling out the tiniest cream-colored cable knit sweater.

"Is someone expecting a baby?" I thought her youngest nephew was two, and the family lived in tropical India. They wouldn't need such a thick sweater.

She held the sweater against her belly. "No, but it's so sweet I can't pass it up."

"We have some other things for a wee bairn," the man behind the counter said. "Everything is hand knitted by the good women of Scotland."

I looked through the sweaters while Anali cooed, yes cooed, over the baby stuff. I picked a white cable knit sweater and one of green cashmere that was the softest thing I ever touched. Looking at the price tags, I flinched. I started to put them back, but they were so beautiful.

"Look," Anali said dangling a pair of knitted baby booties in front of me. "Oh, those sweaters are gorgeous."

"They are, and expensive."

"Oh pish, don't worry about it today. You're here to have fun." Anali smiled. "I'm going to get one , too. Will you hold these while I look?"

"Sure," I said, taking the booties, two baby sweaters, several hats, and a blanket.

"This one," Anali held up a pale blue cabled cardigan sweater. "Let me pay, and then we'll go get something to drink."

I blinked at the whirlwind of emotions coming from Anali and followed. Should I say something? No. She knows I'm empathic. If she wanted to tell me what was going on, she would.

"What would you like?" Anali asked as she set down her bags, tucking them under the wooden table of a tea shop.

I looked at the handwritten chalkboard menu. "A chai latte please."

"Okay. I'll be right back." Anali hummed to herself as she went to stand in line.

I watched as a woman handed a hot chocolate to a little girl, who I thought looked like she might be her daughter. The girl smiled, and her mom brushed a stray curl from her daughter's cheek with a soft smile.

Anali set down two steaming mugs and a plate of cookies. "Here we are."

"Thanks." My fingers wrapped around the mug, soaking in the warmth.

Anali smiled and tucked a lock of my hair behind my ear.

My stomach fluttered. I smiled back

Thank you for reading *Legacy of the Feathered Serpent*, the second book in the *Children of Fire* series. To find out more about me, the crazy thoughts bouncing in my head, what I'm writing, what is distracting me from writing, and when the next book will come out, please connect with me on

Twitter
https://twitter.com/AMckennaJohnson

Facebook
https://www.facebook.com/AlicaMckennaJohnsonAuthor

Goodreads
http://www.goodreads.com/author/show/5755438.Alica_Mckenna_Johnson

My website/blog
www.alicamckennajohnson.com

AND to get information about my upcoming books, book signings, and talks subscribe to my newsletter. It only goes out when I have something of value to share. Cross my heart! **http://eepurl.com/bc5bzn**

FREE DOWNLOAD

Get your free copy of KAYIN'S FIRE when you sign up for the author's VIP mailing list. Get started here: http://eepurl.com/bc5bzn

ABOUT THE AUTHOR

Being told she was a horrible speller and would never learn to use a comma correctly, Alica never thought to write down the stories she constantly had running through her head. Doesn't everyone daydream about flying on a spaceship while walking to school?

Not until she was thirty did Alica dare to write down any of the people living exciting lives in her head. The relief was instantaneous. By giving them life on the page they could be released from her mind and given greater adventures.

As her books grew in size and the voices in her head learned to wait their turn, Alica found a loyal group to journey with. Women who would help her slay her commas, and use their magical gifts to traverse plot holes, transform words into their proper spelling, and release characters from any Mary Sue spells they might be under.

In-between magical adventures, Alica is mom to two personal kids, five foster kids, has one exceptional hubby, a bunny she knows is plotting her death, and some fish, aka her daughter's minions.